The Citadel

a novel
by Alexey Osadchuk

*To my Dear Reader, with gratitude,
Alexey Osadchuk.*

Mirror World
Book#2

Magic Dome Books

The Citadel
Mirror World, Book # 2
Second Edition
Published by Magic Dome Books, 2017
Copyright © A. Osadchuk 2016
Cover Art © V. Manyukhin 2016
English Translation Copyright ©
Irene Woodhead, Neil P. Mayhew 2016
All Rights Reserved
ISBN: 978-80-88231-08-0

This book is entirely a work of fiction.
Any correlation with real people or events is
coincidental.

Table of Contents:

Chapter One

"So you've made up your mind, then?"

Surprisingly, Weigner accepted the news of my relocation casually. "Some place you've chosen, I tell you."I shrugged. "You could say that. You know very well I can't help it."

"You can't. It may sound self-contradictory but this isn't all fun and games. We all have our own problems — and objectives."

"I can't tell you how I hate to go."

I'd told him the truth. I hated changes. For the previous nine days I'd been enjoying some semblance of big city life. I'd met some decent people. Admittedly, I'd also struck up some useful relationships with city NPCs. But as Weigner had rightly said, this wasn't all fun and games. I might appear to be playing but this was my life, however virtual.

"I've only just met you but I think I'll be

missing you," his voice rang with regret. "Doryl, too... We've just been gossiping about you, he he."

I smiled. "Likewise."

"There aren't so many people here you can just sit and talk with. Everybody's in a hurry! Sure it's a game, they've paid a fortune for their accounts. Never mind. No good getting too emotional. Let's move on to the business."

I was grateful to him for not asking any unwanted questions. I was sure he could guess the true reason behind my relocation. Players of my caliber didn't just rent a place in Mellenville only to move to one of Mirror World's most dangerous locations. He knew that better than anybody else.

"So," Weigner went on. "You think you're gonna keep busting your backside for Lady Mel?"

"Exactly. I'm perfectly happy with her. You know it."

He chuckled. "I'm only asking for the record. Obliged to. We have several scenarios to offer in case of such a development: for instance, when a player has leveled up so much that we have no suitable mines to offer him anymore."

It took all of my composure not to betray myself. The thing was, I'd made a decision to keep my Master level under wraps. Emeralds offered decent earnings and a semblance of stability — if you disregarded the need to relocate, of course. What was the point in switching to a new resource? It might pay more but it wasn't going to solve my problem. I had a funny feeling it might even make my situation worse.

My current priority was to get a loan. Then

again, if you think about it... I might gain quite a bit by revealing my identity. I could sign up with a powerful clan like these Steel Shirts. Their locations were well protected. They offered raids to some resource-rich instances. But how sure was I that I could profit from their riches, if at all? No, I wasn't greedy or anything, I just didn't trust anyone anymore. How sure was I they'd want to hear about my problem, let alone see it the way I did? Most likely, they'd simply want to cash in on my weak position. First they'd lure me in and then I could kiss my freedom goodbye. Oh no, thank you very much.

"I understand this isn't your case yet," Weigner continued, unaware of my inner struggle. "But listen to my advice. You need to start weighing up all your potential options. With your perseverance, I wouldn't be surprised if you made Master in the next six or seven months. And this, as you can well imagine, is a totally different ball game," he raised an authoritative finger.

I smiled, struggling to look normal. "Thanks for the tip. The trick is not to bust a gut in the process."

He grinned. "Don't chicken out! If you play your cards well, you'll outlive us all. What was I talking about... yes, so there're several potential scenarios. The best one for you, I think, would be a regular transfer. You signed the trial contract, didn't you? The two-week trial period hasn't elapsed yet. Now listen up. Seeing as Lady Mel has some emerald fields in the vicinity of the Maragar Citadel, what if we simply transfer you there? In theory, you won't even have to report to their bosses. Just go straight to the mine and pull stones to your heart's content. Still, it would be a good idea to pop in at the office and say hello."

This was another proof of the validity of my suspicions and fears. Even this man who was almost a friend was trying to capitalize on me.

If the truth were known, I couldn't blame him. He didn't want to lose an Experienced Digger. He must be receiving some bonuses for having hired me. On the other hand, why not? I too could gain from our cooperation. We were on friendly terms. He could make sure that my two-week trial contract would naturally evolve into a permanent one. What was the point in severing our relationship? Who knew how this relocation could backfire?

"Excellent," I said. "This is even better than I hoped. Every time I think about it, you know... A new place... New people..."

He beamed. "Exactly! You're thinking in the right direction!"

An hour later I left his office and headed for the portal. All the formalities had been settled. We'd signed the transfer agreement. Now I only had to wrap up a few things and I could set off for my new destination. Especially because, according to the quest conditions, I had no rent to pay!

I suspected that the barracks of the Maragar Citadel weren't exactly the most comfortable place in Mirror World. Heh! I was pretty sure I'd be remembering Ronald's pajamas and bathrobes with nostalgia coming back home every night! Actually, I'd already bidden my farewells to him in the Footworn Traveler Inn. Now all I had to do was drop in at Mila's and ask after little Tommy's health. Sure they were NPCs but still I had a soft spot for the boy. He reminded me of my own little girl, my Christina.

That's that, then. I was going to pop by and see them, but first I needed to check on my other employer.

The office of Nikanor the Lawyer met me with a familiar stuffy silence. Cobwebs enveloping the chandelier, dust choking the paintings, the lack of fresh air... Nikanor hated opening windows when he worked. His servant had to air his office in secret.

No idea how the game developers had managed to convey the entire range of nasty effluvia filling the place. It always reeked of old age, moldy papers and — don't ask why — of rotten apples. It must have been my imagination playing up, of course. This place reminded me of something... something from my past... I must have associated Nikanor's room with something I'd seen earlier in real life.

The old lawyer sat at his desk, his quill scratching at a yellowing sheet of paper to the accompaniment of screeching sounds and occasional coughing. His withered lips moved silently, mouthing the words that appeared on the paper. He was clad in a greasy old dressing gown of an unidentifiable dark hue. The image was completed by a three-day stubble covering his saggy cheeks and the unwashed strands of hair adorning his balding head.

"You know, Olgerd," he said without raising his head from his work, "it's a very good thing you're going. And it's a doubly good thing you're going to the Citadel. I have a small job for you."

I'll be damned! How had he found out? Weigner was the only person who knew about my quest, and he didn't have access to Mellenville quite yet. And in any case, what would he want with the old boy? Not good. Even Doryl the dwarf didn't know yet. Not that he minded: Doryl understood there were certain things I had to keep to myself.

A moment later Nikanor answered my unasked question. "When I received notification from the town hall saying that you'd been enlisted into the Maragar Citadel, I knew immediately this was a sign from above!"

Squinting dreamily, he tapped his scrawny ink-covered fingers on the desk. He was anxious, I could see that. His faked indifference had flown out the window. A weak color tinged his pale-gray cheeks.

I'd had a good reason to come and see him. By agreeing to become a "defender of the Maragar Citadel", I had to cancel my monthly Reputation quest — not to mention all the other Reputation mini-quests. Part of me was celebrating the fact that I was seeing this miserable old man for the last time: grumpy, petulant and constantly unhappy with his boring virtual life. Still, I regretted the loss of almost 800 Rep to say the least. Especially because I'd already done so much running around on all sorts of pointless and time-consuming errands for him.

It would have been so much easier to just forget this quest entirely. Still, something made me show up at his office one last time. Of course he was only a lifeless piece of program code... but my entire Mirror World experience had already taught me that everything here happened for a reason.

Okay. Now I needed to find out what this Scrooge wanted from me.

"I want you to listen closely," the old man began in a hushed voice, pointing his gaunt shaking hand at me. "Can't you sit down? My neck has gotten stiff looking at you."

This was my boss. Grumpy and irritable as usual. I perched on the chair he'd motioned me to and leaned forward, obeying the commanding gesture of his bony hand. What kind of Machiavellian scenario was this?

"I'm all ears, Sir."

Never in my life had I ever called Nikanor *"sir"* yet. Admittedly, I'd done it on purpose in the vain hope of scrounging a couple extra Rep points from him. By now, I already knew that NPCs expected you to play your role by the book. Courtesy of the game developers.

The old lawyer seemed to have appreciated my gesture. He even puffed out his lower lip in pride. "I need to tell you something, Olgerd. I've had a lot of messengers in my lifetime. Really a lot. Most of them were stupid, lazy and dumb. I've also seen a lot of rude ones. I hang them from a different tree, if you know what I mean..." he coughed. "But I've never had anyone quite like you. Somebody who's efficient, discreet and, most importantly, trustworthy."

I couldn't help glancing at my sleeve decorated with a colored ribbon. It looked as if it worked. Could be a coincidence, though. "You're very kind, Sir."

"Very well. As I've said, I have some business in

that part of the world. Think you can do it?"

A system message popped up in my view,

You've received a quest: Old Nikanor's Interest

You will collect and daily report all legal and court news in the location known as The Maragar Citadel and Its Environments.

Reward: Unknown

Accept: Yes/No

As I was skimming the message, the old man continued,

"You won't have much to do. I just need a pair of eyes and ears over there. I'm thinking of expanding. If everything works out, there might be a place for you in it too. So what do you think?"

"I don't know, really. I'm going there to serve in the army. I don't think I'll have the time," I shamelessly upped the ante.

The old lawyer curved his toothless mouth in a knowing smile. He might have been an NPC but he hadn't been born yesterday. "Don't worry about your reward. I can be grateful."

As if in confirmation, a new system message appeared,

By agreeing to help Nikanor, you automatically keep your reward for doing your monthly Reputation quest.

So that's how it was, then? It was worth having come here, after all. Well worth it!

"What I'm asking you to do isn't that difficult,"

he continued in a whisper. "Seeing as you can't come here and report to me, all you can do is check the news and make notes in this little journal," he pushed a battered old notebook toward me. "I'm especially interested in inheritance and divorce cases. But you know that already."

I glanced at the notebook.

Name: Nikanor's Old Journal
Type: Quest item

Nothing special, really. Most likely, all his "secret" quests weren't worth a damn. I could only imagine how many players had been forced to listen to the old lawyer's revelations. Unique quest, yeah right! According to Dmitry, all such quests were cyclical. They didn't repeat very often, but repeat they did. Nikanor must have issued them to lots of people before me. But as for the game developers, their agendas were pretty clear. Firstly, they strove for authenticity — and from my own experience, these "Mirror souls" did deliver! This world was as authentic as they came.

Secondly, Reputation quests fell into the category of so-called social quests. And when it came down to it, I really didn't want to second-guess the developers' secret agendas.

Thirdly... yes, it was probably worth it. Not for me, of course. How was I supposed to understand his phrase about "reporting all the news to him"? On the surface, that sounded easy enough. I'd have to spend some time every day checking a few local rags, than entering the results into Nikanor's logbook. Easy peasy. Still, the task wasn't without its hidden dangers. Not too big nor too many, but still. I'd probably have to buy at least a dozen newspapers every day which was going to cost me a few gold. Plus the writing materials. In Mirror World, everything was interconnected. Someone had to play an Alchemist to make the ink; the quills were delivered to the stationery shop by some local farmer like my old friend Zachary. He'd had all sorts of goods for sale on that cart of his on market day. That was how it worked here.

"Agreed," I proffered my hand to the old man.

Having accepted all the tasks and bidden my goodbyes, I finally hurried out into the fresh air. All I had left to do was visit Mila; then I was free to proceed to my new deployment.

I dropped into a bakery on my way and bought some treats for Tommy. Hopefully, he was much better by now.

Ronald's wife Rita answered the door. She beamed and asked me to come in.

"Here," I handed her the pink paper bag containing cream cakes. "They're very fresh."

Tommy shot out of the lounge like a ginger-topped rocket and began pestering his auntie for his share.

"You eat your dinner first," Rita said didactically, "then you can have your sweet."

"They always do this," the kid sighed, following the pink bag with his longing stare as his auntie took it to the kitchen.

"Master Olgerd!" the familiar voice made me swing round.

Smiling cheerfully, Mila was coming down the stairs. Same ginger curls, same funny freckles on her cute snub nose. She was wearing a blue summer dress with a small translucent turquoise scarf. "I'm so pleased to see you!"

"Hi," I smiled. "I decided to check on your invalid — only he's no invalid anymore!"

The woman beamed. "Please come into the lounge! Would you like some coffee?"

"I wouldn't say no. I've been rushing around like a headless chicken all day. Too many things to do."

"Excellent!"

The two women lay the table in no time. A few minutes later we were already sipping our coffees. No idea what they could smell — if they could smell anything at all. It's not that important, anyway. I took another swig and finally remembered this aroma — or rather, I remembered the place where I'd smelled it first.

It had been in early May, when Sveta and I had just gotten married and gone on a Mediterranean break. We used to sit on the terrace of some local coffee shop, drinking coffee and watching the local kids fool around on the beach.

I was so engrossed in my reverie I didn't at first hear Rita addressing me,

"Master Olgerd! Sir! Are you okay?"

I rubbed the bridge of my nose. "I'm fine," I muttered. "Sorry. I was just reminiscing. Did you say something?"

She nodded. "I said we were expecting you."

"Were you really?" I asked in surprise, then slapped my forehead as I realized. "Did Ronald tell you I was leaving?"

"He did," Mila said. "That's why we were waiting for you. We were sure you wouldn't leave without saying goodbye."

I could read in her face that she wanted to ask me about something. Something very important.

"Let me guess," I began. "There's something you want me to do, right?"

A blush flushed Mila's face.

"The thing is," Rita spoke for her, "she thinks you're already fed up with her constant requests over these last few days."

"Not at all," I waved my hands at her. "That's nothing. What's more: I might owe you just as much. Without your recommendation, I might have spent ages looking for a reputable place to stay. I suppose I could say that you and Tommy were the first friends I made in this city."

"Exactly!" Rita said. "That's what I told her myself. Nothing's too inconvenient for good friends, is it?"

A message flashed before my eyes. I very nearly jumped. Good job the other two didn't notice.

Congratulations! Two or more locals consider you their friend.

Reward: +300 to your Reputation with Mellenville.

I did a quick check of my stats. Almost fifteen hundred, excellent.

"You're absolutely right," I replied with a smile. "You can count on me. I'm all ears."

Rita laid an encouraging hand on the other woman's shoulder.

"You see," Mila struggled to find the right words. "What I'm about to ask you is sort of... risky. Dangerous even."

I tensed up. We had developed a friendly relationship, that was true, but I didn't need any unnecessary risks, either. Especially as I already had too much on my plate as it was.

"Before I tell you what it's about, please promise me you'll decline if you consider it to be too dangerous. Your refusal will not affect your relationship with our family, I assure you. We understand perfectly well that you aren't a warrior nor a combat wizard. You are a regular peaceful citizen of Mellenville."

I nodded. What could I say? She was perfectly right.

Mila smiled. "Thank you for being honest with me. I can speak freely now. The thing is, Ronald did tell us where you were about to go."

"He did indeed," Rita agreed. "The Maragar Citadel is not the best place for the likes of you, dear Olgerd."

I only shrugged, as in, *Ours is not to reason why.*

"And we admire you for that! You make a

worthy example for all Mellenville citizens!"

I almost expected a new system message but no, it looked as if there was a limit to their freebies.

So I preserved a modest silence. Had you known, my dears, how I'd have loved to decline your quest.

"I'm not going to beat around the bush," Mila said. "You must be in a hurry. The thing is... I'd like you to pass this letter to my husband."

I glanced at the object she was offering me and very nearly choked, seeing the recipient's name on the envelope.

> *Name: Letter from Mila*
> *Type: Quest item*
> *Deliver to: the Maragar Citadel*
> *Recipient: Captain Gard*

Chapter Two

Captain Gard! A coincidence? Very possible. Another prank of my mysterious patron programmer? Not very likely. Whoever he was, Andrew "Pierrot" Petrov wasn't that influential. Mellenville was way out of his league.

What was it, then? Could it be my Trust characteristic finally kicking in? This was a workable theory. Why not? I would be the first to agree that none of it sounded particularly plausible. Then again, anybody could have been in my place. I'll tell you more: had there been a player back there by the fountain on my first day in Mellenville whose Trust level was one point higher than mine, Tommy would have asked him for help instead — not me.

Then again, what if I was wrong? That was also a possibility. In any case, I had plenty of food for thought.

It looked like I'd managed to lay my hands on

one of those multi-step Reputation quests that Dmitry had described in such picturesque detail. If I stuck to my "theory of non-eventuality", I was looking at a very interesting picture indeed. What had happened could be viewed as some sort of chain reaction. First I meet Tommy. Through him I meet his Mom and his uncle Ronald. Next thing, the system generates a long-term quest tailor-made for me — which was already a bit of a stretch. Actually, had I asked Mila about the name of Tommy's father earlier, it would have clarified a lot of things straight away.

So that man with a scar from the picture was Captain Gard. In other words, my future commander was Mila's husband and Tommy's father. I found it hard to believe that there might be another Captain Gard in the game. Hadn't Mila told me her husband served on the border? At the time, I hadn't paid any heed to her words. Oh well, lesson learned. If I wasn't mistaken, of course.

Actually... I got the impression that an NPC's status in the city directly affected the size of quest rewards. No wonder players flocked around the Mayor's and Chief of City Guards' houses. I could understand them: they wanted it all and they wanted it now. But as a rule, their kind didn't last in Mellenville. It didn't take them long before they gave all these Reputation quests the finger and left for the more mob-rich locations to prove their prowess. I had nothing to do with the likes of them.

I just hoped that Captain Gard was a powerful figure in this game.

I had to stay in Ronald's house for another

half-hour. The moment Mila had learned about my mission, she immediately wrote another letter recommending me to her husband as a friend of the family. Things seemed to be working out. Better still, things were definitely looking up! It's true that some high-paying player might find my petty reputation exploits a worthless waste of time — and my forthcoming trip to the Frontier, an exercise in senility. I didn't care. I didn't give a damn what anyone might think about me. As Weigner had rightly said, each Mirror World player had his or her own agendas.

I walked away and bade my farewell to the city. I especially liked the Flower Boulevard which led directly to the portal station. I could have taken a shortcut via Craftsmen's Alley — my route of preference in my errand-running days. But not today. Today I wanted to take my time to admire the beautiful flower arrangements that the city florists replaced daily.

Many years ago I'd happened to be in Beijing on business. They had put me up in a small, tidy hotel. My windows faced a square. Can't remember its name — nor that of the hotel, either. I remembered surprisingly little of that trip. Everything around me had been happening too fast. Besides, it hadn't been a long visit — two or three days at most.

The one thing I did remember were my awakenings — or rather, what I could see from my window every morning. An enormous flower bed occupied the center of the square. Beijing is absolutely packed with plants. In October, the city is full of flowers and greenery. So this particular flower bed — *my* flower bed — used to change its pattern and color scheme every morning. On the day of my arrival, I admired its blue blossoms. The next morning, I expected to see the blue and green patch from my window — only to be greeted by a red and yellow floral dragon. I froze by the window open-mouthed. Later I was told that a special team did nightly rounds of the city in their van, changing patterns on some of the city's flower beds.

The Flower Boulevard was very similar in this respect with its blossoming turquoise arches, colorful statues of magic animals frozen in fancy poses, its snow-white fountains and bright shrubs fashioned into fantastical shapes. Today of all days I was desperate for my girls to see their splendor. For the first time in the many hours I'd spent in Mirror World, I made myself a solemn promise that one day I would show all this to Christina and Sveta.

The portal station met me with its habitual bustle. Actually, this place revealed the players' respective gaming experience like no other. Newbies stood out like a sore thumb — they always did. And it wasn't even about their yellow name tags: more about their behavior. Take the two Alven girls who'd just stepped out of the portal. Their eyes were about to pop out, their heads seemingly turning at 360 degrees. Despite their rather high levels, the girls grinned from ear to ear, behaving like village schoolgirls on their first trip to a big city. Heh! I'd only stayed here for nine days but already I felt like a local.

I froze in front of the ticket terminal.

Greetings, Olgerd!
This is Portal Terminal # 4578.
Would you like to buy a ticket?

Okay, if you say so.

Please choose your destination.

Last night, I'd had plenty of time to look into this seemingly innocent request. Mirror World's meager info portal had offered me lots of options. Getting to the Maragar Citadel required two transfers. Or three, rather — but the latter, as I understood it, was nothing to look forward to.

My future duty station was located at the very edge of the Lands of Light. Which was probably why the game developers had decided not to create a direct portal jump to the Maragar Citadel. Why would they, if they could extract more gold from the players' virtual pockets this way?

I had several possible routes which didn't differ much, after all. I could make the first two jumps without even leaving the portal stations. Their choice made no difference: they all cost the same.

The Maragar Citadel and Its Environments was an enormous location that was divided into several smaller sub-locations, instances and one-horse towns. My initial itinerary was Drammen Town where Lady Mel's emerald fields were located. That was where I'd have to sign up in her local office. There were quite a few other little towns in the area: our Lady Mel, a.k.a. the Lady of Storms, had laid her manicured hands on quite a large chunk of real estate during the clan wars. Drammen suited me fine — mainly because it was quiet. Or so it was described on gaming forums.

As for the third and last transfer... as I'd said I wasn't looking forward to it. Especially considering the fact that I'd have to take it at least twice daily.

The thing was, the only way to get to the Citadel was by crossing a rather large location known as the Wastelands. And that, let me tell you, was something — at least that's what the few eyewitnesses used to claim. A wide prairie inhabited by all sorts of in-game creatures — which were, unfortunately, equal doses of advanced and nasty. In other words, my zero level precluded me from as much as showing up in that part of the world.

Still, every problem has a solution. As practice shows, human ingenuity knows no limits. Some of the more entrepreneurial players who must have realized that the Citadel would always be a Mecca for Reputation pilgrims had thrown together a quick and quite lucrative business: the Caravans.

I wasn't exactly sure how it was supposed to work but some forum members swore by their reliability. Very well. We'd have to see, wouldn't we?

I scrolled through hundreds of place names, finally settling on Drammen.

The chosen destination requires a double transfer.
Please choose the first transfer point.
I clicked randomly on the list of towns offered.

Cost: 20 gold.

Warning! The effect of teleportation will cause your Energy level to drop 500 pt.

Confirm your purchase: Yes/No

Confirm.

Thank you! Your name has been added to the Portal listings. You can teleport when ready. Have a good trip!

So that was basically it. I'd chosen my destination. I'd bought my ticket. Time to bid this station goodbye. I wasn't likely to come back here for the next month at least.

Before entering the portal, I cast a look around. What was awaiting me there? I just hoped I wouldn't end up as some mob's breakfast on my very first day in service. And I still had to get to the Citadel.

Never mind. Off we go!

As I stepped into the portal, I glimpsed a player standing next to the terminal I'd just used. His face was half-concealed by the hood of a dark cloak. One of the magic classes, apparently. From where I stood, I couldn't make out his name or level. Nothing special really: just some guy standing by the terminal.

It was his eyes. The wizard's glare bored a hole in me. When our eyes met, he swung round and headed toward the exit.

For a few moments, I watched him go but he never looked back. Could I have been mistaken? Paranoid? Probably. Never mind. Now I really had to go.

* * *

This Drammen Town was a right hole! I could already feel that staying here was going to be a bunch of laughs.

Cold rain pelted me from the moment I'd exited the portal. A game it might have been, but I was cold and miserable just like in real life. The local architecture had some leaning toward gothic which made a nice backdrop to the lousy weather and knee-deep mud. Yuck. How had I managed to get into this cesspit after the neat sunlit Mellenville? I only had to hope that the rain wouldn't last.

The system's greeting set my alarm bells ringing too, especially its last part,

Greetings, Olgerd! Welcome to glorious Drammen Town!

Warning! Type of climate: moderately aggressive

Warning! Players below level 80 are advised to abstain from visiting Drammen.

I just loved it. Already I felt like turning round and diving back into the portal in search of sunnier climes.

I hurried to install the *Drammen and Its Environments* app. As if sensing my impatience, the bot helpfully highlighted the route to Lady Mel's offices. Off we go, then!

The first drawback declared itself soon enough. After only a few minutes of walking, I was soaked. Cold raindrops hammered my face, sending rivulets of water trickling down my beard as I waded through the mud. What was the local Mayor thinking of? Or was he simply past caring about his town's Reputation? If the game developers wanted to let players experience the entire scope of the doubtful allure of Frontier life — they had succeeded brilliantly.

Drammen indeed turned out to be a very quiet place. Too quiet, I'd say. Apparently, forum users had been careful not to alienate any potential newcomers.

As I walked, I met no one. The town seemed dead. Actually, I could understand them. They were probably sitting by their nice cozy fireplaces in their nice cozy houses, snug as a bunch of bugs in a rug.

Finally the bot brought me to a dark gloomy edifice with the familiar sign depicting Aquila — the Roman legion's eagle. It was already 11 a.m. but no one seemed in a hurry to answer the door. I couldn't see any potential workers impatient to get down to work, either. Apparently, business wasn't booming.

Never mind. Hadn't Weigner told me not to bother to clock on but to go straight to the mine and start working? Still I thought checking in was a good idea. I went on knocking.

After ten more minutes of unsuccessful door-bashing, I gave up and entered a new address into the bot's memory. My conscience was clear, anyway.

It took my satnav a few minutes to guide me to the town's center. Or should I say, to its poor excuse for a center. The dark gloomy buildings, some in a bad state of semi-repair, created the impression I'd somehow ended up in one of those vampire sagas.

The good news was, the road was getting considerably better as I progressed. Although no one had bothered to switch off the rain, at least the place was relatively mud-free. My first steps along a street paved with ugly uneven cobbles felt like absolute bliss. I'd only been here a half-hour and already I was prepared to run for my life! Which must have been exactly what the game developers wanted players to feel. Very well. In your freakin' dreams.

I still had another five-minute walk to the caravan office that pushed its services under a sign saying *The Guiding Eye* when a system message popped up,

Warning! Your Hat and Boots have lost 1 pt. Durability!

Was this a joke? I reread the message. It didn't look as if it was. No one was poking fun at me. Apparently, local rain had this destructive effect on a player's clothes. No wonder the street was empty!

I stepped it up. I wasn't going to lose my expensive gear to some stupid rain!

As I pushed the caravan office's door, I was darker than the thunderclouds hovering over this abominable excuse for a place. My walk through the town had cost me a few points of my clothes' Durability. I had to look it up on some forum or other. I couldn't remember seeing anything about it anywhere. The admins must have kept a close eye on official resources. Their strategy was quite clear to me: players had to learn from their own experiences. And still I found it quite annoying.

I entered the caravan office and stood there, slightly lost. I hurried to check the bot — but no, it had taken me to the right place. Could the app be out of date? This place was anything but a caravan office. I saw rows of crude tables and wooden chairs and a bar complete with several thugs patrolling the entrance.

Excuse me? As if confirming my doubts, a system message reported that I had the pleasure of entering the Boiling Pot Inn which offered barbecued lamb with onions and assorted veg as tonight's *piece de resistance*.

A few players sat at the tables. The place didn't seem too popular. I studied their faces. They looked drawn and expressionless as if the men were sleeping with their eyes open. They paid no attention to me whatsoever. They must have been studying the info portal to while away the time.

Despite the building's gloomy exterior, the Boiling Pot's rooms looked considerably homelier — cozier, I'd say. An enormous fireplace breathed heat by the far wall. The floor and the walls were lined with wood. I'd expected myself to walk into a dark stone trap — and God was I happy to be wrong!

Mud squelched in my boots as I crossed the room toward the bar. Oh. I'd made a right mess of their floors. I just hoped they wouldn't take offence. Having said that, their cleaning lady needed to earn her skill points too, LOL. She might even make a new level mopping up after me.

"Good morning, Olgerd! How can I help you?"

A pleasant-looking middle-aged woman smiled at me from behind the bar.

"Good morning, er... Talina."

She cast one glance at my drenched clothes and smiled her understanding. "It's some weather outside, isn't it? Wasn't very clever of me to wish you a good morning."

"It's all right," I waved her apology away. "I appreciate your concern. As for the reason of my being here... I have to admit I feel a bit lost. My satnav must be playing up. I was looking for the caravan office but it brought me here instead."

"Don't worry," she answered with another little smile. "There's nothing wrong with your bot. The Guiding Eyes meet here in my inn. There's no point in them renting an office space. They're constantly on the go."

I breathed a sigh of relief. "I see now. I was afraid I might need to go out again, you know. Into the great outdoors."

She nodded knowingly. "That's what we can do," she suggested. "Varn — the caravanners' leader — won't be here for another hour. I suggest you install their app. It's not big but it might take some time for you to study. I can see you're soaked. You must be completely frozen. I insist you take a seat by the fireplace. This way you can combine business with pleasure. In the meantime, I'll fetch you a nice hot cup of tea. What would you say to that?"

"Excellent," I smiled back. "You're so kind. This

place isn't at all as gloomy as I thought it would be. Thank you!"

"Thank *you*," she replied, than added with a bitter note, "*Kind* is an overstatement, I'm afraid. It's just that my brother Varn is a certified penny-pincher. He knows I'm *kind* as you say — and he uses it."

It was true that I'd been slightly puzzled by her involvement with the caravanners' affairs and the fact she'd suggested I install their app. But now the picture was clear. This was a family business.

I could never understand people who were eager to discuss their family in front of total strangers. Not that she'd said anything negative about her brother, but still. Personally, I was a very reserved person in this respect. I could never air my family's affairs in public. Neither did I enjoy listening about somebody else's.

"Actually," I hurried to change the subject, "seeing as your brother isn't coming for a while, I'd love to have a quick bite to eat. The smells coming from your kitchen are irresistible."

She flashed me another smile, followed by a system message offering me a download of the aforementioned app.

I sat back on a broad bench and stretched my legs, offering my feet up to the fire. Oh. It felt too good. A well-deserved meal and some warmth were definitely welcome.

Let's have a look at their app, then.

It was indeed small but very informative. Just as I supposed, The Guiding Eye offered both transportation of passengers and their protection. It had over twenty routes to choose from, complete with security guards. In my particular case, the guards' levels were all 100+, even though the mobs in the caravan's path were below 90.

Never mind. What did I expect? They needed to make their living too. I, however, with my miserable level zero was more than dependent on their services.

The transfer from Drammen to the Citadel took about forty-five minutes. Cost: fifteen gold. Multiplied by two trips a day, that's thirty. Costly but doable. Not as comfortable as portal travel but I couldn't do anything about it. I'd made my bed and now I had to lie in it. It was already a good thing there was a commute available, allowing me to come and work here daily. At least I'd save some money on the rent! I could only hope that living in the Citadel barracks was worth it.

Jesus. How on earth had I managed to walk into all this?

The caravanners had their own discounts too. They offered a choice of travel passes: for ten, twenty and thirty trips each. I could use the twenty-trip one. It cost 260 gold. I thought I might buy one once I finished reading.

Another important thing: I wouldn't have to walk these forty-five minutes' worth of travel. Which in my case was extremely cost-effective. The Guiding Eyes transported their clients in armored wagons which by themselves offered guaranteed protection from local monsters. That's provided the guards failed to defend the passengers — which, according to the caravanners themselves, was impossible.

I also saw some positive reviews of their work left by top players and respectable clan members. All this looked perfectly kosher. No sign of any strings attached.

"You! Are you warmer now?!"

The threatening growl distracted me from my musings. I raised my head. A giant Rhoggh towered not two paces away from me. Name: Varn. Level: 150. He was hung like a Christmas tree with stabbing and slashing weapons. The grimace on his fanged mug was apparently supposed to denote a smile.

This was one tough guy. If all the caravan guards were like him, it wasn't that bad after all. You wouldn't want to mess with Talina's brother.

"Yes, thank you," I managed a smile.

"You're the one who wanted to join a caravan?" he asked, taking a seat opposite. The crude bench creaked its complaint. I got the impression that the inch-thick tabletop was buckling under the weight of his elbows.

"Exactly," I hurriedly assured him. "I'd like to buy a twenty-trip pass. To the Citadel."

Varn bared his teeth in a scowl which seemed to signify his satisfaction with my words. Strangely enough, his toothy grin betrayed no surprise. They must have seen a lot of guys like myself. My mentioning the Citadel didn't seem to throw him, either.

"Oh well," he growled. "If you're happy about everything, I'll forward you the contract."

* * *

Once we'd signed the provisional agreement, he said, "There's one little problem."

I tensed. "What's up?"

"It's this wretched weather, dammit. We can't get to the Citadel until tomorrow night."

"You don't mean it!"

Talk about bad news. I was going to lose another day, almost. And I needed to report to Captain Gard. This was bad. Very.

Seeing my jaw drop, Varn tried to reason with me,

"You need to understand, in weather like this you'd better steer clear of that location. Traveling cross-country in this weather is not a walk in the park. I wouldn't like to be seen there on a night like this. Let alone you, with your zero level and unprotected gear. Cheer up, man. The local wizards say it will clear up by tomorrow night. This place doesn't have weather forecasts. It's all different here."

I fell silent, digesting the news, as he impatiently tapped his curved claws on the tabletop.

"Right!" he finally said. "I'm sending you a friend request. I'll contact you tomorrow to let you know the departure time."

"Okay..." I mumbled, deep in thought, as I mechanically accepted his invitation.

This was a far cry from Mellenville. Mellenville!

This was worse than Leuton even. This was exactly what I didn't need: unscheduled transfers that depended on weather conditions. Between my serving in the Citadel and working in Drammen's mines, popping my clogs seemed to be only a question of time.

When Varn began to rise from the table, I finally came round and hurried to ask, "What did you mean by unprotected, er, gear?"

He chuckled. "It must be your first visit to this kind of place."

"Why, is it so obvious?"

"Sure," he nodded. "Anyone in the Glasshouse can tell straight away you come from more neutral climes."

"*Neutral?*"

"Yep. You might have noticed that it's rather damp here. It's like this virtually all year round. Winter is even worse. We have snowstorms and freezing temperatures. I can see you used to work in starting locations."

"I didn't realize it was that obvious," I said. "Now I'm curious. What else can you say about me?"

He grinned. "That's not difficult. I'll bet you got some cool quest and hurried over to the Citadel to complete it. Which doesn't happen very often to zero levels. The Citadel is not a good place for the likes of you. The best you can do is finish your quest and take your sorry behind back home."

He was right, of course. While I'd been sitting here reading up on them I'd noticed there wasn't a single Grinder in the room. All players here were level

100 give or take.

"You don't see many working-class heroes here, do you?" I asked.

"We do and we don't. But loners like yourself don't come here often."

"I see. I'll keep that in mind. You still didn't tell me what's wrong with my gear."

"There's nothing wrong with it," he said. "For a zero level, it's actually quite decent. Now you need to add some elemental protection to it otherwise it won't last long, not in this kind of weather. Water eats through Durability like hell. If you get soaked, you can expect all sorts of surprises. I can see you already noticed that."

"I did. It's not a good thing. The info portal said nothing about it."

"The info portal!" he guffawed. "You know anyone who reads it? Want a tip?"

"Sure."

"Go to the auction and have a look around. Check out the prices. They have everything there. What you need is elemental protection called Anti-Humidity. That's the only kind you need for the time being. Right, I'm off. See you tomorrow."

He waved me a clawed goodbye and headed for the exit.

I followed his massive bulk with my stare. He might be right — I really should do some market research. Seeing as I had time to burn.

Elemental protection, he said? Let's have a look.

The auction's search engine helpfully offered a

---

dozen pages of relevant results. They had all sorts: protection from humidity, sunshine, cold — you name it. I also saw lots of things that might fit my pet. Not that I needed them at the moment. My Prankster and I, we were doomed to remain level-zero for the rest of our in-game lives.

A message from Varn interrupted my studies. I jumped. I'd completely forgotten I'd added him to my friend list.

Olgerd, I've been thinking. This might be interesting for you. There's a local shop called Rainbow Store. They sell all sorts of cool stuff. I'm not sure but I think they have elementals too. The owner's name is Nilius. Tell him I sent you. Here're the shop's coordinates in case you're interested. Take care! Don't get your feet wet!

The message ended with an active link highlighted in blue. Opening it would make my bot create the optimal route.

I thanked Varn and clicked it. Let my bot do its job. Why not? I could use a walk. I had plenty of time till tomorrow night. Information was always welcome. I just hoped I could glean something from the shop owner.

Before leaving, I made the necessary arrangements with Talina to secure a room for the night. I walked out without saying goodbye to anyone. The rain was pouring down now. If it rained in hell, that's exactly what it would have looked like. Not as wet even.

Apart from the optimal route to the shop, my bot had helpfully offered me a list of all magic-trading shops in the area. The choice was admittedly modest but this Rainbow place had some competition, that's for sure. Supposing that Varn received a commission for every customer he sent Nilius' way, no wonder he'd bothered to PM some humble Grinder. You'd think he had nothing better to do with his time than offer free tips to noobs. But if he received a nice little bonus every time he meted out his advice — that was totally different. Then again, why should I care? Everyone needed to earn a living. He probably had to feed his family or pay for his studies.

I ran all the way to the shop. A couple of times I slipped and very nearly stumbled over the cobblestones but it was worth it. I entered the shop with a satisfied smile: I hadn't lost a single Durability point.

The Rainbow Store's interior was styled like an alchemist's lab: carved wooden cabinets and shelf after shelf of all sorts of little pots and vials.

Behind the counter stood a middle-aged man. A thick black beard hung down to his chest. He was wearing a large beret and a long dark green robe.

I couldn't see the wizard's name even though I already knew it. An NPC, apparently. That was a surprise. How interesting. I understood Varn much better now. Sending me here must have been part of a quest he was doing.

"Good evening, Sir. How can I help you?" the wizard asked with a friendly smile.

"Good evening," I replied, fighting off my desire

to tell him everything I thought about this "good evening" in this wonderful place. "I'm looking for Nilius."

"Who sent you here?" the wizard asked, businesslike.

Oh. So my new friend wasn't his only "agent", apparently. "Varn did."

I struggled to remain serious. He looked so much like that shaggy French comedian, Pierre Richard. If you shaved off his beard and removed his beret you could cast him in the French original of *The Toy*. Heh! Actually, he might look better in the beret...

"Is everything okay?" the wizard asked.

"Sure. Fine. I... I just remembered something. I hope you can help me. Varn says that you might have some protection for my clothes."

"Ah," he smiled, "you've come to the right place."

Once he'd said that, his nametag appeared above his head. Excellent. The ice was broken.

"What exactly do you have in mind?" Nilius paused, then waved his own question away. "Why should I even ask! It's Anti-Humidity, isn't it? You must have already appreciated all the joys of our local climate."

"You could say that. Think you can help me?"

"Of course. Take a look at this."

He produced several small boxes and laid them out on the counter. They looked eerily familiar.

"Runes?" I asked.

"Not quite. Elemental protection."

He gingerly opened one of the boxes. What did

he have here? Small — about half the size of the palm of my hand — flat teardrop-shaped tablets made of glass. He had four kinds of them — or rather, four different colors: green, navy blue, purple as well as some made of regular transparent glass. I focused on the latter.

Name: Vann
Type: Elemental protection, regular.
Effect: +5 to Resistance to Humidity
Restrictions: none

I gave each a quick check. The purple ones were the most powerful: +20 to Resistance to Humidity. The good news was, all of them fitted me. Now all I had to do was ask about the price. Actually, taking the purple ones wouldn't be such a good idea. They were for Master-plus and seeing as I didn't want to blow my cover prematurely, I decided to make do with the blue ones.

"Master Nilius, would you be so kind as to tell me how these undoubtedly wonderful appliances work?"

"Oh! Absolutely! I'd be honored! Seeing as you asked me yourself... Actually, it all depends on the degree of the environment's aggression. For instance, you have no need for these transparent elements. Even if you attach them to each and every item of your gear, it still wouldn't be enough. The easiest and cheapest option would be to buy a regular cloak with +50 to Resistance to Humidity. This would last you the few days it normally takes one to sort out whatever business one has here and leave these rainy climes for good. In other words, the transparent elements are only good against some gentle sunshower in one of the Southern provinces. Now the green ones... they're actually quite popular among office workers, shop assistants and tavern owners."

"In other words, they're good enough for a quick dash from building to building," I said.

"Exactly. They might suit you as well. You're going to work in a mine, aren't you? Having said that, the local mines have high humidity levels. Still, the green elements manage the problem perfectly well."

"I appreciate your being so open with me."

"My pleasure," the wizard hid a flattered smile within his beard. "I'm not a profiteer. I'd never try to capitalize on a customer's ignorance."

"Which means I'm doubly lucky to chance upon you," I played along. "How about the remaining runes?"

"The blue ones are popular with all the local Grinders who work outdoors. They have an excellent track record in this part of the world. And as for the purple ones... a proud owner of a full set of those might even take a marathon swim in our local river without having to worry about the state of his gear. Which is only my conjecture, of course. I'm still going to put this idea to the test. I hate swimming in icy water."

"Likewise."

The wizard laughed happily. He seemed all right. Never mind that he was only an NPC. But the game developers! What a bunch of sharks! The info portal said nothing about damage from the elements. It was, like, *come and get soaked so we can sell you some elemental protection*. As soon as I logged out, I'd have to do some quality research — spend a week looking it up if necessary.

"So, what have you decided?" the wizard's voice shook me from my musings.

"Oh yes," I said, resurfacing. "Sure. I might take the blue ones."

"Good choice! How many would you like?"

"Seven."

The good news was, elemental protection was considerably cheaper than malachite or sapphire runes. A full set of blue ones was going to cost me two hundred and ten gold. Where was the catch?

"A word of warning," the wizard said. "You can't install the elements onto items. They can only be installed onto runes which in turn have to be installed first. In your case, a Vann Elemental Set would only fit a set of sapphire runes."

This was the answer to my question. In order to protect themselves from Humidity, players would have to shell out for both the runes and the protection itself. And one other thing. Had I still been a Seasoned player, I'd have had a hard time battling the local elements. Now I understood why Lady Mel's offices were permanently closed — I wouldn't be surprised if the lock itself had rusted solid. What Grinder in his right mind would come here to work in the mines? To suffer the cold and humidity damage when he or she could happily work in some normal location with a neutral climate?

I wondered if Weigner had known about this. If he had, it might mean that he needed me more than I needed him. Old fox! Never mind. We'd have to have words about it later, that's all.

It looked like visiting the local HR was a total waste of time. I had to follow Weigner's advice and head directly for the mines.

Which was good news, really. I might still do my daily quota, provided the local emerald fields weren't located too far away. I'd have to check the map.

"I'll take them," I said to the wizard. "All seven. They will fit my set of sapphire runes just fine."

"Great news!" Nilius seemed sincerely happy. "No amount of rain can damage your clothes now. Just make sure you don't abuse them. It wouldn't be a good idea to stay out in the rain for hours at a time."

I nodded. "Thank you. May I install them here?"

"Absolutely! Be my guest!"

After about ten minutes, I left the shop. My characteristics sported a new line:

Resistance to Humidity: +105

This was one good thing. At least now I didn't risk losing all my clothes at the least opportune moment. I imagined my gear melting like soggy paper... yuck.

It was a good job I'd come to this particular shop. Firstly, because of the discount. Even though auction prices for elemental protection were cheaper, Nilius' offer had made it worth my while.

Secondly, in the absence of the Internet I'd gleaned quite a bit from my conversation with the wizard. I'd learned a lot about other things — like different kinds of elemental protection to name just one.

Thirdly, I'd received a quest. Which was only natural, considering that Nilius was an NPC. I could understand Varn's enthusiasm much better now. His job was to advertise Nilius' shop to all and sundry. In return, Nilius offered his "agents" some decent discounts and bonuses every time they needed something from his shop. Good system.

The rain was bucketing down. Perfect weather to check out my new acquisitions. I purposefully stepped into the next puddle that chanced my way. My boots stayed dry! Ditto for my clothes: they too were dry as if covered with a layer of protective film. Excellent.

Cold raindrops pelted my face; rivulets of water ran down my beard. Still, I was smiling. Things had turned out not as bad as they had originally seemed.

As I stepped into the next puddle in my way, I noticed that my experiments had an audience. It took me a few more moments to realize:

I was being followed.

Chapter Three

I bent down, as if to tie non-existent shoe laces on my boots, and tried to take a peek at my pursuers. There were two of them, both squat and broad-shouldered. Dwarves? Gnomes?

Gray cloaks concealed their bodies. I couldn't see their faces under the hoods. Then one of them jumped over a puddle, offering a glimpse of a black beard. They had to be dwarves. Or at least one of them was.

That they were following someone was obvious even to me with my complete lack of spying experience. And they were following me. They kept behind me at an ever-constant distance. The moment I stopped, they did the same. As far as spies went, they behaved pretty strange. Either they were out to scare the living daylights out of me — and so far they had admittedly succeeded — or they were just as new to stalking as I was.

Another question was, who were they? Shantarsky's henchmen? But how did he know? Had he really bribed someone in the office? Unlikely. Who would want to risk their job because of small fry like myself? Then again, if the price was right... I had little doubt that father and son Shantarsky wouldn't sleep until they wreaked their revenge on me. And the wizard I'd seen near the portal station — what if he hadn't been part of my paranoid imagination?

But what if these two had nothing to do with Shantarsky? What then? What were they — street muggers? Or some black scavengers who thought me easy prey?

I'd read the admins' warning. Apparently, had someone mugged me here, I'd have to go to the local law enforcement authorities who were conspicuous by their absence. Filing a complaint with the admins wouldn't work. This was gameplay. I'd strayed too far away from the starting locations already.

Right. I had to pull myself together. Nothing had happened yet. I worked for Lady Mel which was a hefty argument in any dispute. In case of a physical assault I could always file a complaint with my employer. Not that it would amount to a lot: who would want to stick up for me? But as a threat, it might just work. At least I hoped so.

I quickened my pace. I had to get to the tavern ASAP. At least there I wouldn't be alone. If push came to shove, I could summon some help. If things got worse, I could always ask Varn to accompany me to the portal station. For him it would be a quick way to make a few gold. But that was the worst-case scenario. I still had to work here — hopefully for a long time. I wasn't going to give in to paranoia.

Having given myself this pep talk, I darted for the Boiling Pot Inn. Actually, talking about Varn... I had an idea. I should give it some thought.

My change of pace must have thrown off my pursuers. When I finally opened the inn's door, I turned and looked back. The street was empty. I hoped they'd lost me. Good. I must have shaken them off.

I entered the inn and breathed a sigh of relief. The room was packed. Almost all of the tables were already taken. Some of the players sported Steel Shirts' logos on their chests. Even though technically I wasn't part of the clan, I could still count on their support.

On seeing me, Talina regretfully nodded at a table by the window. All the places by the fireplace were taken. The area around it was absolutely packed.

I smiled gratefully and took the seat she'd pointed me to. She arrived almost straight away.

"I'm sorry about this-" she began.

I stopped her mid-sentence. "It's fine, thank you. You don't need to apologize. I'm very happy I got a seat at all. Besides, I'm not wet, courtesy of your brother. The tip he gave me was extremely handy."

She smiled. "I'm happy to hear that. Your room is ready. Here's the key. It's number five."

"Excellent, thank you. I'll have a hot drink and go upstairs."

"Would you like some mulled wine?"

"Perfect. Just what I need."

Talina fluttered off to get my order.

Oh. Mulled wine! I'd first tasted it in Dresden at a Christmas market. Sveta and I had spent all day roaming around the town. By the evening, we'd found ourselves embracing the funfair spirit. Lights galore, Christmas arches, tree decorations, pyramids and hand-carved figurines of smoking men...

We had been drinking hot mulled wine and eating Christmas *stollen* packed with raisins and candied fruit. We were happy. Oh yes. A good day it had been. One of the best in my entire life.

Soon my table was graced by a small clay mug filled with steaming burgundy liquid. The mug's side was decorated with a slice of lemon. I could guarantee that the wine was going to taste exactly like it had in Dresden. My subconscious would take care of it.

I focused on the mug and immediately discovered a very touching detail, courtesy of Talina.

Name: Mulled Wine
Effect: every mouthful gives +40 to Energy
Restriction: Only inside the Boiling Pot Inn.

Not much, but so very sweet of her. Wish I'd had some of this on my first day in Mirror World.

I was about to taste the spicy-smelling drink when the front door opened, letting in my two stocky pursuers. Gosh. Just when I thought I had nothing to worry about.

I cast a quick look around. No one in the room had paid any attention to the newcomers. Talina must have popped out into the kitchen. All the patrons were busy eating and talking.

I tensed, shrinking into my chair. I hadn't had time to lower my eyes though. The two "cloaks" had noticed me. Judging by the looks they exchanged, they must have recognized me.

Stomping his steel boots across the room, one of the two headed in my direction. Trying not to betray my anxiety, I cast another look around. Some Steel Shirts' warriors sat three tables away from me. If I protested, would they help me?

My pursuers were barely a few paces away. They'd removed their hoods. I could finally see their faces. Even though "face" wasn't the right word to describe one of them.

I was right: he was indeed a dwarf. The other turned out to be a Dwand. What a strange combination. I already knew that these two races didn't exactly get along. Then again, how could I be sure? It might have been true for Grinders but not for combat accounts. And judging by their levels, these two had to be combat types. Both were level 120.

Wow. Admittedly I was flattered by the fact that Shantarsky might have sent his top fighters just to get me. If it had been him, of course.

I took a screenshot and turned the video recorder on. This way I'd at least have some evidence. My right hand was going numb. Oh! I'd very nearly crumbled the clay mug to dust.

I snatched my hand away — too quickly probably. I had to get a grip. Breathe in. Breathe out. No one should notice my anxiety. Like this. Good.

The two stopped within arm's reach of my table. The dwarf's name was Saash while the gray-faced Dwand's sported *Dan* on his name tag. Strangely enough, their faces betrayed embarrassment. I expected to see just about anything: disdain, hatred, indifference or maybe even glee. But embarrassment?

I decided to take the bull by the horns. "Listen, guys," I forced my voice to sound calm and confident. "I've no idea what you want from me. But I have to warn you that I work for Melorie, the Lady of Storms! Whatever you're up to, you'd better stay away from me. You don't need problems, do you?"

Phew! I'd said it! I was bluffing, of course, but that was the way to do it. Problems, yeah right. As if the wife of the Steel Shirts' leader had nothing better to do with her time than run to my rescue. She didn't even know I existed.

"Are you okay?" the Dwand asked, looking lost. "We just wanted to talk."

"Really," the dwarf echoed. "No need to get so worked up."

"So it's my fault now, is it? You tail me all across town and you're blaming me?"

Surprisingly, the dwarf blushed crimson. His Dwand buddy, however, was quick on the draw.

"So okay, sorry, we overdid it. We first wanted to follow you to wherever you were going. How can you talk in this rain?"

"That's some faulty logic, young man," I said. "Hadn't it occurred to you that it might alarm me? This area isn't exactly welcoming to my types, you know. You could have come over and spoken to me."

I'd called him *young man* for a reason. You couldn't fool me with a person's choice of avatar anymore. I'd already learned to tell a player's approximate age. My gaming experience had begun to show. These two must have been twenty at the most. They too must have realized they weren't dealing with a teenage student.

The dwarf turned to his friend. "I told you!"

"Okay, I'm sorry," he raised his hands in mock defeat. "I thought it was better that way."

I didn't want to alienate them, otherwise I'd have told him which body part he must have been using to think with.

Good. All clear. False alarm. Somehow I doubted that my spiel might have impressed anyone in the real world. There, I was a bespectacled nerd; here I was an Ennan complete with black eyes and beard. My char could look quite threatening.

The feeling was new to me. People like myself have to fend off bullies on a virtually daily basis. And here the slightest pressure forced others into red-faced apologetic obedience. Heh! Wish I could borrow my Ennan for my daily bus ride! For a couple of days, not more. Shame my mug had failed to impress Slayer back in the Spider Grotto.

Rustling her starched dress, Talina reappeared by my table. "Sir Olgerd? Is everything all right?"

I glanced at my reluctant pursuers. "Perfectly fine, thank you. These young men are here to talk to me."

She nodded, then turned to them, "What will

you drink?"

"Two mulled wines," the dwarf removed his soaked cloak and sat opposite me. The Dwand followed suit.

Once Talina had fluttered away to fetch their orders, I said, "Let's get down to business. What is it you two want from me?"

The Dwand wasn't the type to beat around the bush, either. "We'd like to hire you."

I'd expected anything but that. "Excuse me?"

The dwarf gave his partner a nudge with his elbow. "We really should introduce ourselves. My name's Sasha and this is my brother Dennis. You know our nicknames already. We're really sorry. That wasn't the way to do it. We should have approached you straight away. That would have been more acceptable."

The Dwand tried to say something but the dwarf gave him another nudge, pinning his brother down with a meaningful glare.

How interesting. My first impression had been that Dan was the boss but now I wasn't so sure. Another interesting thing about them was that they had turned out to be brothers. I wouldn't have thought so. A dwarf and a Rock Dwand. Brothers. Then again, what did it matter? My Mirror World experience must have already left its mark. I was beginning to think in gaming terms.

I shrugged. "Apologies accepted. You can spit it out now."

The dwarf nodded his gratitude. "I won't be long. It's a quest. My brother and I, we accepted it when we were still in our 70s. We thought one day we might do it but it didn't work out that way. And this particular quest is very important for our Reputation with the House of Stone Lotus."

"We've been leveling this Rep for ages," Dan butted in. "And now this wretched quest stalls the whole picture."

"What have I got to do with it?"

"You'll see in a minute. Our task is to get ten hearts of the Swamp Kardach. That's twenty between the two of us."

"Listen, guys, in case you didn't notice, I'm only a Grinder."

The Dwand chuckled. "If you were, we wouldn't have come to you."

"Nobody's asking you to fight," his brother added. "We're quite capable of smoking the Kardachs ourselves. They're only level 80. A couple of minutes' work. What we need is a mine digger."

"Young people, the more we talk the less I understand."

"Our quest is in fact tied to your profession," the dwarf hurried to explain. "The scheme is simple. We smoke the Kardach and you pick up his heart."

"Why me?"

"Because his heart is made of stone. Of Swamp Ammolite, to be precise. And as you must have already guessed, one has to be at least an Experienced Mine Digger in order to pick it up."

I paused, taking in the information. Seeing this, the dwarf reduced himself to begging,

"We understand you're busy. You have a job

and all that. It's just that when we saw you next to that magic shop... unaccompanied, without a clan logo... we couldn't believe our luck. That's why we decided to watch you for a while. Just in case. We were afraid of getting into trouble."

"What do you mean?"

"You've heard us," the dwarf said. "Clans don't approve of their workers moonlighting on the side. That's why we thought..."

"Ah yes, yes, right, of course," I pretended I knew what he was talking about. "Now I see. No problem there. Let's sum it up. As far as I understand, you have a quest to kill certain mobs and retrieve their hearts. The problem is, the only person who can pick them up is a Mine Digger, Experienced or above. Is that correct?"

The Dwand nodded. "I couldn't have said better myself."

"Good," I said. "Now allow me to elaborate a little. If you're sitting here trying to talk me into it, I presume you can't get those hearts at auction."

"We can't," the dwarf patiently explained. "They're non-drop. Their owner can't pass them on to anybody else. That's the whole thing. Basically, the job is simple. All you need to do is follow us into the instance and pick up the hearts."

"Wait a sec," I interrupted. "What do you mean, follow you into the instance? I'm a Grinder, aren't I?"

"How long have you been in the game?" Dan the Dwand sounded amazed. "Have you ever mopped up an instance as part of a raid?"

I shook my head.

"I see," Dan said. "You see, when a quest is partially tied to a Profession, raiders can accept Grinders into the group. Herbalists, fishermen, you know what I mean. Any kind."

"And what if they don't join the group?"

"Forget it. A quest resource is only available to group members. A lone Grinder just won't see it. He needs to join first. Your job is to pick up the hearts and hand them over to us."

I paused, thinking. "Oh. That's clever."

"We know how busy you are," the dwarf repeated. "Why would you bother? But we can pay you well. Say, ten gold per heart, how about that? Naturally, we'll get you buffed to the teeth. Dan has some wicked incenses. It's on us."

The Dwand smiled. "All you need to do is sit there in the shade and twiddle your thumbs. Every once in a while you hand us a heart, that's it. It's only for a couple of hours. Come on, say you can do it."

"But why me?"

Dan grinned. "Do you see any available Mine Diggers of your level here? We should be kissing Mister Random's feet for sending you our way."

"To prevent any doubts on your part," the dwarf kept applying pressure, "allow me to send you a copy of the quest. Just so, you know, that you don't think we're trying to take you for a ride. It's two hundred gold, nothing to sniff at."

I shrugged and agreed. Let them send their letter. "I need to think about it."

The Dwand opened his mouth to speak. The Dwarf buried an elbow in his ribs — properly this time, judging by his brother's beached-fish expression.

"Absolutely," the Dwarf said, smiling. "We understand you're new to this."

I nodded my appreciation and began reading. What a shame the game had no Internet access. I really needed to look into it. Could it be a trap? I cast a furtive glance at the two brothers, studying their faces. No. Too simple for Shantarsky. Also, judging by the way the quest was worded, everything seemed hunky dory. I couldn't smell a rat.

What was my problem, then? Of course, had I had access to the Internet's collective wisdom, I might have found it easier to weigh up all the pros and cons. But now... the only possible catch might be the price they put on my participation. This I found very easy to believe. They had probably guessed that I couldn't log out. I really had to check out a few forums before making this kind of decision. Unfortunately, for the next month I couldn't afford the luxury of the Internet.

Never mind. I'd have to work with what I had. Let's begin with the dwarf. Judging by his heavy armor, he must have been what they called a tank. He must have had some monstrous shield and poleaxe in that bag of his. Let's have a look.

His characteristics were hidden, just like mine. But his breastplate or, say, arm braces could tell me the name of his kit.

I opened the auction and searched for "arm braces". Restriction: below level 120. No, I'd better check his breastplate. Arm braces, gauntlets, helmet and pauldrons were normally the most expensive parts of any suit of armor.

That's it, then. I pressed *Enter*. Pictures of breastplates flickered before my eyes. Found it! I cast another furtive look at the dwarf. Exactly. Now: his breastplate, as well as his greaves and the chainmail were from the Giants Slayer kit. Color: blue, Class: rare. Not the cheapest one but still quite affordable. Okay.

Now the arm braces. Just as I thought. Part of the Titan kit, Color: green, Class: quality. Ditto for the dwarf's pauldrons and gauntlets. His helmet and weapons must have been in the same vein. Okay. An average tank.

Now. Judging by the absence of the clan's logo, he was a loner. Or should I say, he was quite happy with his brother's company. Rank: Soldier. Such a lowly rank in combination with his high levels meant that he'd leveled himself up by killing mobs. From what I'd worked out already, a player's rank directly depended on his Valor levels which were only awarded for killing Darkies.

I thought I knew what these two were doing here. They'd arrived at the Citadel just like I had. Only I'd come here to level up my Rep and they were after the Darkies' scalps. It looked like our meeting up was indeed accidental. They'd seen me and decided to close an old quest.

I cast another furtive glance, this time at the Dwand. A wizard. His gear more or less in the same league as his brother's. If I wasn't mistaken, by Mirror World standards these two were distinctly average:

two run-of-the-mill players who'd leveled up nicely but had failed to keep up Valor.

I remembered skimming some blog post about Valor. Apparently, the whole thing was rooted in a system of ranks. A military analog of Reputation which allowed access to Mellenville's Arsenal. From what I already knew, the Arsenal armor was the best in the game apart from some truly unique or relic items.

I reread the quest. My head was about to burst as new ideas kept assaulting my brain. Had Dmitry found out at least some of what I was contemplating, he might have had me locked up here for a year at least. Heh! He wasn't here, was he? But the details of my plan had already started to take shape.

I finished reading and looked up at the two brothers. They smiled in unison, apparently reading my answer in my face. No good disappointing them.

"So where did you say those creatures were hiding?"

Chapter Four

As a matter of fact, I didn't have to ask. My bot had already provided me with all the information about the Kardachs' whereabouts. Apparently, quite a few locations had instances called the Swamps which were the Kardachs' natural habitat. The game developers' imagination must have failed them, but then again, they probably knew the importance of keeping it simple.

The nearest swamp was part of a rather large location known as Eyten City and Its Environments. It was to the south of Drammen. In order to get there, you had to use the portal. Perfect, if you asked me. All this constant rain and damp had already begun to get to me.

Dan confirmed my speculations. "The nearest one is in Eyten. The weather is marginally better there, too."

I chuckled. "You two sound as if you're fed up

with this quest already."

"Hah!" the dwarf grinned. "You can say that!"

"Nothing is as annoying as a pending quest," Dan added. "And we have about thirty of them."

"Any more calling for Mine Diggers?"

The Dwarf nodded. "A couple. It's a shame because you won't be able to help with them."

"You need a Master Digger," I said in an expert's voice.

"Yeah. Pending quests are a pain when you need to move on."

I smiled. "Why pending? If you join a strong clan, I'm sure they have their own Masters."

The Dwand sniffed. "Yeah right. As if they're going to help us. I wish! Their Masters have too many orders from the clan's elite. It's so complex, Sir Olgerd, you can't imagine."

I suppressed an inner smile at Dennis' switching gears, calling me "Sir". That was already a plus.

I'd spent most of my life on the road, traveling the world. Naturally, I'd had to follow the protocol which hadn't been easy for me for the first few years. I'd had to deal with too many people, some of them selfish bullies.

I remembered my student years. Our business etiquette teacher had told us that bullies came in several types. Some were just psychos — and, provided they'd already had a taste of power, were incorrigible. You'd have to put up with them while tending to your own interests, like hiking up your rates. That way one might find it easier to ignore their liberty-taking.

But some bullies weren't bullies at all. This was just a defense mechanism they used to protect themselves from the world. They found it easier to get along with people this way. One needed kindness and civility to bring their barriers down, demonstrating you weren't trying to make fun of them. You had to treat them with respect. Admittedly, I'd been burned quite a few times trying to put my teacher's theory into practice in the naïve belief that psycho bullies were few and far between. My youthful love of humanity had played a bad joke on me. But as the years passed, I began to accrue experience. I'd learned to see in people what others couldn't.

I hadn't been mistaken in Dan, either. All his boorish ways were gradually falling away like the skins of an onion, revealing the nice guy within.

"Complex or not, we won't know it until we try," I said. "Seeing as you're here anyway. The way I understand it, you've come to the Citadel to level up Valor, right?"

The two looked at each other. "What makes you think so?" the dwarf asked.

Yeah, I got the picture. You need to go some to pull the wool over my eyes. "There're lots of others like you in this inn," I nodded meaningfully at the players sitting at the tables.

The two brothers tensed up, eyeing the room. I might be a noob to end all noobs but I strove to make the best use of available information. "In my opinion, most of them have arrived to fight on the Citadel's walls."

The dwarf shrugged. "You're right. That's exactly why we're here. Once we've leveled up a bit, we can go out on raids in No-Man's Lands. We're not good enough yet to tackle PvP instances. There, we'll be everybody's whipping boys."

"You could say that," I agreed. "Reminds me of a Plateau battle I watched a couple of days ago."

The Dwand whistled in amazement. "The Plateau! Please. That's only for the elite. There're other instances, easier and not so posh. Still, even they aren't for the likes of us. Leveling Valor is an expensive business."

"It might be, but we know from experience that this characteristic is highly prized in Mirror World," the dwarf said. "Basically, the admins have done everything in their power to make sure people donate as much as they can."

"All right," Dan said. "We can talk about all of this later. Time's an issue. You agree to help us?"

I smiled my acceptance. "I have nothing to do until tomorrow night. If we could do it today, that would be great."

"Deal," the dwarf said, beaming openly. "I'll send you a temporary contract straight away."

* * *

As I left the Eyten portal station, I eyed the evening sky with relief. Not a single cloud. You couldn't believe how fed up I was with all the rain! To spend a few hours away from all the slush and mud was worth the time spent on this little adventure. Especially because I wasn't losing anything. On the contrary. This was much better than spending the whole night stuck in my room. Plus the two hundred gold. I won't lie to you: I was more than happy with this extra bit of income.

It took us about thirty minutes to get to the Swamps. Admittedly, traveling in the company of level-120 players felt good. The roads didn't appear so dangerous. It was true that my bot had been on its best vigilant behavior, but still. I didn't have to fear triggering the aggro zone of any monsters that might jump out at me from the nearest bushes.

As we were about to enter the instance, the dwarf created a group, then sent Dan and myself invitations to join. Much to my surprise, it worked. Honestly, I'd refused point blank to believe in the feasibility of all this. My last doubts were dispelled when Sasha granted me transfer rights. Now I was in charge of the group's loot. That's what they'd hired me for.

We accessed the Swamps via a wide trail snaking through a copse of trees. The already-familiar "parking meters" stood in front of the instance's entrance for Grinders to declare the resources they'd farmed. But today I had no need for them.

Here, we were in for a surprise. Or rather, I was because the other two were apparently used to it. The entrance to the instance was busy. Several players stood there, engrossed in an animated discussion. I counted six of them, their levels not as high as those of my new friends. They too must have had a quest, otherwise what would they want with this low-level location?

The two brothers spoke to the group leader: a thick-set level 110 warrior. I focused on him.

Race: Human
Name: Wolf

Admittedly his and his group's gear was even worse than that of my friends. I stood slightly aside without trying to eavesdrop. I just observed them.

Having exchanged a few phrases with Wolf, Sasha turned round and headed toward me. He was smiling. It must be good news.

"They're busy sharing the loot," he explained curtly. "When they heard about us, two of them asked to join us," he confirmed my hunch. "They're leveling up the Lotus Rep too. There they are. The dwarf and the Alven girl. I told them about your price. If you want, you can make another two hundred gold. What do you say to that?"

"What can I say? I'm all for that," I answered.

"Goody goody," Sasha nodded. "It'll be cheaper for us too."

Once we were done with all the signing of the temporary contracts with the gnome and the girl, Sasha accepted them into the group. Business was done quickly here. Which suited me just fine.

As I crossed the invisible line separating the instance from the world outside, I received a system message,

Warning! You're about to enter the Eyten Swamp!

This location can be too dangerous for players of your level!

Please turn back.

The message was followed by the offer of downloading the instance's map.

I ignored the warning but installed the map. While I walked down the trail, I checked out the Swamp's layout. It consisted of six smaller marshes and a large one. The latter was home to a level-95 boss whom we really didn't need to kill. Our quarry were regular level-80 Swamp Kardachs. Heh! The presence of four high-level warriors who could do this instance with their hands tied behind their backs was admittedly reassuring. There I was, calling mobs "regular" — me who wasn't supposed to cross their paths at all! One such Kardach could make quick work of any quantity of Spider Queens and their retinue.

Finally, the copse ended. We walked out onto the shallow bank of a boundless swamp overgrown with gray and green weeds. The telltale stench of hydrogen sulfide assaulted my nostrils. Actually, that was a good moment to check out my idea.

"Guys, can you smell anything?" I asked.

"It smells of our lake back home," the dwarf said.

"It does," his brother agreed. "Dad used to take us out of town a lot when we were little. That's exactly how it smelled."

"It smells of hydrogen sulfide," the gnome said.

The Alven girl didn't say anything. She'd only uttered a few words the whole time. You wouldn't call her the soul of the party. Her nickname spoke for itself: Shadow.

I could see though that she was hanging on every word we said. She might be just shy. What did I care, really?

Unlike her, the gnome quickly found common ground with the two brothers. He'd just gotten a new level and was happy and cheerful because of that. He was already 119.

He wore the same kind of heavy armor as Sasha, only not as good. Actually, I'd underestimated the brothers' gear. Next to the others, their stuff was quite decent. Especially in comparison with the Alven girl who looked as if she'd just joined the game. Despite her high level, her clothes were rather shabby. It was probably because her class — Archer — wasn't very popular with groups. Then again, I might have been mistaken. Who was I to know?

Despite her reserved looks — cold even — I felt sort of sorry for her.

"Why did you ask?" said Borin the gnome who'd actually introduced himself as Boris.

"Just checking a theory. About my subconscious playing up. I've been in the marshes before, you see. I know what they smell like. And that's the catch. I call it the Mirror World effect."

Dan chuckled. "You could say that. Are you ready?"

* * *

How strange. It had all happened exactly as Dan had predicted — never mind it had been a joke. I was sitting on top of an enormous rock overgrown with dark moss, watching the group smoke yet another Swamp monster.

They did it with remarkable ease. The monsters died quickly. The difference in levels spoke for itself. In a way, I felt sorry for these Kardachs, even though their appearance wasn't exactly pleasing to the eye. The game designers had taken care of it. The creatures resembled a cross between a lizard and a gigantic toad.

The group members acted in synch and with remarkable ease. Their movements seemed choreographed. They fought in silence, which admittedly scared me a little. I knew of course that they must have been using a private communications channel. They probably spoke to each other non-stop, but still it looked spooky.

I'd never been on a battlefield before, if I may call it so. I was actually participating – passively, but still. The scheme was simple. The dwarf and the gnome approached the water's edge and, using their terminology, "aggroed the mob and pulled him", getting him out of the water closer to the wizard and the archer girl.

In other words, the heavily armed players triggered the swamp monster's aggro zone, predictably forcing him to attack them. The tanks would promptly step back, wary of aggroing other Kardachs nearby, then deal their monster several heavy blows to make sure he only attacked them — no matter which one as long as the mob ignored the lightly armed wizard and archer. If they did everything right, the rest was easy.

Once the monster was slain and his body was fading into thin air, the quest item remained lying on the ground. This was when I came into the game. Until I picked up my first heart, I hadn't believed it would work. It was probably time I addressed my paranoia.

There! They'd smoked another one.

"Olgerd!" Sasha shouted. "Your turn!"

I peeled myself off the stone and walk energetically toward the dematerializing monster.

"Throw it to Dennis," Sasha nodded at the stone heart on the ground. "It's his turn. We'll take a thirty-minute break now. It'll give the mob a chance to get closer to the bank. I don't want to pull two or three at once. The difference in levels means there's no loot. We'll only be wasting elixirs," he turned to Borin and Shadow. "How many more do you still need?"

"Three each," the dwarf replied for both.

"I just hope you stay put once you get them."

"Sorry, man," the dwarf took offence. "A promise is a promise. We'll see you through."

Personally, I didn't really care how many were left in the group. I'd already been paid in full. The rest was up to them. I stuck to my part of the deal.

"So, are we taking a break?" Sasha asked me.

"Whatever suits you," I flashed a smile back. "I

find all this very educational."

I handed the heart to the beaming Dennis and was about to step back toward my front row seat when I glimpsed a small object the last Kardach had also dropped.

Okay. What did we have here? I crouched and focused on the item's characteristics.

Name: A Lump of Brown Coal
Type: Quest item
Restrictions: Once dropped, can only be picked up by a Master Mine Digger
Lifespan: 5 hrs
Description: Brown Coal is popular with blacksmiths while the guardsmen of the House of Stone Lotus value it for its magical ability to accumulate energy.
Acquisition requirements: Issued for the killing of any swamp monster. The odds of the creature dropping the item are directly correlated with the monster's level.
For your information: Pryst, the Stone Lotus guard, will be happy to receive the item in exchange for some Reputation.

The name of the guard was highlighted in blue, as was the word *Reputation*. The name was pretty much clear: it was a link for my satnav. As for the Reputation, I'd have to look into it later when the others went back to hunting.

Dennis' voice distracted me from the message. "That's exactly what we'd been talking about. Another pending one."

"You could say that," Sasha agreed. "Wish we could get a few lumps of that coal. Just not our luck."

"Do the mobs drop it often?" I asked.

"Depends on their levels," Borin replied. "It's extremely rare that low level ones drop it. High-level ones, yes. Bosses always drop it — as many as ten sometimes. Then again, depends on their level."

"I see," I said, walking toward my rock seat. "It can't be pleasant watching it go to waste."

"You bet," Dan chuckled. "Never mind. We're used to it."

His brother nodded, wistfully eyeing the fragment of brown coal on the ground. The girl remained silent but I could see in her eyes she too was sorry to see it wasted. Finally some feeling. I'd known NPCs that were more emotional than she was.

Good job I hadn't picked it up. Imagine the surprise. I was sorry for them but not sorry enough to blow my cover. They'd live. There were worse things around.

"Actually," I said when all of us had seated ourselves on "my" rock, "what's so special about it? What's so good about this Reputation with the Stone Lotus?"

"Lots of things," Dennis replied, munching on an apple.

"It's like with all Reps," Sasha began to explain. "Blessings from the House elders, access to their shop, unique quests..."

"I see," I nodded. "And this quest we're doing now, what kind of reward are you getting for it? Don't get me wrong, I'm not trying to double-check you. I'm perfectly happy with the price you put on my humble services. I'm just curious."

"Don't say that," Sasha laughed. "We would never have thought that of you."

"In actual fact," Borin said, "asking questions is perfectly normal in the Glasshouse. The game has too many fine points. Sometimes it takes you a day or two to work something out."

"Absolutely," Dennis agreed. "You open a guidebook to look something up and before you know it the day is gone."

Sasha chuckled. "That's provided there's a guidebook to look it up in. The real problems start when there are none. Then you have to revert to good old trial and error."

"You can say that again!" Borin added. "Sometimes you just keep on leveling as if nothing happened and then there's some bastard problem creeping out of the woodwork and you have to sort it out."

Everyone grinned their understanding. Even the girl allowed herself a barely perceptible nod.

As we spoke, we hadn't even noticed our break time passing. My new friends discussed the game. How they'd started out. How difficult it was to get good gear. Basically, talking shop. I just sat there listening and making mental notes, asking occasional probing questions.

Dennis was the first to come round. He perked up and glanced at the swamp. "It's no good us sitting here. Time to earn ourselves some glory. The mobs are almost climbing out onto the bank."

"Exactly," Sasha sprang from his seat. "I'm gonna pull one. Ready?"

We nodded in synch. The dwarf readied his poleaxe and, hiding behind a full-height shield, trotted toward the swamp. The others waited a few more seconds and then followed, drawing their weapons and readying their combat spells. The hunt was back on!

While the group was busy smoking yet another monster, I got thinking. I'd known it before and I knew it now: sooner or later I'd have to look for allies. I wouldn't be able to tackle Pierrot's questionable "legacy" all on my own. If even these guys were wary of venturing into No-Man's Lands all on their own, who was I to do so? Although I'd decided a long time ago that I would go there one day — and not just go but venture into the farthest and least explored areas.

And as for searching for allies... I knew of course that their motivation was key. In other words, I needed to find others like myself. Which excluded Sasha and Dennis from the list. They were in it for the game. Besides, what did I know about them? Nothing. Just a random meeting. Ditto for the other group members.

True, purely hypothetically our cooperation came with a lot of pros. The kids were useful to me — and I was useful to them. Together we might do a lot.

Now the cons. That's where it got difficult. I might have to tell them the truth. Not the whole truth, of course, but at least some of it. Everything's good in moderation, heh.

I didn't even like the thought of it.

Time was another issue. Or the lack thereof. Any cooperation should be mutually beneficial. Allies have to be nurtured, if you know what I mean. Both of us would have to invest time in solving the partner's problems. Combining our goals would have been even better but that too required time and effort.

Plenty of cons, not to even mention the main one: trust. Who were these people? What were they like? I knew nothing about them. All right, so we've had a nice conversation about the game but it wasn't good enough reason to hand them the keys to my home. Trust: how did people develop it? Just like that? Oh, no. You had to earn it — earn it with your actions. You had to put each other to the test. You needed to develop loyalty.

Admittedly I liked them even though our friendship had got off on the wrong foot. So it looked like I'd come to a decision. We'd stay friends. They might ask me to do another quest with them. But not more.

That was it, then. I heaved a sigh and mechanically rearranged the non-existing glasses. I already felt much better.

Now I could finally check the info portal. No rush. Now... brown coal... brown coal... let's see what's so special about it.

I clicked a link. The next moment I was looking at the House of Stone Lotus official page. The information was minimal. I already knew that upon reaching level 10 every player could commit to a particular NPC Clan, House or Tribe.

Lots of names: it would have taken me a month

of Sundays to check them all out. This was what players called a main Reputation. Naturally, you didn't have to level only one Rep, provided you had enough time, motivation and money. The rule was, your main Reputation shouldn't clash with the secondary ones. Admittedly, the admins didn't bother to warn players about pitfalls like those. Now why wasn't I surprised? Had they ever warned me against anything? Players were supposed to progress by trial and error.

The info portal contained quite a few formal letters from players to the game developers trying to appeal to their consciences. All of which were pointless. Complaints like those remained unanswered — undeleted even. That was the admins' way to make their point. The bulk of players realized that fewer system warnings made for a more realistic gameplay.

Surely you wouldn't like it if you invested all your time, money and effort into two Reputations of more, only to discover later that they were in fact incompatible. But that was what the world's story was for: its history, its media, its legends and even Internet guides, after all. The latter actually advised players to start by leveling their main Reputation first instead of spreading themselves thin. It could backfire.

One glance at the Stone Lotus Reputation chart was enough for me to realize what my fellow team members were after.

Firstly, like all other Reputation rankings, these too had Orders. Five of them. The more important the Order, the better access a player had to the House's store. And that store was something, I tell you. It had some very special spells as well as armor, weapons and elixirs. If you had the Order of Friendship (second in importance) you could even get a pet summoning charm. Judging by the fact that none of the four team members used pets to smoke mobs, apparently their Reputations left a lot to be desired.

Only now, looking into the finer details of other people's Reputations, did I realize how easy Pierrot had made it for me. I'd gotten my little Grison without even trying — and with my zero level, too! I seemed to be the only Grinder with his own pet. Imagine everyone's surprise when they saw someone like me owning a unique beastie like that! Oh no, better keep it under wraps for the time being.

As for the top Order in the ranking — the Order of Veneration — its proud owners had the right to obtain a summoning charm for a combat mount. The Stone Lotus mounts were called Long-Tailed Jandai. Even without checking their characteristics I knew I could use a critter like that. This was more or less clear.

But how about Brown Coal? Let's have a look! Yes... ah... I see. Now I understood Sasha's longing look as he'd eyed the item. The game developers had created an alternative Reputation-leveling system for the more impatient players. I wouldn't be surprised if every NPC clan had a similar system. The trick? You had the choice: either to perform boring tasks for a few meager Rep points, or you could bring them a rare resource. If you wanted an Order, you could fetch a certain quantity of Brown Coal. I did a quick calculation. To complete Reputation, I would need to collect fifteen hundred lumps of coal.

Oh. Without a Master Digger, these kids could spend their entire lives leveling. Gradually I began to realize the importance of my skill. And this was some petty Reputation building! Not to even mention joining a serious raid.

If I was correct, then I had enough to offer any potential allies. All I had to do was find suitable people for the part.

Chapter Five

Just as Varn had predicted, closer to the night the weather improved somewhat, if a nasty drizzle could pass for an improvement. Still, admittedly it was better compared to last night and this morning.

The elemental bonuses performed well. My gear hadn't lost a single Durability point. I only had Varn to thank for that. I really needed to buy him a drink or whatever they bought each other here.

In the morning, I worked in the local emerald fields. What can I say? Two words: silence and desolation. This definitely wasn't the most popular location with Mine Diggers.

I'd popped into the office before work, with zero results. So I headed to work with a clear conscience and registered myself directly in the mine.

Just as the wizard shop vendor had warned me, the local mines were damp — but only the top levels. The omnipresent humidity didn't reach the lower shafts. Funny: I used to like rain and would never have thought that my weather preferences might change literally overnight.

Meeting my daily quota left me unusually tired. I returned to the inn feeling out of sorts. The dinner cheered me up though. Talina served a meat stew — and its taste reminded me of my life with my parents and my Mom's cooking. No idea how the game developers did it, and I didn't want to know either. I liked it, that was the main thing.

When I was finally given the caravan's departure time, I cheered up even more — although it might have been the mulled wine.

Departure was at 6 p.m. I had my dinner, refreshed myself a little and decided to arrive at the meeting point early in order to settle in.

The sight of the armored carts left me speechless. The enormous crate-like wagons resembled the armored train cars I'd seen in old movies. Their Defense stats were going off the scale. I couldn't even imagine a monster capable of peeling off this kind of armor.

Talking about monsters. Each wagon had all sorts of draught animals harnessed to them. A whole menagerie! One was pulled by four enormous black horses, tall and broad-chested, with powerful legs and backs. Truly monstrous muscles rippled under their thick hides. All the horses were level 140. Not bad.

Apart from horses, they also had buffalos, reindeer, elk and dinosaurs. They pulled their respective wagons in twos, threes and fours.

The front wagon was especially eye-catching. I

was a total newb in caravanning business but as I understood the local terrain, the first one had to be the strongest. And it definitely looked that way.

A giant beast was harnessed to the front wagon. The game designers had made it a compilation of several animals; still, the long forking horn on its nose, the thick trunk-like legs and its massive gray bulk reminded me of a rhinoceros.

Level 165. Its name was appropriate: The Hard-Horned Andagar. Oh, yes. None of the Wasteland mobs was strong enough to tackle this beastie. I could see that the Guiding Eyes had invested well into their little enterprise. I could only guess how much this animal might have cost, complete with wagon. Add to it a high-level Riding skill. These guys knew what they were doing.

"So how do you find my Kosma?"

I turned to the voice — cheerful and wheezy. A gnome stood but two paces away from me. Nickname: Uncle Vanya. Level 145. His characteristics were hidden. Clad in heavy green armor, full set — which meant he had all the bonuses that went with it. In other words, he was well protected but didn't splurge on himself, preferring to invest in his animal instead. Which, I began to understand, was a costly pastime.

"What can I say? He's beautiful," I replied in all honesty.

The gnome grinned, pleased. His gray beard and mustache stood on end. "Everybody likes my Kosma," he nodded, giving the beast a hearty slap on his massive armored side. "My breadwinner."

The gigantic rhino ignored the slapping and

continued to chew on something.

"I can imagine him in battle," I said.

"Well, he's not really battle-geared, is he? My Kosma is a regular draught animal, what common folk call a hauler. To go into battle, you need a special combat mount. Because mobs, they ignore haulers as long as the owner is alive. A draught pet can't pull aggro to itself. They don't fight. But in a way you're right. They can be quite useful. They can absorb some of the damage. They can heal. And share some of their protection with you. Still he's no warrior so I don't expect miracles. In battle you can only count on yourself. But a combat mount, that's different! Even though they're not easy to come by, as you well know."

"And how about his armor?" I asked.

"The haulers' armor increases their Strength, Stamina and Capacity, among other things. But I repeat, it can only increase a pet's draught characteristics. Which are definitely my Kosma's forte."

"I see," I said. "So he's a bit like a giant tank with a sawn-off gun which is adapted to be used as a draught horse."

Uncle Vanya chuckled. "Not really. If I can extend your metaphor, my Kosma has never been a tank nor an armored vehicle. He was born a hauler."

"I think I begin to understand. Is there a chance for me to get a similar creature?"

"An Andagar? I don't think so. I won mine last year in an event. They only had fifty of them in the draw. I still can't believe my luck. With your account type you can only have a draught animal if your profession requires one. For instance, if you're a farmer or a coachman like myself. Lots of professions, I can't remember them all. Had you had a Bronze plan, then yes, starting level 15 they have a draught animal quest available."

"I see," I repeated. "But zero accounts can still level up Riding, can't they?"

"They can indeed," the gnome nodded. "No problem there provided the money is right."

"Okay. I'm sorry to bother you. I just like your Kosma very much."

The gnome slapped the beast's giant armored flank again. "It's all right. We're waiting anyway. Time goes faster with a nice chat. And as for my beastie... it may look cool now that it's fully grown and strong. But first you need to raise him; you need to feed and heal him, even play with him. Can you believe I read him bedtime stories? You also need some place to keep him. That's where he respawns if, God forbid, he dies in battle. Draught animals are unsummonable. They don't come with a summoning charm like combat mounts or other pets. I'm not going to complain though. Once the worst is over, your beastie starts to pay for itself. He makes me enough for my bread and butter and then something on top!"

Suddenly he zoned out — apparently receiving a message. "I'm sorry but I have to leave you," he said once he'd finally come back to life. "The caravan needs me. It's been a pleasure."

"Likewise," I nodded as I watched him leave for the far end of the caravan.

While I'd been gawking at wagons tut-tutting at the sight of all the amazing beasts, other passengers had begun to gather by the gates. And I used to think that this was a one-horse town! Judging by the number of passengers, the caravanners were doing very well indeed.

The bulk of the players were low-level, including a few Grinders like myself. The Citadel seemed to be popular among quest-giving NPCs assigning tasks like delivering letters or fetching items. There's apparently no limit to stupid assignments like those.

I could easily tell those of the passengers who'd only planned "to stay overnight". They wore cheap disposable cloaks. They cast studying glances at me, probably thinking I was a local. Of course: the rain kept falling and this midget (i.e. yours truly) kept walking around without taking the slightest notice of the weather.

I could understand them. What was the point in investing in costly elemental protection when there were cheap single-use items available? But as I'd already learned, it was better to invest well once than later repent at my leisure. Especially considering that I'd gotten my money back mere hours after having spent it.

I'd really enjoyed the raid last night. I'd gained some very useful experience.

Once we'd collected all the hearts there'd been to pick up, we'd parted good friends. Even the silent girl archer had condescended to a brief thank-you. Strange creature. Then again, it was none of my business. It takes all sorts.

Finally, Varn announced our boarding time: quarter past six. We had to wait for some less punctual players. Varn's grim glare followed them as they boarded their wagons. As far as I understood from the agreement I'd signed, the Guiding Eyes valued punctuality above everything else. The caravan's route passing monsters' lairs had long been calculated. Had the tardy players lingered for more than a half-hour, the caravan would have left without them. Varn wouldn't have allowed his men and his other clients to walk into the mobs' aggro zone because of a few irresponsible newbs.

The inside of the wagons was vaguely reminiscent of subway trains. *Vaguely* being the operative word. No idea why I'd thought that. Two rows of wooden double-seat benches were separated by a narrow aisle. Oil lamps burned under the ceiling. Luggage shelves lined the walls overhead. The resemblance ended there. Instead of windows, narrow gun slits were cut in the wagon's sides. The floor was strewn with straw. Apparently this was part of the gameplay: everything had to look as realistic as possible.

The cheerful voice of the approaching Uncle Vanya distracted me from further inspection.

"So, would you like to sit with me? Or would you rather sweat here with the rest?"

I grinned. "Sure I'll sit with you. If you don't mind, that is."

"Good," the gnome grinned back. "Come on, then. We'll have to spend almost an hour staring at the road. Boring! This way we can at least talk."

His cab was in the front of the wagon. It was dry and comfortable. The view from the small front windows was much better than from the passenger seats. Uncle Vanya seated me on a soft cushion and climbed in next to me.

He whistled and pulled the reins. Kosma lazily raised his head and effortlessly moved off. The wagon pulled away surprisingly smoothly. I liked it! This was a great way to travel, provided you weren't in a hurry.

I leaned out of the window to take a look back. All the other wagons were falling in behind us.

The gnome whooped a cough and sat back wearily. Silence fell.

"How are things over there?" I asked finally, nodding in the direction of the Citadel.

The gnome buried his hand in his gray beard and coughed again. "Depends. I'd say they're never left alone. If it's not some gory event courtesy of the admins, it's the Darkies craving their scalps. It can get pretty busy. I'm not asking you what you left there, it's none of my business. But I do suggest you grow a spare pair of eyes in the back of your head."

"Is it that bad?" I wasn't overjoyed to go there as it was and this conversation hadn't made me any happier.

Noticing my anxiety, Uncle Vanya added soothingly, "Don't worry. You'll get used to it. Just remember to keep your eyes peeled."

We continued on our way, unhurriedly discussing the game. From time to time we fell silent, thinking each his own thoughts.

The location was true to its name: mud, ditches and low hills interspersed with piles of rock. Wilderness is wilderness everywhere, even in Mirror World. Kosma apparently saw this as an opportunity to show what he was made of. He advanced with effortless ease, paving the way for the rest of the caravan like a giant steam roller. Nothing could phase him: neither the mud, tall grass nor the brambles. He shoved any large rocks out of his way with a single sweep of his enormous horn. Oh yes. A beastie like this could make a dangerous caravan trip feel like a walk in the park.

Uncle Vanya shared his biggest dream with me. He wanted to take Kosma with him on raids over the Wall into No-Man's Lands. According to him, neither of them was ready yet. They still had some leveling to do. Well, in that case I with my zero level had no business being here whatsoever. Still, Pierrot's map clearly showed that all the Ennans' mega bonuses were located in the very heart of No-Man's Lands.

Admittedly, the journey was quite pleasant. I'd expected to be shaken out of my skin — that's when I wasn't being mugged by all sorts of monsters — but the trip turned out to be perfectly uneventful. All I could hear were the guards' occasional hollering and the roaring of the draught animals.

I stared hard into the window hoping in vain to see something interesting. A bare prairie lay around me: nothing but drizzling rain and the squelching of mud under the wheels. No, not so: a couple of times we did see groups of players out hunting. On seeing us, they did their best to clear our path, wary of exposing the caravan to some aggroed monster.

"It wasn't always like that," Uncle Vanya commented. "When we first started out, players didn't give a damn about us. But we quickly taught them some respect."

The closer we came, the harder my heart beat in my chest. My excitement grew when I finally saw the Citadel's walls in the distance. The rain had stopped, replaced by a veil of mist, equally cold and wet. Finally a black shadow, huge and unforgiving, loomed through the haze: the walls of the Maragar Citadel.

I couldn't yet see its towers and merlons, only this cover of darkness hovering over me. It was spooky. The game designers had done their best. I was crushed by the feeling of the citadel's power. I just hoped I might get used to it.

"Eh? Scared, ain't ya?" Uncle Vanya grinned.

I nodded. "Sure."

"Normal," he nodded. "In the mist, it's not as scary. It can give you a fright but nothing too bad. First time I got here in a thunderstorm. That was something, I tell you! I'll put it this way: I'm yet to see the sun shining over the Citadel's walls."

"And this isn't even the front line," I said, turning my head this way and that.

Uncle Vanya chuckled, watching me. "Forget it, man. This wall stretches from the Raldian Range in the South all the way to the Misty Mountains in the North. The Citadel blocks the entire Maragar Canyon. It was built with the purpose of protecting the Powers of Light from the hordes of the Dark and the savage monsters of No-Man's Lands."

I gave him a puzzled look. "Yes, yes, I read the location's history on the info portal. It sounds awesome. The battles of Light against Dark... Legendary feats of fallen heroes... And so on and so forth. But it's only a fancy piece of fiction! A figment of hired writers' imagination!"

The gnome smirked. "One can see you're new here," he shook his head disapprovingly. "Want a tip?"

I nodded. "Sure."

"Don't say anything like that around the old-timers. You might find it hard to understand but for many of us this world and this location are more meaningful than real life. Imagine having to spend several months on the walls of the fortress, warding off enemy attacks, unable to log out. Imagine fellow warriors fighting shoulder to shoulder with you — your friends who've covered your back hundreds of times. In these people's heads, the fine line between the virtual and the real worlds grows ever thinner. It changes them. For them it's much more than just a game. It's their life. A real life, free from the old order and its conventions. And what's more, many of them fight for the lives of their friends. Their gaming objectives don't matter any longer. I'm not saying people forget about them, they just have more important things to-"

"Oh."

"So you see. It's not just a fancy piece of fiction."

I shrugged. What could I say? I'm not the one to teach others how to live their lives. And what's more, I hate forcing my opinion on anyone. "Thanks for the tip. Any other advice?"

The gnome kneaded his beard, frowning. "Going there is not a healthy idea for zero levels. But seeing as you have to... My advice would be: keep your head down, don't play the hero but don't shirk the service either."

I nodded. This was exactly how I'd planned to go about it.

"Another thing," he added. "Lots of NPCs there. Warriors mainly. Don't try to buddy up to them. They aren't gonna like it. There's always some smartass trying to cadge a bonus quest out of the local NPCs. I shouldn't envy them. Just forget it. If a Citadel NPC decides to bestow a quest on you, he'll do it anyway. But he'll do it in his own time and at his own discretion."

"I see. Sounds rough."

He chuckled. "It is what it is. No one forced you to come here."

"You could say that."

The wasteland had ended. Kosma pulled us onto a wide cobbled road. A new system message popped up,

We welcome you, O traveler, to the glorious Maragar Citadel!

Would you like to install our free app: the Maragar Citadel and Its Environments?

It was followed by another message,

Warning! This location can be too dangerous for players of your level!

If you still want to proceed, remember to touch the altar in Central Square in order to make the Maragar Citadel your new resurrection point.

"They're pretty strict here, aren't they?" I chuckled, rereading the message.

"That's game developers covering their butts. They warned you: by touching the altar, you create a new respawn point. To preclude any potential complaints."

"How strange," I said. "As if I might get killed the moment I get there."

"Not you, no," the gnome grinned. "You're a zero level. You might get injured, that's all. But talking about the altar... you did read the contract, didn't you? It says that the caravan undertakes to deliver you directly to the square, right next to the altar. And let me put it this way: a five-minute drive through town is more dangerous than the hour' ride through the Wastelands."

"Oh. Did you say through town?"

"Sure. The Main Citadel is a fortified town. About the size of five Drammens. Further along the wall there're five more fortresses located from south to north. They have their own garrisons. They all make up part of the Maragar Citadel location. It's enormous. Didn't you read the forums?"

He asked me all the right questions. I shrugged.

He stared at me as if I were an idiot. "More free

advice," he added grimly. "Set up your bot now, entering whatever places you need to visit in the Citadel into it. Remember this isn't some cute sunlit new location. Try to move through open spaces as fast as you can. Don't stray away at nighttime. And one last thing. Keep an eye on the sky. Seven times out of ten, what kills you will come out of the sky."

It might be a game but the shiver that ran down my spine was perfectly real.

For the last ten minutes, the wagon had been shuddering over the rocky road. But as the shaking increased, I began to realize: this wasn't a bumpy ride but an earthquake.

The closer we came, the gloomier Uncle Vanya grew. He kept peeking out of his cab, shouting at somebody and nervously pulling at the reins. He paid no attention to me now, too busy doing his job. Only when the wagon jumped from an especially large jolt did I hear him cussing under his breath. I didn't dare annoy him by asking what was wrong. I knew how it felt when someone distracts you when you're busy.

He was nervous. And for him this was just another trip after possibly a hundred similar ones. Me, I was just doing my best to keep my wits about me without betraying how scared I really was.

The wall loomed closer with every minute. A giant of a wall; a behemoth monster. A gentle breeze was gradually dispelling the fog. I could make out the dark outlines of the towers.

Finally I could see the stonework. Some of its blocks were the size of Kosma — and they weren't the biggest ones, either. In places, cement had been washed out revealing ugly patches of brown grass.

Wait a sec. What was that? I noticed several human figures hanging on the wall. Their gray cloaks had prevented me from seeing them earlier. They dangled on the wall at about the height of an eight-story building.

'What's that?" I asked.

Uncle Vanya squinted at the scene. "How do I know? Could be masons refreshing the stonework. Or herbalists cleaning it from grass. Could be anyone. NPCs can find work for all and sundry."

I choked. Some fun they were having here! Wonder what kind of task Captain Gard might have for me? *Bring the stone from the highest point of the tallest tower in the Citadel. Reward: 5 Reputation points.* Uh-oh.

The foggy drizzle parted, revealing the gates of the Citadel. Like the jaws of a giant monster, the fortress' raised portcullis grinned with its steely teeth. We rolled along the road into its black mouth until it devoured us.

This wasn't a gate but a tunnel. High overhead I could see gaping arrow slits interspersed with stone grooves used to pour boiling oil over potential attackers. If this was how they protected their rear, I could only imagine what the frontline was like.

A squad of ten lancers met us in the inner yard. I took a better look at them and froze, stupefied. They were all level 300+, wearing Red Armor and enclosed helmets. They were armed with large full-height shields and long spears.

"NPC guards," Uncle Vanya muttered, seeing

my excitement. "Whenever the Darkies break through, they hold the fort for the first few minutes. Once the players arrive, they make themselves scarce."

I hadn't understood a word of it. Still, I nodded my gratitude as the awesome warriors' silhouettes disappeared behind us.

As we drove through an unnecessarily ornate miniature arc, the system kicked back in,

Greetings, Olgerd!
Would you like to join the Maragar Citadel's common chat?
Accept: Yes/No

I clicked *Yes*.

The moment I accepted it, I was flooded with messages from all sorts of people: some buying, others selling, yet others calling up raids. There were plenty of stupid messages in the vein of *Howdy all!* or *Where do I go now?* Every now and again, the system showered me with details of current events. One, called the Caltean Raid, looked especially nasty. There was one good thing: I'd counted seven invitations to join a raid to the Misty Mountains. That was good news. It meant that the location Master Adkhur had dispatched me to was quite popular with the local war dogs.

Actually, Uncle Vanya had been right. The fortress was swarming with players who rushed around as if the devil was after them, especially in open areas.

What really stood out was the abundance of

scaffolds and building materials. Players, like some gigantic builder ants, were busy repairing the walls, some mixing cement, others lugging up stones. The air was blue with the bashing of hammers, the screaming of saws and an abomination of cussing and swearing. You might think the town had been bombed flat.

Suddenly everything froze. Silence fell. A system message flashed acid-red before my eyes,

Warning! The magic shield will expire in:
05:00 minutes...
04:59...
04:58...
04:57...

Chapter Six

Uncle Vanya cursed and pulled at the reins. Kosma reacted by swinging his powerful head, darting off. Wow. I didn't expect that kind of speed from this behemoth.

Scaffolds, half-repaired houses and players who dropped whatever they'd been doing flashed past the wagon's window. The town buzzed at the double, as if someone huge and invisible had poked a giant anthill with a twig.

The countdown numbers kept dwindling. Something bad was about to happen.

The first minute had elapsed fast — too fast.

I didn't dare look out the window to check on the other wagons. I shrank to the back of my seat, afraid to move.

Uncle Vanya briefly stopped his cussing and said without turning round, "Remember what I said about your bot settings?"

"Yeah," I wheezed.

"Do it. You have ninety seconds. The moment we stop, you gotta run for it."

"Okay. What happened?"

He cringed. "The magic shield over the Citadel is about to expire."

"What do you mean, expire? And then what?"

The right question to pose would have been, *What is the magic shield?* But for some reason, I'd asked what I'd asked.

Uncle Vanya shrugged. "It won't last long. It's always like this. Some stubborn idiot can always hack the shield. That's part of the gameplay. Otherwise what would be the point in the Darkies trying to attack the Citadel walls if they're impervious? It's very possible that our raiders are attacking the Dark Citadel even as we speak. Having said that... no, I would've known."

I tensed. "So is this the Darkies attacking?"

He waved my suggestion away. "I don't think so. It's probably the Calteans. Just my flippin' luck. Now I'll have to repair the wagon again."

I heaved a sigh. I felt sorry for his wagon but I wouldn't mind staying alive too. Who were these Calteans, dammit? Still, I knew better than to ask him. He had more important things to do.

Uncle Vanya took one glance at me and added, "Keep your hair on. You'll live. They'll bring the shield back up pretty quickly. A Caltean Raid is an ordinary event. Not a patch on the Darkies' attacks."

I rearranged my non-existent glasses. The word "ordinary", that's what scared me the most. What kind of universal agitation would something extraordinary inflict?

The wagon jolted over a particularly steep bend, forcing Uncle Vanya to switch his attention back to driving. A minute later, he mumbled,

"Get set."

I was ready. My bot was set up to search for Captain Gard. He lived somewhere in the barracks, apparently not far from the wall.

The wagon cleared the last bend.

The Citadel's main square met us with hustle and bustle of at least two hundred warriors, levels 100+. My eyes watered with the miscellany of races, weapons and gear. The freshly-respawned players stood out in the crowd. They were especially numerous by the main altar at the center of the square. They wore white-linen starting clothes, their faces distorted with fury. I bet! Had I been killed, I'd have been furious too.

Having barely resurrected, the players were off somewhere — apparently, to collect their gear left where they'd been killed. Some respawned partially clothed, a few wearing a full set of gear. This must have been what they called the non-transferable items.

Just over a minute left till zero hour. The doors of several buildings opened, letting out a flood of people who headed toward the caravan. Most were low-level. I could see a few fellow Grinders.

"That's our passengers going back to Drammen," Uncle Vanya said with a wry smile. "Aren't they in a hurry! Nothing motivates one like a couple of

Citadel deaths. The moment we stop, you should make a run for it."

I gave him a quick nod. "Thanks."

He shrugged it off. "You're welcome. Take care, you."

"I will."

The wagon stopped. I had forty seconds left. Uncle Vanya gave me a wink and a slap on the shoulder. I darted out.

I'd set up the bot to No Mercy mode. So! Apparently, I wasn't that bad at short-distance running. At first, my Energy bar plummeted, slowing down at about 80%. Good job I wasn't wearing my Goner's kit. A sprint like this would have bled me dry.

I crossed the central square in one breath. Without looking back, I turned off into a narrow lane. Twenty-two seconds left.

Stone buildings loomed overhead like silent giants. Narrow windows. Closed shutters. Wet cobblestones. Rough curbs. Some place this was!

The gloomy lane ended quickly as the bot brought me out into a wide avenue. Judging by the sheer number of shop signs, this was probably some sort of local high street. All the doors and shutters were already closed. Players were running from a westerly direction. Shit. Ironically, that was exactly where my bot was taking me. The barracks were located in the western part of the fortress.

Fast as I was, the countdown had beat me to it. The system message caught up with me as I ran past some alchemy shop.

Warning! The Citadel's magic shield is down!
The shield will be restored in:
45:00 minutes...
45:59...
45:58...

As I ran past a tiny bakery, I overheard a few phrases,

"Not too bad this time..."

"I don't think it'll reach us..."

Well, if they thought that it wasn't too bad, one could probably live here after all. The players relaxed a little and so did their pace. They were still trotting and galloping about but the spring had left their step.

No, no. I shouldn't even think about it. Relaxing here was asking for trouble. I had to keep going.

Apparently, I wasn't the only one who thought so. Some of the players picked up tempo, too. Which was probably why the disjointed choir of panicky voices hadn't caught me unawares.

"Watch out! Take cover!"

I switched off the bot and ducked into a narrow lane between a couple of three-story buildings, too narrow even for two pedestrians to squeeze past each other, let alone a cart to go through.

I wasn't quite sure yet what exactly I had to watch out for and what to take cover from, but I had a funny feeling that staying out in the open wasn't a healthy idea. A few more players ducked into my lane (quite high-level ones, too), convincing me that I was thinking in the right direction.

I dropped to the ground and covered my head with my hands, checking out of the corner of my eye if anyone would laugh at my behavior. No one did. An Alven guy even gave me a nod of approval. Judging by his gear, he was one of the magic classes. With his level 160, he had no need to grovel in the road dust. He was probably going to magic a force shield for himself any time soon.

For a few moments, the street fell quiet. The air rang with silence: not a shouting voice, not a single sound. The proverbial lull before the storm. Nothing was happening, but I had a strong desire to shrink ever deeper into the ground.

A whooshing hiss, unexpectedly loud, ripped through the silence. I could feel every hair on my virtual body stand on end.

The hiss grew closer, transforming into a roar. Now I could hear that the sound was comprised of dozens of similar ones... hundreds maybe, merging into one blood-curdling wail produced by something very scary and undoubtedly lethal.

I pressed my hands to my ears, my eardrums about to explode with the roar. I didn't look at the other players. They must have felt the same.

The spine-chilling wail stopped.

Once again the air rang with silence.

Then it collapsed on top of me in a torrent — no, a tsunami of dreadful noise. The cracking of wood and the crunching of stone, the tinkling of exploding glass, the clanking of metal and the screaming of human voices.

A God-awful earth tremor resonated through

my body.

And another one.

And yet again.

The walls of surrounding houses swayed. Somewhere behind me the stonework must have collapsed, bringing part of a building down. Dust choked the lane.

A muffled voice came from within the gray haze,

"The Calteans have moved in their trebuchets. These houses make it a perfect trap. One direct hit, and we'll be buried alive."

Obeying the words of the invisible player, I scrambled to my feet and took a peek round the corner. I could barely recognize the street enveloped in dust and smoke.

I peered through the suspended gray haze at one of our unwelcome "guests". A huge chunk of rock the size of my country cottage had ploughed through the street, leaving a long ragged trench in its wake. It now hung dangerously over the bakery where only a few minutes ago I'd witnessed the players' hopeful voices. Another one had landed about fifty feet away like a misshapen bowling ball, knocking several buildings over in its traject.

Screams for help came from within the clouds of dust. Somewhere close, stonework continued to collapse, judging by the sounds of falling masonry, woodwork and glass.

A shove on my shoulder threw me aside. My comrades in misery surged out of their shelter. Thanks a lot, guys, for not trampling over me. I checked my clothes. The push had been strong — but luckily, it hadn't affected my gear's Durability. Big sigh of relief.

I cast a quick look around me. I was about to use this momentary hiatus and make a dash for the barracks when a hand lay on my shoulder.

"Don't rush."

The voice was calm and confident. I turned around. The Alven wizard stood at my side, peering into the dust cloud.

"This is only the beginning," he nodded at the ravaged street. "It's true what the experts say: you should never take cover from bombs in a built-up area. Still, this is probably the safest place to sit out what is about to happen."

I wanted to ask him what he meant when more shouts came from the ruins,

"Watch out!"

"Get down!"

"Hedgehogs coming in!"

The wizard gave a shrug as in, *I told you so.* "There it comes. I strongly advise you to step back and resume your position on the ground."

Silently I obeyed. If I were so lucky to have run into an experienced player, I'd better use the opportunity.

The wizard peeked out, then stepped back and crouched next to me, leaning against his fancily carved staff.

"If I understood you correctly, we're about to be assaulted by some hedgehogs?" I used the brief pause to pick his brains.

He chuckled. "Not just any old hedgehogs. These are Rock Erezes. They're mobs. Other guys may call them hedgehogs but they're anything but cute. All they might have in common is sharp venomous quills on their backs. So I don't think it's a good simile."

"Can they fly?"

"Oh, no. The Calteans trap them in the mountains, then hurl the traps over here with trebuchets. The traps deactivate on impact, releasing these furious spiky monsters."

"And the Calteans, who are they? Are they some Dark clan?"

The wizard grinned. "Some players could use a bit of catching up! The Darkies are players just like ourselves. The Calteans are a race inhabiting No-Man's Lands."

"Does that mean they're mobs?"

"Not really. They're NPCs. Mirror Souls, if you want, only that they're hostile to both Light and Dark. No-Man's Lands are very densely populated and none of their inhabitants stay neutral. And I don't think it's going to change in any foreseeable future."

With every new piece of information offered, I felt less enthusiastic about my potential trip to retrieve the Ennan treasure. That's provided it even existed and that the whole story wasn't some demented programmer's cruel joke.

More warning shouts came. The earth shuddered again, its impact on my body much weaker this time. But considering the fact that these were the echoes of "hedgehogs" landing, I dreaded to contemplate their size.

"That was close," the wizard said, relieved.

He was about to add something else when a lump the size of an elephant landed directly in front of our temporary shelter. The impact sent me trampolining through the air.

The lump rolled on. I glimpsed a coarse-meshed net left at the site of its landing. It wasn't made of nylon or thread but of thick steel links.

A few heartbeats later, I heard the monster's furious roar followed by screams for help.

'That's it. Suppose I spoke too soon," the wizard chuckled and stood up to his full height.

His staff and his armor turned sky-blue. He downed two vials of something or other and stepped forward. As he was about to walk out of our lane into the open, he turned back to me.

"You'd better get out of here," he said.

I nodded. "Thanks for your help. I owe you."

"You do," he said, then darted toward the sounds of the melee.

I took a deep breath. For the umpteenth time, I peeked around the corner. No one seemed to be lying in wait for me. The dust had settled enough for me to get a good eyeful of this "hedgehog".

Oh. Nothing good. The level 270 creature didn't look like a hedgehog at all. If anything, it resembled a Komodo dragon with a long head and a jawful of crooked fangs. His back was covered with long spikes from his neck right down to the end of his long tail. Despite the creature's seeming clumsiness, it moved very quickly.

Several players had already engaged the

creature, including my wizard. I counted seven in total — the wizard being the highest-level of them all.

Three of the fighters hurried to put all of their combat training to good use. Judging by their coordinated actions, they must have been a group. But in general, the melee didn't seem particularly well-organized. The players must have teamed up in a hurry using whatever skills each of them had. A level-150 Rock Rhoggh was doing the tanking, expertly focusing the mob's aggro on himself. Problem was, even I could see he was no match for it.

Despite being outnumbered, the hedgehog seemed to control the situation. It may sound weird but the creature seemed to attack and defend itself by the book.

Its long spiky tail lashed about, meting out blows. Each such hit stripped the mob's opponent of quite a lot of Life; every other hit also added some nasty poison debuff to the damage. That's not forgetting his fangs and his powerful legs.

Even I could see that if the cavalry didn't arrive pretty quickly, these brave seven would die a valiant death without really dealing much damage to the monster.

Very well. It looked like I'd outstayed my welcome here. Time to leg it.

Just as I activated my bot, another couple of players darted out from around the corner of a crumbled house. Their vital stats were in the red. Both were hung with the familiar nasty debuffs. Their eyes were wide open, their mouths contorted by fear and desperation. The two miserable excuses for warriors dashed past me, gasping and screaming for help.

What happened next I'd probably remember for the rest of my life. It was like watching a movie in slow motion. No idea what had saved me: it could have been the warning growl of the approaching behemoth or the aforementioned corner of the demolished house that the giant spiky Komodo dragon had swept away in its stride. Could be a bit of both, I suppose. I leaped awkwardly aside, saving the local road builders the trouble of picking my miserable remains out of the cracks between the cobblestones.

The monster rumbled past, roaring its fury as it caught up with the hapless players. Not only had they failed to stop the creature themselves, they'd pulled it toward us, as well! Now the Alven wizard was toast, that's for sure.

The screaming players never reached the scene of combat though. The hedgehog caught up with them. Even I, snuggling in the dust on a pile of debris, heard the snapping sound of its jaws. The dead players' bodies promptly faded into the air, leaving behind two neat trunkfuls of various gaming goodies they'd earned with their own hard labor.

I wondered if grave robbing was common in the Citadel, imagining the two hapless players — barefoot and in their white starting underpants — scurrying back double quick to pick up their stuff.

In three long leaps the hedgehog reached the scene of combat and joined in the fight, making the situation much worse for the seven players. After a couple of minutes, the two monsters had brought their number down to three. Surprisingly, the last men standing were the tanking Rhoggh, the Alven wizard and a gnome crossbowman. Despite his seemingly cumbersome armor, the Rhoggh fluttered around like a butterfly over a meadow, dealing powerful blows right, left and center. Admittedly, it cost him a great number of Life points. Had it not been for the wizard busy healing him non-stop, the fight might have already been over.

The wizard had it rough. Ignoring his own protection, he poured all of his own mana into the Rhoggh's life support. The gnome looked the healthiest of all three. His Life was firmly in the green. Not a single debuff. He just stood behind the wizard's back, methodically loosing off bolts.

Even I could see that the moment the Rhoggh went down, that would be the end of them. Neither the gnome nor the wizard would last a few seconds without him. What a shame. They were giving it their all. I couldn't take my eyes off them even though I was supposed to be hightailing it for dear life.

I was about to scramble to my feet when the inevitable finally happened: the Rhoggh died. His body dissolved into thin air. The wizard attempted to redirect the leftover mana to his own defense but also flew into the air, struck by a powerful blow from the mob's spiky tail. He landed amid the ruins of the building: I clearly saw some of the brickwork collapse on top of him.

Seeing their luck finally turn, the gnome darted toward the main square. The two hedgehogs didn't appreciate their opponent's behavior. Their disappointed roaring echoed through the streets as they set off after him. Judging by the gnome's impressive head start, he had every chance of avoiding the sad fate of turning into a chestful of goodies sitting on the cobblestones.

Finally, the whole cacophony of the clattering of weapons mixed with the monsters' deafening roar, all the screaming of players and the noise of buildings collapsing died away. Silence enveloped the street. The dreadful sounds of battle still reached out from a distance.

It might be a good idea to stay put and sit it out — or should I say hide out? There was still fifteen minutes left until the magic shield restored. The earth wasn't quaking anymore which probably meant that the Calteans had stopped shelling the fortress. That was good. Pretty good.

While I was still lying about with nothing better to do, I decided to take in my surroundings. The street had been hit hard. It would take a good six months to restore it. Lots of work for the builders. Then again, they shouldn't complain: they'd be looking at a nice growth in skill levels plus all sorts of bonuses.

Actually, I really should seek the Alven wizard out and repay him in kind. He'd saved my bacon, after all. The lane where I'd been hiding was now a mess of rockfall: the house walls had succumbed to the aftershocks. I dreaded to think what might have happened to me had I lingered there a little longer.

But what was that? The Calteans' hedgehog

trap was still there. How interesting. Should I take a peek, maybe? If I moved along the walls, lurking in the shadows... The street looked deserted but I already knew from experience how deceptive could this silence be.

Right, what did we have here?

The trap looked like a cluster of cobwebs made up of chains instead of threads. Judging by the thick layer of rust, the trap's owners didn't care much about its storing conditions. It was approximately six by six foot in size. How on earth had that enormous hedgehog even fit within?

Jesus, what was I talking about? What rust? What size? Wake up, Olgerd! This is a game!

Casting wary looks around, I ventured closer. How very interesting.

Name: A Magic Steel Net

Effect: Thanks to the ancient magic lore of the Founders, it can trap a wild animal and keep it inside for an indefinite period of time.

Restriction 1: Only for animals below level 310

Restriction 2: Only for animals inhabiting No-Man's Lands.

Player's level: 0 and above

Status: discharged

Warning! Binds on pickup!

Warning! The item expires in,

01:49...

01:48...

01:47...

Would you like to pick up the item? Yes/No

I cast another look around. Would picking it up make me a scavenger? I didn't have any right to it, after all. Then again, the hedgehog that it used to confine was still out and about. It was probably out at the main square now, busy laying down the law together with the other monster.

I had very little idea of the game's rules in this respect. Who had the right to this trophy? I'd never thought I might ever need to know things like that. But still, if anyone wanted to claim it, they were conspicuous by their absence. Besides, whoever deserved it must have been busy by the Altar now. No way they could make it here within the remaining minute and a half.

Finally, I came up with a plan. I would wait till the last second, then pick the thing up. It was going to disappear, anyway. Why should I waste it, even if I had no idea what I might need it for? My bag had already become a collection of useless objects. If it went on like this, soon I would look like a walking flea market full of weird artifacts.

I diligently waited another minute, then took a look around. No one. My conscience was clear.

I clicked *Yes*.

With a jolt, the net curled itself into a tight steel ball and disappeared inside my bag.

Let's have a look. Predictably, the item's countdown timer had disappeared. Now the Caltean trap was safe in my inventory until I could use it. Alternatively, I could always discard it. Not necessarily... but if push came to shove...

Talking about using it: I immediately received a

new system message informing me that I could only use the net once. No idea how and when that was going to happen, but it was good to know. And I still had to recharge it! All in all, it was going to cost me a good 2000 pt. Energy.

The item's charging scheme was different from that of the Replicator I'd assembled. The system suggested I synchronize my energy source with the magic network. To put it simply, I was expected to become the item's power supply by channeling some of my daily allotment of energy into the thingy until it accumulated enough to function properly.

So it looked like I'd got myself another leech syphoning off my powers. Having said that, I could now afford to part with a couple hundred points Energy.

I pressed *Confirm Synchronization.* Let the thing charge up. Little by little... you never know, something might come out of it.

I couldn't help thinking about the Alven wizard. Was he already dead — or was he lying somewhere bleeding to death, buried under some collapsed building? I really needed to go and check on him. Of course, the most logical decision would be to switch the bot back on and continue looking for Captain Gard, but I couldn't just leave without first finding out what had happened to him.

As I walked, I kept coming across weird-looking piles of stones. They looked identically neat, each stone like the next. They weren't big: if you topped them with a cross or a tombstone, they'd look just like a proper grave. How interesting.

Finally, I came to the place where, in my estimation, the wizard must have landed. I saw the collapsed wall — and underneath, another one of those piles of stones. Could it really be a grave? Even though, as I already knew, if a player died in battle, he left a chest containing all his in-game possessions behind.

When I walked closer, I could finally see what it was.

Name: A Pile of Brick Rubble
Type: Simple
Name of the casualty: Marcus
Expires in: 2 days

I began reading a rather longish list of item restrictions but was distracted by a voice from behind my back,

"Cool grave, eh?"

I turned round and grinned to the wizard. "You look different."

"This is what they call a birthday suit," Marcus pointed mockingly at his white starting underpants.

"Mind telling me what this is?" I pointed at the grave.

"This is a Pile of Rubble. One of Mirror World's signature tricks. The moment I hit the wall, I got buried by bricks."

"Is it a trap?"

"Unfortunately. Now I'll have to wait for a rescue team or some builders to arrive and dug out my stuff," Marcus heaved a sigh.

"Do you mean that getting buried in one of those means they have to save you in two days max?"

"Yeah. And this is a simple two-day Pile. If you get caught in one of these somewhere in No-Man's Lands, you can safely log out for a couple of weeks and take your family on vacation," Marcus began to explain. "Okay, so normally I don't care about low-level traps like this one. Today was different though. I had too many debuffs plus I got caught, plus the mob had critted me. Shit! My stuff is trapped there now. I've just resurrected in the Central Square and here I am, as large as life and twice as ugly, lecturing you on the dangers of Mirror World."

"Do you want to say that if a high-level player gets caught in a trap like this... especially if he's in good form..."

"Any level 30-plus will get out of it, no problem," Marcus interrupted me, looking around for someone to help him. "But this is a simple one. A player of your level should steer clear of them. Unless you're-"

He cut himself short and turned back to me, beaming. "So stupid of me! You're a Mine Digger, right? Come on, then! Didn't you say you owed me? Quick, dig my stuff out!"

"Can I do that?" I asked, unsure.

"You bet! You're the right person! Shifting rocks is your job!" he rubbed his hands in glee. "Come on, get on with it!"

Unhesitantly I pulled my pick out of my bag and took a swing.

You've tried to clear a Pile of Brick Rubble.
-3 to the item's durability.
Durability: 17/20

I took another swing.

You've tried to clear a Pile of Brick Rubble.
-6 to the item's durability.
Durability: 11/20

"Wow! Aren't you good at it!" Marcus exclaimed. "I almost envy you!"

I couldn't tell whether he really meant it. I took another swing.

You've tried to clear a Pile of Brick Rubble.
0 to the item's durability.
Durability: 11/20

"Oops," he said. "Spoke too soon, didn't I?"

I grinned and took another swing. And again. And another one. After my third blow, the system duly reported,

Congratulations! You've cleared a Pile of Brick Rubble! Reward: 5 Tyllill crystals.

Out of the corner of my eye I saw Marcus beeline for the trunk containing his stuff. Then the half-naked tramp was gone, replaced by a fearsome level-160 wizard.

How weird. Only a moment ago, I couldn't have

cared less about his level, treating Marcus just as a fellow player; if anything, I'd even felt slightly superior to him. That's the power of a person's gear in Mirror World!

"Did you get some tyllill?" he asked once he'd checked all his stuff.

"Yeah. Five crystals."

"Not bad. Congrats. It's the best resource in the whole of the Citadel. At first you could trade it but the admins pulled the plug pretty quickly. Now it's no-drop. Basically, tyllill is one of the reasons people come here for, together with quests and Valor. So? Are we quits now?"

I shook his proffered hand. "We are. If ever you get caught in a Pile of Junk, just buzz me."

He laughed, waved his goodbye and darted toward the West side of the fortress.

I was about to switch my bot on when a system message informed me of the reactivation of the magic shield. According to the script, we seemed to be relatively safe... for the time being. In which case, I'd rather take my time. Let's have a look at this tyllill.

> *Item name: Tyllill*
> *Type: binds on pickup*
> *Player's level: 0 and above*
> *Style: Universal.*
> *Tyllill crystals are one of the ancient mysteries the Founders left behind. Their true purpose is yet unknown. If you stay diligent in performing your quests, defending the walls of the Citadel and being useful to its denizens, fortune might smile on you too,*

rewarding you with one of the precious crystals.

Important! The item is categorized under Precious Artifacts of the Maragar Citadel. To check its exchange rate, Click Here.

The words *Click Here* were highlighted in blue. I followed the link. Oh! This was getting interesting. Apparently, you could exchange tyllill for lots of things: various Rep points as well as elixirs, items and bonuses.

Breathless, I scrolled through the list of Reputations with Mellenville. Got it! The exchange rate was predictably shameless: one to ten, and not in my favor, either. But at least it was something.

A musical voice distracted me from reading,

"Excuse me! Could you be so kind as to help me, please?"

I turned round, meeting the stare of another Alven player. Unlike Marcus, this one still had half of his clothes on, even though they looked admittedly weird. He wore leather pauldrons over his white starting shirt and a matching leather belt. His bare feet were stuck in a pair of boots. Apparently, part of his gear was no-drop. On one hand, it was rather convenient: you didn't have to do a corpse run. But on the other, when you wanted to change your current gear for something more powerful, you'd have to throw all your current items away.

"Sure," I said. "Provided I can do it."

"You can," he pointed at the spot where a leather shop had stood less than an hour ago. "I need to get into that Pile of Brick Rubble to get my stuff..."

Chapter Seven

While I was digging for the Alven's stuff, a long line of half-naked players formed behind my back. Apparently, refusing someone's request for help was considered very bad form here. If you didn't want to end up on some clan's black list, you'd have to comply and do what you're asked: in my case, swing my pick. Expecting any kind of compensation for one's toils was out of the question. Tyllill crystals were my only reward. Which was nothing to sniff at, actually.

Less than thirty minutes into my community work, I realized why it wasn't remunerated. I had competition: some builders, a few rescue workers and a couple of fellow Mine Diggers. An hour later, two stonemasons joined me matter-of-factly, bashing their hammers through my pile of junk. So that's how it was, then? What I'd first thought to be a liability and a waste of time was in fact some sort of privilege?

Still, I soon saw that these two smart guys had

---

no hope in hell of outdoing me. Tyllill crystals went to the player who dealt the most damage to the pile. My stats made me beyond competition. I cracked the brick tombs like walnuts. In the time it took a stonemason to deal a couple of points damage with his hammer, my pick ripped off a good seven — or even ten in one case. So it didn't take long for the opportunistic "rescuers" to realize that they should stay away from me.

Because all these local "rescue teams" started to breed like locusts! I made a quick estimate: the numbers of "casualties" had plummeted, averaging 1 per each 15 rescuers.

I was also quite upset by the fact that tyllill dropped rather irregularly. The five crystals I'd gotten from Marcus' grave was the top. Each pile yielded me one to three crystals at the most. A few times I got nothing at all. So much for my pick-brandishing.

Engrossed in my crystal-farming, I hadn't even noticed that the street had been cleared from debris. Still, the rescue operations were far from finished. From what I gleaned from the players' conversations around me, the entire East part of the Citadel looked the same. Plenty of work for everyone.

An hour later I swung my pick one last time.

Congratulations! You've *cleared a Pile of Brick Rubble!*
Reward: 2 Tyllill crystals.

Good. Enough for today. I didn't see any more piles of rubble left, anyway. The last street had been cleared of debris. I'd done good. I hadn't even had time to take a look into my bag. Let's check our spoils.

Before I could open the menu, a new system message made me freeze like a salt pillar, open-mouthed,

Valorous warriors and denizens of the Maragar Citadel! Congratulations! You've successfully completed yet another event, defeating the Caltean aggressors! Glory to the Forces of Light!

Special thanks to those who helped defend the Citadel with disregard to their own lives!
We congratulate the warriors who excelled defending the fortress walls:
#1: Count, for killing 230 enemies
#2: Turbo, for killing 198 enemies
#3: Irene, for killing 173 enemies
The heroes will receive commemorative Citadel medals or upgrades to those they already have, plus 5000, 3500 and 2000 Tyllill crystals respectively.

We would also like to honor the following citizens of our glorious fortress:
#1: Olgerd, for clearing 254 Piles of Rubble;
#2: Sancho, for clearing 65 Piles of Rubble;
#3: Corinne, for clearing 49 Piles of Rubble.
The heroes will receive commemorative Citadel medals or upgrades to those they already have, plus 5000, 3500 and 2000 Tyllill crystals respectively.

Our congratulations to the winners!

Another system message popped up,

Congratulations, Olgerd! Today you've written your name in the history of the Citadel!
Reward: a medal, Hero of the Maragar Citadel
Reward: a medal, Rescuers Top 1000
Reward: a medal, Pile Buster
Reward: 5000 Tyllill crystals

I stared impassively at the total number of crystals I had. Five thousand nine hundred freakin' eighty. Or, if you wish, almost 600 pt. Reputation with Mellenville.

I hurried to open the menu and indeed discovered three medals: one green and two gray ones. The green one was "Hero of the Maragar Citadel". I'd done quite well — without as much as breaking sweat. I'd also gotten myself a helluva lot of exposure. Which was much worse.

I had to dash.

I activated the bot. I needed to see Captain Gard ASAP. I left the street to the applause of the players. A few seemed to have taken some screenshots. Bummer! What had I been thinking of? On the other hand, how was I supposed to know it might have ended like this?

Calling myself all sorts of names, I finally made it to the barracks.

The number of NPCs was quite astounding. I'd never seen so many non-player characters in one place.

The entrance to the barracks yard was guarded by a lancer who looked very similar to the ones I'd met when entering the fortress. His helmet dangled off his belt, his long hair clotted with sweat. His armor was deformed and dented, his shield covered in scratches. His forehead was bandaged with a strip of white cloth. This event must have cost him dearly.

The sentry frowned, gloomy. Getting on this guy's bad side was the last thing I needed. But strangely enough, his face began to clear as I approached.

"Aha, Olgerd!" he growled good-naturedly. "Great job! As long as we have guys like you behind the frontline, we'll keep going! It makes fighting the enemy so much easier for us."

A nametag appeared above his head. Oh wow. Did that mean my medals had begun to work their magic?

"T-t-thanks, er, Eric," I stuttered. "I do what I can."

"I can see that. Keep up the good work! Now you'd better hurry. Captain's waiting for you. Right through that door, second floor."

I didn't wait for him to repeat it. Still, I couldn't help wondering: if, according to this seasoned war dog, the Citadel was "safely behind the front line", where did that leave Drammen Town?

It took me no time to get to the second floor. All the NPCs in my path exhibited a friendly interest in me. Probably, my situation wasn't as hopeless as I thought it was.

Another NPC stood guard by the door to the Captain's office — or rather, a room which was hung floor to ceiling with all sorts of slashing and stabbing weapons.

The Captain's adjutant, however, didn't look as friendly as the sentry I'd just met. He looked me over with his hard and prickly stare, then nodded at the door. I stepped in.

Captain Gard — because it was him (the portrait I'd seen in his house bore a striking resemblance to him) stood stooping over a huge desk. I was about to step closer when I heard his hard commandeering voice,

"Stay where you are."

I obeyed. Some voice Tommy's Dad had! It literally sent shivers down your spine. Still, it wasn't a nasty voice. Angry, maybe. No wonder. I might be angry too had I not seen my family for months at a time.

The thought scalded me like a cold shower. How sure was I that Captain Gard had even seen his wife and son? Had he ever been on his street or inside his own house? I'd never thought about it before. They were only NPCs, forever locked in their respective locations, doomed to play their parts using a limited emotion simulation tool.

It felt so sad. My heart clenched as I thought about my two girls.

I felt so sorry for this guy — and his family, too. *Easy, Olgerd, easy,* I said to myself. *Thoughts like these aren't healthy. Make sure you don't lose your virtual marbles.*

Finally, the Captain finished studying whatever lay on the desk in front of him. I heard the rustle of paper: he seemed to be rolling a map up, wary of spying eyes. His vigilant glare watched my reflection in a polished cuirass on the wall. Yeah yeah, some spy I was, blowing my cover all over the Citadel. I suppressed a sigh.

Captain Gard turned round. I recognized the firm chin and the scar that ran across his right eyebrow and cheekbone. The sinewy body of a gymnast; the stern stare of the portrait. Still, my first impression persisted: this wasn't a bad man. A *man*?

"Master Olgerd, I received the new recruit list already two days ago. So you shouldn't be cross with me for making you wait a couple of minutes. As far as I understand, you weren't in a hurry, either."

His voice matched his stare. What a predicament! Landing on the wrong side of the local boss was the last thing I needed. I had to talk my way out of it.

"I was, Sir. But as you probably already know, I'm not exactly a recruit. Or rather, I'm not a recruit at all. I'm not a military man. Yes, I reported to the Citadel voluntarily, wishing to be useful, but a different kind of useful. Not the military kind of useful. When I received my, er, orders to report here, I wasn't given a deadline. Had I received one, I assure you I'd have arrived on the dot. And as for today, I couldn't ignore the pleas for help."

"Which is commendable," the cold voice said. "But this is irrelevant. Let's get to the point."

"I'm sorry to interrupt you," I ventured, "but

before we do that, I have a message for you from someone."

It took all of my self-control to blurt this out under his angry glare. Excellent characterization. The game developers earned their keep.

"And who might that be?"

I'd managed to rile him. His jaws clenched.

"It's your wife."

Yes! Dead on. The guy was knocked out. Excellent. Even the room felt warmer. Phew! Those game developers were a right bunch of sadists.

Gard's face changed. His eyes widened.

Unwilling to prolong his agony, I offered him Mila's letter.

Congratulations! You've just completed a quest: You've Got Mail!

Reward: +250 to your Reputation with Mellenville.

Excellent. Very, very good. Couldn't have been better. And this was only my first step on the way to my becoming a defender of the Citadel.

Gard's hands shook. Was I the first one to witness this? How many players had already been here before me? Or was I the lucky one following an unbeaten path?

It was so nice to see a smile on the stern face of this warrior. Oh yes. Tactfully I coughed, addressing the Captain who was already engrossed in reading,

"I'll wait outside, Sir, if I may."

Without receiving an answer, I slid out of the

room. I could very well wait in the reception. It wasn't going to kill me.

Gard's adjutant must have noticed his boss' state of mind. I could literally see his jaw drop. I could have bet anything that this was the first time he'd seen Captain Gard smile.

The reception was quite busy with both players and NPCs. The air reverberated with voices, jokes and laughter. I must have landed in the very midst of the Citadel's defenders, fresh from their battle with the Caltean invaders.

"Ha! There he is, my competition!"

It took me some time to realize they were talking about me.

"Count, look at this Digger! He's definitely not digging it, is he?"

I looked up at the voices. Three players: red-skinned Narches. It was the first time I was seeing examples of this dead race. All three were tall — almost seven foot — with four arms, levels 200+.

The strongest and best-equipped of them was the one called Count. "Best-equipped" was actually an understatement. Compared to the others, he looked like an MMORPG superstar. His armor was speckled with red and purple. His Valor was level 100! I wouldn't have been surprised if he'd taken part in the battle for the Barren Plateau.

"Whatcha stalling for, Dwarf?" Count flashed me a pearly smile. "Let's get to know each other."

I glanced at his friends' nicknames and immediately knew. They were the top three players who'd garnered all the rewards in today's event. All three were sporting small logos featuring a red skull against a black background. The logo of the Dead Clan.

I nodded back. "Pleased to meet you," I said to all three.

"The event sucked," Turbo growled. He was the tallest. "Nothing to write home about. Still, you did a good job."

"Guys, leave the poor Grinder alone."

It was Irene who'd said it — who could be called petite compared to the other two. The powerful crossbow behind her back looked more like some science-fictional missile launcher. Her black hair was pinched in a ponytail. Purple armor hugged her slim figure.

"Please don't take any notice of them, Olgerd," she said with a smile. "It's just that we've wasted two days already on these ridiculous mini-events. We've come here to get us some scalps. Instead, we're hunting mobs."

By "scalps" she must have meant Dark players. Okay. As far as I was concerned, they were welcome to continue wasting their time. As for me, this "ridiculous mini-event" was about all I could stand.

"I see," I said.

"How's the Beast?" Turbo asked me, flexing his enormous shoulders.

"How's who?" I asked back.

The trio exchanged understanding glances. "We can see you're a newb," Count said.

"Beast is what we call Gard," Irene explained with a vague wave of her hand. "He may be an NPC but he's a sick bastard."

"Yeah," Turbo nodded. "He makes you wait for a quest like it's some lottery draw."

I stood there, listening to them shooting the breeze and studying their awesomely expensive gear, amazed by the fact that they treated me almost as an equal. Already in Mellenville I'd noticed the behavior of some high-level types. They treated everyone below level 100 like some kind of human ant. But these guys here stood next to me, cracking jokes and sharing their problems. They might be simply nice; alternatively, my medals might have earned me the right to join in their conversations. In any case, I chose to keep my mouth shut and listen.

In the time that we stood there, several NPCs had walked past. Each of them thought of slapping my shoulder or saying something along the lines of "Keep up the good work!"

Seeing my reaction to their praise, Count grinned, "Don't be shy. It's always like this when you get a medal. Tomorrow it'll calm down. That's the admins' way of encouraging players to strive for new heights."

"Do you mean that tomorrow they won't be so friendly with me anymore?" I asked.

"Oh yes they will," he said. "They'll still have respect for you but it won't be as explicit. Medals are a great thing. You should do all you can to get new ones and upgrade the old ones."

"Thanks for the tip."

"You're welcome."

Irene was about to add something when the

door to Gard's office opened.

"Olgerd!" Gard's adjutant barked. "The Captain will see you!"

When I re-entered the room, I was faced with the same sour-faced Captain Gard as when I'd seen him first.

"Now, Master Olgerd, you said you weren't a recruit. Am I correct?"

He spoke as if there hadn't been any letter at all. Still, I smelled a rat. This looked as if he was testing me.

"You are, Sir. I'm a regular citizen wishing to serve my people. I can't fight. But as I already said, I have other talents that you're welcome to use as you see fit."

Gard theatrically furrowed his brow. "Aren't you afraid I might make full use of your offer?"

I cracked a lopsided grin. "You can see I'm no warrior. Of course I'm afraid. If I lied to you, you'd have noticed it straight away. But despite my fear, I really need these ninety days in the Citadel."

"All right," he said pensively. "I believe you. You can go now. When we have a job that answers your, ahem, talents, I'll let you know. My aide will show you to the barracks. You can go now."

I turned around and headed for the door. His stare seemed to have warmed in the end. I could understand him. Some Digger brings him a letter from his wife, thinking that he would get a cushy posting. Oh no sir, not me. I was quite prepared to give it my all. I needed every Reputation point I could get. The more the merrier.

My hand lay on the door handle.

"Did you know what the letter was about?" Gard's voice asked.

I half-turned to him. "Some of it, yes. I know what Mila wrote about me. She told me herself."

As I closed the door behind me, Gard gave me a curt nod and a faint smile.

Chapter Eight

I thought it was his adjutant's job to take me to the barracks. As if! Too much honor for the likes of me. Did he or the Captain ever leave his office at all? I made a mental note to ask someone about it.

The "aide" meant by Gard turned out to be a limping, old NPC gnome, awfully talkative, clumsy and curious. As he took me up and down numerous staircases, he stopped every now and then to listen in to other players' or NPCs' conversations. A few times he joined their discussions which twice even rose to arguments and finally very nearly ended in a fight with a black-bearded dwarf.

It was interesting to watch two NPCs tugging at each other's beards, panting. Luckily, it hadn't come to blows. The guards pulled them apart just in time. I watched the scene wide-eyed. Where the hell had I come to?

Apart from the guards, another player had

helped to stop the fight. Once the two opponents calmed down, I saw his face light up. I could bet my bottom dollar he'd just completed some hidden quest or other.

After that, the gnome scrambled down the steps without stopping, ignoring conversations and greetings, muttering something under his breath and casting evil glances my way. At first I didn't understand what had caused such a change in this initially so friendly and talkative guy. Then I understood. He was taking me for a dwarf, wasn't he? The "image matrix" that Lyton the barber had created for me worked like a dream. Actually, it was about time I renewed it.

I suffered the gnome's unhappy sniffing for a couple more minutes, until finally we got to my room. Judging by all the laughter, noise and stomping of feet overhead, he'd taken me to the ground floor. There was only one door here, separating a small room from the dark corridor.

Oh yes, I'd been right. This was the ground floor. I'll tell you more: this was an underground floor. No windows. The walls were black with mold, the furniture covered in white spots of fungi. A tuberculosis breeding ground. But strangely enough, it made me feel rather cozy. It must have had something to do with my racial traits. And as for the damp... it wasn't a problem. With my elemental protection, I could sleep in a pool of water if I had to. So if my being billeted here was the gnome's little trick and not Gard's order, I could only be grateful. Imagine the gnome's surprise if I thanked him!

And again I was right. As the gnome left me, he closed the door with an evil grin. He probably thought I hadn't noticed. What an unhealthy individual. I could easily imagine his creator: he was probably just as volatile.

Well, see if I care! I was perfectly happy here. Fewer eyes meant more freedom. It was a good job the gnome hadn't noticed how happy I was.

Now, let's have a look. But first we needed to latch the door. Safer that way.

What did we have here? A rough plank bed without a mattress or a pillow. A wooden crate acted as a bedside table. A three-legged stool... better not to touch you, buddy, or you might fall apart at the slightest prod.

No wardrobe. Not even a table. This wasn't a room in the barracks: this was a prison cooler about to collapse around your ears. Never mind. The main thing was, I was alone here. Away from prying eyes.

Every heavy step overhead showered me with dust and sand from the cracks in the plank ceiling. Only now did I notice that the room had no lighting. Still, I could see everything. Ennan's eyes are the next best thing to a night vision system.

I really had to let my Prankster out. Time for him to stretch his little legs.

Would you like to summon your pet: Yes/No

Come on, cheeky face, out with you.

Prankster appeared out of nowhere as was his habit. He froze, focusing his beady eyes on me as if asking my permission. He'd learned his manners pretty quickly! Yes, little one, you can run around for a bit. Not that the place allowed for much running.

The Grison dashed around the room like greased lightning, sniffing every corner and studying every nook and cranny. Several times he snorted unhappily.

"Oh well," I said, "you might not like it here but at least I do. Why don't you? What's wrong with this place? Do you want to go back to the Steely Mountains? How I understand you. I'd like to go back to lots of places. But I'm afraid we'll have to grin and bear it, little 'un. I'll tell you this: as soon as we get somewhere nice away from prying eyes, I'll let you out for a breath of fresh air."

I reached into my bag and produced a small chunk of cheese. "Here, it's for you. I know you like it."

With a cheerful squeak, the Grison darted toward me, grabbed the cheese with his tiny little paws and sank his teeth in it. He literally rolled his eyes with delight.

I stroked his soft back. Talking about his eyes: the lack of lightning didn't seem to faze him, either. He could find his way perfectly well in the dark — better than myself, actually. I really had to look him up once I logged out. He might not be as useless as he looked.

Actually... how was that trap faring in my bag?

The trap was faring just fine. Its Energy levels kept growing. Very soon I was going to have a net all of my own. No idea what I might need it for but let it just sit there. Waste not, want not.

I was about to check my other belongings and get my wits together when an unceremonious knock at the door put a lid on my best intentions.

I opened the door — which actually was the sturdiest part of my new dwelling. A young guy stood outside. Definitely a player, his level 35 rather low for this location. Ignoring me, he was rummaging through the contents of his enormous bag.

"Wretched place... Dark as a cow's guts..."

Who did he think he was? I really didn't know what to say to this.

Finally he located something in his giant bag and looked up at me. "Are you Olgerd?"

I nodded. Not waiting for my reply, he was already offering me a scrap of gray paper.

"Here. Press your finger against your name in my journal. Like this... good. No, wait for the confirmation. There! You see it's highlighted? It works like a signature, sort of. That's it. I'm off. Bye!"

I poked a finger at his tablet's screen against my name, watching the gray letters turn intense green. The kid had already darted for the stairs while I stood by the door studying the little scrap of gray paper.

Name: An Order
Type: Quest item
Emitter: Captain Gard
Recipient: Olgerd
Read/Discard

Apparently, this kid was a messenger of sorts. That's right. NPCs couldn't use the chat, could they? Besides, it gave players an opportunity to complete petty little quests like this one. Myself, I used to run all sorts of errands in Mellenville even though I'd never delivered any letters to anyone.

Let's have a look, then. Or did they really expect me to discard it?

Master Olgerd,

Soon after you left, I had an idea how we could put your talents which you so profusely praised to good use. The Citadel's Wizard had been asking me to send him a man of exactly your profile and your talents...

Did the man ever stop? Talents! Why did he have to keep harking over the word? Admittedly, as an NPC he had a considerably higher IQ than all those I'd met before him.

With this, I instruct you to report to Master Tronus in his tower and remain under his orders for as long as he has the need for your talents. I've already issued orders and dispatched all the pertinent paperwork. Do not delay carrying out this assignment which is undoubtedly of the greatest importance for the Citadel.

Captain Gard

He was a piece of work, really. One moment

you'd think he was normal, but then... Never mind. I'd earned my Reputation points for delivering him the letter, that was the main thing. If he wanted me to go see the wizard, to the wizard I'd go! You never know, it might actually work out for the best.

New quest alert: Help the Wizard!
Report to Master Tronus and put yourself under his orders.
Reward: Unknown
Accept: Yes/No

I heaved a sigh and clicked *Yes*. What else could I do?

I turned back to Prankster and shrugged my apology, then activated the summoning charm. "Sorry, boy. One of these days you'll have all the prancing around you need. But now we have to dash."

The wizard's name was highlighted in blue both in Gard's letter and in the quest message: a live link for my satnav to follow.

Having set up the route, I turned back one last time, casting a quick glance at my still unlived-in quarters. Oh, well. No peace for the wicked. Now I had to trudge through the night. Never mind: I'd just say hello to the wizard, then go beddy-byes. Tomorrow would be a difficult day.

It didn't take me long to get to the wizard's tower. The end of the day promised no danger. The streets were actually quite busy with players dashing around. This was apparently the bulk of real-life workers who'd clocked out and hurried to their respective module centers to log into Mirror World. Life is but a game, after all...

The wizard lived in the east part of the fortress just next to the wall. His tower was quite ordinary — its brickwork slightly darker, maybe. Either it was a local kind of brick or it was simply covered in grime. And it was at least the size of a nine-story building.

As I approached, the signs of the recent event damage came into view. The wizard must have taken the first blow, which was only logical. He must have been the one responsible for shield-casting. Judging by the fact that there was no other house within a good five hundred feet, this nice little tower must have served to attract the first hits. Which suggested that this must have been both the most protected and the most dangerous place in the entire Citadel.

I started to regret having agreed to be Mila's messenger. I had a gut feeling this Gard was one nasty sonovabitch. Or even, as those Dead clan guys had put it, a Beast.

The street around the tower was deserted — dead even. Not a single blade of grass in sight. The earth here had been ploughed up by explosions: a familiar mixture of sand, cobblestones and fragments of rock left after the recent Caltean attack. Something told me that no one had bothered to repair anything here for a long time. Why would they want to? The next day someone would assault it again.

I came closer. The tower walls were a sorry sight. Oh yes, I'd been right: those were no ordinary bricks. They were black and sort of vitrified as if made of solidified resin. Once restored, the tower might have looked really nice. But now...

I imagined the tower transported to some spooky solitary location — surrounded by a dark forest or a cluster of cliffs. Scary.

As I walked toward the tower's door, I was met by nearby players' stares. The kind of looks they gave me, you might have thought I was a nutcase. Yes, yes, I know. I should have stayed in some warm sunny location farming my little emeralds to my heart's content. But no. I had to do this. I had this gut feeling that declining Captain Gard's quests wouldn't be a good idea. I just hoped I was right.

Warning! This location is not recommended for players under level 100!

I paused in front of the door, staring at the system report and its rather sarcastic message. I held my breath and stepped in.

A navy blue light enveloped my body, then dissolved, leaving me standing at the center of a crumbling, ruined hall. I hadn't even had a chance to get scared. This must have been some clever mini portal the wizard used instead of an elevator. Of course. A small window nearby showed the tops of roofs and dainty tower spires. Nice.

So apparently, I was at the very top of the tower. And if the roofs and the spires were part of the fortress, then an opposite window might offer me a view of No-Man's Lands.

Let's have a look... That's right! I could see the Black Stream, slithering like a giant python in the dark. A thick moonlit forest of ancient trees overhung its opposite bank.

A shiver ran down my spine. One look at the other bank made it clear it was bad news.

Our side of the stream was littered with all sorts of siege-related junk. I could see one hell of a thick log, scorched in places. Judging by a row of shields nailed to it, this was a jury-rigged gate ram. Further away, I could see the burned-out skeletons of either trebuchets or siege towers. Whatever. My meager knowledge of siege equipment was based on Hollywood blockbusters and Instagram pics.

Judging by the vast numbers of still-smoldering fires, the Caltean attackers had been legion. What was it Irene had said? A *ridiculous mini-event*? Oh, well.

"Scary, eh?"

A soft young voice behind my back made me swing round.

Tronus the Wizard, Defender of the Citadel, turned out to be a young man of about twenty-five years old clad in dark leather. He wore a black bandana and a matching necktie. Old-fashioned pilot's goggles sat on his forehead. That's right! That's what he reminded me of: a pilot. His jacket, his pants, his cuffed flying gloves — the guy was a pilot and no mistake. Really, why had I expected to see a long-bearded mage in a dark-blue robe and a pointy hat?

"I've been here for years and still I can't get used to the view," he nodded at the dark bank of No-Man's Lands. "I take it, you're Olgerd? My new assistant, right? I'm Tronus."

He proffered me his hand as he spoke. Despite his puny appearance, Tronus' handshake was surprisingly firm.

"Exactly," I said. "Reporting for duty under your orders for as long as you have need of my talents."

The wizard burst into loud happy laughter. He must have received his own version of Captain Gard's message.

"That's Gard!" he finally said. "He takes some getting used to, Master Olgerd."

"Just Olgerd," I smiled back.

"Agreed. In that case, I'm just Tronus. You're a Mine Digger, I was told?"

"I am."

"Excellent. I've got loads of work for you. You're not afraid of work, are you?"

"On the contrary. I look forward to your instructions."

"Jolly good, jolly good. But that'll have to wait till tomorrow. You need a good night's sleep. You've been working hard today, I know."

He seemed all right. We might actually get on together.

"Talking about sleep," he said awkwardly, "I have lots of space here. So if you haven't yet found a room... you're more than welcome to stay."

His gaze was just as awkward as his voice — and hopeful, strangely enough. I could understand him. He lived alone here — virtually in solitary confinement even though technically this was the town center. He was probably bored out of his mind.

Other players must have been giving his tinderbox a wide berth, declining his invitations in favor of safer dwellings. And judging by the fact that quest-seeking players weren't queuing all around the tower, there wasn't much to catch here.

"So what do you think?" the wizard repeated.

What could I lose, after all? A damp hole in the barracks cellar? And as for dangerous, the game gave us plenty of warning every time the magic shield came down. I could always run for cover if need be.

"I'd love to," I said. "I just hope Captain Gard won't object."

"Oh no, he won't! He's all for it! I'm going to tell him now."

His face lit up with excitement that actually looked sincere. It looked as if the guy really missed company.

"All you have to do is move your stuff here," he said.

I shrugged. "*Omnia mea mecum porto.*"

"Excuse me?"

"*All my things I carry with me,*" I translated for him.

"What language is this?" he asked, curious.

"Latin. It's an ancient language. It's been dead for hundreds of years. This phrase is ascribed to a famous sage."

"How interesting. What happened to him?"

"When his city was seized by the enemy, they took mercy on its citizens and even allowed them to leave with whatever possessions they could take with them. On one condition."

"Which was?"

He was one curious NPC, wasn't he? His eyes were gleaming with excitement.

"Nothing serious, really. The city dwellers weren't allowed to use either draught animals or carts. Only their own backs."

"Oh," the wizard smiled. "I can imagine these people staggering under the weight of their possessions! But what about the sage?"

"The sage walked empty-handed, an unusual sight among his heavily-loaded compatriots. Enemy soldiers by the city gate made fun of him, saying, 'Where are your possessions, old man? Haven't you managed to acquire anything at all in your lifetime?' To which the old sage answered, pointing at his forehead-"

"*Omnia mea mecum porto!*" Tronus exclaimed. "*All my things I carry with me!* That's excellent! That's very clever!"

What an interesting NPC. Then again, why was I surprised? He was probably on the Top 100 list.

"Now then," the wizard smiled, "are you staying?"

"With pleasure," I said.

A new system message came as a complete surprise — probably, because the wizard himself felt almost real. He felt *alive*, if you know what I mean.

Congratulations! You've just completed a hidden quest: Wizard's Invitation.
Reward: 100 Tyllill crystals

What a nice surprise. Ten points to Reputation were always welcome.

"As I said, I've got lots of space," the wizard went on. "Choose any room you want."

"I've been thinking... you don't happen to have anything on this floor, do you? The view is just too good."

"Oh! I can see you have a poetic streak!" the wizard exclaimed.

I shrugged. "Sort of. I'm not sure of that. According to my wife, I'm not entirely lost to fine society."

The wizard guffawed. The game developers must have invested some heart into this toon.

We went on talking for quite a while. Or rather, Tronus did all the talking while I listened. Judging by his behavior, you might think he hadn't seen a living soul for a few centuries at least.

He told me how the Citadel had come about, narrating stories of the glorious Black Stream battle and the famed Maragar Hundred. I learned that the foundations of this fortress of Light had been literally paved with its defenders' bones. Apparently, it had some long abandoned locations — like Zeddekey's Catacombs — a complex maze of underground labyrinths named after one of the Fortress' legendary architects. According to Tronus, these days no one knew where to look for them.

While he elaborated on the subject of ancient legends, I opened the Citadel instance list. There they were, those catacombs. Well, well, well. A secret location, yeah right! I checked the chat. Exactly what

I thought. Zeddekey's Catacombs were quite popular with players. I counted about thirty raid invitations. Recommended levels: 100+. Mobs: various monsters as well as the ghosts of ancient catacomb builders and Fortress defenders. The instance's boss was none other than the spirit of Zeddekey himself. Some place that was!

Lost in reading, I must have missed something very important the wizard was saying. All I heard was,

"...if only I could get a few of those rocks for my tower..."

I shook my head. "Excuse me?"

He stared at me, uncomprehending. "Didn't I just say? Yellow onyx. According to ancient scriptures, catacomb builders came across a small deposit of it. Wizards love this mineral for its energy-accumulating properties. So I just said that I'd love to have a few chunks of yellow onyx for my tower. What do you think?"

New quest alert: Yellow Onyx!
Reward: depends on the volume of the resource farmed.
Deadline: none
Accept: Yes/No

Chapter Nine

I spent some time before bed rummaging through a pile of Mirror World apps until I found one that seemed very useful: Alarm Clock. Apart from the standard options, this seemingly simple device could be set up to alert you to certain quests and other gaming events. For instance, if a player received a quest with a deadline, Alarm Clock had special settings to remind him or her of the time left till deadline. Or, as in my case, it could warn you of the beginning of every event located in the "Maragar Citadel and Its Environments".

The settings offered several notification ringtones. I chose human voice — which surprisingly came in four options: polite, neutral, casual and vulgar. I chose polite, of course. I wasn't even going to try the other ones. I mean, who'd want to listen to obscenities spat at you by *a bot*? I might check out the neutral one later... or even... we'd have to see.

Depends how busy I'd be.

Still, I already knew from experience that Mirror World would keep me busy.

Tronus kept his promise and offered me a decent room with a No-Man's Lands view. What could I say? — I'd asked for it.

The room differed dramatically from my barracks cellar even though it was modest to say the least. Admittedly, I missed my room in Ronald's inn: all those bathrobes and slippers, the shower even. Here I could only dream of such creature comforts, even though here they were all but a figment of my imagination. My body was now lying nice and motionless in the capsule, snug like an Egyptian mummy. It was left in the real world. As was my family.

Before falling asleep, I spent some time contemplating the Logout button. It had already become a habit.

I spent a quiet night — peaceful even. In the morning, I entered the tower's central hall well-rested. The wizard was already waiting for me.

"Morning, Olgerd!" he exclaimed. "Did you sleep well?"

"Excellent, thank you. I can't wait to start."

"Jolly good, jolly good!" he smiled, then added with a hint of sarcasm in his voice, "Very well. You asked for it."

I nodded. "Spit it out. What do you want me to do?"

No points for guessing that a catacomb trip wasn't the only job the system had in store for me. If the truth were known, I was quite happy. Every Reputation point brought me closer to the in-game bank loan.

The wizard rubbed his hands. "You might have already noticed that the area around the tower is a mess."

"You could say that. Strange you don't have any assistants."

He shrugged. "Captain Gard keeps promising but..."

"Can't you hire someone yourself?" I asked. "Look at all those loiterers walking right past your windows!"

With a sigh, the wizard adjusted his goggles on his forehead. "I wish it were that easy. This is a classified location, dammit! I can only hire those with a clearance. For a while, I had a waiting list of players eager to help me. I had to find ways of getting rid of them by giving them impossible jobs to do. Hire! It's never easy with our Captain Gard. Still, he knows his stuff. After the Darkies' last outing it's not easy to find trustworthy personnel here."

That's what it was! And I'd thought that players were afraid to come close to the tower. Did that mean that Mila's letter had worked, after all? My multi-stage quest seemed to have taken an unexpected turn.

I remembered the sideways glances that the players had cast me last night. I could only imagine what they'd thought: an overeager noob Grinder hurrying to the wizard anticipating all the work around him, thinking that the wizard would issue him a yummy epic quest on a silver platter but having no idea that the said wizard's quests were out of even the advanced players' league. No wonder they'd taken me for an idiot!

Which meant that Gard wasn't that much of a beast, really. He might be weird but he wasn't a "sick bastard". Never mind. This was still better than nothing at all.

"I understand," I nodded knowingly. "You don't need to go on."

"Jolly good!" the wizard clapped his hands. "I don't care about all that junk. I have too much on my plate as it is. Still, you have to agree that the square around the tower is not a pretty sight, putting it mildly."

"You could say that," I agreed. "Imagine if some high-ranking officials wanted to visit your modest abode."

"Exactly my point!" he nodded. "I think you and I will make a good team!"

It was a good job Sveta my wife couldn't see me now. A bearded Dwarf craftsman...

"Let's do it!" Tronus summed up.

New Quest Alert: Mop and Bucket.
Clean the square around the wizard's tower.
Reward: 300 Tyllill crystals
Deadline: none
Accept: Yes/No

Okay, why not? *Accept*
"So?" I asked. "Come on, then! Great deeds await us!"

"Well done!" Tronus saluted me. "I've never seen anyone as impatient to get to work as you are."

"It's nothing," I waved his praise away. "Just a bout of youthful enthusiasm, soon to be replaced by rheumatic arthritis. Talking about work: I'm afraid, after lunch I'll have to return to Drammen. I've been contracted to work in the local mines. I might spend the night there, then return to the Citadel with the first morning caravan."

"That's nothing," the wizard replied. "You're a volunteer, aren't you? No one can force you to work."

"Excellent," I said as I headed for the door.

The contrast between what I'd seen outside yesterday and what I was facing now was incredible. Ruin and desolation! I got the impression that the wizard had been spending nights showering his own back yard with bits of rock, pieces of wood, fragments of roof tiles and liberal doses of broken glass. I thought I glimpsed a skeleton, its crocodile-like skull baring teeth the size of my hand. It looked as if this time I was really going to get plucked.

Never mind. I'll just get on with it.

First of all, I had to study the area around the tower which could be divided into two circles: the inner one, surrounded by a crumbling stone fence, and the outer one beyond it, ploughed up by Caltean missiles like a furrowed field.

That decided it. I had to start with the internal part. From what I could see, this was a good week's work. That way at least I wasn't going to be too conspicuous. Already players were beginning to circle the fence, scrutinizing this latest development. Sorry, guys. You've got nothing to look for here. This is my quest, my junk and my mess.

I began to plan how to move the rubbish and where to take it to. Still, as I approached the first heap of debris, I realized that the game developers had thought about everything.

> *Name: a Pile of Junk*
> *Type: Simple*
> *Durability: 30/30*

Aha. These things were basically the same as Piles of Rubble, only those had 10 pt. less Durability. And how about restrictions? Let's have a look... right... found it. So! Hadn't I said that Mine Diggers were always in high demand? We weren't a picky bunch: we could go down mines or we could clear streets from debris... you name it, we could do it.

I raised my head, surveying the square. There were at least fifteen more Piles of Junk lying around. And what if...

I opened my Merry Digger and asked it to scan the work front. It zoned out for a while, then reported,

> *Data analysis completed.*
> *The location contains the following quest items:*
> *Piles of Junk, simple, 25*
> *Piles of Junk, regular, 19*
> *Piles of Junk, large, 12*
> *Piles of Brick Rubble, 35*
> *Piles of Rock Rubble, 46*
> *Piles of Marble Rubble, 28*

Piles of Black Onyx, 11
Blown-down Trees, 6
Clumps of Evil Weed, 107
Trampled Flowerbeds, 3
Broken Windows, 5

The list was rather longish. Generous, I'd say.

Punctured walls, broken doors and windows, trampled flowerbeds and a collapsed fountain — I had enough work for a week, if not more. And all this generous offer for a miserable 30 pt. Reputation? Don't forget I still had to do my daily quota in the mines. No one was going to relieve me of that.

Never mind. We'll get through it.

I walked over to the nearest flowerbed. It looked as if it had been ravaged by a giant mole. The earth had been ploughed up and littered with bits of building stone, bricks and roof tiles. The little fence listed to one side. I wasn't observing any flowers — fresh, dry or otherwise.

Still, I decided to make a start here. This particular quest object was just as good as the next.

As if! Apparently, I couldn't. The flowerbed came with a restriction attached. It could only be tended by players of certain professions. The list was quite exhaustive, starting with landscape designer, gardener and florist. Halfway down it I also saw herbalist. He must have been the one responsible for removing the Evil Weed.

Unwilling to waste any more time on checking the various types of junk piles for their respective availability, I ordered my Merry Digger to search for those I could handle. Much to my pleasure, the list shrank about 25%.

All the piles of rock and junk were mine. To deal with the rest, Tronus would have to hire other professions. One of the items on the list surprised me,

Broken door, 1

What would a Digger have to do with that? Doors were supposed to be handled by carpenters or cabinet makers, weren't they?

I asked my Digger to run a repeat search, just to double-check it. You never know, it might have glitched... but no. My little helper kept offering me this broken door.

Very well. I'd have to look into this later. In the meantime, I had to get to work. What should we start with? — Aha, better the devil you know.

You've tried to clear a Pile of Brick Rubble
-3 to the item's durability.
Durability: 17/20

I brandished my pick some more. Let's see what we have now:

You've tried to clear a Pile of Brick Rubble
-10 to the item's durability.
Durability: 7/20

Excellent. Wish all of my swings were this good.

You've tried to clear a Pile of Brick Rubble
-5 to the item's durability.
Durability: 2/20

Not bad, either. I took another swing, just to check. I was curious. Would I make it?

You've cleared a Pile of Brick Rubble!
Reward: 1 Tyllill crystal.

Yes! Excellent. The wizard's quest began to take on a new shape. What a promising beginning. True, the system could have been more generous, but it was irrelevant. The main thing was, I got some tyllill.

Watch out, junk! Here I come!

* * *

I spent till midday brandishing my pick. Or rather, Merry Digger did. In the meantime, I was doing whatever meager research was available in Mirror World's info portal.

As if confirming the old adage about things being easier said than done, the virtual sky kept up a constant drizzle on me.

It never stopped — a fine, unpleasant veil of moisture that dripped down the back of my collar. What a few hours ago looked like a regular backyard had by now turned into a mud bath. For the umpteenth time I sent rays of gratitude to the caravanners' leader. If I saw him later this evening, I absolutely had to buy him a drink.

I'd already pulled down all the piles of bricks, marble and half of the rocks. Any hopes for the game rewarding me with something worthwhile had dwindled to nothing. Tyllill crystals were few and far between: one or two per junk pile, sometimes three. A lot of piles were empty — no idea why. But it wasn't that bad, after all. Sixty-two crystals: definitely better than nothing.

While my Merry Digger bot controlled my digital body, I read up on the Zeddekey's Catacombs. Had I had access to the World Wide Web, my research might have been more profound but even this meager information was quite enough for my purposes.

Now, the Catacombs. Not the nicest of locations, I had to admit — pretty much like everything else in this part of Mirror World. The most unpleasant thing about them was that their labyrinths didn't have a map. From what I sussed out from reading snatches of forum messages, the Catacomb tunnels had a habit of changing their direction. Each raid down them had to be done from scratch, even for those raid members who'd done the whole instance several times visiting the spirit of the ancient architect in the Main Cave. The time needed to get there also varied: some players reached the Main Cave faster than others.

On top of that, the Catacombs were packed with all sorts of traps and highly aggressive wandering ghosts. And just to give you some idea,

Zeddekey's level was directly proportional to the level of the player who wished to take him on but no less than a hundred. All in all, it wasn't the most accommodating of instances.

My checking of both the chat and raid applications confirmed my gut feeling: there was no way I could do this quest. No group in their sane minds were going to accept a zero-level player. Ideally, group members had to have similar levels. Fighting the boss was a very complex affair that demanded the highest degree of team work. Accepting a low-level player could jeopardize the whole operation, putting everyone else at risk. And I wasn't even a proper player!

Just as I thought, the only Yellow Onyx deposit was in the Main Cave. Or rather, in a small vault located behind it — guarded by Zeddekey's evil spirit.

At first I was even happy: seeing as I was the tough super Digger that I was, I was bound to find someone interested in my mining services. Not so. The forum made it perfectly clear: all the bonuses were pooled and divided equally between group members.

I opened the auction and immediately discovered that Yellow Onyx was a non-transferrable quest item. So it was a double whammy, basically. I might try and join a group, of course, but I doubted it would bring any results.

I checked the clock: half past one. I needed to make sure I didn't miss the caravan. According to the Guiding Eyes' schedule, they would be picking up new passengers at the central square at two-thirty.

Time to wrap up this show. Tomorrow would be

another day. I still had to pop into the shop to get some writing supplies and buy a couple of local newspapers for Nikanor. His quest wasn't going to disappear overnight. I had to live up to my word.

My satnav promptly laid the optimal route to the nearest office supplies shop called *At Tiffany's.* How appropriate. As I walked, I checked auction prices for writing materials. They had loads. Pens, pencils, quills, inkwells and ink in every color, as well as erasers and paper of every possible size and quality. Players didn't sit on their backsides. They were busy making money. They didn't spend their spare time building some weird contraptions from blueprints like some engineering designers did, in the face of yours truly. I could probably have done much better just plucking geese and selling quills at auction.

Lots of writing materials on the auction pages. I could buy something cheap and cheerful right now and save myself a trip to the shop. But firstly, I wasn't even sure what kind of pencil or quill I needed to make entries in the cunning old lawyer's book. And secondly — as I already knew from experience — all these NPC shopkeepers were actually quite useful as information sources. Thirdly, I could compare the prices and buy a few newspapers at the same time.

The nearest office supplies shop was situated at the very beginning of Crooked Lane. Like all other Citadel buildings, it looked rather worse for wear — apparently, Caltean gifts had reached that far. Still, the whole street was in a frenzy of restoration. Another couple of days, and this lane might not look as, ahem, crooked as it now seemed.

The shop's freshly-painted door opened with ease, letting me into a rather cozy room smelling of fresh paper. I'd always loved the scent of new books.

What a great, special feeling when you walk into a book shop and check its shelves expecting to see the book you'd been awaiting for quite a while. The shopkeeper hides a knowing smile as you pay and reach out for the little tome. Seemingly matter-of-factly, you study its cover and open it as if to make sure it's what you've been looking for. It is indeed. You look at the author's familiar name: it feels as if you've known him all your life. The novel's title is printed in large, bold letters, followed by either a prologue or Chapter One. You catch yourself thinking that the book feels pleasantly heavy. You've only opened it to check the design but your gaze can't let go, hurrying from one word to the next, from comma to period. You devour the first paragraph in a matter of seconds... that's it! You've dived too deep to resurface; you're far from here, somewhere on a desert island or in the recesses of deep space.

That's when you pull yourself together and will yourself to stop. Not here. Not now. Tonight. After everyone's gone to bed. You'll make some tea and sandwiches, wrap yourself in a blanket and disappear for a while. You'll be gone. You'll be far from here.

I shook myself out of it. The salesgirl was already giving me funny looks. She must have taken me for some sick weirdo.

I had a brief chat with her which resulted in me buying some writing tools and a stack of local papers. I had my work cut out for me for tonight.

It didn't take me long to get to the main square. It was already getting busy. No one seemed to be particularly cowering. Players stood alone and in groups, talking and laughing. Some had newspapers in their hands.

It all looked like a large bus station medieval fantasy-style.

The Guiding Eyes arrived on the dot. Kosma led the caravan, towering over it like a gray cliff. Today he wasn't in a hurry, moving smoothly like a gargantuan steamboat.

I couldn't help smiling on seeing him. I'd only met his master the day before, but already it felt as if both were part of my family. No idea why. It's probably because you can't feel estranged anymore from someone who used to protect you. For you, they'll forever feel like family.

Uncle Vanya had noticed me too, smiling and waving. "Good job!" he said. "I knew you'd survive!"

"Hi," I squeezed his proffered hand. "How did you know, may I ask?"

He guffawed. "The sight of your clean pair of heels was convincing enough. That was a fine dash — any Olympic runner would have turned green with envy."

"You bet! I'm good at that!"

"I can see you haven't wasted your time," he commented cheerfully. "You're hung with medals like a Christmas tree!"

"Yeah right. If they want to call me a hero, who am I to object?"

"Listen," Uncle Vanya said. "We're leaving in five minutes. Wanna ride with me? You could tell me about your first day."

I shrugged. "I'm all for that. If the truth were known, I meant to ask you about it."

He gave me an encouraging slap on the shoulder. "Deal. You have five minutes. You can get yourself into the cab while I go check on the others. They might need help, you never know."

While he was running around helping other caravanners, I promptly installed myself in my old place. I'd only spent less than an hour in it but already it felt like home.

I hadn't even noticed the five minutes fly past. Uncle Vanya jumped back into his cab. He wasn't alone. A player had followed him. Who was it that said that it was a small world? Mirror World definitely was.

This was Shadow — the Alven girl. She raised a quizzical eyebrow, staring back at me. Long time no see!

I smiled. She frowned.

Oblivious of our little pantomime, Uncle Vanya shifted into his seat, making himself comfortable. "This is my niece. She's coming with us. Liz, whassup? Go sit down."

"We already met," I finally said.

"Really?" Uncle Vanya took in the scene.

"He's right," the girl perched herself on the seat next to me. "Remember I told you about the Swamp? That's him."

* * *

The Wastelands lived up to their name. Ditches filled with murky water crossed out paths blocked in places by brambles and large boulders overgrown with short brown grass.

Kosma didn't give a damn. He kept pulling his armored wagon, occasionally shaking his mountainous head.

We'd been on the road for about twenty minutes already. Liz — Uncle Vanya's niece — had proved not as silent as I'd thought her to be. She wouldn't win any prizes for being Miss Chatterbox of the Year, but at least she pulled her weight in our conversation.

Although we hadn't mentioned her age, she must have been about twenty, twenty-five max. Nor had we discussed any personal affairs. I'd managed to glean that she lived with her grandma. We hadn't mentioned her parents — apparently, this was a sore subject. I didn't insist. I hate prying.

Admittedly, my original not so favorable impression of her had by now completely gone. I was sitting next to a totally different person. What I'd mistaken for an ill-bred coldness back at the Swamp, was in fact a tactful reserve. And besides... I couldn't be sure, of course... but I got the impression that this girl had had her fair share of hardships.

"Dude, you're famous now," Uncle Vanya grinned. "Got three medals for yesterday's event!"

"Yeah right. I hope I won't live to regret it."

"Nah. It's perfectly normal. You just got your fifteen minutes of fame. Most players do. Actually, Liz, how did it go with you and Tronus?"

I pricked up my ears.

"It didn't," she grumbled, staring out the window. "Same old."

"Those developer bastards!" Uncle Vanya sniffed. "They just can't make it easy, can they? You sure you asked him nicely?"

Liz shrugged. "I tried it every possible way. Doesn't work."

"You must be doing something wrong," Uncle Vanya said didactically. "I heard about some dwarf being seen there today."

She screwed up her face. "I know."

I could see that the conversation was painful for her. Me, I just held my breath trying to look normal. No points for guessing they were talking about me. At least I hadn't seen any other dwarves — or should I say false impostor dwarves — in the wizard's household.

"It doesn't mean anything," Liz continued. "He might have bought a guidebook off someone. Why shouldn't he be applying it?"

"I'm sure that's what he did," Uncle Vanya agreed. "You can't do that sort of thing without a guidebook. But you know yourself that not all guidebooks are created equal. What's good for the cat is not always good for the mouse."

The girl sighed. "I know."

Silence fell. It was time for me to butt in. "This Tronus, is he a problem?"

"Not at all, dude. Not if you forget that for the last few weeks, this individual has been generating some truly awful quests. Customer support must be absolutely snowed with complaints. Most of his quests involve No-Man's Lands — and not just any old location but the one which is out of most players' league. You can still do them, of course, but only if you seek help from top-level players. Some poor bastards had to hire whole top-level groups! Imagine how much that costs?"

"I still can't see the problem," I said. "This wizard isn't the only NPC. Why can't they go somewhere else?"

Uncle Vanya and his niece exchanged knowing smiles. He ran his large hand along his beard and explained,

"The thing is, this wretched wizard is a member of the Citadel Council. It's comprised of captains and wizards of all seven castles. Basically, just some local top brass."

"I don't understand."

"You will in a moment. To put it briefly... there's this multi-stage quest. One of its steps is providing help to all of the Council members, may they burn in hell."

"Aha. I see. And?"

"It's basically an initiation," Liz added. "Once you pass it, you get access to heroic quests."

"Let me guess. It doesn't have anything to do with Valor, does it?"

"You got it," he nodded. "Each heroic quest is issued by its respective NPC and is rewarded with quite a bit of Valor."

"I see," I said. "And this Tronus throws wrenches in their works?"

"Not just him," Liz said. "But he's one of a few."

Uncle Vanya shook his head. "I just don't understand all this fuss about Valor. I wouldn't want it if it jumped on me. It's basically extortion."

"If you want to continue leveling, Valor is key," the girl retorted. "You know that better than I."

It looked as if this argument hadn't started yesterday.

Uncle Vanya chuckled. "Key! Yeah right! Remember that Dark Captain who barged into Drammen and started bossing everyone around? We made quick work of him, didn't we? So much for his Valor."

Liz shook her head but chose not to confront him. Whatever counterarguments she had, she wasn't in a hurry to offer them. From what I'd already sussed out, Uncle Vanya wasn't the easily convinced kind.

"Me and my Kosma, we're perfectly happy," he summed up, stroking his beard. "I told you before and I'll tell you again, girl: it's about time you forget your stupid Valor and do something useful. If you had put your mind to it, you could have already got yourself a draught beast. We might have accepted you into the caravan. You could have been making good money, you know."

Still silent, she shook her head.

"Ah, whatever," Uncle Vanya sounded hurt. "As long as you remember that Valor is for those who don't know what to do with their money. And you still have your Bronze account to pay."

She winced. "Uncle Vanya, please. You've chosen what works for you. I have my own priorities."

For the next few minutes, we didn't speak, each thinking his or her own thoughts. I was the first to break the silence,

"Did you say this NPC used to be easier to handle?"

"Absolutely," Uncle Vanya said. "He was one of the easiest when it came to quests. Nothing difficult, just a bit of cleaning. Or fetching him some Yellow Onyx.

I pricked up my ears. "Yellow Onyx?"

"Sure," he nodded. "Tronus has been ordering it by the wagonload. Every quest he issues, he always asks for some. He must be having it for breakfast, lunch and dinner!"

"I don't think I remember any Yellow Onyx mines," I adlibbed.

"You don't mine it," Liz said. "It's a drop from Sand Golems. Alternatively, you can get it from the vault in Zeddekey's Catacombs."

Sand golems. How interesting. Did that mean there was another way of farming this particular mineral so beloved by the Citadel's wizard?

"What's in the vault is nothing though," the gnome shrugged. "It's not worth the trouble."

"What do you mean?" I asked.

"Closing the quest is the tricky bit. The more onyx you bring, the more generous the wizard will be. Take you, for instance. How many free slots do you have in your bag?"

"Eh... a hundred and forty? Something like that."

"Which means you could farm about two thousand crystals. Possibly more. Definitely no less."

"So that's how it works, then."

He nodded. "Exactly."

"You'd never be able to do the quest, anyway," Liz said with a smirk. "You might be able to complete the cleaning and errand-running part... anyone can do that, I suppose. But the onyx... forget it. You'd have to hire a group to take you there. Whether the Blue Hills or the Catacombs, either way it would have cost you a ton of moolah."

"Blue Hills?"

The gnome nodded. "She's right. It's the location where Sand Golems live. They're all levels ninety-plus."

I know it sounds crazy but the funny thing was, the Golems were probably a better bet.

The wagon suddenly jolted, interrupting our conversation. While the gnome was calling Kosma every name under the sun for being a "clumsy blind beast", I opened the map. Let's have a look at those Blue Hills of theirs. Eh? Now that looked interesting...

"So I can see that you too decided to try your luck leveling Valor," Uncle Vanya joked.

I only shrugged.

"He's just being curious," Liz answered for me. "Back at the Swamp, he asked the guys all sorts of questions too."

I rubbed the bridge of my nose, adjusting the non-existent glasses. It looked like it had become a habit. I seemed to be doing it every time I was nervous.

"To tell you the truth," I began, "I had no intention of straying so far from the beaten track. I was never interested in the Citadel. I was going to work in the mines. It just happened. There's little I can do now."

"It's all right, it's all right. Keep your hair on," Uncle Vanya said. "We all have our own goals. As the girl's just said, you have your own way. You're doing everything right."

I nodded my appreciation. The inklings of a plan were already beginning to form in my mind. Now I had to find suitable performers — or even comrades, to a certain degree.

"You're right," I said. "Each of us has his or her own way. Still, sometimes our paths can cross."

Uncle Vanya frowned. "What are you driving at?"

"I'd like to hire you two."

They exchanged glances.

"Meaning?" Liz looked at me with interest.

"The thing is," I touched the bridge of my nose, "I can't handle Sand Golems on my own."

"You're full of surprises, aren't you?" the gnome muttered.

"And another thing," I said. "There's this location just next to the Blue Hills. I need to check it out too. But that can wait."

Liz smiled. "You have any idea how much a raid like that would cost you? Do I understand correctly that you want me and Uncle to handle the golems on our own?"

"Exactly," I said. "Just you and him. And as for your wages... There is a slight hitch here. Once you know all the details you might be just as interested in the Golems as I am. Or not the Golems even. The Yellow Onyx."

Uncle Vanya slapped my shoulder and burst out laughing. Liz seemed to be slightly taken aback by his reaction, looking incomprehensively between himself and me.

"You don't get it, do you?" Uncle Vanya laughed. "The dwarf that's been sighted in the wizard's tower! It's our Olgerd here!"

Chapter Ten

Two days had elapsed since we'd had this conversation. In the meantime, my lifestyle hadn't changed much. Toiling in the mines. Busting my hump in the Wizard's courtyard. Perusing the info portal before bedtime.

I'd always considered myself a patient person, long-suffering even, but these two days had taken their toll on my nerves. Even though the whole raid thing didn't seem to be that difficult, after all. At least not according to Uncle Vanya.

I was sitting at Talina's drinking coffee. It was nine in the morning. The tavern was empty. Today was the day. We were about to take on the Sand Golems. Or rather, Uncle Vanya and Liz were. My combat skills were a little less than useless. So I was probably going to cower behind some rock while those two would have to farm Yellow Onyx. What else could I do?

Even though, if you listened to Liz, my role in the raid was arguably the most important.

We had made out a contract the same evening as we'd had our conversation. According to one of its clauses, I was obliged to help Liz achieve her goal by telling her how to get in the wizard's good books. In their turn, she and Uncle Vanya promised to help me with the Golems. As a bonus, they also offered to accompany me to the location with the Nests of Rocks. They refused the remuneration I'd offered them, saying that helping society's misfits was the right thing to do.

In all honesty, at first I'd been worried whether Liz could pull off the advice I'd given her. My plan was simple. All other players had been so impatient to get the quest that they had gone directly to the wizard. He, in his turn, rewarded them with complex and almost impossible quests. That created a vicious circle that did nothing but anger players and made for a constant stream of forum whining.

I, however, knew of the reasons behind the wizard's behavior. Which was why I'd suggested Liz went to Captain Gard first and only mentioned the wizard fleetingly, inquiring if he needed any help. Considering the sheer amount of her medals received for the defense of the Citadel, Gard just might consider her worthy of the task.

The next morning after our conversation, I'd been working in the wizard's courtyard when Liz walked in. She was beaming. Holding a small knife shaped like a sickle, she cast me a cheerful smile and began cleaning one of the flowerbeds. My plan had worked. She'd done it.

The same night in the tavern, she'd told me and Uncle Vanya about it. The next thing, Varn joined us and offered me a deal. In exchange for information on how to get one of the wizard's quests, he provided me with a lifelong VIP pass with the Guiding Eyes. Judging by the way Uncle Vanya grinned, he must have had something to do with it. I agreed. Why not? It was an excellent deal: a lifelong free ride and a good relationship with the caravanners. And as for my secret... I was pretty sure that the players would very soon have worked it out anyway. All they had to do was track my first day in the Citadel. So basically, it had all turned out for the best.

Uncle Vanya's voice echoed through the empty tavern, bringing me back to reality.

"Right, golem slayer! Are you ready?"

I turned. So! What the hell had happened to the wagon driver in his standard-issue green clothes? The gnome stood confidently with his hands on his hips, enjoying the sight of my drooping jaw.

"How do you like it?" he asked with a self-satisfied smirk.

"Man, what can I say? You're full of surprises!"

Uncle Vanya chuckled. "You're not the only one."

I had to agree. Instead of the humble caravanner I was looking at a gnome tank clad in a complete Purple Set. The precious suit of armor made him look twice as large and ten times more powerful: a super warrior directly from heaven.

I couldn't help smiling. "You've come prepared,

haven't you?"

"You bet," he grinned. "I'll hack them to bits before you even notice. Ah, there's my niece coming!"

The tavern door swung open, revealing our archer girl. Did I say the day was rich in surprises? Her gear was not a patch on her uncle's but still quite impressive. Her Blue Set was infinitely better than the one she'd been wearing back at the Swamp.

"Hi," she sat at our table. "You ready?"

"Sure," Uncle Vanya replied. "A quick coffee, then we'll be off. We should be able to make it back by dinner time. Your auntie wants me to go with her to our country cottage."

"Give her my love."

"Can't you do it yourself?" Uncle Vanya grumbled at her. "Wouldn't you like to go with us to the country? I could get a BBQ going. What would you say to that?"

"Sorry," Liz shook her head. "I have too many things to do."

"Which are what? *Things to do!* You've become completely nuts with this game!"

Liz shook her head and stared out the window.

Uncle Vanya glanced at me, seeking support. "You tell me, Olgerd. Are *you* happy here?"

"Am I supposed to give you an honest answer? Had you asked me twenty years ago... but you want me to be objective, don't you?"

Liz perked up. "Do you want to say that had you been twenty years old, you'd have spent all your waking time in the game?"

"Can't see why not," I replied. "On one

condition.'

"Which is what?"

"I wouldn't ignore my loved ones."

With a sigh, she turned back to the window. Uncle Vanya winked me his appreciation.

"Your coffee," Talina appeared by our table, deftly setting down the cups.

I took a sip. "You know, Liz... my Christina would have loved it here. And my wife. I'd love them to be able to come here one day and see for themselves."

"I don't think you're going to take them to Drammen. Nor the Citadel," Uncle Vanya chuckled.

I nodded. "Christina would have loved to meet your Kosma."

He puffed out his chest with pride. "I bet! Sure she would!"

"But you're probably right," I said. "It wouldn't be a good idea to take them to aggressive locations. Now Mellenville's different. There they might appreciate the whole beauty of Mirror World."

"Lots of nice locations around," Liz said. "There're some really cool ones in the South. And in the East."

"There are," Uncle Vanya agreed. "Mirror World is immense. Right! Time to do some golem slaying! I just hope it won't take us long."

✳ ✳ ✳

The trip to the Blue Hills was quite quick. Three portal jumps from Drammen to a one-horse-town called Toug took only fifteen minutes, followed by a hike along the wide Inunda River: forty minutes in total. Not bad at all. I was more than happy.

As we walked, we came across a lot of people. Surprisingly, the place was literally swarming with zero-level players: mainly herbalists and fishermen. Then again, why was I surprised? This was a river. A perfect location for either profession.

Watching the fishermen was funny. Some were angling off the bank. Others used small boats. To our right, I noticed several teams of five players casting nets into the water. This was probably how you fished in a group.

As we walked through a small forest, we saw lots of hunters, woodcutters and bee keepers.

"This place is a farming heaven," I commented.

"Sure," Uncle Vanya said. "A very good location."

"Aren't they afraid?"

"What's there to be afraid of? As long as you avoid mobs' aggro zones, you can farm all you want."

"Plus the place is chock full of combat players," Liz added. "They smoke the mobs faster than they can respawn."

Uncle Vanya nodded. "The local beasties make up part of quite a few quests. This was one of Mirror World's first locations ever. That's why there's such a disparity in levels."

"I see," I muttered.

'Wait till we come to the Blue Hills," Uncle Vanya grinned. "That's a totally different picture over there!"

"Sure," Liz said. "The Golems aren't very popular, I tell you. Not as quest mobs, anyway. To do a bit of farming, maybe."

After another ten minutes, we finally left the forest. I walked around one last tree and found myself standing on a wide flat river bank. This was some beach, I tell you. Completely deserted, too.

"Slow down, Olgerd," Uncle Vanya warned me. "Better safe than sorry."

As if in confirmation, a system message popped up,

Warning! This location is not recommended for players under level 80.

"Keep next to me," Liz reached behind her back for her longbow. "Uncle Vanya, it's time to create a group."

He sent us invitations to join, then pointed at the beach in front of him, "See that sand? Notice anything different about it?"

"Just sand," I peered at it, trying to make out any peculiarities. "It's very yellow, if that's what you mean."

He shook his head. "You're not looking at the right thing. Look how uneven it is. See those craters?"

I took a better look. "Yes! I see! They're slightly darker than the rest of it."

"They're golems' lairs," Liz said. "Don't go anywhere near them. If he injures you, we'll have to buy a potion for you or go look for a healer. They're all levels 90-95, that's a 20-hour injury. At least."

"I see," I nodded my understanding. "So where do you want me to be?"

"Just here next to the forest," Uncle Vanya pointed. "That's it. Enough lazing around. Lizzie, are you ready?" he waited for her to nod, then added, "I'll go bring the first one, then."

He set off, holding a broad full-height shield in one hand and a battle axe in the other. Despite his seemingly cumbersome armor, Uncle Vanya moved with the flowing grace of an animal.

Reaching for an arrow behind her back, Liz gave me a wink. "He's awesome, isn't he?"

"He's too good," I answered, admiring him.

The girl heaved a sigh. "Such a waste! If he decided to level up Valor, his char would cost a ton of money."

"What do you mean?"

"What do you think? Have you never heard of people selling their chars?"

I shook my head.

'I see," she said. "Never mind. We'll talk about it later. We have a job to do. Look, he's aggroing one already."

Indeed, Uncle Vanya was already about five paces away from one of the craters. The sand around it exploded, letting out the first monster. Jeez, it was fast! For some reason, I'd always believed golems to be slow giants barely moving their massive feet as they stomped along. But the sight of this first Blue Hills golem had busted my ideas of them.

It was short: five foot at the most. It had two arms, two legs and a small head. It moved unbelievably fast, rolling around like a large oily shadow.

Uncle Vanya didn't seem to be nonplussed by its maneuvers in the slightest. Having parried the first blow with his shield, he almost effortlessly twitched his axe, chopping off his opponent's leg and stripping him of 80% Life. Liz's bowstring snapped.

Congratulations!
You've slain a Sand Golem!

Phew. We could go and collect the onyx now.

"We can do it later," Liz said, taking aim again. "Let's mop up this part of the beach first."

I shrugged. If it went like this, we'd be done before midday. Uncle Vanya seemed to be in form, his every swing resulting in a crit. He finished off two more golems without any help from his archer. His level spoke for itself. It was true that we weren't getting any loot or XP for doing this but that wasn't what we'd come here for. We were only interested in the quest resource.

Uncle Vanya had finished off his thirtieth golem — or was it twenty-ninth? — and waved to us.

"Now we can go and collect the onyx," Liz told me.

Softly she moved along the sand. Each mob had given us two or three crystals. Excellent. Another hour, and we could start moving toward the Misty Mountains.

---

* * *

An hour and a half later, the system told me that my bag was now full. After twenty more minutes, Liz let us know that hers was, too.

"Oh," Uncle Vanya said. "Just when I was getting a taste for it."

Liz rolled her eyes dreamily. "Shame we're not getting any XP or loot. Would be good, wouldn't it?"

"It's a good job we aren't!" the gnome snorted. "You'd have run me into the ground then. Olgerd, you ready? Show us the way."

I opened the Der Swyor Clan's Trade Routes map. My bot promptly laid a new route and we set off.

"So what is it you need to find there?" Uncle Vanya wondered, walking next to me.

"There's a Nest of Rocks I need to check."

He looked at me in surprise. "You realize how many there are?"

"I do. But I have the exact coordinates of that one."

"I see. What kind of quest is it? Please don't get me wrong. It's just that I've never seen a zero level performing complex quests like these before."

"I understand. Unfortunately, all I can tell you is that I got it in Mellenville."

I'd rather not tell him the whole truth. Everyone has the right to secrets.

"I see," he said. "Big city dwellers and their secrets. I used to level up Reputation too. Then I got fed up."

"Why?"

He shrugged. "Just a shift in priorities. I got myself Kosma, and a pet like this takes up a lot of time. I couldn't run all those stupid errands anymore. And once Kosma grew up a bit, we started working. And why do you need Rep for?"

"I need a loan from the Reflex Bank," I replied in all honesty.

He nodded. "I see. Well, good luck."

"Is it really possible?" Liz asked us from behind. "To get a loan, I mean?"

"It is," Uncle Vanya said firmly. "I know a lot of guys who've done it. They said it worked out fine."

"That brings hope," I sighed. "Very much so."

"How much money do you need?"

"A lot."

"I see. All I know is that the more Reputation you have, the higher your chances are of getting a big loan. Heh! Now I understand why you came here to the Citadel."

I shrugged. "You'd better tell me why you don't wear your gorgeous gear every day."

They exchanged glances, smiling. "How can I say," the gnome began. "These kits aren't to be worn every day. You need to save them. Their Durability doesn't last forever, and repairs are costly."

"Also, if you flash your expensive kit every day, you're sure to attract some robbing bastard," Liz added.

"Isn't it non-transferrable?" I peered at their armor's stats. "What's the point?"

Uncle Vanya grinned. "You've no idea how

many lowlifes there are in Mirror World. They just don't care."

"For some PKs, smoking a high-level char in elite gear is something to be proud of," Liz added.

I remembered the Spider Grotto. A shiver ran down my spine. "You don't need to tell me. But what's a PK?"

"It's short for a Player Killer," Uncle Vanya said.

"You can tell them by their tags: they have a red skull next to their nickname," Liz explained.

"They love using zero-level players to level up Fury," the gnome added.

"Bastards," Liz mumbled. "My blood boils every time I remember."

"It's okay, Liz," her uncle said soothingly. "They already got their comeuppance. My guys still smoke them every time they see them."

Seeing my quizzical stare, he explained, "Liz had some very unpleasant experiences with PKs. She had it really bad then."

She clenched her fists. "If only they crossed my path now!"

The gnome shook his head. "It's been a while but she still can't let it go."

By then, we'd crossed the river bank and entered a small copse of trees. I could feel the path underfoot go slightly uphill. I glimpsed the first snow peaks above the far-off tree tops. Still distant, they gave you the impression of hanging over you.

Humidity was high here. Uncle Vanya's armor was covered in condensation. Did he use elemental protection? I was about to ask him when he beat me to it,

"We're in the mountains!"

Indeed, the path rose steeply, threading around some of the sharper and nastier-looking boulders.

A system message promptly popped up,

Warning! You're entering one of the most dangerous locations in the Lands of Light! Watch your back for aggressive creatures trespassing from No-Man's Lands!

I already knew about this, as did my friends.

"So how far is your mountain?" Liz asked, admiring the view.

"Less than a mile, according to my satnav," I said.

Uncle Vanya nodded. "It's all right. Come on, then. The place seems quiet today."

"Too quiet," Liz whispered, casting anxious looks around. "I can't see anyone. The Blue Hills I can understand. Golems are boring. But here? Players seem to like it here, normally. They can smoke all sorts of cool mobs."

Uncle Vanya scratched his beard. "I'm afraid you're right. It *is* weird. Never mind. If push comes to shove, we can always use a scroll to port outta here."

"A scroll?" I asked.

"Yes, a portal scroll. It costs a fortune. But it'll jump us directly back to Drammen."

"How much does it cost?"

"Two grand. But you can forget it. Zero levels can't buy them."

"Portal scrolls are only available for players level 70 and above," Liz added.

I rubbed the bridge of my nose. "How interesting. How do you use it?"

"Easy," Uncle Vanya said. "First you activate it. Then you choose a location from the list and press *Apply*."

"How big is the location list?"

"You're thinking in the right direction. To put it short, the entire Lands of Light are divided into four sectors: red, blue, yellow and green. We're currently in the green sector. I'm forwarding you the link to the scroll's description. And here's its page on the info portal. You read up on it later. It's quite a clever system. Can you see that my scroll is green?"

I nodded. "I see. You can only use it to travel around the green sector."

"Or to the capital," he added. "You can jump to Mellenville from any sector."

"If I understand you correctly, does that mean there are more expensive scrolls around? For more advanced players, maybe?"

He nodded. "You're right. You'll have to look them up yourself. I don't know much about them."

I grinned. "Thanks for the tip. I'll buy you a beer."

My bot kicked in, telling me that we'd arrived at our destination.

"Here," I nodded at a towering cliff ahead. "I'd love to know how I'm supposed to climb it, though. As far as I understand, the nest is right at the top."

"That's not a problem," Uncle Vanya tilted his

head upward, shielding his eyes with his wide hand. "There must be steps here somewhere."

Seeing me perplexed, he grinned. "Does that sound strange to you? They're nests, yes. Still, to get to each of them you need to use a staircase cut into the rock. They're actually very well-made. Whoever made them wanted them to last centuries."

"How many nests are there?" I asked.

He shrugged. "Never thought about it. At least a hundred. Each with its own staircase."

"Listen, you two," Liz shuffled her feet nervously, listening in to something, "I understand you can discuss this for hours but don't you think it's time we move it?" she cast a wary glance around and added softly, "I don't like it here today."

Uncle Vanya looked around. "I think she's right. Okay, man, you climb up and do whatever you're supposed to do, then come right back. Go ahead now, chop chop! We'll keep an eye on the area."

They didn't need to ask. I activated the bot to make sure I didn't lose my way and darted off.

I skirted the rock. Indeed, Uncle Vanya had been right. There were some steps going up the cliff, nice and stable, spiraling around it like a giant snake.

The location lived up to its name. The higher I climbed, the thicker the mist was. Sometimes I had to bend down and peer down to see where I was going.

Yet another step unexpectedly proved to be the last. I walked out onto a wide round platform. According to my bot, it was mob-free, but the sheer amount of bones, skulls, scraps of old clothing and rusted pieces of armor put one in a totally different mood.

This was indeed a nest. Made of rocks. What kind of bird was it that had built a nest the size of my old apartment? Judging by the number of skeletons, this monster was hardly herbivorous.

I cast another look around. So what was I supposed to find here? I opened the quest. What did we have there?

You must find the Nest of Rocks and inspect the remains of the last wearer of the Royal Charm. Then come back to Master Adkhur and tell him everything you've seen.

And where was I supposed to find him, this wearer of theirs? The nest was an absolute mess of old bones, bits of rags and chunks of steel. Having said that... What was it Adkhur had told me about the Der Swyor Clan's coat of arms? Could it have been the prompt I needed?

Gingerly I began trawling through the junk. Yuk! Those game designers had some sick imaginations! The charm's last wearer, where are you?

A message from Uncle Vanya popped up in my mental view,

Olgerd, come down quick! We've got problems! Come down now!

Just what I didn't need. What was I supposed to do? I might never get another chance to come back here!

Olgerd come down now!!!

Dammit! Whatever could have happened there? I swung my head around desperately, searching. Wait a sec! What was *that*?

OLGERD COME NOW!!!!

A few paces away from me, a skeleton slumped back as if resting after a hard day's work. Bits of rotting disintegrated clothing still clung to its bones. But the belt still seemed to be in one piece — or rather, the steel buckles that used to decorate it. The leather parts had long gone, either rotted away or consumed by small rodents.

It had been one of those buckles that had caught my eye. It didn't look rusty at all. It was shiny, if anything. Let's have a look...

I reached out my hand. Got it! It was engraved with a triangular shield supported by two Black Grisons, the ancestors of my little Prankster.

I turned to the skeleton. It was frozen in a sitting position, its head slightly skewed to the side, its hands resting in its lap palms up. What could it have been that killed you, buddy?

But what was that? A fluffy ball lay in the skeleton's lap. The man must have held it in his hands when he died. And later, when the flesh of his hands had rotted away, the ball must have dropped into his lap.

It was about the size of an orange, soft and strangely warm. It actually resembled a ball of gray wool. The moment I touched it, a new system message popped up,

Quest alert! Congratulations! You've just completed the first part of the quest: Journey to the Misty Mountains!

New objective: Return to Master Adkhur and tell him about what you've found.

New items received:

A Belt Buckle, 1

An unknown item, 1

I opened my inventory. That's right. Both the buckle and the fluff ball were already in my bag. I heaved a sigh of relief and darted for the stairs.

Chapter Eleven

I found both Uncle Vanya and Liz hiding behind one of the larger rocks. They huddled together, tense as if waiting for a bomb to drop. On seeing me, the gnome motioned me to duck, then pressed his finger to his lips.

Got it. I crouched and lay low, casting wary looks around. Whatever had alerted them so? The place seemed to be perfectly quiet.

Uncle Vanya peeked from behind their boulder, peering at the nearest thicket of trees about a hundred and fifty feet away. He then turned to me and waved an all-clear.

I darted toward them and ducked behind their boulder.

"What's up?" I asked, half-whispering.

"We're deep in it, Sir Olgerd, that's what's up," he grumbled.

"A Darkies' raid," Liz said.

"A what?"

"Apparently, the Rhynn Castle has fallen," Uncle Vanya pointed to the north. "The bulk of the Darkies must still be engaged there. But the first small groups have already infiltrated here."

"They've come looking for scalps," the girl added.

"Liz, you're something," I shook my head in amazement. "Your instincts are unbelievable. Respect!"

"She did good," the gnome gave her a wink. "The moment she noticed the Dark scout, we both ducked behind this rock. I don't think they noticed us."

"How many can there be?" I asked.

"Not the slightest idea. Could be six — but that's unlikely, — or it could be fifty. A raid is a serious business."

"They're probably all levels 200+, no?"

He shrugged. "Not necessarily. They use low-level players too. Those around here are small fry. All the top raid members must be busy now fighting for the castle while all the low-level vultures are on the prowl looking for easy prey."

"How long is it gonna last?"

"Not long," he said. "Soon all the warriors of Light will be here. Everyone can use a bit of Valor leveling."

"So what are we going to do?"

"Stay put and keep our eyes peeled. We can always port out of here if we want to. Still, it would be nice not to use the scroll. It costs two grand, you know. It would be such a shame to waste it."

I sighed. Talk about bad timing. Wretched Darkies and their raids!

We sat there for about quarter of an hour, keeping a low profile. The gnome tapped away in his chat — probably explaining the situation to his comrades.

Personally, I hadn't noticed anyone. But in cases like these it was probably a good idea to trust the more experienced higher-level players. Hadn't I said I was going to "cower behind some rock"? So there I was, doing exactly that.

Uncle Vanya was done with his chatting. He leaned wearily back against the cliff.

"That's it," he smiled to us. "Soon this place will be absolutely packed."

I glanced doubtfully at the forest where our enemies were supposed to be lurking. "It's been almost an hour but I haven't seen a single Darkie yet."

Liz chuckled. "Consider yourself lucky. And pray that *they* don't see you."

"Sir Olgerd doesn't believe us," the gnome winked at her. "You see," he turned to me, "in this game, every race has its own classes. Lots of them. You can look it all up in the Wiki later if you want. But some of those classes have access to the Invisibility skill."

"D'you mean-"

He nodded. "Exactly. They're about a hundred feet directly in front of us, just where the forest ends. At least two or three of them."

Liz grinned. "Four, to be precise."

Uncle Vanya nodded. "You see, Olgerd? Liz has been leveling up Perception. That's her class ability. No wonder she can see and feel much more than you and I can."

"Hush," she brought a finger to her lips. Her pointy ears twitched in a most funny way like two radars.

"They're coming," she whispered. "From the north. They're moving openly."

"Either our guys have won the castle back," Uncle Vanya said, "in which case they're going to mop up all the locations. Alternatively, the Darkies might have broken through. Which doesn't look good."

If I had any hopes for a quick end to our excursion, Liz had now dashed them. "Darkies," she whispered, pressing her back into the rock.

Very soon I got the chance to see for myself. I found a tiny crack in the rocks which allowed me to watch a small area about fifty feet away from us.

There were indeed ten of them: a few warriors, an archer and a wizard, judging by his robes. Actually, no. Not ten. Fourteen. Just as Liz had said. Four more players appeared out of thin air, like the monster in that good old movie, *Predator*.

One of them was a crossbowman, the remaining three also archers. They were saying something to a burly warrior in dark armor. I couldn't hear the words, but judging by their body language, they were reporting to him.

Invisibility, she'd said? What a useful skill. I really had to look into it.

I'd thought their levels would be higher but no, they were all below 180. Uncle Vanya had been right. They'd come here searching for easy prey.

"That's it," Uncle Vanya suddenly said in his normal voice. "Enough hiding. Come on, get out."

"Why?" I whispered. "They're gonna hear you!"

He beamed and stood up, reaching for the battle axe behind his back. "Let them hear! Why not?"

He walked out from behind the boulder and headed calmly toward the Darkies.

I watched him, unblinking. Whatever had come over him? One moment he'd been sitting there quiet as a mouse hushing everyone up, and now he was walking toward them? They'd noticed him, too! What were we supposed to do?

A tap on my shoulder distracted me from the scene. I turned round.

Liz behind me was grinning. "Come with me. It's gonna be hot here in a moment. Not a good place to be for the likes of us."

"Sorry, I don't understand. Can you explain?"

She opened her mouth when a loud popping sound assaulted our eardrums. I squeezed my eyes shut. When I reopened them, a portal already gaped open not fifty feet away, disgorging high-level players with weapons at the ready and happy smiles on their faces. There were at least thirty of them. I saw Varn and a few other Guiding Eyes. So!

Liz gave me a smile. "Do you see now?"

"Yeah... sort of... I think..." I managed, admiring the soldiers of Light.

"What Uncle Vanya did, he forwarded our

coordinates to Varn who threw a group together. They're about to make mincemeat out of the Darkies. Come on now, it's not a healthy place for you and me. If you get grazed by a spell, you'll spend the next few days healing. Same for me. I'm not tough enough to join this kind of fray. I'm still kinda small for this sort of battle. Let's go."

* * *

"You! I thought you'd forgotten all about the old man, dammit!"

The face of Master Adkhur lit up with a happy smile. I looked around, taking in the fresh air. This place just felt so good. Nothing had changed since my first visit: the same hut clinging to the base of a gigantic tree, the same walls overgrown with yellow moss, the tiny window...

Master Adkhur hadn't changed, either: a long gray beard full of twigs, pine needles and bits of dried leaves; the wide-brimmed straw hat and the green robe — he looked just like a big fat mushroom.

That day, Liz had taken me to the nearest portal station as promised. We'd bidden our goodbyes, then I hurried to the Woods of Lirtia hoping to solve yet another one of Pierrot's mysteries.

Unwilling to arrive empty-handed, I'd stopped at a shop to buy two flasks of wine and lots of various treats, including some for the spotted kitty.

It felt so good walking through a warm, sunlit

forest: a welcome change from the drizzly Drammen and the Citadel.

"I've brought you some gifts," I smiled to the old man. "I haven't forgotten anyone, I think," I gave a meaningful nod at the lynx who rewarded me with her signature yellow stare. "Does she like fish?"

"Does she ever! Are you going to lure her away too?" his voice rang with mocking anger. "You must have sold the Grison already, dammit!" his cunning eyes squinted at me.

"Of course I didn't. How could I? I'd feel so lonely without Prankster."

I meant it. The little black joker was the best medicine against any gloomy thoughts.

I activated the charm. Prankster appeared in the blink of an eye as usual. It took him a split second to take in his surroundings. His black shadow flashed through the air as, squeaking victoriously, he darted for the hut and climbed the roof.

"That's it," Master Adkhur sighed. "The roof is finished now."

"Pranky!" I said. "Behave yourself."

The Grison twitched his rounded ears as in, 'yeah, I heard you,' and continued inspecting the straw and moss of the roof.

"No way!" the old Ennan exclaimed. "Lita, did you see that? He listens to our Olgerd!"

The lynx lazily turned her head in the hut's direction, then continued staring at me.

Oh, look! Her name had appeared in a frame above her head. *Lita, a Spotted Lynx!* I froze, stupefied, as I peered at her stats.

Jesus Christ. Level four hundred freakin' fifty? Pierrot played it big and proper. Not every clan could afford a pet like this. You'd need to call up a raid to smoke one of these. And I didn't even know Master Adkhur's level, either. If the truth were known, I hadn't even thought about it.

Secondly, her combat stats. Loads of different kinds of protection from all sorts of magic as well as physical damage. Her attacking skills didn't leave much to be desired, either. Little as I knew about this stuff, I got the impression that this small spotted kitty was a veritable killing machine.

"Ah, so you've already met each other," Master Adkhur hid a smile in his gray beard. "Come in, don't stand outside. I can see you're going to treat the old man to all sorts of fancy goodies."

While I emptied my bag, Adkhur produced some clay cups and plates from a small cupboard. Finally, we sat down at the table. Adkhur uncorked the flask, sniffed first the cork and then the flask itself.

"Excellent," he said. "You seem to know your wines."

He filled the tall narrow glasses with the grenadine-color liquid.

"So, Sir Olgerd? Here's to the future of the Der Swyor Clan!"

"To its power!" I joined.

We clinked our glasses and turned our attention to the food.

"I can see the Grison has accepted you," Master Adkhur took another sip of his wine.

I shrugged. "Not a problem. He's a very good boy."

"A word of warning: don't miss the moment when he begins to grow. They can get quite uncontrollable."

"Thanks for the tip."

"You're welcome," he stuffed a large salad leaf into his mouth. "That's what we can do. When he grows up a little, come back here, both of you."

A new system message came as a surprise,

New Quest alert: Grow Big and Strong

Once your pet reaches level 1, show him to Master Adkhur.

Reward: a choice of two starting skills for your pet

Accept: Yes/No

I clicked *Yes*. But what was the point? My Grison was doomed to forever remain zero-level just as I was.

"Agreed," I said. "What would I do without you, Master?"

"Excellent," his voice rang with approval. "These days young people do things their own way. And once they screw everything up, they come running to the old and wise like guilty puppies."

The wine seemed to affect him just like it had the last time. I'd better close the quest before he falls asleep again. I opened my mouth to speak but he beat me to it,

"I completely forgot, dammit! Didn't you show

me one of Brolgerd's shticks last time? Have you managed to find out anything?"

My hands shook with excitement as I produced the feather from my bag. "Here, Master. I've checked the Nest of Rocks as you told me. I found a skeleton... er... actually, the place was chock full of bones. But that particular skeleton had this buckle on."

He frowned shortsightedly. "Oh. I see. It's one of those buckles our riders used to wear. Useful item. You keep it. You never know, you might need it."

Congratulations! You've received an item: a Buckle from a Combat Belt from the legendary Wings of Death armor set.

I stared at its stats, flabbergasted.

Name: A Wings of Death Belt Buckle
Effect: +150 to Strength
Effect: +100 to Protection
Effect: +250 to Endurance
Effect: +150 to Stamina
Restrictions: Only Ennan race
Level: 50
Warning! This item is non-transferrable!

So much for that, then. Just when I held my breath. If only I could auction something like this! Or at least try it out in the mines.

Once in my inventory, the buckle began to glow a soft ruby color. It must have been very, very valuable. What a shame. Then again, who said it was going to be easy? Judging by Pierrot's sick tricks, he wasn't finished with me yet.

Wait a sec... Why wasn't the quest closed? I'd completed it in full, hadn't I?

Unaware of my inner struggle, old Master Adkhur kept helping himself to more food. He didn't ignore the wine, either.

"Have you found anything else?" he asked complacently. "You said there were lots of skeletons there."

I slapped my forehead and reached into my bag. "There were! I also found this ball of wool. No idea why I took it. Waste not, want not, I suppose."

I lay the gray fluff ball onto the table. How strange. It was warm again – warmer than before.

I watched the old man's reaction. His eyes began opening wide – wide, wider, until they were literally the size of two saucers. Not normal. Master Adkhur exploded in a bout of coughing, probably having choked on the chunk of ham he'd been attacking for the last few minutes.

The lynx's head appeared behind the window, staring anxiously in at him. The creature shifted her gaze to the ball. Oh wow. I'd never seen her in this state. Her feline pupils expanded. Her fur stood on end. Her ears were pressed closely against her head. I could hear her hiss threateningly behind the window pane.

Holy mama mia, what was it I'd just brought them?

Master Adkhur overcame his bout of coughing in record time. "Quiet, you stupid puss!" he shouted at her. "Calm down!"

The lynx's large head disappeared behind the window. Paying no heed to me, Adkhur walked over to the table. His hand shaking, he reached for the wine flask and brought it to his mouth.

After several seconds, I heard a hearty burp followed by a sigh.

"You're something, Olgerd, you really are," he said in a weary voice. "You have any idea what you've brought to my place? Then again, why would you..."

He peered at the ball. I thought I saw some semblance of fear in his eyes. How strange. No, not fear: apprehension. In any case, he kept a safe distance from the thing.

"Is it warm or cold?" he suddenly asked.

"Warm," I said, surprised. "It's even warmer now than it was when I picked it up back at the Nest."

"Aha," he said. "How interesting. Mind picking it up again for me, please?"

I obeyed.

"Is it still warm?"

"It is. It's even warmer."

"I see. Take a seat. I'll be right back."

Mumbling something, he disappeared from the room. A couple of minutes later he returned, holding a large thick book.

"I see, I see," he kept mumbling. "How very interesting."

He clinked the book's bronze buckle open and began leafing through the thick pages. I didn't look. It's not in my character to poke into other people's business. Personally, I hate it when other people look over my shoulder at whatever I happen to be reading. That applied to everything: books and letters, newspapers and even computer screens.

Finally, the rustling of pages stopped. Adkhur chuckled. He cast an appraising look at the ball in my hands and turned back to the book, mouthing the words as he read. He scratched his beard. Then he scratched his head.

Our eyes met. His shone with excitement – with some cheerful, devil-may-care joy. Seeing my state, he finally spoke,

"Well, dammit! You've just managed to find yourself a cocoon of a Hugger the Night Hunter."

Chapter Twelve

Congratulations! You've just completed a quest: Journey to the Misty Mountains.
Reward: a cocoon of a Hugger the Night Hunter.

For a while, I just stared at the message. Then I opened the item's stats.

Name: a cocoon of a Hugger the Night Hunter
Restriction: Only Ennan race
Level: 0
To find out more about the item's characteristics, visit Master Adkhur.

The old man concealed a smirk in his gray beard. "You poor bastard! You don't even know what you've just got, do you?"

Yes, just another useless item to add to my collection, I very nearly said but choose a safe option and shook my head instead.

"There!" Adkhur raised a meaningful (and very dirty) finger. "Then again, who am I to speak? I've very nearly choked on my ham myself when I saw the message. I even had to look this thing up."

"So what exactly is *this thing*?" I asked politely.

"It's not *a thing*, dammit! It's a cocoon."

"So I've heard. But what's the catch?"

He grunted. "Good question! Let's start from the beginning, shall we? A long long time ago the great Master Eilar, my ancestor, rendered a service to the Raldians. And they, as you probably know, are very good at taming all sorts of animals. So Master Eilar who was in fact my great-great-great-grandfather's great-great-great-great... never mind. To cut a long story short, he rescued some high-standing Raldian or other. Their chief's daughter, if I'm not mistaken. It's irrelevant, anyway. So when Eilar — who was still very young at the time — arrived to present himself to the ruler of the Raldian Range — the proud parent of the said damsel — he, er, hem... what was I about... never mind. So he arrived to present himself to him, like, 'Here I am, the rescuer of your sole female issue', dammit. And the ruler asks him, 'What would you, as the rescuer of this mischievous disobedient child, desire to be rewarded with? Would you take gold or do you prefer power over your people? Or maybe something else? You may ask for whatever you want, we have it. As long as you're capable of lugging it back.' And this ancestor of ours found nothing better than to say, 'I have no need for either gold or power. What I'd like to ask you for,

Sire, is some ancient wisdom!' Olgerd, can you imagine? *Wisdom!* Just like that! It runs in our family, apparently. So this ruler of theirs had a good think and then waved his hairy paw and said, 'You can have wisdom if you want. But in order to acquire it, you'll have to live here with us for twenty years. In the mountains.' So he stayed."

"And what was this wisdom about?" I asked.

"Didn't I just tell you? To speak in animal tongues, to command and heal all sorts of beasts and to raise them. This is the skill that now runs in our family."

"All right. But what's this cocoon got to do with it?"

"Everything. It's a very rare beast. Or not the cocoon itself, of course, but rather what hatches from it."

When he said *hatches*, I couldn't help imagining a nasty hairy insect emerge from the cocoon. A spider, maybe? I seemed to be allergic to them just lately.

Oblivious to my inner struggle, the old man kept pontificating, "A Hugger is a rare and very capricious beast. Dangerous as hell, dammit. Probably one of the most dangerous in Mirror World. From what I heard, they might have existed already at the time of the Founders. Never mind. So this Eilar, my ancestor, learned to tame and command them. And once he returned home to his clan, he learned how to choose those of his warriors who would be adept at taming Night Hunters. The Der Swyor clan was the only one boasting Hugger riders."

"But other clan leaders weren't exactly happy with this new development, were they?" I added my two cents.

Master Adkhur heaved a sigh and paused, thoughtful. Apparently I'd touched on a sore subject.

"So what am I supposed to do with it?" I asked, trying to distract him from his sad musings.

"To do with what? Oh yes, the cocoon. Well... what you're about to hear here today is a great secret, my boy. Promise me you'll cherish it and keep it safe!"

"I will."

You'd expect a system message, wouldn't you? Still, this time it ignored me. How weird.

Master Adkhur believed me. "The whole secret of taming a Hugger lies in taking proper care of his cocoon."

I winced. "What kind of care? I hope you don't expect me to hatch it like a broody hen!"

"Not exactly, but..." he paused again, mulling over my words. "You might say so, I suppose."

Jesus. Just what I didn't need.

"You need to keep it on you at all times," he began to explain.

That wasn't a problem, was it? Where else did he expect me to keep it?

"Next. Can you feel that it's warm?"

"Yes," I nodded. "It keeps getting warmer all the time."

"That's because it feels your energy. The Hugger's trying to hatch already. But God forbid he emerges from his cocoon before his time. It's very, very bad."

My hands shook against my will. This thing sounded very much like a ticking bomb.

"Stop shaking!" Adkhur hissed. "Get a grip! He shouldn't sense your fear. That's better... Good boy."

"So what do you want me to do?" I mumbled.

"You need to share your vitality with him," the old Ennan said. "It's a bit like feeding him. That'll calm him down while allowing him to sense you and your superiority. Are you going to try it?"

I gulped. Unblinkingly I stared at Adkhur.

Master Adkhur offers you a skill trial: Soothe the Baby

Warning! Each instance of skill use requires 400 pt. Energy.

Accept: Yes/No

I clicked *Yes*. Did I have a choice?

The item's stats came into view,

Main characteristics:
Name: Cocoon of a Hugger
Type of item: relic
Level: 0
Satiety: 0/400
Would you like to feed it?
Energy required: 400 pt.
Accept: Yes/No

I pressed *Yes*. The item's Energy bar began to fill until it reached 100%. The cocoon seemed to have cooled down a bit. Yes, definitely. It was much cooler now.

Congratulations! Your cocoon is well fed!
Warning! Make sure you feed it regularly!
You might simplify the feeding process by synchronizing it.
Would you like to synchronize the feeding process: Yes/No.

What in the world's name was "a cocoon is well fed"? What had I got myself into again? I might need to consider their synchronization option. Four hundred Energy wasn't the measly ten points I kept investing into Prankster. The Grison was busy now frolicking about outside while I couldn't even feel him syphoning my energy. On the other hand, the cocoon wasn't going to frolic around, was it? It would lie nice and quiet in my inventory. It didn't look as if it was going to release a lot of energy. I might try and synchronize it, anyway. Then we'd see.

Synchronization successful!
Congratulations! From now on, the feeding process will proceed in automatic mode. Check your interface for changes.

I opened my profile to check on my freeloaders. Another smaller Energy bar had appeared directly under mine. The third one, if you counted the Caltean trap.

The cocoon's avatar looked like a gray ball of

wool. Some die-hard gamers might have been overjoyed to see the icon's ruby background, identical to that of Prankster's. I seemed to be collecting myself a menagerie of relic beasts.

The good news was that the cocoon didn't seem to expend any energy. In any case, the system wouldn't let it starve. I just hoped it was worth it.

"I can see you've worked it out," Adkhur said between gulps from his glass.

"So how long am I supposed to carry it around?" I asked, placing the cocoon gingerly back into my bag.

"That's something no one can tell you," he laughed. "It might happen tonight or next week, whenever."

"*Happen?*" I tensed. "What do you mean?"

"You're like a child, dammit. What's a cocoon? It's basically the same as an egg. Soft and fluffy, that's the only difference."

I stared at him. "Am I supposed to play the midwife?"

He guffawed. "I'm not doing it! I have no right to be present at the scene. It's between you and the Hugger. You must be the first person he sees and accepts."

I frowned. "Okay. But what's gonna happen next?"

"*What's gonna happen!*" he mimicked me. "Wait till he arrives, then we'll see. Now you need to relax. Have some wine. Take it easy. You're not the first one to take this route and I sure hope you won't be the last."

I sighed and sipped some wine. Oh no! How could I have forgotten!

"Master, you've never told me what to do with the charm," I produced the feather from my bag and offered it to him.

With a frown, the old man laid his broad hand over it. "Not today. Take it back. Its time will come, don't worry about it. Now you need to eat and drink. You'd better tell me about your family."

We spent another hour talking until he fell asleep in his chair as seemed to be his habit. Just as the last time, I covered him with the herb-scented comforter. I also left some vials of Stamina on the table for him.

As I walked out of his hut, I met the expectant gaze of Lita the lynx. I slapped myself on the forehead and reached into my bag. "How could I have forgotten! Here, take this, sweetheart. I just hope you like fish."

Before setting off, I'd bought an enormous fish from a local fisherman. A red-tailed carp: an Experienced-level resource, apparently, which made me hope kitty might like it.

Lita stretched and rose gracefully. What a beast! She came up to my waist. Standing next to a mob of her caliber felt a bit scary. Last time it hadn't bothered me much as I hadn't had a chance to see her stats. But today... I wasn't even sure calling her a mob was the right thing. She must have been an NPC in her own right. A Mirror Soul. Her gaze beamed with intelligence.

Unhurriedly she walked over to me and began sniffing the fish.

"It's fresh," I said. "Only just been caught. Sorry, I completely forgot. I should have remembered earlier."

In one imperceptible motion, the lynx opened her jaws and grabbed my offering. Judging by her loud purring, she must have liked it. Before returning to her place, she poked my ribs with her large head, allowing me to run my hand over her soft back.

You've received a blessing: Soft Paw.
Effect: +150 to Energy every 30 seconds.
Duration: 4 hrs.

Oh wow. How interesting. This was a buff to end all buffs! It meant that for the next four hours I wouldn't even feel the drop in Energy. How timely was that? I still had my quota in the mine to do.

While I was looking into the surprise gift, the lynx had disappeared — probably, to enjoy her treat.

It was time I was going, too. I activated Prankster's summoning charm and headed for the trees.

The next morning in the wizard's tower promised nothing out of the ordinary. Cold drizzle continued behind the window. The far-off leaden clouds glistened with lightning. I couldn't hear any thunder yet but knowing my luck, the thunderstorm was bound to arrive at the Citadel soon.

Still lying in bed, I checked on my little menagerie. Excellent. I had one leech less: the Caltean trap had finally recharged and switched off from its power supply, a.k.a. humble me. Let's have a look.

Name: A Magic Steel Net

Effect: Thanks to the ancient magic lore of the Founders, it can trap a wild animal and keep it inside for an indefinite time.

Restriction 1: Only for animals below level 310

Restriction 2: Only for animals inhabiting No-Man's Lands.

Player's level: 0 and above

Status: charged

Excellent. Let it sit in my bag. You never know, one day I might need it.

Now, the cocoon. It was still there, consuming next to nothing. Predictably so. That was good. I could live with that.

I'd already made a habit of letting Prankster out every morning for a bit of a run around. Let him have his fun. That way I wasn't so lonely, either. Just look at him frolicking around the room, stopping only to beg for another lump of cheese. He knew already, the rascal, that I always had treats in my pocket for him.

I cast another look at the cocoon. It had been lying quietly in my bag for almost two days now, occasionally drawing some energy from me. Dormant, basically. It was probably how it was supposed to be. Never mind.

Today I could go directly to the mines. I'd cleared the last pile of debris already the previous morning. Oh yes, and the door. I couldn't work out at first why it had kept coming up as an "object available for cleaning". But once I'd finally got around to it, it had become perfectly clear. It wasn't wood at all. The door was made of Dark Lythir which was some kind of local stone. I even received 10 tyllill crystals for handling it. Not bad at all.

All in all, these last two days of my cleaning gig had earned me 600 crystals. Just as Uncle Vanya had told me, I'd received 2,000 more from the wizard — plus another 300 on closing the cleaning quest that same morning.

I had smiled as I'd handed the onyx over to the wizard, watching his jaw drop. At first he couldn't believe I'd farmed so many crystals. He hurried to issue my reward, then scrambled upstairs to his lab. Not that he could have fooled me with his excited face and the compliments he showered upon me. This was, after all, an NPC playing his part, a piece of well-functioning software. His behavioral algorithm was the same regardless of the player. And still I'd enjoyed watching his stunned face: his eyes wide open, his cheeks crimson with excitement.

A poke to my chest cut short my reminiscing. I opened my eyes. It was Prankster back for another piece of cheese.

"You glutton! You'll explode if you're not careful!"

His black beady eyes and his moist twitching nose seemed to be saying, *Come on, master, quit the BS and give me some more and then we'll see who's going to explode.*

"All right, all right. Take it and beat it."

He grabbed his cheese and darted to the top of the wardrobe. That was his habit: he seemed to like sitting up high.

Right. What was I about? Oh yes, the crystals. In total, my little stay in the Citadel had garnered me almost nine and a half thousand Tyllill crystals. Converted to Mellenville Reputation points, that was almost a thousand. Not that I was going to convert them quite yet. I wanted to reach a thousand first: a nice rounded number. Especially seeing as crystals' icons were the same type as money which meant they took up no space at all in my bag.

This morning the system had already bestowed on me my daily 30 pt. Reputation. Which made it 1950 in total. If you added the crystals, it was almost 3,000.

That was much better than I'd initially planned. Another 2,000, and I could approach the bank. Naturally, the 2,000 wasn't the limit. The more I had, the bigger my chances would be of getting a larger loan. And as for a permanent contract... well, if you added up all the days off, my trial period expired today. I'd worked well; I'd never shirked my responsibilities. Let's see what Weigner would offer me now. Somehow I didn't think it was going to be a problem.

Voices outside distracted me from my musings.

What was that? Right under the wizard's windows, too. It had never happened before.

I scrambled out of bed and walked over to the window. So! A motley line of players was forming at the tower's front door. It must have only started a couple of minutes ago because earlier today, the square had been empty.

New players kept arriving. What was going on? Was it Varn's work? I wondered if selling him the quest information had been a bad deal after ll. Just look at that crowd! Quite a few Grinders among them, too.

It was a good job I was done clearing the debris. With such an attendance rate, you could forget farming any crystals. Liz had closed her quest on her very first day. She didn't much care for crystals: it was completing the quest itself that mattered to her. But I really liked clearing those piles of stuff. I kept catching myself thinking that I wouldn't mind if the Calteans attacked the fortress again. Who would have thought I'd become so fearless! Actually, I hadn't. But I was really pressed for time.

The noise grew. What had happened there? Ah, it was Tronus finally opening the front door. Immediately the crowd calmed down as he began dishing out quests. The process didn't take him long: apparently the program could handle several players simultaneously. You might think that the wizard was talking to you alone while in fact he was distributing quests to ten more people.

What happened next puzzled me a lot. The first

ten players had finished their negotiations with the wizard — but instead of heading directly into the back yard, they turned round and hurried away. The next ten did the same. And the Grinders! Why would *they* go? Cleaning junk was something they were meant to do!

The whole thing looked wrong. Varn had nothing to do with it. No, this was something else.

It took about twenty minutes for the courtyard to empty again. I walked downstairs just as Tronus was closing the front door.

"Ah, it's you," he waved a weary hand. "Good morning, my friend."

"It doesn't look very good to you, does it?"

He shook his head. "You've nailed it, my friend. You absolutely nailed it. They all seem to have gone mad! I had to make up a schedule to receive them all. All of a sudden, everybody's dying to help me! For several months they've been giving me a wide berth and now they can't get enough of my quests!"

I was just about to confess when he beat me to it,

"You're gonna laugh," he said. "You remember I told you about those complex quests I made specially to get rid of them?"

I nodded, frowning.

"And," he went on, "this is incredible! Each and every one of these visitors asked me for one of them. Some ragamuffin dwarf demanded several! I decided to teach him a lesson so I gave him the most difficult ones. And what do you think? — he jumped with joy! The world has gone mad!"

I just couldn't understand it. Why would they do that?

"Never mind, my friend," the wizard said wearily. "I still have work to do. But you, you deserve a day off. You did a great job! Tomorrow I'll have to think what else you could do."

"Excellent," I grinned. "Make sure you have a really complex quest for me!"

He burst out laughing. "You be careful," he shook his finger at me, "or I might just do that. If I ask you to bring me some mother-of-pearl spillikins or even some Crast Stones from No-Man's Lands, you'll know all about it!"

After some more small talk, Tronus headed for his lab while I walked back upstairs to my room. I had to contact both Varn and Uncle Vanya and ask them what the hell was going on. They were bound to know.

I was already reaching for my room's door when my inbox pinged.

Sender: Weigner

What was wrong with everybody today? I slumped into the chair and opened the mail.

Hi man, how's it going? Enjoying being a frontier guard? Make sure you don't let the enemy through!

I smiled. Typical Weigner.

Doryl's saying hello. We might actually see you soon.

What was that supposed to mean?

You might be surprised but your temporary contract has already been upgraded to a permanent one. Great job, congratulations! See the attached file with your new work agreement. Take a good look, there's no hurry. And if you're happy with it just sign it and send it back to me.

You've done an excellent job! We're very happy for you. In any case, in five days' time you're to report to our office at 10 a.m. sharp. Lady Mel's representative wishes to meet you. A very big cheese. So make sure you're here on the dot.

Right, I'm off. See ya,

Weigner

I reread the letter and slumped back in my armchair, pensive. A new contract, they say. Issued even before the old one had expired. Why such a hurry? Having said that, there was less than twenty-four hours left. It might be their normal practice. Or just Weigner taking care of my interests. In which case he deserved my gratitude. I had to think of a way of repaying him.

Only an hour ago I'd been wondering about the permanent contract, and here it was! Excellent. Things seemed to be working out, after all. Let's have a quick peek at it, then.

I opened the file and spent some time perusing it. It seemed okay. Actually, it differed very little from my temporary one. The main difference was in its duration. I studied it again. Nothing out of the ordinary. A generic text, generic conditions.

I signed it and sent it off to Weigner.

Almost immediately I received his reply,

Got it! You owe me!

A smilie in the end depicted a cartoon guy raising a beer mug.

I had a permanent job! Which had been one of the Reflex Bank's main conditions. All that was left to do was build up my Reputation well and truly high.

Easier said than done.

I covered my face with my hands. Never mind. I was going to make it. I still had time.

My inbox pinged again. Weigner must have forgotten something.

I opened it. No, not Weigner. Uncle Vanya.

Listen man, there'll be no caravan this morning. Sorry about that. You'll have to take one in the afternoon. Make sure you get to the square by 4 p.m. Nothing to worry about, just a bit overstretched. Little wonder, considering what's going on. We can't sell fares fast enough. By the evening, we'll only run one wagon on the Drammen route. The rest are all taken. BTW, Varn is actively hiring. If you know of any drivers that are not yet with us, feel free to recommend them. Varn will offer them good conditions.

Take care

Excuse me? What exactly was going on? I replied, asking him as much. His answer came in after a couple of minutes.

You're never gonna change, are you? What's wrong with using the info portal? Read the news. You're too much, you!

I hurried to open the news. Now, what did they have there?

The closed auction results. We're happy to announce the lucky winning bidders at our closed auction-

Beautifully crafted boxes, chests and cabinets! Fellow Mirror World dwellers! If you don't know what to spend your hard-earned gold on, don't hesitate to turn to the vendors in your area for...

Not that, either. Next.

A new potion specially for Marium gatherers!

No, not that.

Wait up. What was this? Judging by the pages and pages of comments, this was what I'd been looking for.

Important news for all Mirror World dwellers! Today at 8.07 a.m., the Dark clan known as the Daredevils discovered the ruins of a Medium-class

castle in the North East of No-Man's Lands.
Way to go, Daredevils!

And just next to it...

More important news for all Mirror World
dwellers! Today at 9.15 a.m., the Daredevils clan
handed over the property rights to the castle ruins to
the Dark clan known as the Caste!

I closed the info portal. No need to read any further. The developers had finally opened the colonization of No-Man's Lands.

Chapter Thirteen

Castle ruins! So that's how it was now, then? Let's see if there was anything about it on the gaming forum.

I opened it up. Not much, but still.

I perused it for a while, then closed the info portal.

So what did we have? According to Weigner and Doryl, initially most of the game's territory had been unexplored. The first players had only just begun to level up, creating low-level clans, etc. etc. Gradually their best scouts had begun to venture out into the big unknown searching for new instances, locations and incidentally also castle ruins.

The latter offered not only the ruins as such but also the rights to a certain area around them. All the players had had to do was restore the castles themselves — which came in different classes — then pay the monthly taxes on luxury real estate. In other words, finding the ruins was good news, but then you had to start thinking about how you were going to finance the restoration works, the taxes and on top of that also the castle's defense. It stood to reason that only the most powerful clans — and especially their alliances — were capable of pulling this off.

The Daredevils... the name rang a bell. That's right! I remembered seeing some of them during the battle of the Barren Plateau. If I remembered rightly, they were one of the stronger Dark clans. The reasons of their surrendering the castle to the Caste could be legion but most likely, the clan's analysts had simply decided the clan had bitten off more than it could chew.

And as for the upcoming colonization... even I, a total newb in these things, could sense that something was brewing in the air. Why not? The initial carve-up of the territories had been completed. Mines functioned like clockwork. Everybody was busy working. But at the same time, top players like Count and the like had to sit on the walls, repelling occasional Caltean "attacks". Boring. Declaring a war on the Darkies wasn't a very good idea, considering you had to first cross No-Man's Lands to get to them. Local monsters would make quick work of you. Raids like these exhausted you even before you could get to the enemy's walls.

The best way to add some excitement to the gameplay and improve the cash flow in the process, was to make No-Man's Lands free for all. To put it short, changes were coming. Existing peace agreements between clans would suffer. New alliances would spring up, suggesting a new war. The timing was excellent because, if Dmitry were to be believed, the government was about to buy the game out.

That explained Tronus' sudden popularity and the caravanners' overload — as well as the fact that I'd received my contract a day earlier. From now on, human resources would be precious. Prices for zero-level stones were bound to soar. Most likely, common Grinders like my old buddy Greg might initially receive a productivity bonus to encourage better and faster work until production grew. But emerald prices were unlikely to change. Then again, who knows? We'd have to see.

I'd love to know what Lady Mel's representative wanted with me. I just hoped he wasn't going to look too closely into my history. They had their hands full without me. He might just ask me to work in low-level mines for a while, farming marble with a couple of haulers. Alternatively, he might ask me to joint their No-Man's Lands raids. Too many scenarios to consider.

An urgent system message distracted me from my musings,

Warning! Your Energy levels have plummeted 400 pt.!

And again,

Warning! Your Energy levels have plummeted 400 pt.!

In less than a second, I'd lost 800 Energy! I didn't have a chance to check any of it. The system continued spamming me with messages,

Warning! Your Energy levels have plummeted 400 pt.!
Warning! Your Energy levels have plummeted 400 pt.!
Warning! Your Energy levels have plummeted 400 pt.!
Warning! Your Energy levels have plummeted...

My body jolted. My lights went out.

* * *

I struggled to come round. An instantaneous loss of all Energy is no joke. I had a splitting headache. I looked at the timer. I'd only been unconscious for forty minutes but that was well enough for me.

I felt awful. Colored circles swirled before my eyes. My sight blurred as if I was looking through murky glass. I couldn't hear a thing. My ears felt as if blocked with cotton wool.

With a shaking hand I pulled a vial from my belt, then activated a Stamina stone.

Phew. That felt a bit better. Come on, Energy, grow.

Yes! I felt human again. Both my eyesight and

hearing were back. I could finally move my arms and legs. What the hell had it been?

I opened the menu. Oh wow. It was plastered with new messages, all red!

Warning! Your Energy is dangerously low!
You're about to lose consciousness!

Ten minutes later, they'd sent me another one:

Warning! Your pet is hungry! It's exhausted! Its Energy is plummeting!
Your pet is tired!
Emergency activation of the summoning charm initiated!
You cannot summon your pet for the next three hours!

I glanced at the clock. Less than two and a half hours left until the summoning. I might need to have some cheese ready for Prankster by way of apology. Then again, it wasn't my fault, was it?

I checked the next message,

Warning! The Cocoon of a Hugger is gone!
A new Hugger the Night Hunter is born!

What the hell? What did they mean, *'born'*?

Congratulations on your new mount!

My bag's icon kept blinking. I opened it to a new system message,

Warning! Some of the items in your bag have undergone transformation!
New name: Feather of a Hugger
Effect: use of the medallion summons your mount.
Restriction: Only Ennan race
Level: 0

This was my feather! So that's what it was, then: a summoning charm. Its effect must have been unblocked the moment the Hugger had been born.

I cast a zoned-out stare at its stats,

Main characteristics:
Name: [...]
Type: Hugger the Night Hunter
Class: Relic
Level: 0 (1st stage of growth)
Satiety: 500/500
Experience: 0/50
Damage: 0 (activates when your mount attains Level 1)

Not much. I seemed to have a knack for collecting useless creatures. Let's have a look at its parameters, then.

Abilities: Hidden (available upon reaching 3rd stage of growth)

Experience received: 20% of the owner's combat experience without detracting from it.

Riding the Hugger increases your speed 20% (available upon reaching 3rd stage of growth). It also allows you to carry two additional heavy items.

Nourishment: The owner can feed his pet at any given time by sharing some of his Energy with it.

Warning! A pet's level may not exceed that of its owner!

This creature had some appetite! 500 pt. Energy just to feed it! And this was supposed to be the 1st stage of growth, whatever that might mean?

I opened the info portal. Let's have a look what they had on mounts. Aha... I see...

Apparently, mounts had three stages of growth. The first meant I'd have to nurse my new pet like a human baby. The longer my baby pet remained summoned, the better: that way he or she could learn by interacting with the world and getting to know his or her master. In other words, if you wanted a mount you had to spend all your waking time in the game.

The next two stages, although less problematic, also required certain attention. All in all, raising your mount was a boring and laborious process — but animal lovers didn't seem to mind. Some of them even complained in the comments that their mounts had grown too fast. This especially concerned all sorts of felines, extremely popular in Mirror World.

I wasn't really interested in all these games. Quite honestly, I hadn't counted on this scenario at all. All I had "gained" from it was yet another useless pet.

Where was I supposed to ride it without attracting attention? I could forget going into battle. This was just another Prankster, and a baby one at that.

Actually, what did it look like, this Hugger the terrible Night Hunter?

I activated the summoning charm. Admittedly I felt uneasy after what Master Adkhur had told me.

The air rippled, forming a weird-looking creature in my lap. Oh. How interesting.

So, kiddo, what were you supposed to look like? This Pierrot had some truly psychedelic imagination. I got the impression that he'd simply put together body parts from various animals, run the result through a simulator, then played with colors until he'd finally decided on ash-gray. *Eh voila!*

The pet's body looked like cheetah's with long but disproportionally muscular legs. His tail was long like that of a snow leopard. A rather wolfish head sat on a long neck — probably also taken from *canis lupus*. The ears were definitely wolfish, pricked and sensitive like two radars. But instead of a pair of jaws, the creature had an aquiline beak and a pair of eagle eyes. Trust me to get a mutant pet. Actually, he reminded me of something I couldn't quite put my finger on.

"So what am I supposed to do with you, kiddo?" I asked an utterly rhetorical question.

He craned his head to one side, watching me attentively. He must have arrived at some decision as he squeaked softly, placed his front legs onto my chest and rubbed his beak against my chin. How interesting.

Gingerly I laid my hand on his back and ran my fingers through his fur. Actually, no, not fur: more like a bird's down. He squeaked again and looked into my eyes.

"I think I know what you mean!" I opened his interface and habitually located the Satiety icon. It was at 150. Not enough. How I understood him. Very well, let's have a bite to eat. Where's this Nourishment tab...

Would you like to feed your pet?
Energy required: 350 pt.
Accept: Yes/No

I clicked *Yes*. The Hugger's Energy bar filled up. His eagle eyes closed — hopefully, with pleasure.

Congratulations! Your pet is well fed!
Warning! Make sure you feed your pet regularly!
You might simplify the feeding process by synchronizing it.
Would you like to synchronize the feeding process: Yes/No

I had my doubts, considering what the last synchronization had cost me. I just hoped I wouldn't have any more problems. Then again, five hundred points were five hundred points.

"You're an expensive brat, aren't you?"

Synchronization successful!

Congratulations! From now on, the feeding process will proceed in automatic mode. Check your interface for changes.

I opened my profile. Below the Energy bar, the cocoon's icon had been replaced with one of a Hugger. I really had to sort out this Energy issue. Then again, it was doubtful that I would summon him often.

"What are we supposed to do about your name?" once again I ran my hand along his back. "Wish I knew what you would look like when you grow up."

I looked at him from one side, then the other. For some reason, I remembered an old Russian cartoon about a wolf who adopted a calf. "What if we call you... eh... Boris? It wasn't in the cartoon but I like it. What would you say to that?"

He didn't seem to mind. With another squeak, he started to try to chew the table top.

"Oh well. Welcome to our kindergarten."

✷ ✷ ✷

I spent the next two days toiling in the mines. Not exactly crowded before the recent developments, now they stood completely empty. No one gave a damn about emeralds anymore. Just as I had supposed, every pair of hands had been employed to farm building resources. Back in the Citadel, I'd received constant propositions from clan head hunters offering work in marble and granite mines. Still, the moment they learned the name of my employer, they didn't look so eager. Leady Mel had some reputation in this part of the world. Which suited me just fine.

Seeing as the mines were empty anyway, I began letting my beasties out for a bit of a run-around. Prankster accepted his new friend as if he'd always known him. As I worked, they dashed around the tunnels, making a nice dent in my Energy. Actually, the Hugger didn't spend as much as I'd originally thought. Although no comparison to Prankster with his measly 50 pt., Boris wasn't such a burden on my body resources after all.

Last night he'd had the biggest drop in his Satiety levels yet. He only had 100 pt. left, but only because he'd learned to scale walls. I must have looked a sight. Imagine my little Boris gingerly stepping along the ceiling, his ears pressed down to his neck in a most funny way — and me following him below with my arms outstretched, ready to catch him if needed.

Having studied his little paws later, I realized that they had changed. His feet had developed sets of narrow ridges of hair, just like a gecko's. How interesting.

When I finally completed my quota and headed for the terminal to declare it, a system message popped up.

Congratulations! Your mount keeps growing!

Your Hugger the Night Hunter has just entered his 2nd stage of growth!

I turned round for a look — and froze, stupefied. Prankster hadn't changed. But instead of the cute and cuddly Hugger baby I was now looking at a fine animal the size of a young lion walking along the rocky path.

Prankster didn't seem to notice the change in his friend. But me, I admittedly chickened out.

My pets followed me, occasionally growling their indignation: like, *we haven't played enough and we don't want to go back into those tiny summoning charms.* When they finally caught up with me, Boris gave me a look of incomprehension, as if asking, 'What on earth is going on here?' Staring me in the eye, he gave me a gentle poke in the chest with his massive beak. I staggered. Reaching out a shaky hand, I touched his powerful neck.

"You're not so fluffy anymore, are you? You're covered in feathers. And you're too big now to sit on my lap. Sorry, kiddo. You seem to have grown awfully fast, don't you think?"

Boris didn't reply. He rolled his eyes in delight and shoved his massive flank under my hand, very nearly dropping me again.

"You're a right little elephant, aren't you?"

In the meantime, Prankster jumped onto his friend's wide back, studying his recent metamorphosis.

"Ah, you've noticed the changes in him too, haven't you?" I asked him. "I dread to even think what he's going to be like in the third stage of his growth..."

* * *

Today the wizard's place was busy again — just like it had been every day recently. Everyone was bending over backwards to get No-Man's Lands quests. Quite possibly, Lady Mel's representative too was going to offer me a trip down there in the company of some high-level scouts. Having said that, they only knew me as an Experienced Digger. They'd probably only send their Masters on raids like that. I'd have loved to meet one of them and ask them a few questions. What were their lives like? Did they enjoy working? What if I didn't have to worry about unveiling my status at all? Should I stop looking for "devious routes" maybe and throw myself at rich employers' feet?

If things didn't work out with the Reflex Bank, I might just do that. I'd simply have no choice.

Tronus the wizard was cheerful again today. He seemed to find this entire quest rush quite funny. "Ah, Olgerd! Any news?"

I nodded. For the last few days I did nothing but run a few errands. At the moment, he didn't have time to appreciate my "talents". He'd been writing an awful lot of letters just lately which I then had to run around and deliver. I'd seen Captain Gard a few times — and one letter had even been addressed to a fellow player. Basically, the moment I completed my daily

---

quota in the mines, I had to go back to the Citadel to do my messenger bit. The local quest system seemed to be identical to that in Mellenville: you had to find your way around the place before you could qualify for more complex quests. Not that I minded, really. Every completed quest gave me 50 pt. Reputation with Mellenville. I could actually use more of them. Three or four such quests a day would have suited me just fine.

"What did the Lieutenant say?" Tronus asked me.

"It went well," I replied. "He was very nice with me. He even wrote a quick note to give to you."

He beamed. "Excellent!"

I offered him a small envelope. A quest completion message popped up. Fifty more Reputation points into the piggy bank.

"Thank you very much, Olgerd. That's all for today," he turned around and strode off to his lab.

Very well. He was probably right. Time to catch a few winks. Having said that... I might do one last thing before going to bed.

A few days previous, Tronus had given me a guided tour of his tower — as a sign of goodwill and to show his trust in me. I'd quite enjoyed our thirty-minute excursion which resulted in me getting 100% access to virtually all of the tower's premises.

If you asked me whether I'd liked it... Oh well. A tower is a tower. Even though admittedly this was the first proper wizard's tower I'd ever been to, it was interesting but not particularly impressive.

Apart from one place, that is. The roof. Or to be

more precise, a large terrace on top. And that was where I was heading now. I wanted to enjoy a bit of a view before calling it a day.

And some view it was! The tiny figures of players scurried below. Tiled roofs were topped with colorful little flags and chimneys, both round and square. The far-off wall towers looked like toys. That was beautiful. I didn't even mind the constant drizzle so much. I was actually getting used to their weather.

Having said that... should I let my beasties out, maybe? Let them enjoy the view too.

Good idea. I activated the charms.

Prankster materialized instantly as usual. He froze, then began darting around the terrace like a black bolt of lightning, studying his new playground.

Boris appeared to my right. He always did. He must have been preprogrammed to do so, to allow a player to mount him straight away.

He arched his back and stretched, protracting his foot-long claws, then tilted his head in a most peculiar way and stared at me quizzically.

"Go ahead," I nodded. "Check the place out. I'm sure you'll like it here."

For a while, Boris watched Prankster dart around. He then stood up slowly and laid his front paws onto the stone parapet. His ears rotated like two radars as he moved his head slowly up and down. His powerful leonine body tensed, his shoulders bulging with muscles. Wasn't he beautiful!

I slapped his back. "So what do you think?"

He didn't react, unmoving, as he stared upwards. How strange. His tail began swishing violently.

"Everything all right? Whatcha lookin' at?"

The feathers on the nape of his neck bristled. A growl escaped his throat. I'd never seen him like this before.

Slowly I removed my hand. I knew of course that this was my mount — and a mount couldn't possibly attack his own master, it simply wasn't in their makeup. But on the other hand, simply looking at this monster gave you the shivers.

"What's up there?" I whispered. "What can you feel?"

The rest seemed to have happened in slow motion. Boris dipped slightly on his haunches. His body turned into a steely knot of cable-like muscles. The screech of his claws on the parapet made me cringe. His head sank into his shoulders. He pressed his ears to his neck, the feathers on which bristled ever higher.

I'd never expected what happened next. He jumped! With a curt growl, his ashen body disappeared into the darkness below.

"You stupid idiot! Where d'you think you're going?" I leaned over the parapet, trying to make out his falling outline in the dark. I couldn't see anything.

"Hold on, kiddo! I'm coming!" I yelled and swung round, about to dart for the door.

A system message made me freeze in place.

Congratulations! Your pet is fully grown!
Your mount has received a new skill!

The flapping of powerful wings distracted me from the message.

"I see," I whispered. "I think I know what skill it is."

Chapter Fourteen

When Boris finally landed on the terrace, I realized that my plans might need a bit of tweaking. My kiddo had a fine pair of wings now. He'd also doubled his previous size. We could fly now!

A thorough check of the forum made me wonder. Apparently, Boris was the first flying mount in Mirror World. Don't get me wrong: the game had plenty of dragons, eagles, manticores and wyverns in place. The problem was, they were all Relics – unknown entities which, according to lukewarm forum discussions, weren't to arrive for quite some time yet. It looked like I'd stolen a march on everyone else.

Apart from the purely physical changes in his appearance, Boris had received a new skill – Flying — as well as a new characteristic: Stamina which boasted a number 10. I thought I knew what it was: Stamina must have been responsible for energy regeneration.

His Satiety had also grown to 1,000 pt. His Level and Damage stats both sported miserable zeros. Until I received some combat XP, neither he nor Prankster could level up. This seemed like a Catch 22 situation. Still, Boris' ability to fly changed a lot of things.

I opened his skill tree. What a disappointment. All the slots were dark, sporting small locks next to them. The Flying alone was accompanied by a brief description according to which, using it increased Boris' Speed 30%. It was an expensive pleasure which would cost me 15 pt. Satiety per minute. In other words, Boris' own energy would last him an hour-plus — or considerably more, if you added the synchronization to the equation. Admittedly, it might backfire later but I already had a few ideas how to circumvent the problem. It was going to cost — but it was probably worth every penny.

The first item on my new list was to acquire the Mount Riding skill. Without it, I could forget flying or riding anywhere. But once I studied the relevant info portal page, I realized that this skill was little more than yet another money extortion machine.

So you've got a mount summoning charm? Then you'd have to pay.

Name of skill: Mount Riding
Restrictions: None
Description: Not one warrior in Mirror World would say no to a strong brother in arms and a fast mount.

A mount will never betray you. It can't flee a battle. It'll never shrink back under you. Ask Rotim the Riding Instructor to help you learn the art of mount riding. His experience will turn you into a perfect rider.

Yeah right, provided you paid five hundred gold.

According to the page, Rotim the Riding Instructor lived in a small village called Tikos in the vicinity of the Tallian Prairie. One needed to take a few transfers to get there. Never mind. I could use a walk. Once I finished my daily mining work and closed the wizard's quest, I might go there. I needed a change of scenery. I was fed up with this constant drizzle.

"Hey, dude! Move over, wouldja?"

An enormous level-90 Rock Rhoggh barged at me like a shell-proof tank. Oh wow. Their race looked awesome in their armor. They sent shivers down your spine.

I leapt aside before he had the chance to trample me.

"Hey, man. What do you think you're doing here?"

I turned round. A level-70 Dwand was hung with ribbons, bone charms and bits of colored string. He must have belonged to some magic class. Having said that, had the game had a jester class, this guy should consider swapping.

"Excuse me?" I asked.

The gray-skinned Dwand frowned. "I'm asking what the hell you're doing here! Being a zero level and all."

"I see," I said. "Why? Are they, as you called them, 'zero levels' banned from this location?"

He shook his head. "They're not. But what's the point, anyway?"

Mirror World was crawling with guys like this one. Always meddling into other people's affairs. They couldn't live without telling others what to do. Always ridiculing and criticizing others. Always celebrating others' failures. Always ready to add an inane comment before they even knew what the discussion was about, then being rude to those who disagreed with their short-sighted views. Such people tend to neglect their own mental skills — instead, they keep insisting on their ignorant philosophies.

It looked like I'd chanced upon one of them. Time to make myself scarce.

"Thanks for the tip... Drox. I must be off now. Enjoy the game," I swung round and, accompanied by their mumbled contempt and snide giggles, headed for the large courtyard.

The next moment I'd forgotten all about the Dwand. You had to see this.

A courtyard? — more like a football pitch covered with sand.

It was crowded with what looked like at least a hundred players. But that wasn't what caught my eye. All the mounts! They must have been brought here from every corner of Mirror World.

I didn't see any Grinders. Probably, a riding instructor wasn't their most popular NPC choice. Never mind. I couldn't turn back now.

I walked across the sandy yard, staring at this collection of beasts. They had all sorts. Reptiles, ruminants — but predominantly, felines.

Aha, I'd seen that one over there before! Not in real life, of course, only on a web page. What was its name again? Yes! A long-tailed Jandai! A battle mount. To get a summoning charm for one of those, you had to level up Reputation with the House of Stone Lotus. It looked scary — a bundle of muscle, albeit admittedly slightly smaller than Kosma.

I cast another look around, realizing that Uncle Vanya's draught animal could compete for the title of super giant of Mirror World.

The Jandai's owner was a level-260 wizard sporting the Steel Shirts' insignia. Both his armor and the gear of his mount glowed a reddish purple. I dreaded to even think how much money he'd poured into the game. Then again, who knows? He might have started off a Grinder like myself, farming stones or growing pigs at some rich bastard's farm. Hadn't Greg said that most top players had started off as Grinders?

My satnav — which I had prudently set up at the portal station — brought me to a large hangar. Its interior resembled a stable with countless stalls for all sorts of animals. Despite their sheer number, the passages between the stalls were sparkling clean.

Could they possibly have Grinders to do their dirty work for them here too? A place like this probably needed a whole army of us.

I jumped at the calm sound of a male voice behind me,

"Good day, Sir! Can I help you?"

I turned around. The speaker was about forty years old: suntanned, his hair cropped, his face cleanly shaven. His slanted eyes focused on me.

My satnav pinged happily, reporting my arrival at the target location.

I smiled to him. "How do you do, Master Rotim. I suppose you can help me, yes. I've actually been looking for you."

The riding instructor raised a surprised eyebrow. "Do they use mounts in mines these days?"

"Not yet. But you never know."

He sized me up and down. "You don't have a mount yet, I presume?"

"How can I?" I replied with a deadpan expression. 'Where would I get one from? A friend suggested I gave it a try. It might be nice to learn at least the basics."

Somehow I didn't think I was the first Grinder asking to join his class.

"It's five hundred gold per lesson," he watched my face closely for a reaction.

I shrugged. "It's by no means cheap, I agree. But it can't be helped, can it?"

He smiled. "Very well. We can start now if you think you're ready."

"I am."

He motioned me invitingly into the passage that ran the whole length of the stalls. "Please."

I walked down it. The passage ended with a large gate-like door.

What did we have here? A riding hall. About ninety by two hundred feet. It was covered in sand just like the yard outside.

There was no one inside. Excellent. The fewer eyes I attracted, the better. Sunlight beamed through the wide windows lining the arena.

"This is where we're going to practice now," Rotim said.

"Fine."

"Wait for me here. I'll bring you a mount," he disappeared behind the door.

A few minutes later he re-emerged, leading a small horse just a tad bigger than a pony. "Here's your mount!"

He spent the next hour teaching me various riding tricks. Admittedly it was a lot of fun but hardly worth half a grand. I wouldn't be surprised to see other players voice this concern at forums.

I wasn't even sure this lesson could teach me anything useful. This pony was a far cry from Boris. I found solace in the thought that all players must have started with this little hobby-horse.

An hour and a half later I paid Master Rotim, received the Riding skill and left the arena.

My next port of call: a saddler's shop. As the name suggested, I needed to buy a saddle. Why in a shop and not at auction? I was too paranoid to do that. A zero level buying that sort of stuff was bound to attract attention. It might have been much ado about nothing but still... better to be safe than sorry. For the same reason I preferred to avoid places like Doryl's little shop or the good old Digger's Store owned by my friend Rrhorgus.

That left me with NPC shops. They were bound to be more expensive but at least NPCs didn't talk. The least amount of fuss made, the better.

It didn't take me long to locate a saddler. I shouldn't have even used my satnav: his shop was a stone's throw from the riding school.

Predictably, his trade wasn't exactly booming. Why would anyone bother with overpriced NPC merchandise when the auction was brimming with much more interesting offers?

I got the impression he was happy to see me. I might have indeed been a rare customer. Alternatively, this could have been just part of his player-friendly program.

Yeah right. Friendly he may have been — but not enough to allow me to talk his prices down. Grudgingly I parted with another hundred and fifty gold. At least the saddle's stats pleased the eye with ten more points Stamina. That brought my Boris up to twenty.

The saddler attempted to sell me yet more gear — but once I told him my mount's level and explained why I wasn't going to buy anything to grow into, he seemed to lose interest.

As I left the shop, a familiar voice spoke behind my back,

"You're one funny guy, that's for sure."

I turned around. Drox, as large as life, was grinning at me.

"Oh," I said. "It's you. Why do you think I'm funny? Actually, don't bother. I don't really care."

I cast a suspicious look around and set off toward the portal station.

"If you say so," his sarcastic voice echoed behind.

I hurried to the station, checking my back as I ran, and dove directly into a portal. Good job I'd thought of pre-paying all the transfers. Every time I changed portals I peered around me for any sign of Drox's cunning fanged face. Luckily, it didn't look as if he'd followed me. Still, the fact that he'd remembered me was already bad enough. Never mind. It might be nothing. Just a nosy guy, as simple as that.

I only allowed myself to relax when I finally got to Drammen. The station was empty. I'd never thought I'd be so happy to come back to this wet, muddy little town.

It looked like I had everything ready for the trial flight. Last night I'd decided on what seemed the best place: the cliff that housed my emerald mine. Initially I'd been toying with the idea of using the wizard's tower as a landing pad, but then I'd reconsidered. Not now, anyway. Even though I planned to only practice at night, the risk of being discovered was too big there. You never knew how many eyes might be focused on Tronus' tower at any given moment. The Citadel was a very busy place, and the tower had recently regained some of its popularity.

And as for the emerald mine — in all the time I'd been working there, I hadn't come across a single fellow player. Which made perfect sense. Who in their right mind would volunteer to work in this miserable excuse for a location? Apart from me, that is.

I reached the Crooked Cliff without further ado. The place was predictably quiet, its silence disturbed only by the rustle of rain and the squelching of mud underfoot.

I passed the entrance to the mine and began climbing a narrow trail that led to the cliff top. I used to take it quite often in the past to enjoy an after-work view of Drammen by night. The flat cliff top wasn't exactly large but it just might suffice for my purposes.

Soon I stood there. The wind had abated; even the rain seemed to have calmed down. I wasn't really sure I could perform my first test flight under these conditions. Then again, last night's downpour hadn't been an obstacle for the Hugger.

I'd never been afraid of flying. I'd taken enough plane trips in the past. Still, Boris wasn't exactly an airplane, was he? So admittedly I was nervous. All day I'd been trying to put the thought of it out of my mind. And now it was all coming back with a vengeance.

I exhaled and activated the summoning charm.

Boris appeared to my right as usual. He was almost twice the size I'd seen him last, with a formidable beak and a large powerful neck. His wings were folded behind his back. He was awesome.

"So, kiddo? Are you ready?"

Reaching into my bag, I produced the saddle.

Immediately a new system message popped up, offering me to saddle up my pet. I pressed *Yes*.

And there he was, my very own Hugger the Night Hunter, ready for his maiden flight.

"What do we do now?"

Boris seemed to have understood me. He crouched down on all fours.

"Excellent!"

For a while I shifted from one foot to the other. Awkwardly I leaned my hands against his powerful back. "This is definitely not a pony, is it?"

Boris sat there nice and calm, as if oblivious to my tentative attempts. Strangely enough, it gave me a little more confidence.

I pushed myself up. Phew! There I was, up in the saddle. I seemed to have mounted it right. If the forums were to be believed, you couldn't fall out of the saddle in Mirror World. Which was good news, I suppose: at least my backside didn't risk familiarizing itself with the rocky surface of this clifftop. Already during my riding practice I'd noticed that sitting in the saddle was in fact quite comfortable.

And so it was now.

"Listen kiddo, before we go flying, mind if we just walk around here for a bit?"

Indeed, why start with the hardest bit? You should always master the basics first. His saddle was designed a bit like the seat of a sports motorbike: I was half-lying in it face down, rather than sitting. My elbows rested in special moldings. The saddle's pommel was shaped like handlebars. My stomach rested on a leather cushion but there were no

---

stirrups. Not that I needed them, either. Apparently, the game designers hadn't even bothered with them. How strange. When I'd bought it, the saddle had looked totally different.

Slowly Boris rose to his feet and walked toward the rock face. That seemed all right. I focused, sending him a mental command to change direction just as the instructor had taught me.

Boris obeyed. Excellent. It wasn't that much harder than controlling a pony, after all.

"Now let's try and climb that wall over there. You can move a bit faster if you want."

He obeyed instantly. In three leaps I found myself halfway up an almost vertical slope. Boris moved effortlessly, ignoring the rider's extra weight.

I could feel my digital heart flutter in my chest. I glanced down. Oh wow! The rocky cliff top below kept shrinking in the distance, its gray rocks looking like toys. Boris climbed the wall confidently, his powerful muscles rippling under his skin.

I didn't dare move but I was perfectly comfortable. I must have looked like a scared baby monkey desperately clinging to his mom's back.

The higher we climbed, the stronger the wind grew. Drizzle battered my face. Boris seemed to be indifferent to either: he just kept scaling the wall ignoring the elements.

We'd been at it for about ten minutes already, and Boris' Satiety was only 90 pt. down. Considering the climb, the weather and his impressive speed, the Energy drop was negligible. I felt fine. Fine? — I was thrilled! I had this amazing feeling of having just conquered half the world.

"All right, kiddo. Now climb all the way up to the top. We can fly from there."

As if sensing my excitement, Boris rushed up, raindrops pelting my face, the gray rock ledges flashing before my eyes.

He was on top of the cliff in a heartbeat. I looked around me. The view sent shivers down my spine. Occasional disjointed bolts of lightning ripped through the darkening skies. The leaden thunderclouds resembled giant mountains about to squash all living things underfoot. Somewhere far below at the foot of the cliff lay the forest. I knew it was safe but it looked gloomy and threatening from up here.

My fingers sank into the pommel. I leaned forward. "Are you ready, kiddo?"

He growled an affirmative, swinging his large head as if to say, *Come on, let's do this already.*

I heaved a sigh, activated the Flight skill and squeezed my eyes shut.

I could feel Boris leap forward. I opened my eyes. The sharp gray rocks below were approaching rapidly, growing in size. The hiss of the wind in my ears grew to a roar. Then his powerful Night Hunter's wings billowed open, parachute-like. In two powerful thrusts, he headed for the skies. Strangely enough, this gave me no unpleasant sensation. The game developers must have been too busy to have bothered with the authenticity of flying experience. But as far as I was concerned, the less authentic it was, the better.

Boris continued to gain altitude with fast, powerful thrusts, catapulting us into the gloomy skies. There was no stopping him, his enormous eagle wings ripping through the dark with ease. I couldn't see earth anymore: only the gray and black tatters of thunderclouds below. Now I knew what Boris reminded me of: a gryphon. It wasn't a hundred-percent match, but the idea was there.

We exited the darkness in a few powerful thrusts, flying above the thunderstorm. Here, it was quiet and rainless. A huge moon hung dead ahead. I'd almost forgotten what it looked like with all these constant thunderclouds constantly hovering over both Drammen and the Citadel. Later in the daytime you could probably see the sun here. A skyful of stars twinkled overhead. What a shame Boris couldn't climb higher: this was all he could do in the game. But even this was plenty. I had this feeling of being alone in the whole universe.

Somewhere below, the rain showered the dark sleepy streets of Drammen; the wind, damp and cold, whistled through the hated tunnels of my emerald mine. But here it was quiet, warm and dry. And then there was this moonlight, soft and gentle.

"Right, kiddo. No good getting all soppy about it. Let's go to the Citadel now."

Obediently he flapped his powerful wings, changing course. Now we were soaring toward my temporary abode.

Even better news was that he followed the satnav settings to a tee. This was very useful as I didn't need to double-check his course every five minutes.

"Do you think Prankster will like it?"

Boris squinted his eagle eye at me, as if saying, *you won't know if you don't try.*

I activated the charm. Prankster materialized on my shoulder. He momentarily froze as was his habit, taking in the sights, then clung to my back, swinging his head around in surprise. Soon he was over his initial shock, busy climbing over Boris' back. The Hugger greeted his old friend with a quick turn of his head and a hoarse croak.

"So you like it, don't you?"

It took us about fifteen minutes to get to the wizard's tower. The thunderstorm was stronger over the Citadel which made me hope that no one had noticed our landing. They must have mistaken Boris for yet another thundercloud in the sky.

I unsummoned both critters and stood on the terrace alone. My heart was heavy as I glanced at the dark expanse of the woods in No-Man's Lands.

"No idea what awaits me there, kiddo, but I'd better come prepared."

I didn't even notice the next week fly past. I spent mornings performing the wizard's quests, trying to complete them before midday to catch the caravan to Drammen. There, I toiled in the mines, then tried to get a few hours of sleep after dinner before going out at night for some flight practice.

We took care to stay unnoticed. We only landed in deserted places, mainly clifftops.

Gradually we built up range, making sure to stay within Boris' own Energy limits. By the end of the week, we'd completed our longest journey yet, crossing the entire breadth of the Lands of Light.

As a result, I already knew from experience that a flight to Mellenville took me forty-three minutes while the town on the shore of the Azure Ocean, the farthest in the Lands of Light, was all of two hours away.

Unfortunately, flying over the ocean was strictly forbidden. It felt as if Boris just hit an invisible wall. A system message would then pop up,

Warning! Mirror World's submarine locations are still undergoing testing. Please check back later for updates.

I could only guess at all the game's immense potential once they were opened.

We'd been practicing for a week now. On Sunday we had to go and visit Master Adkhur, for several reasons. Firstly, I couldn't wait to show him my Boris. Secondly, the old boy just might impart some secrets concerning him. Thirdly, I really needed a good buff — and at the moment I only knew of one creature capable of casting it on me for free. Well, almost free.

Chapter Fifteen

Sunday evening.

I'd spent the afternoon visiting Master Adkhur. Admittedly, Boris had been a blast. The old man studied him for well over an hour. He must have inspected every feather of his wings. He checked Boris' beak, massaged his legs and felt through his tail, then dove into his hut and emerged with an armful of ancient books. He pored over them for quite a while. Finally he reached into his pocket for a long piece of knotted string and began measuring Boris with it, comparing each result with the books and tut-tutting delightedly every time.

Boris had remained nice and quiet all along, sitting motionlessly and apparently lapping up all the attention.

Later over a cup of wine, he imparted to me that our Boris was apparently the gold standard of its species. "Our Boris"! I didn't mind him saying this —

not because an NPC couldn't rob me of the summoning charm but simply because it felt so good to see Boris being admired. Besides, to be brutally honest, by saying "our Boris" the old man had sort of accepted me. It didn't matter that he was only a cleverly designed in-game character. Even so, I wasn't alone anymore. Which meant a lot to me.

We'd had a nice day as usual. As I left, I offered his gorgeous feline another huge fish. It had cost me an arm and a leg but it had been worth it. This time the kitty generously issued me a five-hour buff of +250 to Energy every 30 seconds. Now we could fly around the world without stopping to refuel: the spell would have lasted both of us.

Before soaring into the skies, I humored Adkhur by circling the place a few times. I thought I saw tears in his saucer eyes.

I waved our goodbyes and told Boris to climb. In a few powerful wingbeats we rose over the clouds. Time to head for No-Man's Lands.

Admittedly, it felt scary. I kept telling myself this was only a game, even if it looked too much like real life.

I was heading for the North Mine where, if my satnav was to be believed, I could farm some of the Blue Ice necessary to create an Unworked Charm of Arakh. I only had the Map of the Der Swyor Clan's Trade Routes — or rather, the omnipresent Pierrot — to thank for this bit of intel.

In fact, it had been Boris growing himself a pair of wings that had prompted my decision to risk delving into the very heart of No-Man's Lands. Before that had happened, I'd had not a hope in hell of leveling my second profession. But now my mount's surprise development might just pay for itself.

According to the satnav, we were flying over the Citadel although I couldn't see a thing through the clouds. And once we'd crossed the invisible line marking the frontier of the Lands of Light, a system message popped up,

Warning! This location can be too dangerous for players of your level!
Please turn back.

Apparently, this wasn't the place for the likes of me. Never mind. They couldn't scare me with these kinds of warnings anymore. I was too used to putting my butt in the fire.

I won't lie to you. The message had made my heart miss a beat. But if you want to get anywhere in life, you shouldn't indulge your fears.

I ordered Boris to descend. He dove through the dark clouds and re-emerged directly above the woods. Strangely, it wasn't raining. The wind had abated too. Overall, the weather was much better here than it was in the Citadel.

Spreading his wings wide, Boris soared the sky above the primeval woods. The sheer thought of my being the first player to ever set foot here gave me goosebumps.

I peered hard, trying to make out the land below. Pointless. The dark woods weren't in a hurry to divulge their secrets to me.

After another twenty minutes, the forest had become sparser.

Warning! You're about to enter the Quartan Valley!
This location can be too dangerous for players of your level!
Please turn back

Ignoring the message, I checked the Der Swyor map. Everything was going as planned.

Gradually the night clouds parted, revealing a gargantuan Moon. Now I could see the land below much better. If you disregarded the fact that this was apparently one of the most dangerous locations in the whole of Mirror World, it actually looked quite pretty.

This moment of admiration, however, was immediately cut short by the arrival of a group of huge arachnid mobs. I hiccupped and ordered Boris to gain some altitude. Even though the creatures couldn't have possibly noticed me, let alone reached me, it was more prudent this way. I hadn't had the chance to read their stats but I had a funny feeling that this wasn't the right place to encounter low-level mobs. Talk about goosebumps: I wouldn't like to meet them in the woods after dark. Having said that, proper players who farmed monsters for hours on end, probably didn't even notice their appearance anymore. I must have been the only impressionable one.

In another quarter of an hour, we'd left the Quartan Valley and were flying over the Rocky Desert.

Here, it was considerably colder. And the worst was yet to come. Judging by the map, we were heading toward Mirror World's northern extremity.

I glanced at Boris' stats. His Satiety was nearing zero. Immediately the Synchronization kicked in, but — thanks to the kitty's buff — I didn't even feel the drop in my Energy. It definitely paid to do things properly!

The night before I'd bought myself a few Stamina stones just in case, so I was pretty sure my little flying pony wouldn't run low on gas. The buff would last another four hours, plus my stones: plenty for Boris to feed on. Especially because once we got back to the mine he'd have more than enough time to recuperate.

The Rocky Desert lived up to its name. From above, it looked like a moonlit sea of solidified lava. That's what it probably was. I glimpsed a few silhouettes flashing past amid the fire-polished rocks but they moved way too fast for me to see them properly. Their speed was mind-boggling. For the umpteenth time, I congratulated myself. Personally, I was safe here — but I couldn't say the same of those players about to conquer these lands on foot. Having said that, I kept forgetting that encountering local monsters was exactly what players like Count needed: to loot and level up. Wasn't it exactly what they joined the game for?

And talking about the cold, a couple of days previously I'd popped into Nilius' shop. The wizard had greeted me like an old friend. He wanted to know everything about the Anti-Humidity protection he'd sold me. My appraisal pleased him a lot. And once he'd learned of the purpose of my visit, he couldn't have been happier.

I have to admit that all this flying practice had very nearly made me forget the nature of the place I was heading for. Only when I'd overheard a tavern conversation between a newb and one of the old-timers did I realize the importance of it. So that day I'd been treated to Nilius' half-hour lecture on the importance of cold protection and left his shop perfectly equipped for the journey. The good news was, the Anti-Frost Elemental Protection cost considerably less than the drop-shaped Anti-Humidity. And before I left, Nilius had asked me to pop in once I was back to report on the protection's performance.

Finally, the Rocky Desert was over too. We approached a body of water that the map identified as the River Quiet. The night before, I'd imagined it might be a sleepy little stream. As if! The sight of this mighty body of water, as wide as the eye could see, took my breath away. When you reached its middle, you couldn't make out the ancient pine trees lining its banks anymore: they looked like a brown stubble covering gray cliff sides. The cliffs themselves, black and gloomy, loomed over the river's mirrored surface, threatening to squash any humble intruder.

This place was an angler's dream. I dreaded to even conceive all the kinds of fish you could catch here.

Just as I was thinking this, a jet of water rose a good hundred feet above the surface. Some beast that was! Judging by the size of its broad back, Kosma was a kitten compared to this little fishie. Oh no, any angler might be in for a very nasty surprise.

After I'd left the mammoth fish far behind, I noticed several outlines in the water that looked suspiciously shark-like. Oh. The local mobs would make quick work of Boris and myself. If these were river monsters, I dreaded to think what upcoming surprises the developers had in store for any submarine pioneer.

The satnav pinged, prompting us it was time to turn right. Obeying its directions, Boris banked a simple turn, changing course. That was it. All we had left to do now was cross the Ardean Range.

A few minutes later, the black mountains topped with white snow appeared on the horizon. I was getting cold. My nose and ears tingled with frost. Had it been happening in the real world, I might have already turned into an ice statue.

"I think we should climb a bit higher, kiddo. We don't need no unpleasant encounters."

In one powerful wingbeat we left the snowy peaks far below.

Suddenly I glimpsed a tiny light glowing on a mountain top. The sight made me jerk my head, so out of place it was. How interesting.

Obeying my command, Boris banked, diving toward the speck of light. Could any of the players had already gotten this far? I decided to get closer and investigate. Whoever it was, they were unlikely to notice me from below. All they might see was Boris' belly — and No-Man's Lands were crawling with all sorts of critters.

The light came from a bonfire. But whoever was sitting around it weren't players — even though they might have passed for such from a distance.

Boris soared above them like a silent shadow. We descended some more. I took in the surroundings. Aha! I could see a small rock ledge just above the fire.

Boris didn't need words. After one last wingbeat, he sank his talons into the black rock. No one could see or hear us from there.

"Great job," I whispered into his ear.

We were about the height of a three-story building. I could easily see the creatures sitting around the fire. There were five of them. Same size as myself, only burlier with slightly broader shoulders. What a strange race. Well-built midgets, they did have something in common with dwarves and gnomes. Thick beards. Large noses. Clad in furs and armed with long spears. Each had a short wide knife dangling from his belt.

Even in the fire's failing light, I could clearly see their dark skin which distinguished them from both gnomes and dwarves.

They sat there in silence, casting an occasional wary look around as they listened in to the night's sounds. No one had bothered to look up. Apparently, they didn't expect any danger to come from the sky. Which was good news, I suppose.

I'd love to know what they were doing up here. Who were they?

The answer to the first question I might never know. But as for the second one, the game promptly informed me,

A Caltean advance team

Well, well, well. Fancy seeing you here. So that's what you look like, then. How very interesting.

All five had rather high levels, especially the team leader: level 230. The others were only twenty levels below him. They looked like nothing special but you wouldn't like to bump into a group like this!

What had Marcus told me about them? They were NPCs, not mobs. Mirror Souls, hostile to the players of both Light and Dark. Now what might they be doing here? Wait a sec... Yes! Hadn't Marcus said that "hedgehogs" lived in the mountains?

Mechanically I cast a wary look around me. Being attacked by one of those spiky monsters was the last thing I needed. A few dozen of those had completely demolished the Citadel's West side in less than an hour. Still, admittedly I was curious. I'd love to see the Calteans trap these gargantuan beasts.

A powerful growl from below made me jump. Goosebumps erupted all over my spine. Talk about the devil.

Boris strained his muscular back. Strangely enough, this brought me out of my stupor.

"It's all right, kiddo," I said, stroking the nape of his neck. "We're too high. They can't get to us here."

Previously impassive, the Calteans jumped to their feet — admittedly without any fuss. This was a well-choreographed group. Each team member seemed to know what he was doing.

The repeated growl sounded even closer. The Calteans formed a semicircle bristling with spears. Their leader produced something out of his bag. Now only their tiny bonfire stood between their flimsy ranks and the monster-harboring darkness.

Somehow I doubted they'd make it, even despite their levels. Then again, I still seemed to be thinking in real-world categories. Everything was different in Mirror World. Earth's laws weren't applicable here.

Yet another growl rose to a roar. The darkness parted, disgorging a leaping beast. Oh wow. This was big. Either I was too scared or this hedgehog was twice as large as all the others. Level 300+, it was much darker than those that had ravaged the streets of the Citadel. His elongated muzzle was covered in old scars. This was an animal tempered in battle.

The Calteans seemed to have noticed it too. Their ranks stirred, anxious. They couldn't have expected a visitor of this caliber.

The ginormous Komodo dragon peered shortsightedly at his opponents. He didn't seem too impressed. He must have sensed their fear but wasn't in a hurry to attack. Slowly he turned his head from side to side which only seemed to unnerve the dark-skinned dwarves further.

Their leader snapped a few brief commands, making even me jump. The Calteans' attitude transformed. Their stance gained confidence. Who was is that said, *A commander's spirit is his soldiers' courage?* He was dead right there.

Finally the beast decided it was time to quit the staring game and get himself a bite to eat. His enormous bulk shifted. He advanced. Much to my surprise, instead of walking around the fire, the hedgehog headed directly for it.

The Calteans didn't seem to have expected this, either. A few more commands, and their semicircle widened. The five squat figures froze, awaiting the beast's attack.

His growl made me jump. I might never get used to the sound. Boris, however, was cool as a cucumber.

The beast was about to step into the fire when the leader took a big swing and hurled something right under the creature's feet.

Aha! This was the famous trap! The tiny rolled-up ball unraveled into a large net. The Calteans began shouting as if on cue, teasing the beast into taking just another step: one more step, then it would be over.

Unfortunately, the hedgehog had other ideas. He ignored the trap, clearing it in one long leap. I wouldn't be surprised if he was already familiar with these kinds of surprises.

The Calteans, however, didn't seem to like it. And seeing as their leader wasn't in a hurry to use another net, I realized he'd only had one.

In a few more snapped commands, the Calteans' ranks broke. Without awaiting the monster's next leap — which was bound to be his last — they charged at him themselves. Were they raving mad? This was like attacking an elephant with a feather!

The hedgehog took his time to strike back. It assumed a combat stance. Oh, yes. I'd seen it before. I knew what was going to happen.

His long spiky tail swished through the air like a giant sickle. Still, the Calteans weren't stupid. Some of them ducked while others leaped high, foiling his attempt to destroy all his enemies in one clean sweep.

Then it was their turn to assault the giant. He seemed to be taken aback by such brazenness. Using his tail to parry their blows, the hedgehog began to back off. A few more feet, then he'd trigger the steel net.

The Calteans doubled their effort. Then they made a mistake. Even I could see they'd underestimated their opponent. Seemingly awkward, the beast lunged forward, scooping a squat NPC up into his large clawed paw. The next moment his jaws ripped through the poor Caltean's chest, showering the rocks with blood. One down, four to go.

The Calteans screamed but didn't budge. I had to give their leader his due. Those were some well-trained fighters.

In the meantime, the tables had turned. Now the hedgehog was on the offensive, forcing the Calteans back, cornering them. They could still flee but I had a feeling that they wouldn't do that.

I was right. The Calteans charged.

Almost immediately their leader found himself alone. The bodies of his men lay listlessly like broken dolls. The hedgehog hadn't had it easy, either. His left eye socket oozed blood. A spear shaft protruded from his right side. Remarkably, the Calteans' leader was still unharmed. You couldn't really count the shallow scratch on his shoulder. But I could already see that the beast's wounds wouldn't prevent him from finishing the brave NPC off. Unless a miracle happened.

No idea what made me do it. It could be the sight of the warrior frozen in an en-guard position. The expression in his eyes. His spirit. His willingness to stand to the last. I don't know. It could have been my situation too, of course. Cowering in the safety of the cliff while smugly watching someone die... never mind. It wasn't the right moment for soul searching. I had to act fast.

I snapped a brief command. Noiselessly Boris dove. His wings flapped open directly above the monster's head. The Caltean's eyes were like two saucers. He'd been ready to die and there we were, a bearded guy astride a flying monster.

I gave him a wink. Which was a big mistake.

The hedgehog swung round, glaring its remaining eye in search of the new opponent. Then he froze. Admittedly it looked weird, as if the image lagged due to a slow internet connection.

It only lasted a few seconds but the Caltean leader jumped at his chance.

He somersaulted toward the trap, deactivated it, then threw it again right under the awakening mob's very feet. It all happened simultaneously: the creature stepped forward while the Caltean reactivated the trap.

The hedgehog disappeared in a bright flash of

light, leaving behind a huge glowing lump of flesh. I watched the Caltean move it into his bag. This was virtual reality for you: something the size of a whale fitting into a shabby backpack. Having said that, it had probably taken at least twenty slots in his inventory.

Boris and I prudently returned to the safety of our perch, curious about what he'd do next. The Caltean seemed to ignore me entirely but I knew he was watching me out of the corner of his eye.

First he moved his men's bodies away from the fire. He knelt on one knee before each of them, whispering something. Having finished, he turned round and headed for me.

I thought against descending. You never know what kind of thoughts were brewing in his boisterous head. It was probably safer to sit it out. He might have looked worse for wear but he was still an almost level-300 NPC.

"These aren't your lands, Lightie!" the Calteans' leader shouted. "They belong to us! The fact that you helped me is the only reason you're still alive!"

Hadn't I been right keeping a safe distance? But before it sank in, I received a very interesting system message,

Congratulations! You've completed a hidden quest: Helping Hand!
Reward: +100 to your Reputation with the Red Owls clan.
Warning! You need to watch out! Now the clan's enemies will double their efforts in pursuing you

wherever you go!

There you had it. I didn't know whether to laugh or cry. What kind of enemies did it mean? On the other hand, I was in the very heart of No-Man's Lands where every rock underfoot was supposed to be an enemy.

As I reread the message, I realized that the Caltean was still speaking to me.

"You, Lightie! You deaf or something?"

"Oh. No, I'm not. I'm very sorry. I'm just a little bit confused," I finished in a small voice.

"You gotta get outta here, Lightie. My kinsmen will be here in a minute. They might not like your company."

"I'm happy to oblige."

Effortlessly Boris took off the cliff, spreading his wings nice and wide. The Caltean's eyes gleamed with admiration. Good.

"Fare thee well!" I shouted. "Hope to never see you again!"

He crossed his arms and gave a curt nod. I cast a parting glance at the ground below. The Caltean's name glowed bright over his head.

Chapter Sixteen

The place which my satnav identified as the North Mine was located in one of the numerous crevices of the Ardean Range. Had it not been for my useful little app, we'd surely have flown past it. How many such discreet locations were there in No-Man's Lands? The game developers must have done their best to ensure that a pioneer's life was anything but boring.

Before landing, I thoroughly studied the area. It would be little fun becoming some mob's lunch with my objective already in sight.

The place seemed to be quiet. Down we go, then!

I jumped off Boris' back, sinking up to my knees in snow. Had it not been for my elemental protection, my boots would surely have lost a few points Durability. Here it was noticeably colder than above the clouds.

I had no problem finding the entrance to the mine. Or rather, whatever was left of it. The upper beam had been shattered. The caved-in entrance was blocked with huge jagged fragments of rock, leaving only a small crevice just the right size for someone like myself to squeeze through.

When the entrance was within arm's reach, the system sent me another message,

Congratulations! You've just discovered the North Mine! Be careful! The mine is so old it can collapse at any moment. The resource deposits are long gone. You won't find anything but piles of slag inside!
Would you like to unseal the cave?

Excuse me? What did they mean, I *won't find anything*? What kind of trick was this? Had Boris and I made this journey for nothing? We couldn't have. I needed to check.

I stepped back and entered *Blue Ice* into the search box. The search engine unhesitantly offered my current location, pointing directly at the collapsed entry. What a bunch of jokers!

Never mind. It wouldn't hurt me to "unseal" the mine, would it?

I pressed *Confirm.*

Immediately a new message sprang up,

Congratulations! You've just unsealed an ancient mine! No one farms resources here anymore. The resource deposits are exhausted. The resource itself is depleted.

*The Lord of the Underworld must have fel.
ignored and grown angry with the miners' greed,
shaking the rock and burying the decayed remains of
the Dwarven cohort which used to develop the mine.*

Only high-level Diggers are granted entry here!

*But hurry! The old God's curse is still active! The
rock walls can close in on you at any moment!*

Start countdown:

02:59:59...

02:59:58...

02:59:57...

They had the cheek to congratulate me? First,
there was no Blue Ice here. Second, I could expect to
be buried alive at any moment. Nice little excursion,
thank you very much.

"So what do you think, kiddo? Do you agree
with me? Or should we go down and investigate?"

Boris moved his shoulders which could be
understood either way. He looked calm, staring
curiously into the cave's dark mouth. For some
reason, his behavior gave me an added boost of
confidence. And having said that...

"Prankster? Come out, buddy, have a bit of a
run around! And while you're at it, check out the
premises, will ya? Three pairs of eyes are better than
two."

The Grison materialized in a flash and
disappeared down a snow bank. Immediately he re-
emerged, screaming indignantly, and sprang onto
Boris' back with one long leap.

"All right, all right! Stop it already! You'd better

keep an eye on where we're going."

With a heavy heart I stepped into the darkness. My Ennan eyes adjusted promptly. What can I say? I was quite pleased with my racial peculiarities. The darkness wasn't so dark anymore. It felt comfortable, cozy even. I wondered if this ability of mine — this positive feeling that underground tunnels seemed to give me — stretched to my real-life body too. In any case, I'd have to try it and then I'd know.

As I scrambled over the piled-up masses of rocks, sand and wood debris — apparently the remains of the support frame — I came across my first pile of rocks. Aha! This was getting interesting!

Name: Old Pile of Rubble
Type: Advanced
Name of casualty: Thorgryr
Expires in: 2 hours

Unhesitantly I produced my pick out of the bag and took a swing.

You've tried to clear an Old Pile of Rubble.
-3 to the item's durability.
Durability: 97/100

Oh wow. Some piles they had here!
Let's do it again.

You've tried to clear an Old Pile of Rubble.
-6 to the item's durability.
Durability: 91/100

In total, it took me twenty swings to clear it. Finally, a new system message popped up. My arms shook as I leant against my pick handle, peering excitedly at the words,

Congratulations! You've cleared an Old Pile of Rubble!
Reward: 1500 Tyllill crystals.
Reward: 50 Crast stones
Reward: Blue Ice (2 pc.)
Reward: a wooden box, carved (1 pc.)

That's what it was. The mine was indeed depleted, but it had rubble deposits instead. And these deposits were the most interesting bits here. Tyllill alone was great news. Fifteen hundred — and that was only the beginning. Crast stones... it did sound familiar... whatever these were... never mind. I'd have to sort it out later. The fact was that these stones had the same icon as both money and tyllill crystals. It was probably some trading resource. Once I crossed back from No-Man's Lands, I might look it up on the info portal which was unavailable here just as the auction and the messaging service were. Which meant that a player should have done his or her homework before venturing into the neutral zone. At least now I could understand the raids' demand for high-level Alchemists, for instance. Having a player like this in your group, you wouldn't have to worry about running low on elixirs while raiding the vast expanse of No-Man's Lands.

Unfortunately, the game engine hadn't been too

generous with Blue Ice. It must have been a very rare resource.

Now, the carved wooden box. Strangely enough, I already knew about these sorts of items. I'd first heard about them from Flint's group when they'd discussed hidden treasures. A few forums and open clan sites sometimes mentioned various "goodies" that were apparently stored in similar boxes. The more precious the carving, the bigger a player's chances were of a nice fat reward.

Oh by the way, one more thing. Experienced players warned newbs against opening the boxes straight away. On a long-distance raid, every bag slot is priceless. The box only took one slot but its contents could easily fill the entire bag. Some of the more curious players were known to have emptied their entire inventories just to accommodate the long-desired goodie. So the boxes would have to wait till I came back home. No, not home. I couldn't open them there. What was I supposed to do with all the loot, then? Never mind. I'd have to sort it out later, wouldn't I?

"So, guys? Not bad for a start, eh?"

My two pets stared at me eagerly. They seemed to be enjoying it too. Apparently, the emphatic link between us kept growing stronger every day.

We moved on.

We discovered the next Pile of Rubble very close to the entrance to the mine's main room. Its Durability was considerably lower which took me less time but was accordingly poorer paid. 700 tyllill crystals and 15 Crast stones, plus a Torn Pouch, whatever that was supposed to mean. I shoved it down my bag, too. I'd check it all later.

In total, I counted 32 Piles. I had just over two hours left. I should be able to make it. Plenty of time — I might even have an hour left.

"Listen guys, I'll work here for a bit and you can check this place out if you want."

Boris and Prankster seemed to be waiting for the offer. They darted toward the opposite wall, trying to outrace each other. I smiled watching them. Kids!

Never mind. Time to do some work.

My hand shook with excitement as I grabbed the pick and took a swing.

You've tried to clear an Old Pile of Rubble.
-3 to the item's durability.
Durability: 97/100

I kept swinging my pick like a crazed gold-digger. Every Pile I opened increased my hope of seeing my two girls even earlier.

Fifty-eight minutes before the mine's self-destruction, I had cleared everything there was to clear. I'd done two or three rounds of the cave, checking every nook and cranny twice.

So what had this Aladdin's cave given me? 48,000-plus tyllill crystals. 1200 Crast stones. 70 pieces of Blue Ice. 3 wrought chests, 12 steel boxes, nine carved ones and 10 holed pouches. I couldn't believe my luck.

My legs gave way under me. I collapsed onto a rock, feeling as if someone had removed a steel rod from my spine: the rod that had kept my back straight all this time despite all the problems that had showered us over those last few years. I knew it was too early to relax. I still had the bank to persuade. But the fact that I'd met each and every one of their requirements cheered me up. Had I really made it? Added to those I already had, the tyllill crystals I'd farmed today way exceeded the required Reputation quota. The Blue Ice would allow me to raise my profession level. And then there were these Crast stones. And the boxes which were a very nice big fat bonus in and by themselves. I just couldn't remember where I'd heard about those blasted stones... never mind. It would come to me later.

Prankster's excited squeak disrupted my musings. He was jumping around me, apparently trying to attract my attention to something or other. I raised a weary head. Boris froze by the far wall.

Had they discovered something else? I hadn't checked that particular direction very well. Also, there might have been something in this cave invisible to my human eyes. A hidden treasure, maybe. Still, there wasn't much I could do about it. I just didn't have the Piercing Vision ability which was mentioned so often by other forum users.

I struggled to my feet. "Prankster, that's all right! I'm coming! Let's have a look at whatever you two have found there."

Oh. How interesting. I was pretty sure that this one tunnel hadn't been there before.

It was small and neat, located in the shadows which was probably why I hadn't noticed it before.

Somehow I doubted that my both pets had suddenly developed an ability to see what's hidden. Most likely, my clearing the last pile had automatically granted me access to this tunnel. It sure sounded like it. Game developers love creating chain reactions like this one. They make you do something which in turn would allow you access to something else...

Right, should we go and investigate?

My heart missed a beat as I stepped in. The tunnel was indeed small. It was dark and dry. It was also short, ending less than twenty paces away. I was about to exit its far end when another system message popped up,

Warning! You're trying to enter the second part of the North Mine! Watch out! This is the habitat of the Diadem Serpent!

Not recommended for players below level 200!

So that's how it was, then? This wasn't a mine even — this was a mini instance. Not that it changed anything for me, really.

"Come on, guys! There's nothing for us to catch here. Let's go back. We still have to get home. The cave's mob is way out of our league."

Was it my imagination or did I indeed see disappointment in their eyes? Or could it simply be the reflection of my own? Why not? I wouldn't lie to you: whoever smoked this Diadem Serpent might receive a nice hefty bonus. If I could only take a peek at this creature!

My pets perked up, sensing my indecision.

"Are you serious? It'll make mincemeat out of you — or me, as the case may be. You might get out of it relatively lightly. In any case, how are you going to fight it?"

Wait a sec. And what if... The thought made my ears itch. No way. Too risky. How much time did we have? Forty minutes. It only took a few seconds to vacate the cave. These weren't the deep emerald mines. In other words, it wouldn't hurt to take a look.

Inhale. Exhale. I stepped forward and took a cautious peek around the corner.

So what did we have here?

The game developers hadn't bothered to splurge on detail for this one-off instance. This cave was a carbon copy of the one I'd just been to. It was much cleaner, though: not a single Pile of Rubble in sight. By the same token, their proverbial Diadem Serpent wasn't around, either. Having said that...

Holy mama mia! They might have saved on adding detail to the cave but they sure hadn't skimped on the creature's size.

It was the color of gray stone, with a triangular head. No wonder I hadn't noticed it earlier. And your level, buddy? 260. Not that terribly high, either. Plenty for me, though. Being the location's boss, the monster was bound to possess some very interesting abilities.

I glanced at the other two. Both had grown quiet. Their fur stood on end. The Grison resembled a coiled spring.

Tauntingly, the giant snake coiled its enormous body around a shiny box. I dreaded to even think what the game developers might have filled it with. I gulped and shrank back behind the corner. The other two stared at me inquiringly.

"So, my little desperados? Think we can take him on? I have an idea — but Prankster might not like it, I'm afraid."

I had indeed come up with a plan. Admittedly iffy, but in this particular case it just might have worked 100%. In any case, we could stop (read: flee) at any moment.

For the first time in the game I regretted not having a combat account. Killing a mob like this — and in a No-Man's Lands instance, of all places — could have reaped me a handsome reward.

But even someone like me had a solution available for this scenario — as the Calteans' leader had demonstrated some two hours previously.

The trap.

This was the "flight or pocketfuls of loot" situation. I had to try it. It would also give me a chance to see Prankster in action.

Time left: thirty-five minutes. That should do it, provided I didn't get carried away.

I took another peek from around the corner. The cave hadn't changed. But the moment I stepped into it, the setting would change dramatically. Just one step — that should be enough. Prankster would do the rest.

"Are you ready, boy? I don't need to ask, do I? Off you go, then. Make sure you don't go too far."

Inhale. Exhale. Let's do it!

I stepped forward, ignoring the barrage of

system messages. I didn't need to read them to know I was an idiot.

On my command, Prankster darted forward like a black bolt of greased lighting.

The serpent's body shuddered. His head the size of a truck's cab rose a good fifteen feet in the air. His forked tongue quivered anxiously as the Diadem Serpent awoke from its slumber.

By then, Prankster had already reached the center of the cave and had frozen bolt upright. He resembled a prairie dog — one that was black and lethal.

I hoped the snake would fall for it. My pets' levels were the same as mine: zero all around. Which meant that the mob was bound to *aggro* us, as gamers say.

Yes! It worked! The serpent's unblinking eye focused on the bold little animal. The coils of his body shifted.

"Prankster, now!"

He flowed sideways like a blob of black mercury, then zigzagged straight for me.

The snake hissed, enraged by our skullduggery. He thrust forward, shifting his entire giant bulk. He was very fast. Very. But not for Prankster. My little brute was almost on me, getting closer with every leap.

The sight of the infuriated monster thrusting his body toward me must have thrown me into a daze. A dig in my chest — rather powerful considering Prankster's humble size — brought me out of my stupor.

Would you like to activate the trap: Yes/No

Yes! I hurled it forward, watching the steel net unfold in the air, parachute-like. Unlike the hedgehog before him, the serpent must have never encountered this kind of thing before. He barged directly into the trap, his body disappearing with a flash.

"Yes! We've done it!"

Both my pets tilted their heads with interest, watching their master dance a celebratory jig.

Oh wow. I'd never thought that victory could be so intoxicating. What an incredible, unforgettable feeling. This was the first time in my life I'd actually experienced it. I'd had my fair share of triumphs and achievements, sure. But this! Outsmarting a dreadful monster! I was beginning to understand all those players capable of defeating mobs like this one, then enjoying the blissful moment of sifting through the loot. Talking about which...

I hurried toward the huge, glowing ball of flesh.

What would you like to do?
1. Activate the trap again
2. Move the trap into your inventory.

The second option, of course.

Success! The trapped animal has been moved into your bag.

Excellent. Now the trophies.
I dashed for the chest. It was big, wasn't it?

Name: a Precious Wrought-Iron Chest
Type of item: Relic
What would you like to do?
1. Open the Chest
2. Move the Chest into your inventory

I gulped and pressed Move. Immediately my bag became ten slots poorer. Oh! It was heavy now, wasn't it?

Still, I felt as pleased as Punch. A few more trips like this one, and I might become Mirror World's best fan.

A quick search of the cave for any hidden treasures produced no results. Never mind.

The ground shuddered underfoot. The ceiling showered me with dust, sand and small rocks. I glanced at the timer. I still had twenty minutes left on it.

"Come on, guys! Time to get going before we get whacked by something heavy."

As we ran, more shocks followed. It must have been the "ancient curse" waking up; the forgotten god remembering about this place.

We hurtled out of the cave and dove into the snow. Day was breaking. Excellent. The first morning sunrays tentatively peeked through the thunderclouds. The fresh frosty air burned my lungs.

Phew. We were back in one piece.

I chose not to wait till the mine collapsed. I mounted Boris and told him to take off. In one powerful leap and a single wingbeat, my mount took to the skies.

Chapter Seventeen

Drammen met us with a furious gale and a downpour. It looked like the rainy season had started. Bad news for the Guiding Eyes. This kind of forced downtime was the last thing Varn's caravanners needed. Especially considering the latest developments.

I could only congratulate myself on the fact that I didn't have to depend on them now. Mechanically I slapped Boris' powerful neck.

The idea to go to Drammen first to investigate my trophies had come to me during the flight. Initially I'd been too tempted by the thought of going upstairs to my room in order to open all those chests and boxes. I just couldn't wait. Still, while we were leaving No-Man's Lands, the impatient mentality of a treasure hunter had given way to the cold calculations of a bookkeeper. Who rearranged the glasses on his nose and began his reckonings.

The problem was actually in the following. If I opened all the boxes now, very soon all the available slots in my inventory would be taken. Which in a way was a good thing. Question: what was I supposed to do once my bag was full? The game mechanics didn't allow you to just unload all your stuff and keep it on the table or under the bed. You could unload it, of course, but only for a few minutes. Then, if you failed to collect your possessions promptly, they would disappear into thin air.

I remembered reading some forum discussions on the problem. At the time, I'd just skimmed through it as I'd had no idea I might ever find myself in a similar situation. I'd even wondered why other forum members were so unhappy about it. But apparently, it wasn't that easy.

When you first start out in Mirror World, you don't have the storage dilemma. Wish all problems were like that, you might say. But as days turn into weeks and weeks into months, all sorts of junk somehow find their way into your inventory. Bits of old maps, rock fragments, quest plants, empty vials... I know it sounds weird, but you need all this stuff in the game. Here, every scrap of paper or length of old rope has its use. All these odds and ends have been meticulously and sometimes painstakingly collected. An inventory purge is the last thing a Mirror World player wants to do.

Property owners solve this problem with relative ease. Every house, apartment or castle has all kinds of storage areas: from cellars and pantries to strong vaults and warehouses. Why relative? Simple:

having storage areas means there'll be people willing to burgle them. This is another chain reaction created by the game developers: in order to secure their storages, their owners would have to pay to install various magic traps or hired guards. Everything in the game is interrelated.

The safest places where a player could keep his hard-earned artifacts were safe deposit boxes. Banks offered their users a 100% safety guarantee. Renting them was quite costly but it was worth it. Imagine I began to open all these chests and boxes filled to the brim with all sorts of paraphernalia. What was I supposed to do with it all? Auction it? But I risked blowing my cover by auctioning the stuff that a regular Grinder couldn't lay his hands on. Because unfortunately, the game admins had denied Grinders the Anonymity option.

If the truth were known, I had no idea why they'd done so. They must have had their reasons. But what if one of these boxes dropped something that binds on pickup? I could forget selling it, that's for sure.

All in all, even though I still had enough available slots in my inventory, it was probably time for me to start thinking about finding some safe storage. Which brought me back to the bank.

That settled it, then. All the chests and boxes would have to wait until I got myself some vault space. It wouldn't be nice to blow it all simply out of greed and impatience. I wasn't a teenage newb. Better just to forget about the loot's existence for the time being.

The nearest Reflex Bank branch was in Drammen. It was nothing compared to its main office. The Drammen branch only offered a few staple services. Vault rental was one of them. I didn't know the rates yet; I just hoped that the game developers would abstain from ripping off their players.

The wind had abated but not the rain. It was bucketing down.

After a confident dive, Boris landed onto a narrow cliff ledge. We could have arrived directly in the city, no one would have even noticed in this kind of weather. Still, my prudence had served me well in the past. Better safe than sorry.

I gave the bedraggled Boris a hearty hug. "Time to get some rest, kiddo. You've done a great job. No idea what I would have done without you."

I activated the summoning charm. Apparently, even zero-level pets could be useful. I dreaded to think what might happen once they started leveling up.

The rain grew ever stronger. This was exactly the kind of weather I'd encountered on my first visit to Drammen. Mud and more mud. Actually, at the moment I was lucky: the rocky trail down to the mine was quite clear.

The mine was almost in sight, behind this one last bend.

I took a step toward it. Or rather, I tried to. Something powerful jostled my chest and sent me flying backwards. It knocked the wind out of me. My vision darkened with sharp pain.

"What in the devil's name-"

System messages began flashing before my eyes,

You've been attacked by another player: Lance.
A Fire Arrow has bored through your chest!
Damage received: #%@&*.
You've received a Burn to your chest.
Effect: -150 pt. Life every 40 sec

Through the haze of pain, I realized that had it not been for my Grinder's account, I'd already have been dead and sent to my resurrection point at the Altar. As it was, I'd received a rather useless debuff and a nasty injury.

My jacket dropped to the ground, losing 15 pt. Durability. I quickly picked it up and shoved it into my bag. As my college teacher used to say, "poverty learns you a few tricks".

"Lance, did you hear that? He called you a devil, the bastard!"

I turned my head to the sound. The voice was high-pitched and sneering.

The speaker's appearance matched his voice. He was small and lean, with green skin and pointy ears. A Forest Dwand, apparently. His level... oh wow. Level 240.

I racked my brains, trying to work out what such high-level players might want with me. Had Shantarsky, this psycho, finally got to me?

"Mind your tongue, Glitch, before I give you a dose of lightning."

This must have been Lance. I still couldn't see

him no matter how hard I tried.

"Be my guest," the Dwand parried.

"Do shut up, you two!"

Oh, there were three of them there. I couldn't see the third one, either. But judging by the fact that both Lance and Glitch promptly shut up, he must have been the alpha dog here.

His voice resounded somewhere very close to me. "Cheeky, take him and get him to the camp!"

They were *four*, then? Wait a sec... What camp was he talking about?

A warrior, wrapped in a dark cloak, walked out of the torrential rain. Race: Human. Level: 210.

"Move it!" he barked.

"I'm very sorry but could you please be so kind as to explain what's going on..." I mumbled, forcing my feet into a trot.

Without saying a word, the warrior strode behind me, giving me an occasional shove in the back. I was tormented by doubts. Somehow I didn't think these were Shantarsky's people. He didn't have to hire top-level players to trap the humble me.

Then all my doubts were gone.

The clearing before the emerald mine, deserted only yesterday, was now packed with players. There were at least a hundred raid members. Portals flashed open as more people kept coming. Strangely as it sounds, I was glad to see this. They couldn't have all arrived just to arrest me.

Admittedly they had come prepared. Their wagons were even sturdier than Uncle Vanya's, placed strategically in a circle in the middle of the opening like some kind of a siege vehicle. I could make out the outlines of archers and crossbowmen through their narrow window slits. The wagons were packed, but not *packed* packed. They had all sorts: dwarves and gnomes, Dwandes and humans, I even glimpsed a few Horruds and Rhogghs. At least 80% of them were levels 200+. I hadn't noticed a single person below level 100. Warriors in purple armor were especially eye-catching. I also saw some wizards and snipers. Swordsmen and lancers kept a select distance from the rest. The others were enjoying an eyeful — covert or otherwise — of the elite warriors' gear. The latter behaved as if they owned the place. They didn't look around, they just stood there talking in low voices, casting occasional impatient glances at the portals. No one had bothered to check me out, though.

What the hell was going on here?

We approached the center of the camp. Cheeky put me in front of a giant Horrud and froze, apparently awaiting orders. The monstrous creature simply had to be their commander. Next to his bulk, my friend Greg would have looked like a starving artist.

The Horrud's armor gleamed scarlet red. Level 280. If I wasn't mistaken, the legendary Romulus from the Steel Shirts was only five or six levels above him.

"You didn't gag him, did you?" the Horrud asked calmly. Or should I say, roared calmly.

A new system message popped up,

Warning! You've been gagged! You cannot

contact other players for the duration of: 2 hrs.

"It's all right, Armat. I've done it," an Alven wizard in magic-class armor stepped forward from behind the Horrud's back.

With a curt nod, the Horrud turned back to Cheeky. "Tell Critter he really blew it this time. This Digger must have already messaged half his friends about us."

"I don't think so," Cheeky replied calmly. "He didn't know what hit him. Lance really did his best. He still can't get over it."

Ignoring his explanations, the Horrud turned to the Alven wizard. "Jed, I want you to leave some extra guards in the camp."

The wizard nodded, then zoned out, apparently forwarding the order to the raid chat. I had no doubts that this was a Dark raid. The players' clan logos spoke for themselves. These were the Independents, one of the four clans that had fought at the Barren Plateau. I could see a few other clan members too, but still the Independents seemed to be in control. What would one of the game's most powerful clans want with the tiny one-horse Drammen?

Then again, trying to second-guess it wasn't worth my time. I had very little idea of Mirror World's political layout. I had nothing to do with it. I was just a little guy farming mines, earning Rep points and hoping for a bank loan. They might have been in the middle of a major clan war for all I knew. One thing I was sure of: I had to keep a low profile while these big guys played their war games.

"Jed, get your men to keep an eye on this Grinder at all times," the Horrud roared, then turned to me. "All you need to do is keep your head down. You've already ruined our surprise attack as it is. We'll let you go once it's over. Or maybe even before that. Don't worry, no one's gonna hurt you. Nod your head if you understand."

I nodded enthusiastically. We seemed to be thinking along the same lines.

Having finished talking, the Horrud seemed to have lost all interest in me. He turned away and walked toward the opening portals. What a beast. Somehow I didn't think this was a schoolboy playing. The player must have been quite old — and used to ordering others around. Just look at all the players fussing around him. In real life, he was probably a very influential person. Somehow I doubted I was lucky enough to have stumbled over the Independent Clan's leader but you never know. In any case, I could always look him up later.

A light nudge in my back motioned me toward a wagon.

My guard was a whopping level 260. I didn't know whether it was supposed to make me feel sad or proud. Level 10 would have been plenty for me.

The guard's moniker was Mammon, a Dwand. Some magic class, judging by his gear. Affiliation: the Wasters clan. Interesting name. He looked as sour as a lemon. He wasn't looking forward to the prospective of sitting the entire raid out in the camp guarding some worthless newb. He must have invested a lot of money into all sorts of buffs and elixirs. Other raiders shook their heads or smirked as they walked past.

No wonder. They couldn't wait to lay their hands on Drammen and its loot.

Another Dwand stopped a few paces away from us, grinning from ear to ear. He looked very pleased with himself. "Mammon, dude! Make sure you keep an eye on this wonder warrior! We don't want him escape!"

My guard snorted.

"No good snorting, man. He might be a Lighties' spy. You never know, he might grow a pair of wings and report on us to his bosses! Heh!"

He had no idea how close to the truth he was.

"Listen, Bob," my guard said. "Do me a favor. Go somewhere and die a hero's death. Think you can do that?"

As if! His buddy was only warming up. "No, but really, Mammon. It's not for nothing Jed entrusted him to *you*! Heh heh! If he gives you the slip, that's gonna be fun! Is there anything you can do without messing it up? I'm surprised they still take you on raids."

"Shut your mouth," Mammon hissed.

If Bob had heard him, he didn't show it. "Actually, no. I think I know why they do it. Everybody does. It's your sister, isn't it? Had it not been for Clo, no one would have touched you with a barge pole. Guarding newbs is the only thing you seem to be capable of."

"Right, I've had enough!" Mammon put his dukes up and planted his feet wide.

Bob grinned. "And what do you think you can

do?"

As if in confirmation, a pale green haze enveloped his body.

This must have been some kind of magic shield. Bob's voice rang with confidence which didn't promise anything good to my reluctant guard. Still, Mammon couldn't stop. Had it not been for a barked rebuke from a passing Alven warrior, an Independent clan member, I'd have become witness to a magic duel.

"Watch out," Mammon murmured, stepping back. "I've blacklisted you."

Bob burst out laughing. "I'm really scared! You can shove your black list where the sun don't shine! You can't frighten a hedgehog with a hairy backside!"

He waved a mocking goodbye and walked away, whistling an upbeat tune.

What I liked about this whole situation was that I had a school student for a guard. These kids were neither particularly observant nor responsible. I might indeed be able to give him the slip. He knew nothing of my bag of tricks.

Predictably the Darkies began leaving their camp — some on their own two feet, others riding their mounts. In about ten minutes, a hundred-plus top-level warriors were going to invade Drammen. No idea what they needed it for. They might be doing some quest. Or just for the kicks. The fact remained, they weren't going to encounter much resistance.

By now, there were only ten raiders left in the camp. Portals kept flashing open, disgorging even more players in a hurry to get to the war. None of them lingered in the camp, desperate to catch up with the main raid — worried about missing all the fun. Interestingly, these late players were mainly of the low-level type.

After another twenty minutes, the portal traffic stopped too. I estimated about three hundred Dark players looting Drammen while I was sitting here. Three hundred! Warriors of Light had their work cut out for them. I just hoped they'd be prudent enough not to assault the enemy in small numbers as new players kept trickling in. Oh, no. This called for a completely different tactic. We were dealing with a top clan, after all.

"Mammon?"

A raspy voice behind my back made me jump.

"Yeah?"

"I've been thinking."

The raspy-voiced speaker walked out in front of me. A Human. Nickname: Raven, level 140. He had a longbow by his side. The quiver behind his back was packed with arrows.

"What is it?" my guard sounded disinterested.

Raven gave me a sly look. Our eyes met. Then he said something I'd been dreading hearing all along.

"Have you checked his bag? The guys said our scouts apprehended him as he was leaving the mine."

"Well, I don't know," the guard hesitated.

"Look at him, look at him!" Raven was almost jumping with joy, pointing at me. "Did you see his shifty eyes when I mentioned his bag?"

I had to keep my cool. I took a few inconspicuous breaths. I had to get a grip.

"It's an emerald mine, isn't it? If he was exiting it, it means he's got a whole bagful of them."

"You think?" Mammon asked, doubtful.

"Sure! A hundred percent!"

"Someone told me Armat had promised him immunity. Said no one was gonna touch him."

Raven waved his suggestion away. "Please. Armat has already forgotten all about him. He has more important things on his plate. In any case, we aren't going to touch him, are we?"

"Meaning?"

"Meaning he's gonna give us the emeralds himself. He knows better than to get hurt because of something that's not even his. Am I right, my good man?"

I gave a non-committal shrug.

"Oh! Mammon, look at him! There might actually be something better than emeralds in his bag. Look, he's all shaking!"

My guard attempted to talk himself out of it. "I really don't know. Robbing a Grinder... it doesn't feel right."

"Cool it, man. This is a game. Anybody can rob anyone. You'd better ask yourself what we are doing here. Why such disrespect toward us, of all people?"

Mammon scratched his head. "But how can you do it?"

Sensing his friend giving in, Raven rubbed his hands and turned to me. "You'll see now," he said with a dirty smile.

Chapter Eighteen

"You sure it's a good idea?"

I might have underestimated my guard, after all.

"Mammon, give it a rest," Raven hissed.

"It's easy for you to say. He's not your responsibility. If Jed finds out, it's my neck on the line," Mammon repeated, firmer this time.

"Aha!" Raven rubbed his hands. "I knew it! You wanna rob him yourself and take all the loot!"

"Are you nuts?" Mammon looked embarrassed. His cartoon nature prevented him from turning crimson.

"Well, what do you want me to think? Look at it my way. I'm offering you to rob a Lightie. And you're trying to get rid of me, saying Jed this and Armat that. They've already forgotten all about this stupid Digger! Don't you understand why he's still here? Aha! I can see you do!"

"But Armat promised him..."

"Oh, do give it a break!" Raven switched to an angry whisper.

He was too cautious to shout at him. But he was trying to apply pressure to the guy. I wondered if Mammon would have been as unyielding had he known what I had in my bag. Or would he be the first to rob a helpless Grinder?

"Leave Armat alone!" the archer kept fuming. "Who is he? Is he your commander? The leader of your clan? He has no right to boss us around! We're not his soldiers! This isn't an army! I didn't sign for this!"

"This is an alliance," Mammon offered.

But Raven had already got on his high horse. Angry with the top brass, he'd finally found an audience to pour out all the negativity he'd accumulated. If the truth were known, I could understand him. Clan members weren't a regular army. They'd paid to play the game and wanted to get their money's worth. And here they were, stuck in camp while all the others were busy looting Drammen.

Raven grinned. "And? Why should it be us remembering about it? They didn't think about leaving *us* without loot!"

"Hold on! You're dead wrong there! Once the raid is completed, everyone's gonna get his share."

Raven snarled. "Yeah right. You really are simple, aren't you? Okay, let's presume we'll get something out of it. But how about Valor? Have you even thought about it?"

"You might be right," Mammon mumbled.

"Just imagine how much loot and Valor we could have gotten! After a high-level attack like this!"

"Probably," Mammon didn't sound too sure.

"I view this guy's stones as a small compensation for the damages. Robbing a Lightie is a sacred right. Especially because the stones don't even belong to him. They're the property of whoever owns the mine. And that's the Steel Shirts, if I'm not mistaken."

He turned to me. "Am I right?"

I gave a reluctant nod.

"You see? He doesn't mind!"

My guard shrugged.

Oh, Mammon... I thought better of you. Then again, why should he care? I was a stranger, wasn't I?

"Actually," Raven squinted at me, "He's not so simple, either. His Profession level is good. His gear is quality. I bet it's got runes installed. You see his cloak?"

Mammon shook his head.

Raven grinned. "Neither do I. What does that mean?"

"That he's got elemental protection installed on all his clothes."

"Exactly! Good boy!"

Raven crouched next to me, studying my gear. I didn't like his expression at all.

"You know what, Mammon? The more I look at him the curiouser I am. I'd love to know what he's got stashed in his bag."

Mammon walked closer. "So how are you gonna

do it?"

"Haven't you ever robbed Grinders in raids before?"

Mammon and I cringed simultaneously. "Nah," he said.

"Injuries!" Raven raised a meaningful finger.

"Excuse me? Are you going to-"

"But of course. Their gear has no Defense installed. You cast an injury on him, then strap him up and share out his stuff."

Mammon opened his eyes wide. "You nuts?!"

"It's tricky, sure," Raven mockingly agreed. "His stuff's Durability will suffer. But if even some of them have runes installed, they'll still be auctionable."

"I'm not talking about that! Are you suggesting we mug him?"

"Not *mug him*, stupid. Just *act in self-defense*," Raven grinned. "This is enemy territory. I can understand leaving our Dark Grinders alone, but you can't expect me to ignore a Lightie! Do you think their raiders spare our Grinders? Well, don't. Right, enough whining! Let's do it!"

His last arguments must have worked. Mammon's expression changed. Doubt had left it, replaced by a threatening squint. He must have imagined poor Dark Grinders being attacked by the army of Light. Shame I couldn't ask him how I fitted into the picture. But even if I hadn't been gagged, somehow I didn't think these kids would have listened to me.

Raven turned to me, his face a mask of mock sympathy. "Listen, dude. Neither I nor my partner here wish to hurt you. Why would we want to? We can't even level Fury on you: all we'll get is a miserable +1 if anything. But you're gonna suffer. Not only will you lose your gear, you'll end up paying a lot of money to a healer. With our levels, you'll get injuries for 24 hours at least. You know that, don't you? You have a Burn already: thirty hours plus the level of the injury. It's gonna cost you, I tell you."

I sighed. He was damn right.

"I can see you're a smart dude. You know how these things work. You were in the wrong place at the wrong time, that's all. It can't be helped. Sure it's a game but we're at war: this is martial law, as simple as that. No hard feelings, eh? You would have done the same yourself. We're offering you a chance to cut your losses."

Oh, yes. He was generosity itself. Damn those Grinder account options! At least combat classes could die if necessary.

Admittedly Raven was a crafty bastard. If ever he had to report to Armat, he'd have an ironclad alibi saying that the "Grinder" had removed his gear willingly. Then again, I somehow doubted it would come to that. Raven had been right: Armat must have long forgotten all about me.

Oh well, I'd have to play for time, wouldn't I? I had a few surprises for them up my sleeve, provided I got the timing right.

And now it seemed to be just perfect.

"Whassup, guys? Why are you stalling?"

A Rock Horrud stopped a dozen paces away from us. Level 170: a walking ten-foot destroyer. He sported the logo of the Independents: the alliance's leading clan. Apparently the highest level around, he must have been running the coop in Armat's absence.

"Hi Morph!" Raven stood up to his full height. "We're just having a chat with this Digger here. You have a problem with that?"

"Chatting?" the Horrud growled. "Jed cast a gag on him. You, Mammon, are supposed to guard him. And you," he turned to Raven, "were supposed to be with the wagons ten minutes ago. I suggest you leave him alone."

Raven chuckled, turning to Mammon. "You see? What did I say? Too many chiefs and not enough Indians!"

Mammon didn't reply. He stood there silent, closely watching the potential developments.

"Raven, quit being fresh. I can see the guys were right about you."

I'd only known Raven for the last five minutes but even I could see this wasn't the way to speak to him. Not if you doubted your chances against him. Morph didn't seem to have a problem with that. I could see a few other players appear behind his back, walking toward us. All sported the Independents' logo. Morph must have already posted about the upcoming show in the chat.

"Morph, you sure you haven't hurt your head dropping from the piss can?" Raven's smile promised nothing good. "You watch your filthy mouth, dude. You think if you suck up to Jed you're the boss here?"

The timing was perfect. The moment Morph went for Raven, I'd... but no. The Horrud apparently wasn't that tough, after all. He just stood there grinning.

"So much for you, Raven. All you can do is make trouble. And that's on a raid, right under the Lighties' nose. Well done, dude. Once the raid is over, our clan's blacklisting you."

Raven forced a chuckle. "Be my guest!"

A level-120 Alven archer stopped next to Morph. "Is he stoned again?" the archer smirked knowingly.

Morph gave a curt nod.

"You idiot!" the archer snapped at Raven. "You wanna be blacklisted by all of the Glasshouse? The Loafers clan leader will kick you out, and rightly so! I'm surprised he enrolled you at all! You're a real pain in the butt!"

"There he comes," Raven shrieked, "another brownnoser! Phil, dude, how does it taste like?"

The archer didn't boast Morph's self-control. As if in slow motion, I watched a mask of fury distort his handsome Alven face. His right hand darted for an arrow behind his back.

Raven reacted fast: the level gap was in his favor. He dropped to the ground, rolling over and loosing off three arrows in a machine gun-like succession. All three smashed against a translucent pale green cocoon that had enveloped the figures of Morph and Phil. It must have been the work of a Dwand wizard who'd stopped a few paces away from them.

"Now you're toast!" Morph growled and went for the bully while Morph's arrows pierced the ground where Raven had just stood.

"Mammon, help me!" Raven shouted.

"You keep out of it," Phil stopped Mammon. "I don't think Clo's gonna like her little brother side up with junkies stoned out of their heads."

"Mammon, I'm your clanmate!" Raven insisted. He'd already received two arrow wounds: one to his leg, the other to his shoulder.

I didn't wait for him to make up his mind. This was a perfect moment for me to escape. The gaming gods wouldn't send me a better one.

Step by tentative step, I moved toward a trail to my right: the one I'd taken not fifteen minutes previously.

I glanced back. It looked like Mammon had sided up with his clanmate, after all. Not the smartest of decisions but apparently chivalrous. I was pretty sure other raid members would forgive him, chalking it up to his young age and lack of experience. But as for Raven... I didn't even want to think about what awaited him now.

I was ten paces away from them. No one seemed to notice me, engaged in a short-lived combat.

Twenty paces. I stood up almost to my full height and ran. When I stopped and turned back for a look, Mammon was performing wonders of bravery — even though I had the funny feeling that others were sparing him. A deep blue haze enveloped his body as he adopted a defensive stance.

The nearest wagon was fifteen paces away. This was the most dangerous leg of my escape. If they failed to notice me now, I might have a chance. I could always have summoned Boris, of course, but I didn't want to risk it. Firstly, because I had no desire to expose myself to them. And secondly, no one could guarantee they wouldn't shoot us down as we took off. Then we'd have a real problem. No, I'd have to try and slip out on my own. It seemed to be working, anyway.

"Going somewhere?" a raspy voice asked.

I'd celebrated too soon, hadn't I?

I turned around. Bah! This was the Dwand wizard who'd cast a shield over Morph and Phil. He was quick, wasn't he?

Mechanically I attempted to speak. System messages flooded my mental view, informing me of my temporary handicap.

"Take it easy, dude," the Dwand offered, his voice hopeful. "No one's gonna hurt you, I promise."

Oh no, thank you very much. I'd had enough of the Darkies' company. Their leader had already promised me that, and what was the result? They'd very nearly mugged me right there and then. True, as a Lightie I couldn't have expected a red-carpet treatment. So it was probably better I just left.

My eyes must have betrayed some of the above because the Dwand stepped forward. I stole a look around. No one close enough.

"Hey, keep your hair on," the Dwand offered me one last chance. His voice rang with threat.

Too late.

I opened my inventory. A small glowing ball of light appeared in my hand.

The Dwand's eyes reached the size of coffee saucers. His hands shook. His frog-like mouth opened in a silent scream. A pale green haze enveloped him. Doubtful it would help him though.

Our eyes met. He seemed to know what it was in my hands and how things were going to progress from there. Well, wrong guess. This was a surprise.

Would you like to activate the trap: Yes/No

I mouthed a silent *Sorry!* to him, then hurled the glowing ball in front of me and pressed *Yes*.

In a fiery flash of yellow light, my prisoner materialized in the clearing. I barely glimpsed a system message,

Warning! The Caltean trap has expired! It's about to evaporate into the game's cyberspace!

Instinctively covering his eyes, the Dwand shrank to one side.

For a brief moment, the Diadem Serpent froze in an awkward pose. It was the second time I was seeing something like this. The first one had been back in No-Man's Lands where the hedgehog had seemed to exhibit the same kind of behavior. It was as if the creature was rebooting, processing new information. It looked admittedly weird. Imagine if he failed to come to life at all!

My inner pessimist heaved a sigh of relief when the snake's giant body began to quiver. Being a game mob, he paid no heed to me: there was a much juicier morsel within his aggro zone.

I watched, transfixed, as his reptilian head the

size of a truck cab darted toward the Dwand's tiny figure.

Would I ever get used to game mechanics? And how would this affect my real-life perceptions? Back in the real world, a blow of this power would have turned the Dwand's body into a blob of crushed flesh. But here their combat followed a different scenario.

The wizard's force shield had withstood the blow. He hadn't even budged — even though, judging by his grimacing face, he hadn't enjoyed it. No wonder. The level gap between the two was impressive.

Our eyes met. Surprised, buddy? Sure. The sheer fact that a Grinder had produced a Caltean trap out of his tatty bag must have been unfathomable for him. But the creature that had come out of the trap... I could bet my bottom dollar it wasn't listed in the game's bestiary.

The Dwand's glare finally shifted from me to the monster. The man was silent but I knew that reinforcements were already on their way. The problem was — and both of us understood it — that a dozen players were unlikely to smoke the furious snake. Only now did I begin to realize that once the last camp defender fell, this place would turn into a trap for all new portal-traveling raiders.

The cavalry didn't make it. The Dwand's flimsy force shield gave up the ghost after the serpent's second attack. With the third one, the player disappeared into thin air.

Having finished off his opponent, the snake curled up and froze, awaiting a new enemy. He didn't

---

see me: I'd prudently made myself scarce, sitting it out behind a large rock and waiting for the sentries to arrive who'd earlier blocked my trail. It was still too early to let Boris out.

Finally, Morph came running — and two more players with him. They barged directly into the serpent's aggro zone. Apparently, they weren't new to battling this sort of mob.

Even though I couldn't check the logs, it was clear that the serpent had surprised them. They cringed — he must have attacked all three at once or, just like Steel Widow, cast some nasty debuff over them.

The Guardian of the Cave isn't some humble bot. The spells he casts are in direct proportion to his own level. Judging by how the Darkies' arrows kept bouncing off the serpent's body, his protection was up to the challenge, too.

As his heavily armored status suggested, Morph did the tanking. The level-120 Alven archer was small fry for the monster. Another Alven player next to him seemed to be casting a spell — apparently some protection for Morph. That's right. While the tank was distracting the mob — "aggroing" him, as gamers would say, — his stats had to be topped up.

The little group was dragging it out, biding for time. I could see more players coming. Three tanks, their levels barely over 100. You never know, they might do him.

Just when I thought that I must have overestimated the No-Man Land critter, he offered another surprise to his attackers. The serpent's body coiled like a taut spring. A lightning-fast blow of his tail sent the Alven archer to his resurrection point.

Oh wow. I wiped my eyes in disbelief. Indeed, the archer wasn't there anymore. Apparently, the snake had a particular dislike of distance weapons.

The loss of yet another fighter seemed to have really upset the Darkies. They stepped up; their tanks formed a semicircle, pressing the mob. The serpent wriggled about, dodging their attacks while responding to them with sharp precise hits. Two more players joined in the combat: a dwarf and a human. The former was holding a powerful crossbow, the latter brandishing his double swords. The serpent didn't like the swordsman at all: apparently, this class could deal maximum damage.

Finally, what I'd been waiting for happened. The sentries walked down the trail. Archers, levels 150+. Those who had captured me must have left with the Dark army. Good. The serpent would have a hard time fighting them.

The sentries dashed past the rock where I was hiding. They hadn't noticed me. Big sigh of relief. Excellent. I'd wait another minute, then be on my way.

The archers engaged. No one seemed to care about me. Time to leg it.

My virtual heart fluttered in my chest. I didn't even breathe as I cleared the remaining dozen paces, expecting to hear an angry shout behind my back at any moment. It didn't come. Luckily.

I'd made it to the trail and scampered off, zigzagging between rocks and swinging my head in every direction. I wouldn't put it past the Darkies to have left another sentry on the trail despite the desperate combat unfolding below.

The rain grew stronger. Perfect. You'd think this was the right moment to let Boris out and bid a hasty retreat. But I had this feeling that something was wrong. I sensed it with my back: a watchful eye following my progress.

I swung around. I thought I'd glimpsed it — but no. Nothing but the pouring rain, the gray cliffs and a deep ravine to my right.

I continued zigzagging in brief bounds. The sensation of a stranger's presence kept growing. By then, I was 80% sure I was being followed.

Finally, I reached the last bend and ducked behind it. The sensation of being trailed was gone. So there was someone behind me, after all.

I was standing on a small platform where I'd first let Boris out. I cast a desperate look around. This was it. Nowhere to run. End of the line. If I'd been followed by an archer, he'd have no problem shooting both me and Boris down. Boris was a zero-level mount: one arrow would be enough to down him. And falling from this height could only mean one thing: an emergency logout. Which threatened to sabotage my entire mission here.

I drew in a deep breath and tried to concentrate. Now I could clearly hear the splashing of my pursuer's footsteps. Then he stopped. He probably thought he'd cornered me.

I waited another couple of minutes but nothing happened. I strained my hearing. I even closed my eyes to focus on the sounds — but all I could hear was the patter of the rain. Could this pursuit idea have been a figment of my overwrought imagination? What if there was no one here? In which case, I was losing precious time. Or could it be my paranoia playing tricks with me?

As if answering my question, a familiar high-pitched voice reached out to me from behind the wall of rain.

"Is that it?" Raven asked wearily, materializing not a dozen paces away from me. "Is this where you were trying to get to? What have you got here? A portal? A stash? A secret tunnel? How the hell did you get here, anyway? Speak!"

His eyes burned with malice. His lips trembled. The broken-off shaft of an arrow protruded out of his left shoulder. A dark-red spot covered his right side. His right leg was wounded. Morph and his men had done a mean job on him.

I shrugged.

Raven cringed. "Of course! You're gagged, aren't you? Well, point your finger, then! And don't you dare lie to me! This trail is exactly where our guys collared you."

I made a helpless gesture and shrugged again.

"Very well, mister. You asked for it."

He raised a bow in his left hand. Slowly he slotted an arrow into the bowstring.

"This is my last arrow, Digger!" he snarled. "I've been saving it for you! Couldn't you've just given us your gear nice and quiet? You could always have gotten yourself some new stuff. But no! Oh well, you're gonna regret it now. *Really* regret it."

I watched detachedly as he raised his bow. The bowstring grew taut, finally stopping by his cheek. The arrow's dark tip faced my chest.

This was his last arrow. The *last* one. There was no way I could duck it But-

Before I could finish my thought, my left shoulder exploded in burning pain. A powerful jolt swung me about-face, throwing me back. A red haze clouded my eyesight. I gasped.

You've received a wound to your chest!

"So how did you like that?" Raven asked in a calmer voice. "That's just for a start," he said, slapping the short sword dangling from his belt. "Just wait till I start cutting you to pieces. This Caltean trap, did you activate it? Excellent, bro. Perfect timing. They'd very nearly finished me off."

He took a short step toward me. "Regret it now? Sure. I know I would. Having said that, I wonder where you might have gotten all these thingies from. Never mind. Plenty of time for that. You're gonna tell me everything you know. Trust me. I know just how to make you speak."

He pulled out his sword and limped toward me.

Trying to ignore the arrow sticking out of my shoulder, I scrambled back to my feet. Raven was already almost within reach. His eyes glowed with hatred, his mouth a smirking mask. Well, well, well. Sorry, bro. You're not gonna make it.

Come on, Boris. Your turn. Time to leg it!

You should have seen the expression on Raven's face when Boris materialized. Mechanically Raven recoiled but tripped, very nearly landing on his backside. He barely kept upright while getting an eyeful of my beastie. This moment of hesitation was enough for me to spring into the saddle and order Boris to take off.

Already at a safe altitude, I could still hear the shrieking curses in my wake. At the moment, Mirror World was on my side. I was too far for Raven to either launch his sword or hurl stones at me. The only weapon that could have aborted our escape was now sticking out of my shoulder.

Chapter Nineteen

Once Boris had soared to the skies, leaving the cussing Raven far below, my first impulse was to fly to Drammen to warn its citizens about the impending danger. Then I reconsidered. The damage to the town had already been done. Besides, how could I warn anyone about anything being gagged and all?

So after careful consideration, I finally told Boris to head for the Citadel. I'd had enough combat for one day.

As I approached, I activated my satnav. After my little adventure back in the Spider Grotto, I'd spent some quality time looking into gags, injuries and other related subjects. I just wanted to know the scoop, as they say these days. As a result, I'd bought a useful little app called the Healer Finder. You enter the name and level of your injury into the search box, and it offers you a list of all the local healers capable of treating it. Same applies to gag-removing wizards.

This was how I'd found Nyra.

* * *

"Don't move. And most important, don't look at the wound," the female Alven wizard and a level-8 healer, Nyra bit her lip, working on my shoulder.

"Why?" I asked.

"Don't you know?"

I shook my head.

She sighed. "I see. Well, the thing is, it's not proven yet..."

"What are you talking about?"

"I'll tell you. Have you ever wondered how the combat account players overcome phantom limb pain?"

"Which pain?"

"Well, it's not exactly what it's called. We just call it phantom pain. You know, when someone loses a limb."

"I know what phantom limb pain is! I just never thought I'd hear it mentioned here."

"Have you already been to a real-world hospital after a mob attack?"

"Yeah."

"Then you probably know that getting wounded in the Glasshouse is not a good idea. And if you do, you shouldn't think about your injury or even look at it. The human brain is a complex thing. You can't imagine how much extra work it made for all those egg-headed researchers."

"I see. I actually wondered about it myself."

"Of course I wouldn't know how to explain it

from any scientific point of view..."

"You're not alone," I said. "I have every reason to believe that those 'egg-headed researchers', as you so eloquently put it, have only scratched the surface. I dread to think how much stuff they're yet to discover — things that are both interesting and scary."

"Exactly my point," Nyra said, then warned me in all seriousness, "Now sit still. Don't move."

"Yep."

Obediently I closed my eyes and tried to distance myself from what was going on.

For a few seconds, I felt nothing. I was about to open my eyes when my interface was flooded with messages reporting my miraculous cure.

I looked up at the girl. Her face was flushed with pleasure. She must have received some Profession points — both for healing me and for removing the gag. As far as I knew, the lower the level of the victim and the higher the level of his or her torturer, the bigger the bonus the healer would get.

"Plus four to skill!" Nyra reported, confirming my suggestion. "Wish you got more injuries like these!" she added with a smile.

I chuckled. "I bet you would!"

"A special thanks for the gag," she said. "A very rare debuff. And cast by Jed himself!"

"He's quite well-known in this part of the world, isn't he?"

"Yeah, sort of," she replied, putting all her pots and vials back into her bag.

"How much do I owe you?"

"Nothing," she dismissed my question. "Our

clan deputy leader told me to give you a free heal."

"Why would he do that?" I didn't like this sudden show of generosity. Free lunches are rarely a healthy idea.

"Jesus," she sighed. "You really should visit forums more often. You need to study the game. You've just given me the Dark camp's coordinates. This is very valuable intel. My clan is probably storming it as we speak. If we win, it means tons of bonuses for everyone."

"But you weren't the only person I told about the camp. The moment you removed the gag, I PM'd a couple of friends..."

She smiled. "You mean Varn and Uncle Vanya?"

"Yes. But how did you-"

"Cool down. Keep your hair on. There's plenty of work for everyone there. From what I've heard, most high-level Darkies are still alive. Armat and Jed aren't the kind of people you can smoke easily."

"I see," I mumbled, pensive.

"Don't sweat it," she waved her goodbye. "Go get some rest. Better still, click the logout button and get some proper shut-eye. The big bad guys can sort it out between themselves."

I bade my goodbye and headed for the wizard's tower.

Despite the constant rain, the Citadel's streets were packed. The Darkies' Drammen raid had caused quite a stir in the unhurried local lifestyle. The Citadel's inhabitants hadn't been quite so agitated even after the Calteans' bombings.

When I opened the chat, I learned that Armat and his men had given the Lighties a good hiding back in Drammen. I also read a few things I didn't like quite so much. Messages were coming in saying that some very weird mob had put a quick end to the Independents' raid, adding that videos of the combat would be following soon.

Videos! They were the last thing I needed. I just hoped they focused on the brave camp defenders while drawing no unwanted attention to the humble Digger lurking in the background.

I walked down the street deep in thought. Pensive, I paid no attention to the NPCs around me — who admittedly behaved strangely. They cast frowning sideways glances at me, nodding to each other knowingly. They exchanged whispers. I thought at first that it must have been the result of the overall mood in the Citadel, but when I took a closer look, I realized this kind of behavior was reserved for me alone. A dwarf knotted his bushy eyebrows, his glare boring a hole in me. An Alven serving girl looked out of a tavern and gave me a squinted look.

What's up? Anyone? What the hell was going on?

I ran all the way to the wizard's tower.

The NPCs' behavior wasn't good news. Could it be a glitch? Or problems with my account? Or could it be some secret nutty-programmer's setting suddenly activated?

Talk about bad timing. Things had only just started to work out.

I strode across the inner yard and literally

stormed into the tower. I slammed the door shut and sank to the marble floor, heaving a sigh.

The reception hall was dim and quiet: a soothing change after the bustle outside. That was it. I'd had my share of adventures for the day. I could finally climb upstairs and catch forty winks.

"Anybody here?"

The wizard's voice sounded so hostile I nearly jumped. The room's stone walls crackled as if surging with electricity. The distinctive smell of ozone filled the air. My reply stuck in my throat. What was wrong with him?

"It's me," I squeaked like a mouse.

"Olgerd? My friend! Is it really you?"

The electrical tension ceased somewhat. I found I could breathe easier now. Phew. That was close.

"It is... It's me."

"But how on earth-" Tronus sounded genuinely puzzled. "Only a moment ago I was sure I had an intruder in here, an enemy. How is it possible?"

I felt myself shaking again. "An en-enemy?" I remembered the NPCs' distrustful stares in the street.

The sound of footsteps came from the staircase. Tronus was coming down. Had he been talking to me from his study? That was several floors above!

The wizard appeared in the reception hall. "You see, my friend, my tower is packed with all sorts of useful spells which can only be activated using this little crystal," he tapped a fingernail on a small stone dangling from his neck. I had a funny feeling I'd seen it somewhere before.

I nodded my understanding. "A burglar alarm, sort of."

"Burglar alarm?" the wizard rubbed his chin. "What an interesting word combination. I must remember it. You're right, I suppose. When fibers of magic encounter something out of the ordinary, they send a signal to the crystal. It's professional, you know. But why are you sitting on the floor? Are you all right?"

"I'm fine, thank you," I said, scrambling back to my feet. "I just got the impression I was about to get an electric shock."

"Get what, excuse me?"

"Eh, how can I say it... struck by lightning, if you wish."

"Aha!" he beamed. "You've no idea how right you are!"

"What do you mean?"

"This room was about to turn into the Hall of a Thousand Lightning Bolts. One of my best traps, you know. Look, you've turned pale again! Come on, Olgerd, pull yourself together. Allow me to help you..."

The wizard hurried toward me, then froze not two steps away. "Wait a bit, my friend. What is it you've got there?"

I glanced at my jacket and shrugged wearily. "It's blood. I've been wounded. According to the healer, the spots should disappear after a few hours."

Judging by the expression on the wizard's face, he hadn't even noticed the blood. He'd meant something else, but what?

"I see..." he finally managed. "Go ahead, tell me. Where did you manage to pick up a Caltean Mark?"

* * *

For the next hour, Tronus was plying me with his herbal tea — which incidentally offered an Energy buff just as powerful as the touch of Adkhur's kitty.

He tried to reassure me saying it wasn't serious. Things happen. Just some stupid coincidence.

Admittedly, I came slightly unstuck. Too much had happened in one day. No-Man's Lands, the Darkies' camp, the combat and now this Caltean Mark.

I was forced to tell Tronus all about my escapades: where I'd been and what I'd done there. I told him how I'd looted the abandoned mine and trapped the serpent, then set him free later. I told him how I'd helped the Calteans. This "Caltean Mark" was actually their clan's Reputation I'd received. Somehow NPCs seemed to sense its presence. *Sense?* What was I talking about? They were pieces of program code!

Now I'd have to check the box against *Make your Rewards private*. Problem was, this would automatically make private all the other little prizes and medals I'd earned. Which wasn't a good thing when you had to deal with local guards and such. I got too used to their friendly attitude — and not only theirs but that of all Mirror World's NPCs. It saved one a lot of time. Opened virtually all doors. And now... never mind. We'd make it.

Tronus talked me into showing him my little menagerie. The sight of Boris made him childishly happy. Admittedly he was impressed by Prankster too. Tronus even allowed me to let them out for a walk any time I wanted. He didn't mind them at all.

I sat there talking to him, feeling greatly relieved. I didn't have to lie or conceal anything from him. Such precious moments had to be relished. I was so happy Mila had given me that letter! Had it not been for her and the Captain, I'd have never met Tronus. And I didn't give a damn about him being a piece of program code.

"Actually," the wizard turned away from Prankster and looked up at me, "you can always remove the Caltean Mark at the Obelisk of Light. If one day you discover it's too much of a liability..."

"The Obelisk of Light?"

"You really don't know?"

I shook my head.

"The more I know you, my friend, the more amazed I am at your... eh..."

"Ignorance?" I offered to the embarrassed wizard.

He grinned. "Heh! I was going to say, your recklessness. But your definition is admittedly more, heh, more encompassing."

I grinned back. "I prefer to call a spade a spade. It makes life easier this way. Living in denial progressively lowers your chances of success."

"Absolutely!" he saluted me with his herbal tea mug.

"Talking about ignorance, I think I resemble one very famous detective."

"Oh! How interesting! Never heard about that! Come on, tell me!" Tronus shifted in his armchair and prepared to listen.

"Very well. This detective had a friend, also a healer and a very educated man who, however, was constantly amazed at his detective friend's professional knowledge. He seemed to know everything about poisons, chemicals and weapons. He was always up to date with current court cases and criminal reports in newspapers. At the same time, he had very little idea of most common facts known to every schoolchild. His healer friend was always surprised at this peculiar trait of the detective's mind. So one day they talked about it..."

"Oh! I'm very curious to hear what the detective told his friend. Even though I think I already know..."

"Simple," I smiled. "This is what he said in a nutshell. Imagine that the human brain is an empty attic. Most people use it to store all sorts of garbage — furniture and stuff. And remarkably, they keep it there all their lives."

"But the detective seems to be more practical," Tronus nodded, laughing. "He only stores what he really needs. How entertaining! Heh! I'm actually a bit like him too! Now I understand what you mean."

"Which is why I try not to overload my brain with useless information either."

"I wish our priests could hear you," Tronus

leaned back in his chair. "But I assure you, the Obelisk isn't some useless worldbuilding detail you can easily forget. If we continue your detective friend's analogy, I might agree with him on most accounts — most but not on all. Obelisks play an enormous role in our world."

"Did you say 'obelisks'? Are there other ones?"

"But of course! No one even knows how many of them there are. I only have reliable information on two but I've heard about two more. I think there must be lots of them around."

"How interesting."

"You could say that, my friend. You definitely could say that."

"And these obelisks, what do they do?"

Tronus took a sip of hot tea and began,

"If ancient legends are to be believed, our world was once inhabited by gods. Lots of them. Not the nicest of creatures, I have to admit. Constantly quarreling between themselves, plotting and allying against each other. Not that different from us mortals, if you ask me. These gods were divided into several ranks and classes. Each mortal race had its own patron god in the heavenly pantheon. And it happened one day that these quarrelsome creatures took it too far. They started a war. This is how Mirror World was split up into factions..."

"Of Light and Dark?" I helpfully suggested.

"Not only. There were many of them."

"Oh really?"

"Each god had his or her own followers, temples, statues, sacrificial altars and other religious props. And as you can well imagine, gods are highly selfish creatures with an overblown idea of their own importance, for which reason the number of factions mushroomed with an incredible speed."

"I think I know what happened next."

"Exactly. The divine war couldn't but affect us mortals, each of whom sided up with their own patron god, defending him or her. As a result, war was waged both in heaven and on earth."

"Did they really live in heaven?"

"Not exactly. The gods' world was connected to this one by an enormous portal. Our ancestors used to call it the Mirror of the First God."

"Aha. The Mirror! I thought I'd heard that word before."

"The richest of the countries started wars, throwing the strongest of armies into battles over whose god was better. For several centuries, the mortal world choked on its own blood. Then a new force entered the conflict."

"How interesting," I said.

"I wouldn't even call it new. They were still mortal — but different. Let's put it this way: they were my colleagues."

"I see. Wizards and mages."

"Exactly. Only their powers were ten times greater than mine. I'll tell you more: not every god could take on a mage like those."

I shivered. "I dread to think."

"Hah! So do I."

"And what about this new force?"

"Oh! You had to give them their due. They

proved much wiser than gods themselves. In the name of peace keeping, they developed a cunning plan on how to stop the war. Their solution was simple and quite elegant. Assuming that the absence of gods would mechanically stop the war, they decided to destroy the Mirror of the First God."

"Sounds easy enough."

"Easier said than done. I'm not going to bore you with a detailed description of their undoubtedly heroic actions. Let's just say they brought their plans to a successful conclusion."

"And these obelisks, do they have something to do with the portal?"

"Exactly, my dear friend. You're very insightful. The obelisks are nothing other than the fragments of the First Mirror. By breaking the most powerful portal in the history of this world, the wizards were left with a vast number of mirror fragments of various sizes and, simply speaking, various magic hues. With that, the Era of Gods was over. The mirror fragments were dispatched to all the corners of the world, as far from each other as possible — because someone had come up with an appropriate prophesy, as was the habit in those bygone days. Which said that when mirror fragments reunite, the gods will return, furious with the mortals' treachery."

"I see. Funny story. Did you just say you knew of two other obelisks?"

Tronus nodded. "I do. Apart from the two known ones, I heard of two more: the Azure Obelisk and the Twilight one. The first is supposedly located at the bottom of the Scyllian Ocean. The other is somewhere in No-Man's Lands.

"How interesting," I murmured. "Wonder why they're called so? And what have they got to do with the Powers of Light and Dark?"

"Simple," the wizard replied. "In our world, magic comes in different hues. Our power shimmers with every color of the rainbow. Have you noticed that our races don't differ from those of the Darkies? You really can't tell the difference."

I nodded.

"The only difference between our two sides is the hue of our power. Of our magic, if you like. This is yet another curse: the more we fight, the fewer are the chances of the gods making a comeback. Actually, there're rumors that the ocean dwellers have managed to locate the Azure Obelisk. In which case we might soon hear of the arrival of a new political force on our map."

Oh wow. That was some food for thought.

"That's basically it," Tronus concluded. "And now I'm dying of curiosity to find out how your trip to No-Man's Lands worked out for you. Did you manage to get anything nice?"

"Well, it's a bit too early to-" I stopped mid-word as my gaze alighted on the charm around the wizard's neck. Wait a bit... But of course! This was...

"Olgerd? Are you all right?" Tronus' face betrayed concern.

"I am," I reassured him. "Don't worry. I just thought about our earlier conversation."

He chuckled. "I thought you might."

"Do you remember telling me about some

complex No-Man's Lands quests you might have for me?"

His eyebrows rose in surprise.

I was pleased to see his reaction. "Let's see what you say when I tell you how many Crast stones I have in this bag of mine."

Chapter Twenty

I took a day off today. I needed a break.

Apparently, Drammen was bubbling and boiling like the proverbial magic pot. From what I'd heard, it had been the first Darkies' raid in quite a while. Which provoked the arrival in Drammen of not only the expected loot hunters, but also of lots of regular tourists as well.

I had to stop flying for a few days and use portals instead. My mine had become a major tourist attraction. If it didn't stop soon, I'd have to find some other farming location.

Liz sent me a few pictures and videos of the town street with a caption saying,

They did a nice job of our damp little town! Finally our backwater has its fifteen minutes of fame!

Depends on what she meant by it, of course.

Burned houses, collapsed brickwork; stone fences that had melted away like candles. Once again I commended myself on not having gone there last night. I could understand Liz' excitement. She must have received plenty of Valor and this, for her, was the only thing that mattered. For adventure seekers like herself, moments like these were in the same league as major raids to smoke a location boss. If anything, they were more important.

Uncle Vanya sent me a line too,

Hi dude,

How do you manage to always be in the wrong place at the wrong time? This is crazy. He never leaves his mine and still he's always in the thick of it! Me and my guys had a chat and we're going to give you your cut of yesterday's spoils.

Oh, and one other thing. You didn't notice anything strange in their camp, did you? By the time we got there, the Darkies had their hands full with other things. I'll tell you later.

Go get yourself some sleep.
See ya!

Uh oh. I could sense their questions coming from miles away. They even offered me a cut, just to stay on my good side! I had to urgently come up with a convincing cover story. Last night I'd already spun Uncle Vanya a tale about my supposedly lucky escape from the camp and the subsequent hike across the Wastelands to the Citadel with the help of some high-level dudes. It looked like my story had failed to satisfy him.

"Never mind," I said out loud. "We'll think of something."

Hearing my voice, Prankster turned his head from his nest on the wardrobe's upper shelf. Now that Tronus knew about my little menagerie, I could safely let the Grison out into the tower corridors for a bit of a trot. He cost me next to nothing Energy-wise, so let him have his fun.

Talking about Tronus. Last night I'd thought he'd have a heart attack when I'd told him about Crast stones. They turned out to be a very important resource for him. Then again, which of Mirror World's resources wasn't important? Everywhere you turned, you could find something valuable here.

Oh, yes. The wizard had been ecstatic to see the stones. Why would I complain? Not many can boast results like mine in this respect. Unfortunately, what Tronus had offered me for them hadn't lived up to my expectations. To say the least. My account just wasn't up to it.

It felt like I was having my wings clipped. I could still fly after a fashion but it wasn't the same thing, of course.

If the truth were known, I'd counted on the Crast stones to get a bit more Rep. But what Tronus had offered me was completely different. Better in a way but unavailable to Grinder accounts.

Firstly, when I'd handed the twenty Crast stones over to him, I'd received a new system message closing yet another hidden quest. This was turning into a habit.

Secondly, this latter development had improved my and Tronus' relationship to Brotherly. Or something like that. I didn't quite remember how the message had been worded.

And thirdly and mainly... I'd received access to the tower's *sancta sanctorum*: Tronus' lab. You couldn't even imagine the amount of stuff he had there — portal scrolls, elixirs and runes, tons of useful goodies. Crast stones served as some kind of exchange currency, allowing Tronus to swap his inventions for rare No-Man's Lands resources. Which was the catch.

Grinders had no right to own them. Our type of account had some sort of "do-not-touch" policy on rare resources. Like some freakin' museum. In my case, this was a disaster. The thousand-plus Crast stones that I had in my bag would have allowed me to stuff my inventory stupid with all sorts of goodies. Actually, Tronus seemed even more upset than I was.

I slumped onto my bed. Prankster turned his curious little head to me.

"Wait up, Speedo. I'm not going anywhere. Let's do some Engineering. Time to level it up a bit."

So, what did we have here? I opened the Engineering Designer tab. Assembling the Replicator had brought my skill level to 200. Plus the two blueprints I'd studied, each more useless than the other. And the completed Replicator, whatever that was. Now I could start on the Unworked Charm of Arakh. Let's have a look.

I activated the blueprint.

In order to build an Unworked Charm of Arakh, you will need:
   A fragment of Blue Ice
   Warning! Building an Unworked Charm of Arakh will deprive you of 100 pt. pure Energy!
   Would you like to build it?
   Accept/Decline

Well, compared to assembling the Replicator parts this was a good deal. I pressed *Accept*

Congratulations! You've just built an Unworked Charm of Arakh!
   You've received +1 to your skill.
   Current skill: 201.
   The maximum skill limit for your current profession level: 400.

All right. What did we have here?

I took the item in my hands. It vaguely resembled a rune made of a murky fragment of blue glass. Or ice, rather. I could see some scribbles at its center. What was I supposed to do with it? It had no prompts, no activation messages — nothing.

And if I studied another recipe, would that help me solve this mystery, maybe? But I might not get such an opportunity until I leveled up some more. Four hundred points sounded like an awful lot. And I only had 69 fragments of Blue Ice left. I might need another trip or two to No-Man's Lands.

In any case, I could forget new adventures for the time being. For the moment, my priorities lay elsewhere. The bank. I had to make sure I came prepared. I needed to do some math. Tomorrow morning I'd have to go to Mellenville.

As I was finishing the seventh Unworked Charm, my mailbox pinged. Uncle Vanya just couldn't give it a rest, could he?

I opened the letter. No. Not Uncle Vanya. Weigner. What might he want with me?

Hi there, O brave defender of the Realm! Are you guarding our frontiers well? Good for you! Why I'm writing, do you remember the bigwig guy who wanted to talk to you? The one you failed to meet?

Did I ever! That was Lady Mel's representative who'd wished to see me earlier. Later, Weigner had written me an apologetic letter saying the guy was terribly sorry but something had come up and he couldn't make it. He said the moment he got business out of the way, he'd contact me. At the time, I'd been even happy it had gone the way it had: I was too busy throwing my solo raid together. So now I had every reason to believe this "bigwig" was going to schedule another meeting. Very well, let's take a look.

So basically, this guy is over there now, in the Citadel. He's apparently dying to meet our valorous warrior. Between the two of us, his desire to meet you has only increased. He was very insistent I contacted you.

I'd really appreciate it if you could write back at

your first convenience.
   Weigner

   Surprise surprise! Let's write back, then.
   I jotted a brief note saying I could meet him straight away. Weigner replied at once.
   Ten minutes later, I strode down the Citadel streets to meet Lady Mel's impatient representative.

   "So how do you find Mirror World?"
   Tanor — which was the bigwig's name — sipped the fragrant coffee from a tiny bone china cup. He didn't look as if he enjoyed it. From his greeting I'd understood that he was my immediate boss who supervised all the mines in the area. Or rather, those of them which were Lady Mel's property.
   I shrugged. "Takes some getting used to," I studied him out of the corner of my eye. Because, let me tell you, taking stock of a character and their appearance can tell you a lot about the player himself lying motionlessly in a capsule.
   Take me, for instance. I often asked myself: why Ennan? What had prompted me to have chosen this character and this type of appearance? Because of his characteristics? Please. At the time, I'd known very little about the game. You see, my Ennan was a generalized idea of a gray, mousy little person, quiet and inconspicuous. Few notice him, leaving him alone

with his thoughts. To tell you more, I was even happy in my solitude. That's what I'm actually like, to a point. Gray. Silent. Reserved. The only ray of light that made it worth my while were my two girls: Sveta and Christina, my wife and my little daughter. Without them, my life would indeed have been sad and dark.

Likewise, I could tell a lot by looking at the man in front of me. The first thing that caught your eye was his neat appearance. Buttoned-up even. It showed in everything: his meticulously clean clothes; his well-calculated movements; the unsmiling, non-committal absence of any unnecessary facial gestures; calm speech that gave you the impression that he'd rehearsed his every line in advance.

It wasn't for nothing he'd chosen the Alven race for his character. It suited his intentions like none other: sophisticated and highly adaptable, unlike the cumbersome awkwardness of a dwarf or a Horrud that would have failed to communicate his human traits.

His account was another surprise. He was a Grinder like myself. His Profession and other stats were hidden. He must have been using some rare and costly settings. But I still could glean quite a bit from his clothes. He was dressed like a lawyer. Well, everyone couldn't be diggers and herbal doctors.

"If you don't mind me asking... what are your plans for the game?" he asked matter-of-factly. The guy seemed so cordial and laidback. Still, every word he uttered seemed to add to my doubts of his real intentions.

"I'm here to stay," I replied curtly.

That's how you should speak to these guys. No word mincing. No trying too hard. Not giving them a leg to stand on. The longer he was sitting there next to me, the stronger was my desire to show him the door.

"Excellent!" he exclaimed.

"You think so?"

"But of course! Workers like yourself are very important for us."

"Eh... I did say I was here to stay, but I didn't mean I was planning to stick to one particular employer."

"Ah! Of course," he waved my response away. "This world may be virtual but it still has to comply with the principles of democratic society. Am I right?"

"This is exactly my point."

"I see. You want to put the record straight right from the start."

"Exactly. No promises means no responsibilities. Apart from the contractual ones, of course."

He nodded. "Only the facts."

"Yes. Including all the possible legal ways of canceling the contract."

"Well, I hope it won't come to that."

The more he smiled, the less I liked the whole situation. This may have looked like an ordinary conversation. Still, I had a hunch that something wasn't right.

"How do you like your working conditions?" he asked.

I shrugged. "Same as everywhere. Farming stones, then scrambling out to declare them. That's it."

"This I understand. But there're other places one might go to in order to farm resources. Should I say, more-" he looked over the tavern, "more *comfortable* ones."

I shrugged. "Makes no difference to me. A mine is a mine."

"This I doubt," he said. "I can't see your gear's stats at the moment but I'm pretty sure that you have humidity protection installed on all your items."

Cold protection too, Mister Smarty Pants.

"My job has made me a good judge of character," he continued. "Now my gut feeling tells me that your gear's protection is above average. Am I right?"

I shrugged again. "You won't find many people who don't have it. It would be penny wise and pound foolish. Skimping on these little things might cost you."

"That's right, of course, but... we come back to where we started. Wouldn't it be easier to work in a mine situated somewhere with neutral weather conditions?"

I nodded. "Sure."

"Then why?" he squinted at me. "Why would a professional of your caliber make his own life difficult? Do you really need all these unnecessary risks, facing Dark raids and such? Spending your hard-earned money on elemental protection? You can't even imagine the number of people who've been playing for over a year and are yet to leave their locations!"

He flashed me a pearly smile. "Compared to them, Olgerd, you're a seasoned pioneering traveler."

"You flatter me."

"Not at all. These people log in, do their quota and log out. They're protected. They have occasional bonuses, like mopping up instances and such. Lots of other things, too. I assure you that lots of workers of a lower level than you have much better working conditions than you do. Why would they want to move to a nasty, unpredictable location?"

"No reason."

"So what's stopping you, then?"

"Just that you know nothing about me."

"Here's where you're wrong."

Our eyes met. His, the dark Alven grey, exuded a relaxed confidence. Not a grain of sarcasm or disdain. Only a light squint: he's curious to see my reaction. This was one hell of an experienced head hunter. He'd pressed all the right buttons, appealing to my self-preservation skills. He'd given me a brief run-down on how happy other Grinders were in the tender care of his masters. He'd even thrown in a dash of flattery.

"Oh, am I?" I said. "What is it you know about me, then?"

"Heh heh! We know enough to realize how badly we need you."

"And still?"

"Very well. If you insist. You came to Mirror World for a reason."

"You could say that about any of us."

"I could. But you — you have a purpose. Christina, your daughter, is very sick."

I frowned.

"We know," he gave me a calm nod. "She needs expensive surgery. We even know how much it costs. Finding out such things is not a problem for my employers."

My face must have changed because he added even more smugly, "It didn't take our analyst long to work out what keeps you in this God-forsaken hole. Tracking your movements allowed us to conclude you're here to level up Reputation with Mellenville. You need a loan in Reflex Bank. It's a large amount so you need lots of Reputation. I hate to be the bearer of bad news but according to our estimate, you won't make it. And even if by some miracle you do, you still risk a lot."

Oh yes, mister, you know a lot about me. A lot — but not everything.

I attempted to calm myself down, trying hard to disregard the unpleasant chill in my chest and belly. "I see," I forced a smile. "You've worked out my multi-move super plan. There's only one thing I don't understand."

He arched a quizzical eyebrow. "Which is?"

"Why would you invest so much research in a regular Digger? You even had your analysts on me. Strange, don't you think?"

He flashed me a smile. "That would be strange, I agree, provided you described yourself correctly. The thing is, your situation has nothing to do with how you've just described yourself. Don't look at me like that. I haven't come here just to offer a job to an Experienced Digger. I'm here for the actual Master."

Chapter Twenty-One

There are moments in life when you just expect something bad to happen. Some might call it a premonition. Oh well. You might say so, I suppose. The word isn't a hundred percent accurate, but it conveys the meaning quite well.

In my case, it wasn't just a premonition. Oh, no. I'd known all along that sooner or later I'd have to suffer through this kind of conversation. That someone was bound to call my bluff. That's why, strangely enough, Tanor's words had brought me an enormous relief. Why, was I so fed up with living undercover? No, not really. It was something else too. But I was still curious what plans they might have in store for me. Had I been right all along?

There was a glint of interest in Tanor's eyes. "You're not really surprised, are you?"

I shrugged. "It's not going to change anything, is it?"

"Olgerd, please. What is it with you? Why all this defeatist talk?"

"It's not. I've long given up looking at the world through rosy-tinted glasses. I always prepare for the worst. It helps to roll with the punches."

"Then I suggest we quit the overtures and speak openly. This would save both of us an awful lot of time."

"Can you speak openly?"

He smiled. "Try me. You think *you* can?"

"I might actually beat around the bush for a wee bit longer but that's because I have a very vague idea of who you actually represent. So much effort invested into wooing even a Master Digger — that's too much, you know."

He clapped his hands. "Bravo! You're full of surprises. I think... No — I'm absolutely sure we'll make a good team."

"Dear Tanor, or whoever you are. Will you please leave all the sales pitch for Mirror World fans? I have other objectives in this game. Massaging my own ego fortunately isn't one of them."

He forced a smirk. "In other words, you don't give a damn that one of the most powerful coalitions in the Glasshouse has sent you a personal head hunter? Hah! Quite a few players would have given a lot for this kind of attention."

"I didn't say I wouldn't."

He snapped his fingers. "I think I know! Correct me if I wrong, please, but had this conversation taken place within your first few weeks into the game... would your reaction have been different then? What do you think?"

"There's nothing to think. It would have been. The problem is, normally a worker is supposed to prove his worth to a potential employer before starting to talk up his price. Am I right?"

"You are indeed. We need professionals. Yes, I can see you disagree. Of course it's a game, of course you're forced to do work you would never have accepted in real life. Things are different here, I agree. A lawyer collects rare herbs, a surgeon farms marble down a mine while a clergyman sneaks out every night to climb into a virtual capsule and head for a far-off instance to kill yet another monster. Mirror World dictates its own rules."

"Meaning, you have to adapt in order to survive?"

"Not exactly."

"How is it, then?"

"*We* don't adapt We make the world adapt We just follow its development."

"I see... if you don't do it, someone else will."

"Of course. It can't be otherwise."

"Probably not, no... not for your type of person."

"What about your type?"

"For my type, things are much simpler in the long run. My goals might seem too boring for the likes of you. A home, a family, a steady life that throws no unpleasant surprises at you."

He shrugged. "To each his own. I'm pretty sure we can manage that."

I was pretty sure they could. Problem was, I

wanted to manage my own life. Still, I asked,

"So what do I need to do?"

He nodded his understanding. "We have several suitable scenarios."

"Suitable for whom?"

"Both for you and for us."

"I'm all ears."

He brought his coffee cup to his lips and took a tiny sip. "Allow me to expand on this a little."

"Be my guest."

He gave me a curt nod.

With every word he uttered, I sensed there was more to it. This wasn't about my Master level. There was something else they wanted from me. And I had a funny feeling I knew what it might be.

"As I already said, the game keeps evolving," Tanor was saying. "It has already been through several stages in its development, all equally important for its formation."

"Let me guess. Clan wars?"

"If you wish," he replied. "You got the idea, anyway. All the known territories were carved up. The clans of Light signed a peace agreement which makes our part of the world a relatively quiet place. The Darkies can't say the same, I'm afraid."

"Are they still at war with each other?"

"They are. But everything's relative, according to Einstein. What would have weakened them in the real world, makes them stronger here."

"Sorry, I don't quite understand."

"What's a war? It's primarily human losses. You can't bring your soldiers back to life. Here, the opposite is true. The more battles you fight, the more XP your players get. If you look at the rankings, you'll see that already we're lagging behind the Darkies. This last raid of the Independents has shown everyone how weak we are. They managed to invade our territory with three hundred fighters whose levels averaged 200. If you had told me this was possible a month ago, I'd have never believed you."

"Does that mean that the clans of Light need an internal conflict?"

"That's what we used to think until very recently. Especially seeing as we had plenty of reasons for our own conflict. Too many issues have accumulated over time."

"If you'll excuse me... but doesn't it sound cynical to you?"

He gave me a sarcastic smile. "You think it's any different in the real world?"

I shrugged. I had nothing to say to that.

"The recent announcement of No-Man's Lands available for colonization has shifted our priorities," he continued. "We have to set aside our internal differences. This is the beginning of a long-term confrontation."

"So you think a war is inevitable?"

"Of course," he replied with a smile. "And I assure you that everyone in Mirror World is looking forward to it. The game developers first of all. This sort of war will call for exorbitant resources. Money, workforces, the army... Neither us nor the Darkies are ready for a conflict of this proportion."

"I see. You have your work cut out for you

before you can even come to blows. Waging war in No-Man's Lands is no walk in the park."

Oh no! I'd put my foot in it, hadn't I?

Tanor's gaze alighted on me, attentive. "You know what? Had it not been so absurd, I might have thought you've already ventured out beyond the Citadel's walls."

I flashed him a naïve smile. "Now that would be a bunch of laughs. With my super pick for a weapon and my armored pants for mob protection."

He grinned. "You would look a sight, you're dead right there," he appeared to be smiling but his eyes remained pensive. "So where was I?"

"The war expenses."

"That's right. You can't even start to imagine the costs. The changes involved — this world hasn't seen anything like it. Which is why we're currently deploying all our resources."

"Including me?"

"Absolutely. First and foremost."

"I already said it looked like too much effort for even a Master player."

"Well, firstly, your progress has been impressively rapid. You promised a certain person you would do that-"

"Ah, so it's Shantarsky..."

He smiled. "And not only him. You were quite naïve if you thought that you could keep your account's true potential under wraps for very long."

"But who, apart from Shantarsky-"

"I assure you that Shantarsky only confirmed what we already knew."

I decided to test the waters. "This is classified information, isn't it?"

He beamed. "Not at all! We don't have any secrets from you. You'd like to know where you made a mistake, wouldn't you? Heh! Very well. It might be useful for you to know that all good clans monitor the progress of all workers who show a certain potential. We received the first signal when you first leveled up. It just happened too quickly."

"Wait a sec..."

"Of course. The Mine Diggers Guild. Did you ever ask yourself why it was manned by players? Shouldn't NPCs be doing this kind of work?"

I remembered the smiley she-dwarf teller in the Guild's locket. How she'd congratulated me on reaching a new skill level... "Aren't you afraid I might file a complaint with the admins for disclosing my personal data?"

"You wouldn't be the first. By the time they get to it, find the culprits and close the case..."

"What do you mean, *close*?"

"Easy. What do you know about the Reflex Corporation?"

"Oh. Not much. I know they own the game."

"Is that it? Know anything of their other business activities?"

"No."

He massaged his chin. "You're a virgin case, aren't you? Then again, why should I be surprised? You didn't have time to frequent forums, did you? You virtually live in the game. So basically, Reflex controls lots of social programs. One of which is called World

Without Borders."

I frowned. "I think I heard something about them in the news. Some kind of international program for people with disabilities? What's that got to do with me filing a complaint?"

"Everything. It wasn't just people with disabilities they mentioned on TV, remember? Large families in difficulty, single mothers, senior citizens, orphaned children... now who do you think work as guild clerks? Aha. I can see you understand. Then you need to realize another thing: we're involved in lots of social programs. World Without Borders is only one of them."

"You don't mean they rat on other players!"

He smiled. "Sort of. I can assure you that our informants sincerely believe they're helping people like you find better employment. So if you begin to protest and file complaints, no one will understand you. The most you might achieve is public condemnation."

I scratched the back of my head. Oh. Surprises never cease.

"Come on," he said happily. "Cheer up. Everything is working out fine, isn't it?"

This I was yet to see. "Did you do a check on my friends too?"

"A very superficial one," he said casually. "Which only confirmed our previous suspicions, albeit indirectly. Your escape from the spider instance was especially amusing. Flint and his men are still trying to work out what happened there. Very clever. My congratulations."

"I see. Then you received another signal from the guild about my upcoming leveling, after which you..."

"We had a brief talk with Shantarsky which made everything perfectly clear. And then you disappeared. You've given our sleuths a run for their money!"

I chuckled. "I can imagine how happy you were to discover the contract I signed with Lady Mel."

He laughed. "You can say that! We'd never have thought of looking for you in the capital, of all places. And then we received the news..."

I closed my eyes and rubbed the bridge of my nose. "I still can't wrap my head around it. The Analytic Department. The sleuths. All for the sake of a Grinder?"

He shrugged. "Why not? You're a Master. My gut feeling tells me that had you had the chance to farm higher-level resources, I'd have been talking to an Expert now. The top office gives the runaround to its workers for much less important cases. You're a Godsend for the clan. Your input will boost the power of many of the clan's top players. Which will result in the clan's growth too."

"I'm sorry. There must be something else to it. Has to be."

His stare leadened. Even the color of his eyes seemed to have darkened. This was the real Tanor: cruel, hard and unsmiling. Something told me this wasn't just a humble head hunter.

"Enough pussyfooting around," he quipped. "We're losing time. You need the money, we need your skills. We can offer you the sum you need and a highly paid job to go with it. Plus a bonus from all the raids and war campaigns."

I nodded. "Generous enough. What do you want in return?"

"To join the clan with all the rights and responsibilities it entails."

"You want to say that the current contract won't cut it?"

"No," he snapped. "We can't take the risk. Too much at stake. We're on the brink of war. We need all the resources we can muster. We can't afford a freelance Expert Digger. Only a clan member. It's much better for you, trust me. A calm location. Excellent weather conditions. Quality gear on the house. Finally, protection."

"What about my responsibilities?"

"Working for the clan."

"Is that all?"

"It is."

Wearily I rubbed my forehead and looked up at him. "I need some time to think."

With a heavy sigh he slumped against the back of his seat. "Please do. You have a week. There're a few things you need to consider though."

"Which are?"

"I doubt the bank will give you the sum you need. We can give you more. In either case, you'll have to pay it back."

"Of course. I'm quite prepared to work for it."

He curved his mouth in a grin. "We know. As long as you understand that if you refuse our offer,

---

you might find it extremely hard to find another employment."

* * *

Our parting was rather subdued. The representative paid for the coffee and left the tavern. I sat there for a while, staring out the window.

My mind was racing, thoughts fluttering around like moths trapped in a glass jar.

Had I done the right thing? I really didn't know. Honestly, I was at a loss. I used to wonder when and how it might happen, and now it had. Meeting the Steel Shirts head hunter had left a bad taste in my mouth but apart from that, their conditions were very acceptable. More than acceptable even. They had lots of upsides, all of which he'd laid in front of me. True, I was already getting used to my new life in the Citadel but admittedly this place was one of the game's most dangerous locations. Especially for someone like myself. How many times had I wished I could simply log in, do my quota in the mine and log out straight away? Oh, no. There I go again. I just missed my girls so much.

What was there to think of? The game's most powerful clan had just offered me a job. Wasn't it exactly what I'd been looking for? Why did I have a bad feeling about it, then?

Never mind. Time to grab some fresh air. Tanor could say all he wanted but I fully intended to see my plan through. Whether it would tank or succeed, only the bank could tell.

The Citadel streets bustled relentlessly as usual. The weather seemed to have picked up. No, don't get me wrong, it was drizzly as usual but, as Citadel old-timers would say, "This is nothing like yesterday's downpour".

On Tronus' suggestion, I made my entire achievement list private — both the good and the "undesirable" properties. Once I'd done that, NPC passersby stopped paying any attention to me altogether.

Amazing what a difference my little medals used to make. The change in the NPCs' behavior was tangible. Before, they were all smiles, winks and cheers. Now they were stone cold with me. That's the power of habit for you. Before, I used to take it all for granted, and now...

My memory promptly offered a few snippets of past days. A black-bearded dwarf player, watching thoughtfully as I chatted with an old lady NPC baker. A female archer player, staring in surprise at NPC guards giving me friendly slaps on the back.

Similar moments were legion, only I'd long stopped paying attention to them. Now that it was gone, I was beginning to understand why I never considered the Citadel as gloomy as others pictured it. That's human nature for you. To appreciate something, we need to lose it first.

I decided to give it a check. There was a greengrocer's within walking distance, just opposite Tronus' tower, where I used to buy the occasional

---

fruit and veg to restore my Energy down the mine. Stephen, its owner, and myself had often chatted about things like the weather and the latest Citadel news. Not that what he said ever had any informational value. But for me conversations like those were like a breath of fresh air.

Interestingly, you didn't often have these kinds of relaxed chats with other players. Gamers had a very limited conversation spectrum: they mainly discussed loot, buying and selling, locating certain items, that sort of thing. Now I could better understand Weigner who liked to shoot the breeze. Such hunger for company was typical of players in extended immersion.

When I was only a few paces away from the greengrocer's display of fruit and veg, I heard a short whistle coming from my right. I turned to the sound. A squat figure hovered in the dark narrow lane. Had it not been for my Ennan eyesight, I'd never have noticed.

The stranger motioned with his hand, inviting me to approach.

How strange. I cast a look around, just in case. A dozen feet to my left, two guards were busy discussing something. To my right, a group of three NPC builders were having a smoke break on a bench.

I cast another glance into the darkness. The squat stranger gestured to me again. Interesting. I might venture a little closer and find out. Doubtful that anything bad would happen: only an idiot would attack a Grinder in the heart of the Citadel. This was one of the unwritten rules.

I took a few steps toward the edge of light and darkness. The stranger kept motioning. I thought he'd even brought a finger to his lips, signaling for me to keep quiet.

How weird. What kind of spy game was this?

Judging by his silhouette, he was either a Dwand or a puny dwarf. No: a Dwand, rather.

"I'm not coming any closer," I said firmly. "If you need me, I'll be waiting for you here."

The stranger didn't say anything. He didn't even move. Instead, my chat window blinked.

A character called Max would like to start a private conversation with you.
Accept: Yes/No

I pressed *Yes*. What would he want with me? Let's see.

With every word I read, I could feel the corners of my lips stretch into a smile.

Hi Olgerd,

This is Max. Do you remember me? Dad's sending his regards. He wants to see you. He says it's urgent.

Chapter Twenty-Two

Algar was a one-horse town like any other. Had it not been for the Gothic spire of the town hall, the portal station, the bank and a few more institutions securing its status as a town, it would have easily passed for a village.

Players were few, mainly Seasoned Grinders. I could see a couple of Warriors too, most of them below level 30. Basically, this place had still a lot to grow. To a newb player, Leuton might seem like a megalopolis in comparison.

Despite their relaxed lifestyle, the inhabitants of Algar were no slow coaches. Which made sense. Time waits for no man, whoever said that. This game dictated its own harsh rules.

Closer to the night the streets might actually grow busier. A lot of players were out smoking forest mobs. Herbalists crowded all the nearest meadows. And my colleagues, fellow Diggers, spent all their waking hours underground. No point staying behind the town walls when you had work to do.

It felt good. I wasn't used to this kind of weather anymore. It was warm, the evening sun casting its gentle rays on the town. What a nice location. Especially after that humid Drammen.

This was the place Rrhorgus had suggested as our RV point.

At first I'd found Max's behavior quite funny. Still, a lot had become clear when he began to speak. I'd meant to question him at length but he only said that his father would explain everything himself, adding that he personally didn't know much. He was only a messenger, sent to me with a brief note,

Hi Olgerd,

If you're reading this letter it means Max has found you. Add me back to your friend list please, this way we can stay in touch. I need to see you. It's important. I can't come to you. They might smell a rat. It's best we meet on neutral ground. There's this God-forsaken town: Algar's the name. Let's meet up and talk.

RSVP

I read the letter, unblocked my friend list and contacted him. We decided not to drag it out and set up an RV for the same evening. I had a hunch that the mysterious "they" mentioned in his letter might have something to do with the arrival of the Steel Shirts head hunter. Before leaving, Max instructed me to be on my guard and keep my eyes peeled at portal stations to make sure no one noticed where I was porting to. All this had only strengthened my suspicions.

I hadn't risked using portals, especially seeing as today's caravan to Drammen had left the Citadel already an hour ago. If the truth were known, I hadn't considered using portals to begin with.

My satnav had had no problems locating Algar — and Boris had taken me there with an equal ease. We'd landed in one of the numerous forest clearings. Less than ten minutes later I was standing by the front door of the White Goose Inn where we'd agreed to meet up.

"Had I known you'd be such eye candy for all the Grinders in the area, I'd have invited you somewhere else."

I grinned, turning to the familiar voice. "Rrhorgus!"

"Hi there, man. So good to see you."

We hugged; then he eased me away, holding my shoulders. "You've changed. Are you posing as a dwarf these days? That's clever."

I shrugged. "I do my best."

He nodded and nudged me toward the inn door. "Let's go in and have a taste of the local brew. Then we'll talk," he paused and added in a whisper, "Were you being followed?"

I shook my head. "No. A 200% guarantee."

"Oh really?" he sounded surprised. "Now I'm curious."

"Not as curious as I am."

He slapped my shoulder. "Go in now. I can

already see we'll be there a while."

As if following the already-established tradition, Rrhorgus went for the table in the farthest and darkest corner. We didn't have time to sit down before a waiter arrived, promptly took our orders and dashed back toward the kitchen. It looked like my friend had been right: players sporting my kind of gear were rare visitors here.

He smiled. "Before we begin, I have a few hellos from your family to impart."

My heart fluttered. "Did you see Dmitry?"

"I did."

"How are they?"

"Sveta and Christina are fine. Your wife says that Christina is stable. She says they both miss you. They can't wait to see you. That's all Dmitry told me."

I'd always been amazed how much one can convey in a few short, simple statements. I wanted more. One always does. Especially in my situation. But I could understand my brother. He was playing it safe. You can't share your family affairs with a stranger, they're nobody's business. And Rrhorgus *was* a stranger. But even this brief message was like a breath of fresh air for me.

"Dude, I really appreciate it. You can't even imagine how I needed it."

He nodded.

For a while, we didn't say a word. I was thinking about my own problems. Rrhorgus was tactful enough to give me time to recover from the news.

The waiter broke the silence. "Your order,

gentlemen!"

He unloaded his large tray, placing several steaming platefuls, two beer mugs and two sets of cutlery onto the table. "Enjoy your meal!"

With a curt bow, he disappeared.

"Ah! That's useful!" Rrhorgus rubbed his hands. "I haven't eaten anything since this morning! Cheers, man!"

We clanked our beer mugs and tucked in.

"The service is good here," Rrhorgus nodded approvingly in the direction of the waiter.

"Just as good as in Mellenville, if not better."

He guffawed. "Oh, yeah! You're a big city boy now, aren't you?"

I decided to move to business. "Who did you mean by "them" in your letter? Steel Shirts head hunters?"

"Not necessarily."

"Shantarsky?"

"Also. A few other top clan representatives, too. Including the Dead Clan."

"Oh. So many?"

He chuckled. "Did you say they'd already found you?"

"The Steel Shirts, yeah. Tanor."

Rrhorgus nodded. "I know him. He's a piece of work. Anybody else?"

"Not yet. But judging by the expression on your, er, face it might only be a matter of time. Did you know they had their spies in all guild central offices?"

"Sure. It's not mentioned very often but those

who need to know are in the know. They approach me quite often about new players. I sell gear, don't I? No newb can escape my shop."

"I see. When was the first time they asked you about me?"

"Right after your Spider Grotto gig. Shantarsky's men started grilling Max, like, you and I were friends so we were bound to know your whereabouts. At the time, I was in occupational therapy."

"Health problems?"

He emitted a short laugh. "You could say that. I've been unable to walk for many years now. I'm wheelchair-bound."

"You never told me. Sorry."

He grinned. "What for? It wasn't you who fell asleep at the wheel. You didn't crash your car into the ditch. Did you? In which case, shut up! And don't you dare feel sorry for me. I don't like it. If you absolutely need to know, I'm allergic to sympathetic stares and tearful exchanges about my everyday challenges. Just forget it. Don't make me regret telling you."

"It's all right, it's all right," I raised my hands in a mocking gesture. "I got it. I'm not saying a word."

"Much better," he took another sip of his beer. "Where were we? Oh yes. Shantarsky. Dmitry told me all about you and him. What a bastard! You might be interested to know that all of our guys quit and moved town after that incident. All but me, that is. You need to understand. The Digger's Store is my domain."

"Of course," I said. "It would have been stupid to pull the plug on it. Listen, I feel really bad about leaving without explaining anything to anyone. The guys must be mad at me."

"Leave it," he waved my apology away. "They weren't born yesterday. They understand you didn't mean to drag them into this thing you had with Shantarsky. Who are we to you, anyway? Nothing really. Fellow players, that's it. And even then... So just don't sweat it. On the contrary: Flint, Sandra, Greg, they all appreciate what you did. But Shantarsky's dogs have no shame, I can see. And the worst thing is, you can't put them in their place without harming yourself."

I waved his warning away. "It doesn't matter anymore."

He chuckled. "That's where you're wrong. It's only just starting, now."

That came as a surprise. "Or really? Don't you think it's too much fuss about some humble Digger? Even if he *is* a Master?"

"A Master, already?" he opened his eyes wide. "Dmitry told me you were one busy beaver, but this... Oh, well. You're right, anyway. We have a feeling that their unhealthy interest in your persona has more to it than just your skill level."

I sucked in a deep breath and mechanically touched the bridge of my nose, trying to rearrange the non-existent glasses. "You know what, man... I might actually accept Tanor's offer. Or his bosses' offer, rather. You need to understand. Time is an issue."

He smirked. "How much did they offer you?"

"Enough," I said, serious.

"Make sure you don't bust your gut."

"Why should I? It's a dry location and a nine-to-five job. All I need to do is farm some resources for the clan. It's night and day compared to what I'm doing now."

"They offered you to join the clan?" he sounded surprised. "They didn't waste their time."

"I was worried about it too. Then I thought that it might be proof of their serious intentions toward me."

He smirked again. "You bet."

"Listen, dude. If you have something to tell me, just spit it out."

He heaved a sigh and leaned back in his chair. "That's why I was looking for you. Not only to explain things but also to warn you, if possible. Apparently, I'm too late. They're going to monitor your movements now. I'm surprised you got here without a tail. Did you splurge on a portal scroll? Never mind. We'll talk about it later. Something in your cheeky mug tells me I'm in for a surprise."

I gave an all-knowing smirk.

"Well," Rrhorgus tensed up, "I think they know everything there is to know about your char."

I nodded. "That's Shantarsky."

He made an impatient gesture. "That's not what I'm talking about. This is something totally different. Basically, you see... I've been here for quite a while. I saw some of the top players in their newb underpants. The clan wars. I was one of those who started the Glasshouse."

"I know, you told me."

"Right. So. The Darkies had one hell of a scrap

once. The mother of all battles!"

"What's that got to do with me?

He frowned. "Let me finish."

"All right, all right."

"At that time, the Light players were quite strong. They would habitually raid the Dark side. It was probably because they had a lot more registered players. Being a player of Light was sort of cool at the time. Forums were full of claims that all Darkies were wusses. You get the idea."

"I don't think they enjoyed it."

"They didn't. But as the saying goes, whatever doesn't kill us makes us stronger."

"You mean this scrap?"

"Exactly. Apparently, it was quite serious. They were fighting over some large castle that made up part of several instances."

"Heh! I can imagine."

"So basically, once it was all over, dozens of clans went bust. But the two strongest ones were born: the Caste and the Independent Clan."

"From what I remember, they now have all of the top Dark players."

Rrhorgus nodded. "That's right. But there's one other thing. Very few people know about it. I do because at the time I used to follow it. I was curious, you know. I've even tried to look up the old forums that discussed it at the time."

"And?"

"Nothing. No search results. My old bookmarks all lead to some new promotional sites."

"It happens."

"Probably. Who am I to argue? In any case, I'm not too eager to look into it."

"Listen, dude, I'm sorry to interrupt you but what's that got to do with me?"

"It's what caused the conflict that's important," he went on as if not hearing me. "I had no idea! And I should have guessed, if not immediately when I met you, then at least when we celebrated your promotion. I sifted through the whole auction that day trying to find something for your race. And all I found was that ring. Statless, as well. Just a piece of junk jewelry."

He glanced at my hands, then looked me straight in the eye. "Funny I don't see it. Did you sell it?"

I felt uncomfortable under his gaze. "I can explain."

He shrugged. "Never mind. It can wait. I was talking about what triggered the Darkies' conflict. I did speak to you about the Mirror World phenomenon of dead races, remember?"

"Do I ever! I'm one of them myself."

He shook his head. "Not exactly, dude. Not quite."

Goosebumps broke out all down my spine. "What do you mean?"

"You're much more than just the last of a dead race. Both Dmitry and I think your char might be some sort of key."

I shook my head, uncomprehending. "A key. To what?"

He rubbed his chin. "How can I tell you... It probably hasn't manifested itself yet..."

"Don't drag it out, please."

"Well, basically, we have every reason to believe that you may be the key element in some major quests. It can be anything. A hidden instance, an old mine, a dungeon... I understand it sounds crazy to you. But if you add up all the data and give it a good thought, it looks like Pierrot has set you up big time. I can see it in your eyes you don't understand. Let me explain. The Darkies' scrap I told you about, what do you think had caused it?"

"Please don't tell me it was about a Grinder like myself."

"Oh no, no Grinders there. That guy was a Warrior. But he was a unique race too. All of a sudden he began to advance real fast. Relic gear, pets, some cool quests... the works. Problem was, clan leaders kept tabs on him. They didn't waste time appropriating him. They're just like vampires: they won't stop until they suck every drop of blood out of you. That guy was a well-known forum rat, he never stopped bragging about his successes. And then he just disappeared. As if he'd been moved and made incommunicado. Just like that. So Dmitry and I, we basically think you're heading in the same direction... Hey, whassup, dude? Don't go all pale on me like that! Olgerd! Olgerd, are you all right? Talk to me!"

I may look like a bespectacled wuss but I used to be quite tough when I was a child. I got in fights almost every week: either for being called four-eyes or beanpole, or otherwise to defend my pocket money. There was always something. The problem was, our local bullies were right: I really used to be the four-eyed beanpole that they'd called me. I hadn't taken after Dad. I was pretty sure that Dmitry, who'd inherited Dad's giant mitts, hadn't had such childhood worries.

But I had never suffered in silence. Which had resulted in even more beatings. Sometimes they'd call me names simply to have an excuse to beat me up. Now, too, I was flooded by this desperate feeling of getting into a fight I could never win.

Someone might say it's not possible. There's always a way out. Well, they're either overly optimistic... or they've never been beaten to near death in dark alleys.

One thing I could say: this opponent definitely wasn't in my weight category. I could forget winning. Apparently, clan leaders had some idea — or even knew for sure — that my skill stats weren't my only fortes. And I used to think that they were only interested in my profession! Apparently, they needed some information on the Ennan race.

Rrhorgus' cautious touch of my hand made me jump.

"Olgerd? Are you all right? You're all pale."

I nodded.

"You don't need to worry," he insisted. "It might all come to nothing. Could be a false alarm, you never know. Why are you looking at me like that?"

With a sigh I slumped back in my chair. "I don't think so."

"You mean-"

"Exactly," I said. "They got the ball rolling. And you'll never believe what started it. It's that ring of yours."

Chapter Twenty-Three

We talked till midnight. I had to tell him a few things. Not all of them but still. When the inn closed we went into the forest away from the town walls where I presented my little menagerie to him. To say that Rrhorgus was in shock is an understatement. He couldn't believe his eyes as he was admiring Boris. This Mirror World old-timer just couldn't wrap his head around the fact that a noob like myself and a Grinder to boot could have laid his hands on the game's top flying mount.

He didn't like my story about the Darkies' raid at all. Now they knew about me too. As it turned out, Dmitry and Rrhorgus had been working on a plan for me to defect to the Dark side. And now it was off limits too.

Rrhorgus suggested I scrapped my current char and started playing from scratch. But that wasn't even an option. Too much at stake.

We spent a lot of time talking, debating, offering all sorts of arguments. Pretty pointless, really. It's not easy to plan anything when a powerful clan has got tabs on you.

I didn't hold my breath that they might treat me as I'd like them to. I wouldn't be their slave but I wouldn't be a free man anymore, either. They would pay for Christina's surgery, thus tying me even stronger. They would decide when I could log out — and I was pretty sure they might keep an eye on me in the real world too.

So basically, I was caught between a rock and a hard place. I doubted very much that my humble character could trigger a clan war. The Light side had long been carved up, its priorities established. I was pretty sure that whoever located the guy who was the key to Legendary-class quests would receive a nice bonus on my head. That, yes, but a war? — no way. The colonization of No-Man's Lands was about to begin, anyway.

Still, right as it may be, there was still a catch. Nobody seemed to know yet that all my "secrets" had something to do with No-Man's Lands. This was something I'd kept from Rrhorgus, too.

I might have to tell him, though — and pretty soon, as well. I had the inklings of a plan. Had anyone found out that I owned a detailed map of an abandoned Ennan castle in the very heart of No-Man's Lands... I dreaded to even think what might start then. Fur would fly.

Finally, we decided to stick to my initial scenario. I would apply for a loan in the in-game bank, seeing as the looting of the abandoned mine had given me enough crystals to raise my Rep with Mellenville to the required limit. The only condition I didn't answer was their requirement to have spent at least a month in extended immersion. But a few days couldn't make such a difference, really. In any case, I needed to go to the bank and find out. Pointless delaying my trip to Mellenville. On the contrary: the sooner I got there the better.

Tomorrow – or rather, already today – everything might come to a head. I couldn't avoid joining the Steel Shirts, anyway. I might have tried to provoke a conflict and join the Dead Clan but a clan war with me at its epicenter was the last thing I needed. I'd watched a nature program on TV once, about a school of sharks ripping apart some poor seal. I didn't want it to happen to me, thank you very much.

Or should I really defect to the Dark side? Heh! If Sveta could hear me now! Me taking the Dark side! Unfortunately, that wasn't an option, either. I'd have to start from scratch. According to Rrhorgus, I could save my char's stats, but lose all of my Rep with Mellenville. This was one of the defection requirements. Only one of them, eh? There were others, including making an offering to the Dark Obelisk which had to consist of a mind-boggling amount of resources that probably cost an arm and a leg. Even if everything worked out well, I simply wouldn't be able to promptly raise the required sum. And, as an unsavory bonus, at least three of their top players must have already blacklisted me. That's the way the cookie crumbles.

Rrhorgus and I parted ways just before dawn. He promised to send a word to my family saying I was all right. Dmitry was the only person supposed to know about my problems. I had to spare my wife. Sveta had enough on her plate as it was.

I used portals to get to Mellenville. The stations were crowded as usual: some gamers played night shifts, others lived in other time zones: for them it must have been late morning or even early evening. Some were in a hurry to get to work while others had already called it a day and were unhurriedly discussing the latest game news. Strangely enough, I found the bustle soothing.

Mirror World's capital city met me with the mixed aroma of freshly-baked buns and springtime blossoms. Flocks of little birds crowded its trees and statues, twittering in their own language. NPCs rushed past, each on their own business.

I needed to check if my achievements were still hidden. Getting on the local guards' wrong side was the last thing I needed. I glanced over my interface. Good. No problem there.

It didn't take me long to get to the city center even though I kept checking the street behind me for a potential tail.

As usual, the views of Mellenville pleased the eye. A lot had changed in less than the month of my absence. There were some new statues... and those two fountains didn't seem to have been there before, did they? And those flowerbeds over there had grown even bigger. Here, life carried on. The players who'd chosen Sculpture, Floral Design, Architecture and Landscaping as their respective skills must have leveled up nicely. Why not?

In a way, I couldn't help feeling a bit jealous. Life wasn't about toiling in mines or smoking mobs in God-forsaken locations. These were big city dudes, whichever way you looked at them.

Finally, I arrived at the town hall. Before going to the bank, I first needed to exchange my Tyllill crystals to Rep points.

In the morning, the place wasn't at all crowded. And there it was, my old friend — terminal can't-remember-its-number...

Greetings, Olgerd!

This is Mellenville administration Terminal #312.

Would you like to check the Reputation Quests available?

No, I wouldn't. I clicked on the Menu. What did we have here? Aha... *Resource exchange.* So! The list was impressive. They had all sorts of things: Red Coal... Turquoise Manyl... Imitra Stone... and there they were, my Tyllill crystals. The exchange rate hadn't changed: still 1:10. I clicked on it.

You currently have 57,700 Tyllill crystals on your account.

Would you like to exchange them for Reputation points?

I heaved a weary sigh. *Yes*, please.

Congratulations! You've just added a valuable resource to the city treasury!
Reward: +5770 to your Reputation with Mellenville.

Phew. That seemed to be it. The things I'd suffered to lay my hands on those crystals! In total, I now had 8,550 Rep points: more than enough to view the desired page. Time to get going. I was finished here.

A surprise awaited me as I exited the building. Tanor, as large as life and twice as ugly, was standing there cross-armed, grinning.

"Morning, Sir Olgerd!"

I looked around me in surprise. Doubtful he was there alone.

"Don't worry. No one's going to bother us."

I sighed. "Your name should really be Tanor the Ubiquitous."

He laughed and made a mocking bow. "I'll have to think about that. Thank you."

"You're welcome. If you'll excuse me, I have things to do."

"You don't seem to have taken our offer seriously, do you?" he shouted at my back.

He was too much. I swung round. "You can't even imagine how seriously I've taken it. You've been the only person on my mind for the last few hours."

"Then what are you doing here?" he nodded at the building behind my back.

"I can't remember selling myself into your slavery yet to be hold accountable for my every move."

He smirked. "Please don't be like that with me."

I shrugged. "That's the way I am. You think I don't know what you need?"

"Well, if you do, what's the point of complicating things?" he raised his hands in mock incomprehension. "What did you expect to exchange here? A miserable handful of crystals that the Citadel NPCs mete out to players like yourself? You're about to run to the bank to apply for a loan. This is all children's games. You'd better think of all the prospects of your joining our clan."

"I thought you gave me a week to make up my mind. Is that correct?" I'd have loved to see his face if he found out the exact number of crystals I had just declared.

He nodded. "I remember. I'm just trying to save you from any hasty decisions."

So much for freedom of movement. I hadn't even signed up with them yet and already they were applying pressure.

I walked over and got in his face. "Tell your bosses they shouldn't worry about me. I will inform them of my decision before the deadline expires. And please stop following me! Do you really think I don't understand I have no choice?"

He tilted his head to one side. "That's exactly what we thought. Well, what did you expect? Last night, you and I had a really nice talk, and now we receive a report that my Ennan friend has just been sighted in Mellenville. You've no idea how important

---

you are for us."

Yeah right. Pull the other one. "Talk about important," I said seriously. "Has it even occurred to you that I might make a deal with some other clan?"

What an interesting reaction. He didn't flinch a single facial muscle.

"Sir Olgerd," he sounded bored. "This was the first thing we took care of. Have you ever wondered why not a single head hunter tried to approach you in these last few hours?"

He was right. Rrhorgus had indeed told me about a few clans wondering where they could find me.

"That got you thinking, eh?"

"I'm pretty sure you have an explanation."

He smiled. "Of course. We came to an agreement about you a long time ago. We had to make a few arrangements and pay off a few people, but that's irrelevant."

"I see," I added a note of sarcasm to my voice. "Really, why ask me if you can do it behind my back?"

Tanor stepped towards me and pinned me down with his glare. "Listen, Sir Olgerd," he said through clenched teeth, "if someone has already put you in the picture regarding your char, we'd better be brutally honest. Surely you didn't think anyone would allow you to control it yourself?"

Oh well, at least I'd managed to throw him. "I can't see why not. I read the Terms and Conditions before registering. They're very clear that no one has the right to interfere with my gaming experience."

"Who says anything about interfering? The

game offers plenty of ways to influence a player's decision without interfering with his or her gaming experience. You've just been lucky enough not to come across it yet. Having said that... oh yes, you have. If I remember rightly, some time ago you had quite a close shave with some instance mobs... arachnids, if I'm not mistaken. I can see that you remember! And this is peanuts compared to some other things one can do to you. The funny thing is, the admins won't lift a finger. They're the ones who made such scenarios possible to begin with. I suggest you give it some good thought."

"I'll do my best," I tried to keep my voice firm and level. "Now, if you'll excuse me, I have other things to do."

I turned my back to him and headed for the bank. So much for their promises. A nine-to-five job! A quiet location! A friendly atmosphere! Yeah, right, dream on. The most unpleasant thing in this situation was that I really saw no other way. I was like the proverbial fly caught under a glass. The freedom was just out there, I could see it but I couldn't break free. For the first time in all my time in the game I regretted not having deleted my Ennan. Dmitry had suggested I did it, too!

I should have chosen a dwarf. Joined the Stonefoot guild. Too late to think about it now.

The bank's doors loomed in front of me. I was dying to turn around for a look. But no, I wasn't going to give him the pleasure. He was probably standing there grinning.

The Central Office of the Reflex Bank was

deadly quiet. I looked around me. Not a single person; nothing at all apart from row after row of the already-familiar "parking meters".

I delved deep into the thick of them, trying to get as far from the front door and any prying eyes as possible. Stop. This one might do.

Greetings, Olgerd!
This is Reflex Bank Terminal # 567

Hello to you too, tin can. Now! Let's click on the Menu. The Loans page.

I was still shaking with anger. Calm down, Olgerd man. Calm down. This Tanor was only a pawn in a much bigger game. Even though he admittedly annoyed the hell out of me.

Would you like to apply for a loan?
Accept/Decline

Accept, definitely.

Available services by Reflex Bank:
Express Loan:
Maximum 3000 gold for up to 10 months.
Medium Term Loan:
Maximum 20,000 gold for up to 6 years
Long Term Loan:
Amount: Negotiable
Term: Negotiable

My virtual heart was thrashing about in my

chest, trying to break free. I was only interested in Long Term Loans.

Verifying the applicant's personal data

A download bar appeared on the terminal's monitor, its color gradually changing from yellow to green. A percentage count began flashing inside the bar. Very well. I could wait.

98%...
99%...
100%

It looked like it was finished.

The applicant's personal data analysis completed.
Name: Olgerd
Race: Ennan
Account type: Daily Grind
Profession: Mine Digger
Skill level: Master
Workplace: Drammen and Its Environments
Employer: Melorie, the Lady of Storms
Work contract type: Permanent
Reputation with Mellenville: 8550 pt.
Time in game since last login: 28 days
If the above information is correct, press Submit Application.
If you discovered an error, please contact Customer Support.

Okay, let's check it again... all right. Everything seemed to be fine. I pressed *Submit Application*.

Thank you! Your information has been submitted. Processing it might take several minutes.
We appreciate your patience.

Very well, then. Several minutes was nothing. I'd been waiting for almost a month already. I could wait a bit more.

I might actually check out some deposit boxes to keep my little chests and boxes in. I had a bagful of loot on me, didn't I?

Right, a safe deposit box. What did we have here? The choice wasn't that big, after all. The smallest volume allowed was twenty slots, followed by fifty, a hundred, etc.

There were several things to keep in mind. You could rent a box: either on a monthly, quarterly or yearly basis, depending on your needs. Long-term rent was more interesting, considering all the potential bonuses and discounts. That was good news. Price per slot, too, was considerably smaller on large boxes. A 20-slot one would cost you 60 gold a month while a 50-slot one was only 125 gold, saving you 50 silver on each slot.

And what if I rented a 100-slot one? Firstly, because I tended to deal mainly with stones, and this particular resource had the tendency to quickly take up all the available bag space. Secondly, I liked the price. Two gold per slot. That was two hundred a month: costly but on the other hand it was worth it.

Knowing that all your possessions are safe under lock and key makes you feel better. The only problem was, they could freeze your cell if you missed a payment and you wouldn't be able to get your stuff back until you paid it plus all the relevant dues.

That wasn't so bad, really. I remembered forum members saying that the rules used to be much tougher when the game had just started out. The unpaid stuff simply disappeared, once and for all, and couldn't be reclaimed. It hadn't lasted long, naturally, because it had caused a godawful outcry among forum members. The admins had to handle kilotons of messages, mainly threats and complaints. Because everyone was complaining! Who would like to lose a valuable item to a stupidly missed payment? Especially if the payment had been missed due to some justifiable real-life problem. One could fall ill or get married — even have a baby, after all.

That was it, then. I'd better take a 100-slot one. And pay for three months: they had a discount running.

My wallet became almost 600 gold poorer.

Congratulations! You've created a safe deposit box!

What now? Should we start opening Christmas gifts?

What a strange feeling. I wasn't really angry with Tanor anymore — but my hands kept shaking. The situation was unconventional, I had to agree. There I was waiting for the bank to grant me a loan,

---

and I found nothing better to do in the meantime than to open my hard-earned loot. Crazy.

So, let's do it. Where do we begin? The biggest prize, obviously. Off we go!

I pressed the scarlet-red icon of the Precious Wrought-Iron Chest, its iridescent surface exuding rays of magic. This was the treasure guarded by the giant serpent.

Are you sure you want to open the Precious Wrought-Iron Chest?

Accept/Decline

Of course I was sure. No need to ask.

The moment I clicked *Accept*, the system offered the following cynical message:

Unfortunately, your level isn't high enough to perform the requested action.

Level required: 50

Bummer! They can shove their restrictions up their- Actually, what about other boxes?

Are you sure you want to open the Wrought-Iron Box?

Accept/Decline

Yes, I'm sure, dammit!
Calm down, Olgerd. Get a grip.

Unfortunately, your level is not high enough to perform the requested action.

Level required: 30

How could I calm down when this was happening? With a heavy heart I began opening the remaining items: first the Steel Chests, then the Carved Wooden Boxes and finally, the Pouches. I wasn't holding my breath. Predictably, the result was the same everywhere. Even to open the Torn Pouch, you still had to be level 10-plus.

Oh well. I closed my weary eyes and rubbed my temples. Strangely enough, my anger seemed to have disappeared. I'm not the kind of person to hold grudges. At least I'd tried. And I could still auction everything which was good news. Still, I had a hunch that it would have been much better for me to open these sorts of things myself. Unfortunately, with my account type I could forget it. And as for the auction... I shouldn't rush it. I absolutely needed to talk to Rrhorgus first. He was the expert.

What a shame I'd rented a 100-slot box! Fifty would have been plenty. Never mind. It's always better to leave it here out of harm's way. I'd very nearly been robbed once already.

As I moved the items into the safe deposit box, the terminal offered a new message,

Dear Olgerd,

We have processed your personal information.

To receive a consultation regarding your request, please proceed to Floor 2, Office 1 of the banking center.

Chapter Twenty-Four

Did they even have a Floor 2? The building looked one-story from the outside. Never mind. Where was I supposed to go?

I wandered around the hall for a bit until I finally found a short passage leading to a stairwell. The narrow marble stairs and the wrought-iron banister reminded me of an old house in Madrid where I'd once stayed on business for a month. Outside, it had been scorching hot, the sun was blazing but inside it was cool and shady. They don't build houses like this anymore.

I hurried up two flights of stairs and stopped on a banistered landing facing the only door. A number *1* glittered gold on the dark-blue sign. Looked like I'd got to the right place. I cast a cautious look around me just in case and tapped on the wood.

"Come in," a calm voice said.

The door handle turned with ease.

I had to rub my eyes. I hadn't expected to see this at all.

After all the medieval halls, inn beds, tavern rooms and magic shops, the sight of a modern office took me slightly aback.

Dark gray filing cabinets, boxfuls of papers, a printer, a black computer screen, the rustle of an old aircon... Vinyl windows...

Windows? I couldn't believe my eyes. They opened *into the real world!*

Ignoring the office worker at the desk, I walked slowly to the window, unable to take my eyes off it.

It was cloudy outside. Judging by the wet tarmac, the rain had just stopped. The sun tentatively showed its pale yellow flank from behind the dispersing clouds. People filled the sidewalks below. Real people. Not dwarves, not Alves, not goddamn Horruds but real breathing human beings.

Jesus. It felt so good seeing them. Children, teenagers, old people and young couples — all wearing normal street clothes, jackets and raincoats, many with umbrellas. A white bus drove past, closely followed by a yellow taxi. The cabman signaled left, trying to overtake the cumbersome behemoth. The rich green foliage of the maple trees lining the road was still loosing off occasional raindrops.

"How do you like the view?" a calm, dry voice made me jump. Reluctantly I tore my gaze away from the window.

A man of about fifty years of age sat in an office chair behind a large desk. His bald patch glowed like a polished billiard ball. He had an aquiline nose and small dark eyes under bushy eyebrows. His intelligent gaze was sort of weary.

His skinny shoulders shuddered. "It's wet, isn't it?" he added without waiting for me to reply. "They promise more showers tonight. Would you like to take a seat?"

Slowly I lowered my body into the chair he'd pointed me to. I must have really looked out of place in this setting.

As if second-guessing my thoughts, the man wheezed, "You're quite a sight, Sir Olgerd, I tell you. Still, it's better than being a Horrud, I suppose. I doubt my office would survive a visit from one."

He said it matter-of-factly without even a shadow of sarcasm. Strangely enough, he hadn't even looked up at me yet. He kept staring at his computer screen, occasionally clicking the mouse.

"And as for this view," he went on, "it shouldn't surprise you. We're still in the game. This is a different server, that's all. The street view is an illusion. A video clip. All thanks to our wretched shrinks and their ideas. They think that this kind of scene sets the right tone for our customers for the upcoming conversation. Judging by your expression, they were probably right. Now!"

He fell silent as he tapped his long fingers on the keyboard. The glow of the computer screen reflected in his glasses. His thin lips moved as he mouthed something.

Finally he coughed into his fist and turned his attention from the screen to myself. "Allow me to introduce myself. My name's Victor Pavlov. No, please remain seated. I don't think we'll be able to shake hands in this environment. I'd rather save both your and my time and not explain to you the nature of this phenomenon."

"As you wish."

"Excellent. So let's move straight to business. We know you need a large sum of money."

"That's right," I offered weakly.

He nodded and glanced back at the screen. "You've made some impressive progress, I have to admit. In less than a month, you've managed to meet all our conditions."

I sensed my lips stretch into a tentative smile.

"You've found permanent employment," he continued, reading from the screen. "Let me tell you that you're the first player in my experience who's managed to raise his Reputation so high in such a short period of time."

"Thank you," I said cautiously. "I'll take it as a compliment."

"Despite your lack of experience, you've braved almost a month's immersion."

"This is the only clause on your list of requirements that really worried me," I admitted. "Should I have waited some more?"

He pursed his lips and waved my question away. "That's not a problem. Two more days don't really count. But your skill level is impressive. Congratulations! This is a big fat plus in your favor."

"In yours too," I said softly but he didn't seem to have heard it, busy peering at the screen.

The tapping of the keyboard stopped. With one

last click of the mouse, the worker looked up at me and produced some semblance of a smile.

"Congratulations, Sir Olgerd! Our bank can offer you a loan of eighty thousand gold in in-game currency. Which corresponds to the same amount in dollars at the last rate. Sir? Are you all right? You're pale."

"But," I whispered. My throat was dry. My temples felt as if being caught in a vice. A tell-tale sharp pain pierced my chest.

"Are you okay? Would you like some water?" he asked sympathetically.

"No thanks," I slowly shook my head. "I'm sorry to bring it up but actually I counted on a bigger sum."

His bushy eyebrows shot up. "That's the biggest we can do! Please have mercy on us! You have neither security nor guarantors... If it were a mortgage, at least we'd keep the property."

He was absolutely right. "Yes... sure... of course. I understand."

"No bank in this country can make you a better offer."

"You're right, of course. I'm sorry about this. I just need the money really badly. Can't you do something?"

He glared at me, about to reply, when the phone rang softly. "If you'll excuse me, I'm obliged to take this..." he picked up the receiver. "Hello?"

While he spoke into the phone, I lowered my head, staring thoughtlessly at the floor. Eighty thousand. Only eighty. Where could I get another hundred? As if I didn't know...

"Yes. Absolutely. I won't be a moment," he replaced the receiver and turned back to me. "I'm afraid I must leave you now. My boss will be with you in a moment. Have a nice day."

He rose from his desk with an agility remarkable for someone his age and strode out through a door in the far corner.

No idea how long I remained alone but by the time the door opened again, I was all shaking.

The door opened, letting in — or should I say, spewing out — a young woman about thirty years of age. She was tall with black hair, a chiseled face, slim waist and legs that seemed to go on forever. She looked more gorgeous than any amount of Alven girls here in Mirror World.

Despite her stunning appearance, her clothes reminded me of what our business etiquette teacher used to call "standard-issue office fatigues": a gray pencil skirt ending just below the knee and a matching fitted jacket. A no-frills (literally) ivory blouse, nude tights and kitten heels completed the look.

"Good morning, Mr. Ivanenko!" she beamed at me from the doorway. "Your capsule readings indicate your heart is about to jump out. I've come to put your mind at rest."

She walked over to the desk and fell gracefully into the chair that Mr. Pavlov had occupied only minutes ago. Looking me in the eye, she went on,

"I'm Vicky, the head of the Mellenville branch of Reflex Bank," she said with a disarming smile. "I'm sorry about this circus. Mr. Pavlov is quite capable of smothering anyone to death with his calculations. I'm going to tell you something, but first please promise you won't be angry with me."

The smile lingered on her face.

"If the truth were known," I said, "I'm past caring. I feel completely burned out. So no, I won't be angry with you. I promise."

"Good," she smiled again. "All this time, we've been watching you, analyzing your progress."

I waved her confession away. "That's pretty clear, isn't it? The fact that I can see no cameras here doesn't mean they're not there."

She half-lowered her eyes and gave a light shake of her head. "You don't understand. I don't mean now."

"Excuse me?"

"We started following your progress as soon as you chose the Ennan race."

I sighed. "I know. My brother told me. It's because of your ex-worker, isn't it? Andrew Petrov, a.k.a. Pierrot. It was him who channeled me into this race."

"Not exactly. You don't know all of it."

"Meaning?"

"Pierrot doesn't exist. Andrew Petrov does, of course. But he has nothing to do with it."

"Wait a sec..."

"Do you really think that a company like ours would allow some programmer to wreak havoc on us?"

"Well, in that case..."

"That's right. It was us who channeled you toward Ennans. I'll tell you more: you're not alone."

"But as far as I know, I'm the sole Ennan player. Do the Darkies have them too?"

"We're not talking about Ennans."

'Wait a sec! Does that mean that-"

She nodded. "We have quite a few other such races in the game. We call them Unique, or First-Born."

I frowned, rubbing my temples. "This is something I don't understand. My brother Dmitry..."

She raised her hands in a soothing gesture. "You don't need to worry about him. He still thinks it was Petrov who caused the glitch."

I sat back and interlaced my fingers. "I should probably listen to what you have to say."

"Good decision," she flashed me an encouraging smile. "Let's start at the beginning, shall we? As you well know, we're about to release a new Mirror World project: Water World. Marine races and species, ships, pirates, lots of islands — tons of stuff. Only not everybody knows that the project has just been frozen for a few more months."

"I see. I think I know why. Might it have something to do with the company's plans to sell the majority stake to the government?"

"That's right," she said. "Apparently, the rumors have already leaked into the game. Or was it your brother who told you that? Actually, it doesn't matter."

I shrugged. "Every player knows that." I couldn't allow Dmitry to have problems because of me.

"We've invested a lot of money and effort into

the new project," she said.

"And now it'll be the government reaping all the dividends," I added knowingly.

"As if! The government I wouldn't have minded so much. It'll be those in control of the project who'll do all the reaping. We might be looking at considerable losses. Losses! We're basically giving our baby away for free."

"This sounds scary."

"Don't worry. Very few know that we're having this conversation. That's why we've chosen this old backup server to meet you."

"I still don't understand why you might need me."

"You don't?" she arched a thin eyebrow.

My back erupted in cold sweat. "Wait a second... is it the Ennans' map you want?"

She nodded. "You're our Plan B. Others too, of course, but they haven't progressed a quarter of your route. Which is perfectly understandable."

"What do you mean?"

"I mean your motivation. You would move mountains if it helped your daughter to get better. So let's stop beating about the bush. Mr. Ivanenko, I have a proposal to make."

"I'm all ears."

"You're right, it *is* about the map. Or rather, the Ennans' Twilight Castle."

"You want the clans to start a new war over it?"

She shook her head. "Not exactly. The Twilight Castle isn't really a castle. It's a city. And not just any city: it's the capital of the Twilight Zone."

For a while, I fell speechless. Cross-armed, Vicky seemed to be enjoying my reaction.

Then I knew it. "You can't activate Water World quite yet, but you seem to have a backup scenario in No-Man's Lands. You want to launch the Twilight Zone."

"That's right," she smiled. "We would like to ask you to activate the Gray Obelisk. By doing so you will trigger a war the kind of which this world hasn't seen yet."

"But why me? I'm only a Grinder!"

"If we strike a deal with any of the big clans, this will immediately become known to those who we'd like to remain in the dark for as long as possible. So you're actually the perfect solution. Whoever might try to look into you, will soon come across Pierrot's defection story and won't dig any deeper. The whole corporation knows about him. So you, in disregard of our warnings and propositions, insisted on sticking with this char. Yes, it brought you quite a few bonuses but you earned them yourself, without any help from the admins. And you only have the crazy programmer to thank for it."

"All right," I lowered my eyelids. "Let's presume I agree to all this. How am I supposed to do it with my account type? And most importantly, why would I need to do it?"

"Oh," she smiled. "Now we're talking. Firstly, we'll give you the loan to finance your daughter's surgery. Secondly, you'll have to upgrade your account. Yes, that'll cost you. You'll have to pay to keep all your current characteristics, professions,

---

items and such but, as you might have already guessed, we just might offer you another loan to do that."

Clever bastards. That way, they were still behind it all but none was the wiser. And once all hell broke loose, it would be too late to ask questions.

So, Sir Olgerd? Out of the frying pan into the fire? Still, if I had to choose I'd rather go with the bank.

Did I see a pattern here? My every step seemed to take me further away from quiet locations. Very well, then. Time to head to No-Man's Lands.

End of Book Two

About the Author

Alexey Osadchuk was born in 1979 in the Ukraine. In the late 1990s his family moved to the south of Spain where they still live today.

Alexey was an avid reader from an early age, devouring adventure novels by Edgar Rice Burroughs, Jack London and Arthur Conan Doyle.

In 2010 he wrote his first fantasy novel which was immediately accepted by one of Russia's leading publishing houses Alpha Book.

He also used to be a passionate online gamer which prompted him to write the story of a man who joins an MMORPG game hoping to raise money for his daughter's heart surgery. In 2013, the first book of *Mirror World* was published by EKSMO, Russia's largest publishing house. The original Russian series now counts three novels. The second book of *Mirror World, The Citadel,* is now being translated into English.

Want to be the first to know about our latest LitRPG, sci fi and fantasy titles from your favorite authors?

Subscribe to our NEW RELEASES newsletter:
http://eepurl.com/b7niIL

Thank you for reading *The Citadel!*
If you like what you've read, check out other LitRPG novels published by Magic Dome Books.

Dark Paladin LitRPG series by Vasily Mahanenko:
The Beginning
The Quest

**The Dark Herbalist LitRPG series
by Michael Atamanov:**
Video Game Plotline Tester
Stay on the Wing

The Neuro LitRPG series by Andrei Livadny:
The Crystal Sphere
The Curse of Rion Castle

**The Way of the Shaman LitRPG series
by Vasily Mahanenko:**
Survival Quest
The Kartoss Gambit
The Secret of the Dark Forest
The Phantom Castle
The Karmadont Chess Set
The Hour of Pain (a bonus short story)

Galactogon LitRPG series by Vasily Mahanenko:
Start the Game!

Phantom Server LitRPG series by Andrei Livadny:
Edge of Reality
The Outlaw
Black Sun

**Perimeter Defense LitRPG series by Michael
Atamanov:**
Sector Eight
Beyond Death
New Contract

Mirror World LitRPG series by Alexey Osadchuk:
Project Daily Grind
The Citadel
The Way of the Outcast

AlterGame LitRPG series by Andrew Novak:
The First Player

The Expansion (The History of the Galaxy) series by A. Livadny:
Blind Punch

Citadel World series by Kir Lukovkin:
The URANUS Code

The Game Master series by A. Bobl and A. Levitsky:
The Lag

The Sublime Electricity series by Pavel Kornev
The Illustrious
The Heartless
Leopold Orso and the Case of the Bloody Tree

Moskau *(a dystopian thriller)* by **G. Zotov**

Memoria. A Corporation of Lies
(an action-packed dystopian technothriller)
by Alex Bobl

Point Apocalypse
(a near-future action thriller)
by Alex Bobl

You're in Game!
(LitRPG Stories from Bestselling Authors)

The Naked Demon (a paranormal romance)
by Sherrie L.

In order to have new books of the series translated faster, we need your help and support! Please consider leaving a review or spread the word by recommending *The Citadel* to your friends and posting the link on social media. The more people buy the book, the sooner we'll be able to make new translations available.

Thank you!

Till next time!

Made in the USA
Middletown, DE
16 November 2018